MW00912782

An Adirondack Life

An Adirondack Life

by

Brian M. Freed

Cover photograph of Lake Abenakee in Hamilton County, New York was taken by Dr. Lisa Geiselhart of Yale University.

Copyright © 1996, 2000 by Brian M. Freed

All rights reserved. No part of this book may be reproduced,
restored in a retrieval system, or transmitted by means,
electronic, mechanical, photocopying, recording, or otherwise,
without written consent from the author.

ISBN: 1-58721-066-5

1stbooks – rev. 04/13/00

About the Book

John David Marten is accused of killing his best friend, Jack O'Neill, just three weeks before their high school graduation in 1971. He eludes capture by disappearing into the Adirondack Mountains and, despite a massive manhunt that lasts all summer, he is never captured. A newspaper reporter discovers that John David and Jack were in love with the same girl, who later gives birth to a daughter, Danielle. Danielle's lifelong quest to discover her father's identity spurs the emergence of the legendary John David Marten almost twenty years later.

For Gisele

Forever and ever ... and then some

Part I

Chapter One

The baseball park in Henoga Valley was located at the end of a narrow road leading out of the village. The road was covered by a canopy of elms, and the Raquette River flowed along one side. Those of us who walked to the field would stop to throw stones at the remains of the blast furnace located on the distant shore, and then we would follow the road until it dipped down into a bowl, formed by the receding glacier ten millennia ago, where neatly groomed fields were morticed against the slate blue Adirondack Mountains. There has never been a professional baseball stadium so beautiful, nor one that inspired such awe.

The 1965 Henoga Valley Little League All-Stars were behind 8-7 with men on first and second when John David Marten stepped to the plate at the bottom of the last inning. The coach, Bernie Masurkiewicz, didn't really want John David on the team. Bernie was a perfectionist. Swing at the right pitch, he intoned, a walk's as good as a hit. Steal second, win the game on a wild pitch if you have the chance. Any other Little League coach might have loved to have been in his situation, having the league home run leader coming to the plate with the tying and winning runs on base. John David had hit six home runs over the course of the season. Unfortunately, he also led the league in strikeouts and had the lowest batting average (0.167) of any kid on the all-star team. Other than the six home runs, he had just one other hit. On that occasion the pitcher had thrown the ball high and inside, and in ducking away John David's bat had fortuitously dropped into the path of the ball. The infield had been playing deep, and by the time the third baseman picked it up John David was safely on first.

Unlike his only single of the season, John David Marten's six home runs were incredible displays of power. John David stood nearly six feet tall and weighed 165 pounds and, although only in the seventh grade, he was bigger than most of the kids on the high school team. Mothers of opposing first basemen held their breath when John David came to the plate. He was left-handed, so *their* sons were directly in the line of fire. Over the course of the season John David's strikeouts mounted and some of the mothers relaxed more, but the first basemen never did. John David's batting was, both statistically and aesthetically, a game of Russian Roulette. One for six, all or nothing. John David's first home run was a line drive that cleared the plywood church steeple in center field by eight feet and traveled a tape-measured 314 feet-6¼ inches. It was still early in the season, the last week in April, and the ground was soft enough that the ball didn't bounce, so the measurement was more accurate than it might have been in June. He hit one to left field, which landed in the front of the shortstop on the Babe Ruth field and caused no small measure of confusion in *that* game. John David's third, fourth and fifth home runs were hit to right field and cleared the fence by thirty or forty feet. His sixth home run was spectacular. He took a low and inside pitch on a two-and-two count and hit it over the black ash trees beyond the right field fence.

Had the coaches ever thought to study John David's batting performance, they might have noticed a curious connection between his home runs and the weather. John David hit well in bright sunlight, when he was forced to squint. It had escaped even John David's attention until just before coming to bat with his All-Star team behind 8-7 in the bottom of the sixth. The *All-Star* team. John David had made the team in spite of his abysmal batting average. He was a pretty good outfielder, certainly, but his judgement at the plate was questionable. John David considered a walk a waste of an at-bat. He didn't think there should be such a thing as a "walk." It was a safe bet that he'd swing at an outside pitch, *way* outside, on a 3-2 count. Once, during the regular season, he struck out during an intentional walk. Wouldn't let the ball go by that late in the game, knowing he wasn't going to get another at-bat that night. The coach wanted to pinch-hit Tony Massillo for John David now. The Henoga Valley All-Stars typically didn't win many games. They played against more experienced teams from Wells and Minerva, Johnstown, Gloversville, bigger towns with bigger boys, kids who probably shaved.

Bernie hated to leave the game to chance. And John David

had been standing at the far end of the dugout for the entire inning, seeming not to notice the game at all. John David hadn't cheered when Chris Miller hit a bloop single over the shortstop's head with two out and the game hanging by a thread! He didn't notice when Frank Massillo hit the ball only two feet to the right of the second baseman, and everyone held their breath fearing the worst. But the ball was hit hard and the second baseman bobbled it long enough to allow Chris and Frank to get on base. Bernie looked over to see if John David was ready and, to his horror, he saw that he *didn't even have his helmet on!*

"*John David!*" he shouted.

Bernie's mind raced frantically between the possibilities. Rush to get the helmet on, find the kid his bat. Send him to the plate looking like some hick who doesn't even know when it's his turn to bat. What a joke!

He thought of Tony Massillo, Frank's little brother and the only ten-year-old on the All-Star team. Tony was a great hitter, but Bernie had used him sparingly out of deference to the older kids. The thought of using Tony in place of John David quickly left Bernie's mind. John David's father was in the stands, probably drunk. Bernie had only inserted John David into the lineup in the fifth inning; he hadn't even batted yet. If Bernie pulled John David, Dutch Marten would be in the dugout in seconds, throwing punches. So Bernie held his hands over his face and gently shook his head while John David walked over to the helmets.

John David picked up his 34-inch Louisville Slugger. He was the only kid on the team using that bat, but he had been splitting wood for his family's woodstove since he was seven years old. He could cleave a six- inch thick block of maple with a single blow, and the snap of his wrists at the final moment would send the two halves spinning end over end. He could stand a one-inch piece of wood on the chopping block and split it perfectly in half. Every time. Once, several years earlier, John David was forced to explain to his disbelieving mother and sister how their cat *Tiffany* had been accidentally killed by a block of oak that had flown off that chopping block. There was no question that he could handle a 34-inch bat. As he walked to the

5

plate, though, his mind still wasn't on the game. He had always wondered why he couldn't hit a baseball like his friend Jack O'Neill. It embarrassed him. But moments before he had discovered something that had oddly eluded him for a long time. Standing near the end of the dugout, he had been closing one eye and then the other. Then both were open. Right eye closed, left eye closed. Both eyes open looking left, both eyes open looking right. It would be several months before he could explain it fully to the optometrist, but he noticed that when he looked over his right shoulder, he saw double. It didn't happen when he looked over his left shoulder. He had tried it several times. Standing facing the pitcher's mound on the top step of the dugout, he looked to right field. Slowly, two identical right fielders emerged from the same body. He blinked and they became one. But as he stared they began to separate again. It would dawn on John David after the game that all of his home runs had been hit when the sun was setting low over the outfield, forcing him to squint. He'd never hit a home run when it was overcast. Now he walked to the plate and stood outside the batter's box, closing one eye then the other. If he had to close one of them, it should be the left eye, he decided. The Johnstown All-Star team noticed his squinting, one eye then the other, his face contorting like a man with a pretty bad tic. They laughed and pointed. *Batter needs glasses, batter needs glasses.* John David took the first pitch with his left eye closed. It was a called strike, but John David couldn't follow it with one eye. It didn't look right. So he asked the umpire if he could switch to the other side of the plate.

"Sure, son," the umpire answered. "You sure you want to do that this late in the season?"

John David nodded and crossed the plate. Bernie Masurkiewicz was shocked. He looked as if someone had hooked jumper cables to his ears. He ran out onto the field calling time out, not even waiting for the umpire to acknowledge him.

"What are you *doing*!?" he pleaded, his hands outstretched.

John David was at least three inches taller than his coach. John David didn't really answer, except to say *What?* Like it

6

was a common occurrence, a kid switching his stance in the middle of a game. *What?* What options did Bernie really have? He couldn't yank the kid, not with one strike on him already, although the thought did cross Bernie's mind as he walked out to the plate. The crowd from Johnstown loved it. The hometown crowd was typically quiet. They weren't used to winning these all-star games. The season was over, really. This game was a ritualistic honor bestowed on the better players for having excelled at the local level. The All Star game was more like a sacrificial rite when Henoga Valley actually faced the bigger towns, and it didn't really matter whose kid was served up on the altar.

So John David stepped up to the plate, right-handed, amidst peals of laughter from the Johnstown dugout. The pitcher went into his stretch, looked down at second base, lifted his leg and threw the ball waist-high, slightly inside. John David swung and hit the ball foul. It wasn't *just* a foul ball, not the kind of foul ball that would make you think *maybe* this kid has a chance to connect. John David took the pitch with a long stride and his arms fully extended, snapping the bat around so fast that it came all the way back to his right leg. There was a tremendous crack that sounded like one of the bleachers had snapped. The ball flew over the backstop on the Babe Ruth Field and bounced on an access road more than 300 hundred feet away.

"What the hell was that?!" was all the Johnstown coach could say. He looked to the assistant coach, who was already out of the dugout trying to see where it went. The entire Johnstown infield moved in unison back to the edge of the infield. Actually, they were about four feet beyond the edge of the grass, so now, technically, the Johnstown team had a pitcher, a catcher, and seven outfielders. The pitcher looked at his coach, dumbfounded. They hadn't seen John David before, had no idea how to pitch to him. Couldn't walk him, that would load the bases. Low and inside didn't look like a great idea either. Billy went back to the mound rubbing the new baseball with both hands.

"You can do it, Billy!" the coach shouted, his hands cupped over his mouth. Billy probably didn't hear him because everyone in the Henoga Valley bleachers was screaming at the tops of their lungs. The Johnstown coach tried to wave his infield back in, but they ignored him. They knew there was more than baseball at stake here. If that last shot had been a line drive, somebody might have been killed. The third baseman had a look on his face that said 'please let it hit the ground once before it gets to me.' The pitcher felt especially vulnerable. If that ball had come right back at him he might not have even gotten a glimpse of it before the lights went out. He wished his coach would protest. Who was this kid? Why all of a sudden does he show up? In the last inning. It was like Frank Robinson had just stepped up to the plate. And his coach might have protested if they hadn't just laughed at the kid.

"Come on, Billy. Just throw to him. Make him hit it," he said. The Johnstown coach meant 'don't walk him,' but it didn't sound right. John David ignored the crowd behind him. Mothers were yelling at the tops of their lungs, their voices fused into one high-pitched scream, like Millers saw mill on a busy afternoon. The men were, by comparison, almost silent. They were studying the game, watching the drama unfold. They offered useful, somber advice. *Okay John David. Just hit the ball. Get a piece of it. Don't try to kill it.*

But John David fully intended to kill that ball.

Had the Johnstown pitcher regained his composure, a classic struggle between good pitching and good hitting might have ensued. But the good pitching side of the duel didn't show up. Unnerved, Billy from Johnstown hesitated midway though his windup, thinking that perhaps a change-up would catch John David off guard. The hesitation was not enough for the umpire to call a balk, but it was enough for Billy to lose the momentum he would have needed for his best fastball. The ball came across the plate a good ten mph slower than was prudent under the circumstances, and John David drove the ball into the Raquette River, a hundred and eighty feet beyond the right field fence.

No one ever found *that* ball.

And so it was that John David's seventh and last home run of the 1965 Little League season came to be legendary long before he disappeared into the Adirondack Mountains. His little brother Stephen claimed to have found that ball, running up to the front porch of the O'Neill house later that summer with Ralph and Joey Miller. The three of them were soaking wet, their hair matted down, shirts spattered with mud. They had been playing along the eastern bank of the Raquette River for hours and came upon a water-logged baseball wedged between two rocks.

"This is the ball!" Stephen shouted. "This is it. I know it is!"

He had one foot planted on the first step of the porch. His right elbow was perched on his knee and he held the ball like a young Hamlet. John David was sitting on the top step and looked at the little treasure hunter indifferently. The rest of the kids jumped up to look at the ball, to determine its authenticity. But how could anyone tell? One water-logged baseball pretty much looked like another, and everyone had a few water- logged baseballs. Balls left out on the lawn, or hit into the tall grass behind the Marten's garage and never found. Stephen could have soaked one on purpose. He was at that age when reality and fantasy were just a couple of points on the same compass. He had claimed, at one time or another, to have seen an eagle swooping down in the backyard and pick up a cat, then drop it in a tree, and a snake swallow a turtle, and even wolves descending on the back yard and stealing an entire box of Oreos from the picnic table. All of these things happened when Stephen was alone and were therefore not quite believable. But Stephen looked convincing now, holding the baseball with uncharacteristic authority. And he had two witnesses. The boys were more likely to believe Stephen if he had witnesses. None of them had mastered conspiracy yet and you could never get three kids to tell a lie the same way, even if you rehearsed it for a week. So Stephen had found a ball in the general vicinity of where John David's legendary blast went. And it was soaking wet. They all grabbed at it. All except John David. He just sat on the top step of the O'Neill's porch with his elbows resting on his knees. Chris Miller was the quickest and got it first.

"It's definitely a Little League ball," he said, turning it over. "You can still see the letters."

"All baseballs have that," Bobby O'Neill said. He was

Jack's eight year old brother. Like all little brothers, he was quick to argue.

"No they don't," said Chris. "Do you think the pros play with Little League baseballs?"

"We're two thousand miles from Yankee Stadium," Chris said, trying to get everyone back on track. "Any ball around *here* has to be a Little League ball."

"We're not two thousand miles from Yankee Stadium," Frank Massillo said. "We drove down there with my uncle. I think it's more like a thousand."

"Oh, right," Chris countered, "so maybe you think Mantle can hit a ball *one* thousand miles."

"It would have to be a foul ball," Frank added, "I think Yankee Stadium faces the other way."

Stephen Marten looked up in wonder at the complexity of these arguments. He was hoping to one day master the font of knowledge needed to be an articulate twelve-year-old. He stuck with the cautious approach, the bare facts. This baseball was found in the river. There were no houses down by the Little League Field. No kids played there except for Little League.

"It can't be the ball," Chris decided. "The real ball would have floated down the river to the ocean."

That led to several minutes of discussion on whether or not baseballs can float. Through it all, John David sat and listened, slightly bemused. Finally he asked to see the ball. He held it in front of his face and rotated it once.

"It can't be the one I hit," he concluded, tossing it back to his little brother. Stephen caught the ball off his chest, bobbled it a little, then looked up at John David, bewildered.

"How can you tell?" he asked.

John David leaned closer to his little brother and said, "Because the one I hit should be *flat* on one side."

And we all laughed.

Chapter Two

River Street. Hardly a street at all, barely wide enough for a single car to pass. In the 1840s, the narrow, poorly-lighted alley between the tannery and a row of taverns was frequented by loggers, guides, and trappers. Surprisingly little had changed over the ensuing one hundred and twenty years. The tannery business was gone, having moved south to Gloversville in the late 1800s. The building had been occupied over the years by an assortment of warehouses, general stores, supply stores, but was now long abandoned. Few residents of Henoga Valley were old enough to remember when the building was last used, but everyone still referred to it as "the tannery." Many of the windows were boarded up, and those that weren't, were broken. On the other side of the street were several taverns. Smokey's Grill, the River House and the Tahawus Hotel, which wasn't really a hotel, but a bar with eight rooms on the second and third floors. They, too, were more than one hundred and thirty years old, and together they represented the 'historic' district of Henoga Valley, although hardly anyone spoke of it in those terms.

The buildings along River Street were erected shortly after the prospector, William Spencer, arrived from New York City in 1835 to mine his newly acquired lode of iron ore. He formed the Adirondack Iron Works a year later and built several blast furnaces. He dammed the Raquette River just north of River Street and built a sawmill and a gristmill three years later. A general store appeared the following year. William Spencer then starting selling parcels of his vast wilderness to farmers lured by the prospect of both jobs in the Adirondack Iron Works and farming. By 1845, Henoga Valley was a bustling village with more than three hundred inhabitants.

The Adirondack Iron Works and the village it spawned was buoyed by the shear optimism of the era. *Weren't all things possible*? Spencer reasoned, riding his quarter horse through the Adirondack wilderness after traveling from New York to Utica on the newly constructed Erie Canal. *Wasn't the canal built against all natural odds? Weren't all things possible if one simply willed them to be?* He had invested $40,000 of his family's money and borrowed another $80,000 from associates. The pig iron he produced was generally acclaimed to be equal to the finest in the world and even won a gold medal at the 1854 Paris Exposition.

In spite of these accomplishments, the burden of mining so far from civilization eventually eroded Spencer's spirits. Despite the awards, fortune seemed ever distant. The ore was particularly difficult to extract. It contained strange impurities that even the 'experts' from Albany, brought to Henoga Valley at great expense, could not identify. And the iron had to be hauled by wagon to Lake Champlain, sixty miles to the east, over roads so crude as to be treacherous in the best of seasons and impassable in the worst. William Spencer had tried to build a narrow gauge railroad to the lake, but the project was abandoned after two years with only *seven* miles of track laid. The forest had proved to be impenetrable. And then ore was discovered near Lake Champlain, a lode with fewer impurities than Spencer's. The Champlain lode was particularly valuable because it was located only a few miles from the western shore of the lake, which was linked to Albany by the Champlain Canal. The iron could be shipped from the mine to Albany by canal boat at a fraction of the cost that William Spencer paid to ship his ore. Spencer became despondent and sullen, knowing that the forces of nature and economics were ganging up on him.

Although profoundly religious during more prosperous times, and rarely known to drink strong liquor, Spencer began spending more time in the taverns. His mood blackened for days at a time. Unable to believe that fortune could be so fickle, he began to see enemies lurking in the shadows of his misfortune. *Why is this happening to me?* he thought. But his enemies continued to multiply. When the heavy spring rains of 1857 made it impossible to ship any iron to Champlain, William Spencer ran short of cash. He could no longer pay the iron workers on a regular basis. He tried to borrow more money, but neither his family nor his associates would invest any more (they had long ago given up on the project and had even tried to recover some of their investment, but with no success), and the banks refused to give him a loan. A financial crisis, they told him. A national crisis. There was no money to lend. He scoffed at their notion of a crisis. *His* was the financial crisis. Nearly one hundred miles into the wilderness, and it might as well have been a thousand.

A little-known historian wrote years later that the failure of the first foundry in the Adirondacks had been unavoidable. He described the enterprise in military terms. Spencer had been overconfident in his abilities, waging the battle in hostile territory with supply lines that could not be maintained. The enemy, the wilderness, was always flanking him. These analogies were undoubtedly accurate, but in the end it was a simple act of God that closed down his mine. The heavy spring rains of 1857 simply washed away the dam one cold, drizzly morning. The dam had powered the bellows that stoked the blast furnace, which went cold like a candle snuffed. That night, William Spencer went into the Tahawus Hotel and drank heavily from six o'clock until almost midnight. Everyone later agreed that Mr. Spencer must have been trying to drink himself to death, and he might well have succeeded had he more time. But standing at the bar he began to curse the valley, the forest, the mountains, and every creature, man or beast, that resided therein.

"The whole fuckin place can go to hell!" he finally concluded, slumping against the bar.

He was speaking to no one in particular, but the dozen or so patrons in the bar clearly heard him. Spencer was a strange sight in the Tahawus Hotel. He had never been inclined to mingle with the trappers and miners, a breed, in his estimation, just slightly above the forest creatures. They came to Henoga Valley like crows to carrion. One of the miners, who had been sitting with his friends at a table near the door talking in hushed voices, walked up to William Spencer and asked him when they were going to receive their back wages, now six weeks overdue.

"Back wages!" Spencer bellowed. *"Back wages!* Where have you been, my good friend?"* he said, slapping the man on the back and laughing at the comic tragedy. "The dam is gone and the money with it. All of it washed away," he said, his hand rising. He placed his hand on the man's shoulder, a friendly gesture, though Spencer had never been friendly with miners before. "If you want your money, you best look downstream."

The man brushed away Spencer's hand.

"Oh, come now," Spencer said. "Do be a sport about it. Come, let me buy you a drink. What will it be? A draft? A shot of whiskey?"

"I don't want nothing from you but my wages," the man said. "You owe me for six weeks."

Had William Spencer known these men better, he might have sensed the danger. He might have recognized the pitch in the man's voice, the way that he issued words with a hiss from pursed lips, with tiny droplets of spit forming at the corners of his mouth. He might have observed the furrow of the man's brow and the downward tilt of his head, like that of an angry dog. But Spencer didn't know the man, couldn't even be sure he worked for the Adirondack Iron Works. So he foolishly placed his hand on the man's shoulder a second time. The act of Spencer's hand squeezing his shoulder infuriated the miner. He drew a knife from his belt and slashed Spencer's throat, all in a single motion. It happened so quickly that William Spencer never comprehended what had happened. He simply stared at the man while his right hand reached instinctively for his throat. He felt the warmth of his own blood, yet he knew not that it *was* blood, and he collapsed onto the floor like a tree felled.

River Street, narrow and dark, the name itself so ominous that I continued to avoid like-named streets long after I grew up. We were warned by our parents never to take shortcuts through River Street, never to fish off the ruins of the old dam. Older boys sometimes told stories of fights that had taken place down there. Big brawling fights that younger children couldn't possibly comprehend. Broken noses, men getting their teeth kicked out, and we wondered, but dared not ask, how the boys relating the stories even knew about these fights. John David Marten must have known about them. His father was often involved. Dutch Marten seemed to delight in punching someone out over the smallest infraction, a mere glance, a casual bump in a crowded bar. Fighting was as natural to Dutch Marten as golf

14

and tennis were to people who frequented the Tupper Lake Country Club. But John David never spoke of these fights, never even seemed to know that they had occurred. He was asked about them in school by upperclassmen, kids three and four years older than him who seemed to know many of the details. John David would shrug his shoulders and smirk, which made the older boys think that the real details were a secret between him and his father.

The Martens were an unusual family, one of the few that could trace their roots back to the Adirondack Iron Works. Dutch Marten's great- great grandfather had moved his family to Henoga Valley from Elizabethtown in 1846. He was rumored to have been the miner who killed William Spencer, though no one at the time ever testified to that effect. His descendants, for better or for worse, had stayed ever since. Dutch Marten worked at Valley Auto, where he was known to be a hard worker. His face was weathered and old for a man of 38. There were deep creases in his face and he looked at people with his head tilted slightly downward. He stood nearly six feet tall, with broad shoulders and heavily muscled arms. He never drank on the job, but at quitting time he walked two blocks to River Street and stayed until well into the evening. Many nights he never went home, which suited his wife, Diana, just fine. She would have been content if he *never* came home. She hated it when he came home drunk. Drunk and violent. There was a crack in the back door from the night that Dutch found the door locked at four a.m. He knocked loudly and when no one answered in the next thirty seconds, he smashed the door with his fist. He was prone, when drunk, to throw objects around the house, break lamps, and even, on one occasion, to rip down all the curtains in the living room.

Other than drinking, Dutch Marten's only interests in life were the cars he repaired out in barn behind his house. He was always rebuilding the engine from an old wreck. He bragged about how he'd bought it for $50 and was going to sell it for $500, but Diana never saw any of the profits. Whatever money he made must have gone to the bartender at the Tahawus Hotel.

John David somehow managed to keep himself and his little brother Stephen out of his father's way most of the time, but there wasn't much he could do for his older sister. Eva was fifteen in 1965, three years older than John David. She was tall like her brother, with auburn hair that hung past her shoulders. She inherited her father's broad shoulders, and sinewy arms. Her legs were long and muscular, even though she had never participated in sports. She came home after school and studied. She helped her mother take care of Stephen when he was a baby, she cleaned the house, she waited on her ungrateful father. She did this without ever complaining, which, as the years went by, John David found increasingly remarkable. Her father had beaten her just once, when she was twelve, but she had not forgotten how it felt. Or how it *looked*. She hated him, but she was careful not to show it. But when she left home for college, she never again set foot in Henoga Valley.

John David treated his father with veiled contempt. He too had received beatings from his father, even when Dutch Marten was sober, but he had stopped crying about them when he was seven years old. The last time he had been beaten by his father was a year earlier. His father slapped him repeatedly for moving something in the garage, a wheel barrow or the mower, leaving it too close to where Dutch parked the car. And Dutch scraped the car door against it after a night of drinking. He was so infuriated that he hauled his son out of bed at three a.m. to show him what had happened.

"I'll move it," John David answered, still groggy.

"*Now's* too late," Dutch yelled, slapping him across the back of the head. "You shouldna put it there it the first place."

"Do you want me to move it or not?"

Dutch followed his son to the garage. He continued to hit the boy across the face and head, backing him into the corner. John David blocked the blows, most of them, the ones that would have hurt. Finally, Dutch backed away, nearly tripping over the garbage can. John David stood there looking at him, but he couldn't help but smile. His father's fly was undone.

"Jesus, Dad, you're losing something off the hook."

"Don't get smart with me, you little wise-ass or I'll kick the shit outta ya."

Dutch Marten came back in at John David and swung, but

John David ducked and easily avoided the punch. Dutch's fist hit the tip of the metal support that held up a shelf and a huge gash opened on his knuckles. His father swore. John David couldn't help but wonder how pathetically drunk the other guys must have been, the ones his father actually managed to beat up.

"Get back to bed, you little wise-ass," Dutch said. He slapped the back of John David's head as he walked past.

John David had been in only one real fight that anyone could remember. There had been the minor skirmishes over the years, wrestling matches between John David and his best friend, Jack O'Neill. Two boys pushing each other, tempers flaring, gripping each other in a headlock that made them appear as Siamese twins. And punches thrown, but not aimed to where they would inflict real damage. Never to the face or stomach, because neither one wanted to hurt or embarrass the other in a way that might ruin their friendship. It was strange to watch John David in a *real* fight because it made us realize that we didn't know him as well as we had thought.

John David, then only thirteen years old, had been taunted by a high school senior named Frank Tomecki for almost a week. Frank was the center on the football team. He was a big kid weighing 220 pounds, fleshy, but strong and perpetually picking on smaller kids. It would last for a week or two and then he would start on someone else. Usually it was a boy, and mostly confined to his own classmates, but he was not averse to picking on girls and very young children. John David had been standing in a crowd that was waiting for the morning bell to ring. Frank was talking in a loud voice, speaking to his friends nearby, but loud enough for everyone to hear. He had been razzing Mike Missek, a fat kid in John David's freshman class, for weeks. Now it was Monday morning and he was taking up where he had left off the previous week. Mike had large lumps of flesh that looked like breasts, and Frank grabbed one of them.

"Bout time for that training bra, Missy." Frank said, and his friends exploded in laughter. "If I had tits like these, I'd go out for cheerleading."

Missek did not say anything. He knew instinctively that it was best not to engage Frank Tomecki at a time like this. He

17

wasn't the kind of bully who taunts you to answer him. He didn't expect answers, didn't want them. So when John David, standing on the other side of the Mike Missek, said, "If you had tits like that you'd look a whole lot better bending over on football," Frank Tomecki was simply dumbstruck. Frank's friends laughed even louder, slapping him on the back. One of them, Joey Cassillo, the quarterback of the varsity team, turned and placed his head and hands against the school wall and howled in laughter.

"Fuck you, Marten," Frank said.

John David only smiled.

"Hey Marten, your father get drunk again last night?" Frank asked, as if Dutch Marten's state of intoxication was somehow relevant at eight o'clock in the morning, at school.

"Wouldn't surprise me," John David answered. He had stop being embarrassed by his father, or at least showing his embarrassment, years ago.

"Wouldn't surprise me if I punched your fuckin' face in this afternoon," Frank answered. He was referring to the fact that the varsity and junior varsity football teams practiced together. John David was only a freshman, Frank a senior.

"You mean, before I put on my helmet?" John David asked.

"Well, maybe I'll just rip your helmet *and* your fuckin' head off."

And so it went for the rest of the week. Every morning Frank maneuvered close to John David and talked about maybe beating the shit out of him today. John David would smile, even laugh when the taunts were actually amusing, and all the while Mike Missek was thankful that nobody noticed him anymore. John David didn't even know Missek, who had moved to Henoga Valley a couple of months ago with his minister father. He was in the 'smart group' and John David wasn't, so they didn't spend any time together. Missek felt sorry for John David now, listening to him being bullied. But it didn't seem to bother John David. He laughed along with the older boys, and some of them started to admire him for it, which only pissed Frank off even more.

Eva stood up for John David on Thursday morning, telling

Frank in front of everybody to pick on someone his own size. Frank could have made it into a joke, but Eva was so beautiful that he had difficulty speaking in her presence. So out of frustration he simply went up behind John David on Friday morning and grabbed him in a bear hug, pinning his arms to his side.

"How's it feel to have your ribs crushed?" he whispered into John David's ear.

Although John David would never admit having learned anything from his father, he had, in fact, learned at least one lesson. 'No such thing as a fair fight,' his father told him on several occasions, as if imparting the wisdom of the ages. Dutch meant that he should never wait for the other guy to get ready. And John David didn't. He threw his head back so hard that it cracked against Frank's face with a loud pop, like two bowling balls colliding. The force of the blow flattened Frank's nose. Blood gushed forth and quickly covered his face. He released John David from the bear hold and held his nose with his hands, trying to staunch the flow of blood. Pain shot through his face and his ears were ringing. He felt dizzy and started to stumble.

Frank was bent over, his head down almost to his waist. In another second he might have recovered and erupted in rage. Under those circumstances John David might not have had much of a chance against the much larger boy. But John David had already swung around and grabbed Frank by the hair. His right hand was cocked. At that instant everyone in the schoolyard realized that John David was about to throw an uppercut, a blow that would again hit Frank squarely on his crushed nose. They gasped, seemingly in unison, because Frank's hands were covering most of his face. He couldn't even see the punch coming. Fortunately, it never did.

"Oh, I'm sorry," John David said, as if he had just realized he'd made a big mistake. "You were just *kidding*, weren't you? I thought you really were going to beat the shit out of me." His voice was genuinely apologetic, even submissive.

"I *was* just kidding, you dumb son of a bitch," Frank said, still holding his nose. He was barely able to stay on his feet. A searing pain rushed through his face and jaw, and the sight of his

19

own blood made him woozy. He was trying to stop the bleeding, but the blow left him dazed. He was holding his mouth, perhaps thinking that it was the source, but the blood continued to rush from his broken nose.

"Really, it was, you know, like a reflex," John David said.

He took off his flannel shirt and held it up to Frank's face.

"Shit, I thought you were going to kill me or something," he repeated.

"I still might," Frank answered, but there was no intimidation left in his voice.

John David helped him sit down on the school stairs. Frank's head was throbbing with pain and he was drifting in and out of consciousness. Someone had gone to get the principal, Mr. Dalton, who showed up in a huff and asked the usual What's-the-meaning-of-this type questions. It was an odd thing to ask about a fight. There didn't seem to be any appropriate answers, since fights rarely had any intrinsic meaning. They were just fights. Years later I might have been able to answer that question, but not then. Not there.

Frank was driven to the emergency room by one of the bus drivers, and we would learn later in the day that he had suffered a concussion. A concussion! The words reverberated throughout the school with electricity, the implication being that John David had not merely beaten up the bully, but had nearly killed him.

John David was suspended from school for two days. They had been horsing around, he admitted, that was all. It had been an accident. He never argued that it was self defense, or even that they had been fighting. They had been just horsing around, he told the principal. But Mr. Dalton was no fool. He knew enough about Dutch Marten to draw the appropriate conclusions.

"You don't have to grow up like your father," Mr. Dalton said. "You can make your own decisions, live your own life."

John David only nodded in agreement. He accepted the suspension without a word of protest.

Oddly enough, John David and Frank Tomecki apparently became friends for the remaining year they shared at Henoga Valley High School. When they passed in the hallways, Frank would pretend to throw a punch and John David would cringe.

20

Then Frank would stop and talk, ask John David about the JV team, tell him a crude joke. He pretended to protect John David on the football field, grabbing him around the neck and warning the rest of the varsity players not to take any cheap shots at his 'little buddy.'

No one ever spoke of the 'fight' in the schoolyard again. It was unusual for kids not to talk about such things. After a while most of them came to believe what John David had said, that it had been an accident. They were able to convince themselves because they did not want to believe that one of their friends was capable of such an act of violence. They did not want to think of the possibility that the second blow, the one not thrown, might have killed Frank Tomecki. And that their lives would have been forever changed by witnessing death in a schoolyard.

Late one afternoon, weeks after the fight, Eva stopped to talk to Frank outside of the school. They were alone, each waiting to be picked up by a parent. Frank had stayed for football practice and Eva had stayed to work on the yearbook. It was one of her few extracurricular activities. The sun was beginning to set behind the school, casting a long angular shadow onto the schoolyard where the fight had taken place. A gentle breeze blew through the red maples growing along side the building. Beautiful Eva, wearing a plaid skirt slightly above the knee, holding her books to her chest. She walked along the side of the building and stood not five feet from Frank. A month earlier she would have stood fifty feet away and pretended not to see him.

"Hello, Frank," she said. She barely spoke above a whisper. He had heard Eva speak in the school play the previous spring and had gone to all three performances, even though his father derided him over 'gettin cultured.' But she had never before actually spoken to *him*. Frank would have liked to have carried on a real conversation with Eva, but he simply could not. Just hearing her say his name made him blush. Beautiful Eva. So tall, her thick auburn hair blowing across her neck. Her lips open slightly, her perfect teeth. Were he able to articulate his feelings, he would have simply asked, *was there ever a woman so beautiful?* He was grateful just to look at her, to be *able* to look at her without feeling ashamed, because she had spoken to him first.

Hi was all he could say.

"How's the team this year?" she asked.

Could this be happening? Eva? Asking him about football? Asking his opinion, about anything?

"Real strong," Frank managed to reply, trying to sound like an authority. He could feel the veins throb in his neck.

Eva nodded.

"That's good," she said. "I hope you win a lot of games."

"Thanks." He thought for a second, then added, "You like football?"

"Well, no, not really," Eva said, and then laughed. "But I can see why it appeals to boys."

"Yeah, well, you know . . . it helps you keep in shape."

Eva nodded again and smiled. Her mother's car turned into the long school driveway and coasted to a stop in the schoolyard. A tiny cloud of dust drifted by their feet. Eva reached for the door handle. Frank, suddenly remembering manners he had been taught long ago but had never used, quickly stepped ahead of her and opened the car door.

"Thank you, Frank," Eva said, surprised. She was pleased to discover that he was capable of chivalry, in any form.

She slid into the car and her skirt crept up her thigh, revealing her long thighs. Frank began to feel dizzy, but managed to close the door without catching her skirt or banging her on the leg. Eva turned to him as the car pulled away and, in the last second, she lifted her left hand in a delicate wave.

Chapter Three

John David Marten got up from the table. It was Thanksgiving of 1969 and the snow was already falling. He could see it coming down heavily from where he sat at the table, looking past his mother to the large windows on the north side of the house. The snow had begun around noon and several inches had accumulated by the time Diana served the pumpkin pie. Diana noticed her son looking out the window. She glanced at him several times, only to catch his eyes moving away.

"John David, you're not thinking about going out in this, are you?" she asked. She knew it was a silly question. Of course he was going out. Going out for days, in fact. He'd be back on Sunday afternoon, dirty, smelling of campfire smoke, carrying the pelts of a dozen or so animals, perhaps the remains of a deer. It wasn't the simple fact that he went hunting or trapping for days at a time that bothered her, but that he went alone. It bothered her the first time he spent the night in the woods alone. She didn't sleep at all that night. But it had become so common over the last three years that she accepted these treks. He left with a small tent and a sleeping bag and would return with dozens of muskrat and mink pelts stuffed in the bottom of a wicker knapsack. His traps were stashed out in the woods God only knew where. Some of his friends said that John David had built a log cabin out in the woods, but he never admitted to that and no one could possibly hope to find it in the hundreds of square miles of mountains and swamps north of Henoga Valley. Rumors circulated that he killed six or eight deer each year, far beyond the legal limit, but there was no proof of that either.

"Why don't you leave in the morning?" Diana asked.

"Can't Mom," he answered. "I got traps to check in the morning."

"Where the hell did you set them?" his father mumbled. "Vermont?"

John David had tried on several occasions to explain to his mother where he was going, but she never seemed to comprehend. Once he gave her a detailed description of an unnamed pond near the eastern tip of Lost Creek, where he intended to trap during the week school was out in February. Diana listened to him, dumbfounded.

"Do *you* know where this is?" she asked, turning to Dutch.

"Yeah, I been hunting out there a couple times," Dutch said. "It's okay."

But, in fact, the pond that Dutch Marten was thinking of was twelve miles further to the east, and it had a name. John David hunted and trapped along creeks and lakes that no one ever visited, some of which were fifty miles from the nearest road. Diana asked him once to show her *exactly* where he was going, but he presented a map unlike any she had ever seen, with oddly shaped concentric circles and symbols that she did not understand. She pulled the map out of his coat pocket after John David had gone to bed and studied it closely. The map was covered with her son's pencilled notes. He had named some of the ponds and streams and mapped out places along the swamps with little dots. There were tiny boxes with dates written next to them, which she decided probably indicated deer that he had shot. Twenty-seven of those little boxes. Could he have really killed that many? At age sixteen?

Two weeks earlier a man had come to the back door, a *stranger*, asking if John Marten could guide him into the woods to hunt deer. Diana hadn't known what to say. *You mean John senior? Dutch?* But, of course he meant John David. Dutch had shot only one deer in his life, and that one had wandered into the backyard.

"Can you imagine," she told a friend afterward, troubled, "a stranger coming to my house and wanting John David to take him into the woods? Can you imagine?"

John David went into his bedroom and finished packing while his mother and Eva cleared the dishes. He emerged a few minutes later wearing a heavy canvas coat, a wool cap, leather boots, and an aluminum pack frame. He set the backpack down near the back door and strapped a pair of snowshoes onto it. Diana watched as he went to the cupboard and took down a box of rice and poured it into a plastic container. He mixed in some sunflower seeds and raisins and screwed on the lid.

"That all you're going to take to eat?" she asked.

"Enough food for a week, Mom," he said, stuffing the container into the pack. "Besides, there's plenty of fresh meat out there."

"Be sure to send me a postcard," Eva said. She stood at the kitchen sink, but did not turn to face him.

"Well, you can't live on rice, that's all I know," Diana added.

"No, you can't live on rice," John David agreed. "But you can survive on rice. I'll live when I get back home."

Did he say these things to tease her, she wondered, or was he serious? He hoisted the heavy pack onto his back, nodded once to his mother, and walked out the back door. Eva looked up from the kitchen sink and watched him cross the backyard and disappear into the woods.

"He's strange, Mom. He's going to set up a tent in the snow, in the dark. Don't you think that's strange?"

"Well, from my perspective, yes."

"Where's he going to sleep?"

"Same place he always does," she answered, "wherever *that* is."

"Don't you worry about him? Don't you think it's just a little bit odd?"

Diana rubbed Eva's back gently.

"I appreciate your concern, dear," she said, "but I'm sure he can take care of himself."

"I can't even stay out until midnight, but you let him stay out for a week?"

"That's different, Eva, and you know it."

Eva had come home late only once, which shouldn't have caused great alarm, so seldom was it that she dated. But her father had called her a cheap tramp, and her mother had defended her only half-heartedly. Eva was not disappointed in her mother's pathetic behavior because she could not have imagined her standing up to Dutch Marten. But the pity she felt for her mother was so great that it made her feel sick to her stomach.

Diana Marten, Diana Boutin for the first seventeen years of

25

her life, had married John "Dutch" Marten in her senior year of high school. He had graduated the year before and gotten a job at the sawmill. It seemed logical to marry him when he asked, like taking algebra as a freshman. People did that sort of thing, married whom you happened to love when you reached marrying age. She never considered for a moment that she might have had choices. Certainly no one else had shown much interest in her back then. She had been an average student, pretty, perhaps, in an awkward way, but not popular. What possible reason could she have had for saying no to Dutch Marten almost twenty years ago? He drank, but so did a lot of men. It never crossed her mind that she should consider her choices, even if it was simply whether to marry Dutch Marten or to remain single with no immediate prospect for marriage.

Perhaps if Diana had been beautiful, or bright and outgoing like some of her classmates who went off to college, she might have allowed herself to believe that she had options other than marrying Dutch Marten. Ironically, Diana became more beautiful as time passed. She had been exceedingly skinny as a teenager, with sunken eyes and jutting cheekbones. Her fingers had been so long and bony. But she gained weight during her first pregnancy and did not lose all of it after Eva was born. Her face was fuller, her arms and legs 'filled out' (her mother's expression), her breasts grew the way she thought they were supposed to when she was fifteen. Her cheeks became flushed, replacing a rather chalky complexion. Even her hair color changed subtly. Auburn highlights that had been unnoticed before now seemed to streak her chestnut hair, and it glowed with an almost unnatural sheen.

So great was the change in Diana that people could not help but comment, even men who worked with young Dutch Marten at the sawmill. Older men, who meant no harm at all, simply had to comment on the remarkable change in Diana Marten, as if Dutch himself might have missed the transformation. And there were others who *meant* to tease Dutch, who cautioned him to 'keep an eye on her,' thereby unearthing his latent jealousy.

Diana received so many compliments that they made her slightly dizzy. Nineteen years old, never even noticed by an adult as far back as she could remember, now stopped on the street by people she hardly knew, who fussed over the baby in the carriage, then fussed over *her*. Teachers she'd had in school only two years earlier, and who hadn't paid much attention to her then, so busy were they with the best students, now stopped in Woolworth's and chatted with her for ten or fifteen minutes. Not talking *to* her, like they had when she was in school, but *with* her, as though she was someone whose opinion might be important, someone who might say something amusing that you wouldn't want to miss. *Why is everyone so much more friendly now?* she asked herself.

She attributed all this attention to her baby. It was only much later, several years later, in fact, when a man at a wedding reception said that 'she was the most beautiful woman he had ever seen and not to take it wrong, for he meant no offense, he just wanted to be able to tell her,' that she allowed herself to think that she had actually become attractive. She had attended the wedding alone. Dutch Marten did not like weddings because Diana refused to go with him if he was going to drink, and he could think of no reason to go if he wasn't. The stranger's compliment had made her lightheaded. He was a distant cousin of the groom, in town just for the wedding and headed for Syracuse that evening. She had seen him in the church, sitting across the aisle from her. She thought she noticed him glancing at her at the reception, but she was still not capable of thinking that people noticed her. She was surprised when he followed her out onto the patio. He was so straightforward. He walked over to her and introduced himself, then asked her to dance. She agreed and he led her back to the dance floor. It felt so strange to be held by another man, whose arm gripped her around the waist so that their bodies were pressed together. He looked into her eyes and, for the first time in her life, she looked back. He asked of her relationship to the bride and groom. He told her where he lived and asked, like it was the most natural question in the world, if she was married.

"Yes, I am, " Diana replied, showing him her wedding ring. In retrospect, it seemed so childish to *show* him her ring like it was a certificate of authenticity. But her lack of sophistication made her more attractive to him.

"I guess I should have known that," he said, smiling.

They returned to the patio. He turned to lean on the stone wall. His voice was playful. "It's just that now that I have seen you, I'm afraid I'll be unhappy for the rest of my life."

Diana laughed, a chuckle really, but blurted out like a sharp cough. Women who knew they were beautiful might not have been taken by surprise, or might have even been offended by his effrontery. Diana was just amused.

"Oh, please," she said, incredulous. Diana had no experience carrying on this type of conversation. She could not remember Dutch ever telling her she was beautiful.

"It's my lot in life," the man said, "to be perpetually late."

She could not remember the rest of the conversation because her mind went numb when she realized that he was serious. Had he actually said those things, that she was not just beautiful, but the *most* beautiful woman he had ever seen? This stranger, who looked to be at least thirty years old, and was himself so very handsome. Then he excused himself, saying that he shouldn't detain her any longer because her company was certainly much in demand. *Detain her? Her company in demand?* She had never heard such words uttered by real people. No one in Henoga Valley ever spoke like that.

And so later that night, while Dutch Marten snored loudly in a drunken stupor, Diana stood naked in front of the bathroom mirror and studied her reflection unashamed.

Chapter Four

John David walked into the woods on a trail behind his house, a trail that all the neighborhood kids used. He followed it for about a mile, then picked up one of the state hiking trails that went past Indian Brook. It was already past four o'clock, later than he had wanted to start out, but it *was* Thanksgiving and his mother had prepared a turkey dinner that he hadn't wanted to miss. He figured he still had plenty of time to make it to the small hill overlooking Beaver Pond, where he would pitch his tent for the night. The next morning he would set over one hundred traps along the streams behind Raquette River Mountain. A full day's work. He had stashed the traps in bundles of twenty at five sites two weeks earlier. He would set them Friday, check them Saturday and Sunday, then spring them and leave them in place until the next weekend. He figured on catching at least forty muskrats and a half dozen mink over the weekend. He could make a hundred bucks easily. But there would be a lot of work. He'd return to the campsite each night, skin out the day's catch, bury the carcasses so as not to attract bears, then fall asleep exhausted. It was hard work, but he loved it. He loved to sleep in the woods alone. He loved to hike through the damp forest in the morning, coming upon each site in anticipation of a catch. His friends thought he was a little crazy. They called him Daniel Boone, "Daniel" actually, trying to sound like Cincinnatus on the television show. But they also envied the amount of money he made and the way that he made it. There were rumors that he shot deer for other hunters, that he left the tagged deer in the woods and told the men where to look for it, and was paid *twenty* bucks for his work. John David denied these stories, but several men in town who hadn't killed a deer in years were suddenly telling pretty incredible hunting stories. Old Mac Driscoll, who was eighty pounds overweight and smoked three packs of Pall Malls a day, told everyone in the Barkeater Coffee Shop how he had *stalked* a six-pointer for two miles over dry leaves. It was hard to believe a man like that would be capable of such a feat, and even harder to believe that a wild animal wouldn't see a man like Mac Driscoll coming.

There were a lot of fantastic stories that corresponded remarkably with John David Marten reaching his teenage years. How much money did he earn, his friends wondered? John David didn't spend his money like most kids. He didn't buy records or sneakers or leather jackets. He didn't hang out at Murphy's Drug Store buying sodas and talking to girls. But he had the best backpacking gear anyone had ever seen. Tents, snowshoes, backpacks, eider down sleeping bags that allowed him to sleep on the snow. And rifles, several rifles, a side-by-side Winchester 12-gauge shotgun with a walnut stock, a .30-06 bolt action Savage, a .220 Marlin. All purchased by special order. He received dozens of catalogs, with pictures of guns and boots and mess kits, all kinds of turkey calls and deer musk, and strange devices to mount on trees to allow the hunter to perch among the branches. His mother marveled at the gear her son carried, marveled at the fact that he knew how to use it. Her son, who, as far as she knew, had never even operated the washing machine.

John David reached the crest of the hill by Beaver Pond shortly after six o'clock. It was already dark, but he worked quickly to set up the tent. He could do it with his eyes closed. He rolled out his sleeping bag, then hoisted his backpack up into the trees with a rope to keep it out of the reach of any animals. He stripped down to his underwear and climbed into the sleeping bag. In bed by seven o'clock; pretty strange for a teenager, but there was nothing to do in the forest at night but build a fire and watch it burn, and he considered that a waste of time. So he closed his eyes and listened to the sound that came forth from the darkness. A gentle breeze rattled the dry oak leaves that still clung to the branches overhead. In the distance he could hear a hum, like a river flowing. As a young boy he had often been fooled into believing that it was the sound of a nearby stream. But the subtle drone had no origin that he could detect, so he accepted it as the life blood of the woods coursing through invisible veins.

John David awoke the next morning long before the sun

rose. He lit a can of Sterno and boiled water for his rice and tea. He ate quickly, washed his dish and repacked his utensils. A half hour later he was standing beside Indian Brook, a small stream that connected a series of ponds in the narrow valley alongside Raquette River Mountain. He was less than two miles from Henoga Valley, but the forest was so thick with spruce and hemlocks that it seemed utter wilderness. He began the long tedious process of setting his traps, following the stream to Rock Pond and Beaver Pond, then beyond to the nameless streams and ponds north of Raquette River Mountain. He would trap this area only once this year. On Sunday he would collect all the traps and stash them along the North Branch of the Raquette River and trap that area for two consecutive weekends. Then, during the Christmas break, he would trap the swamps to the north, along Independence River, Shaw Creek, and Lost Creek. He wouldn't need his tent for that trip; he had built a small log cabin on the south shore of a pond ten miles north of Henoga Valley and he would spend the nights there. The cabin was only nine feet tall, eight feet by eight feet, made from hewn logs. He had originally planned to build the roof out of plywood, but it proved too clumsy to carry. So he built it out of small logs and covered it with cedar shingles that he bought at the lumber yard. He framed a doorway only six feet tall, then carried in a small door with a window so that the cabin would have some light during the day. For warmth he put in a small Franklin stove.

It was almost three o'clock on Saturday afternoon when John David pulled his last trap out of the water. His catch had been bigger than he'd expected. He'd caught 36 muskrat that day alone. Only two mink, which disappointed him because a mink was worth $15, and a muskrat only $2 or $3. But he figured he made at least $150, and the holiday weekend was only half over. He had been skinning the muskrats on the spot because there were too many to carry. He was quick. Two slits, from the tail to each hind leg, then he pulled the fur off inside out with a single motion, like removing a glove. His pack weighed over fifty pounds now, and he'd already decided not to head back to his tent. He was east of Blackfoot Pond and the state trail was only a few miles away. The state trail was cleared six feet wide and was easy hiking. So he followed the stream south from the Blackfoot Pond, planning to pick up the state trail on the other side of Little Simon Pond.

The stream ran through a narrow valley with steep 200 foot walls on either side. John David followed the stream through the ravine until he came to the crest of a small knoll. He stopped suddenly when he noticed something move ahead. He always reacted to movements in the woods by standing perfectly still. It was as natural to him as it was to all of the other forest creatures. An object, a *person,* not fifty yards away, was sitting on a rock with his head in his hands. John David crouched down and slid his pack off quietly. *What the hell is he doing out here?* he thought. He'd never run into anyone this far from town before, and certainly never this far from a major trail. Maybe it wasn't a hunter. He couldn't see a gun. After a moment the figure raised its head and he realized it wasn't a man, but a *woman.* And she appeared to be crying! He could not tell at this distance who it was, but he could hear her talking to herself. He moved a few feet to the side to try to get a better look. The woman stood up and looked around, startled. She seemed to shout into the trees.

It took John David a minute to realize that the woman was lost. John David always knew generally where he was, even without a map. He'd heard stories about people getting lost from time to time. Hunters separated from friends and wandering around for hours until they were discovered, embarrassed, by the state police. He'd even heard of hikers being lost and never found, although that hadn't happened in the last couple of years. He watched as the woman walked about fifty yards and then stopped. She turned east and started following the stream. Wrong way, John David said to himself. She was headed further away from the state trail that John David assumed she must have taken into the woods.

Then he recognized her. Emily Davignon. They were in the same grade at Henoga Valley High, although he didn't know her very well because they didn't take any classes together. She came from a wealthy family, the only daughter of Dr. Davignon. Her family owned a mansion on a rocky point on Raquette Lake. She was the smartest kid in the class, probably smarter than his friend Jack O'Neill. Emily was beautiful, too, although there was considerable disagreement among his friends on *that* point. Emily had long chestnut hair and skin of cream and silk. Her dark brown eyes were perfect almonds and her nose looked like it had been sculpted from polished Italian marble. Her hands were delicate, her fingers gently tapered. She walked with such exquisite posture that her body appeared to waft through the corridors. She was exceptionally small- boned, so even though she was almost 5'-5" tall she appeared much shorter. Anyone seeing her for the first time would find her striking, but later they might come to question their first impression, She rarely smiled, not even in her senior class portrait.

John David had seen Emily's beautiful paintings in the glass cases in the school hallways, where the teachers displayed the works of the most talented students. Nothing of John David's ever appeared in those cases. They weren't likely to display a muskrat pelt, pulled taut inside out on a wire stretcher, but one of Emily's paintings was always on display. They were oil paintings of trees and rocks, close-ups of oak leaves on a pond, or ferns covering the forest floor, rendered in exquisite detail. They were unusual because she sometimes omitted parts of the subject. Sometimes it was the middle of the painting, sometimes the edges. Her strokes ended abruptly, sometimes with perfectly square edges, sometimes tapered to fine points. Unusual paintings, John David thought, but unquestionably beautiful.

Emily Davignon had started out along one of the state trails early that morning after telling her parents that she was driving up to Raquette Lake to buy new brushes. She had to lie about it because her parents forbid her to go hiking alone. Sixteen years old and she couldn't go on a clearly- marked hiking trail alone. She wanted to take pictures of the bogs and had tried twice before to do it with a friend, but it was impossible. Most of *her* friends wouldn't walk more than a mile in the woods, and they talked too much. She needed to be alone to take pictures, the kind of pictures she would later paint. She had left the trail around ten o'clock, planning to hike along the shore of a pond whose name she did not know. Emily had been experimenting with different techniques to show light reflecting from beneath

33

the surface of the water and she wanted to study light reflecting from different angles. So she stopped every fifty yards or so and took another picture, crouching down to capture the light reflecting off the smooth black surface. She was almost three quarters of the way around the pond when she came to a marshy area. One of her sneakers sank into the black mud hidden beneath the grass. She should have backtracked around the pond, but it had taken her three hours to walk through the dense brush to get this far, and she guessed that she was close to the trail. Maybe if I just go up along the marsh until I find a dry spot, she thought, then cut across. I'm almost back. But the forest played tricks on her, luring her deeper and deeper away from the trail, her umbilical vein to the civilized world. The marsh veered back and forth for almost a half mile before narrowing to a point where Emily decided to try crossing. She hopped between clumps of thick grass, assuming that they were drier, and holding onto small trees. But she slipped and her right foot sunk deep into the black mud halfway up her calf. She panicked, pushing on across the marsh even though she was getting wetter with every step. Twice more she stepped deep into the soft earth. She felt hands come up from the ground and grab her ankles. Let go of me, she shouted, perhaps out loud. I want to go home. But the forest teased her. *You are home, Emily. This is where you belong, with us. Stay here and take our picture.* The small trees that she held onto for balance dipped beneath her weight, as if *trying* to make her to fall. Don't fall, she told herself, whatever you do, don't fall. Her legs were beginning to feel numb from the cold. The mud was sucking body heat out through the soles of her sneakers. So cruel, so devious.

She finally reached dry ground. She climbed a small knoll covered with hemlocks and walked along a ridge toward where she thought the pond was. But she was more than a mile from the pond and walking away from the very trail she thought was just out of sight. The hemlocks reached out to touch her face. She brushed them aside, which angered them. They began to strike her harder, whipping her across the neck and shoulders and slapping her across the face. Her cheeks stung and angry

34

red welts appeared. She swung her arms to fend them off. Get away from me you son of a bitch! *You're the bitch, Emily.* Leave me alone. *We are leaving you alone, Emily. All alone.* The wind howled in delight and the hemlocks swayed back and forth like children, laughing at her, taunting her. One of them yanked her hat off her head and dangled it out of her reach. Give it back, give me my hat, Emily said, pawing at the branches. But of course it did not. *Reach for it, Emily. Jump Emily.* And another branch came down and slapped her face again, really hard. The game was getting out of hand. The hemlocks were no longer playful. They were brutal and cruel in their mocking. They huddled around her like bullies in a playground, forcing her to run to the only open area. They were leading her away from the trail.

Emily finally came out of the stand of hemlocks and walked along a stream balancing herself by leaning on the larger rocks. She sat down on a boulder and began to cry. *What have I done? How could I let myself get lost?* She looked up and down the stream but saw not a clue of her whereabouts. The forest was unwilling to offer even the most meager hint. The trees looked the same in all directions. Without a trail to follow she knew she might walk for hours and end up only a quarter mile from where she started.

The stream. She remembered something about streams. How did it go? *When you're lost, follow a stream.* Unfortunately, like many of the Adirondack streams carved by the receding glacier, the stream she was following flowed north, away from the village.

A shadow passed over her face. It startled her. She looked up at the sun, which had begun to dip below the spruce trees on the stream bank. She stood and stared at it, then looked at the horizon in all directions, spinning, as if caught in a vortex. *The sun! The sun is setting! It's getting dark! No. No, it can't go down!* She held her hands to her face in horror.

The darkness sets in quickly in the narrow valleys. There were no street lights to warn her of its impending arrival. She had not planned to spend the night and now she would have less than a half hour before it was dark. A fresh wave of panic came over her, gripping her stomach. She was wet and cold. She knew that she would not survive a night in the forest in her condition. She remembered camping out with the girls scouts. How cold it had been, laying on the ground in a sleeping bag, even in the summer. Tonight would be much worse. She didn't even have that cheap sleeping bag to keep her warm.

In panic she began running along the banks of the stream. *I've got to get out of here*, she thought. *I've got to get home before dark.* Suddenly her eye caught a familiar shape, a human shape. She might not have noticed the silhouette on the streets of Henoga Valley, where it looked like so many others. But out here it was unusual and it drew her focus. She looked up and gasped so loudly that it sounded almost like a scream.

"How long have you been watching me!?" she shouted, terrified.

She recognized him immediately. John David Marten. Who *didn't* know him? He had practically killed Frank Tomecki a couple of years ago, she remembered. A big tough kid whose father was a drinker, and hadn't *he* killed someone years ago? What was he doing here, she wondered? How long had he been stalking her, like an animal? And what might he be thinking, finding her alone in the woods?

"How long have you been *watching* me?" she repeated, her voice shrill like a cat's screech and her eyes brimming with tears.

"Long enough to figure out that you're lost."

"I am not lost!"

"Oh, well then, sorry." John David turned and pretended to walk away.

"Wait!" Emily shouted. "I was ... hiking, you know, taking pictures. I was on my way home."

John David nodded as if he understood, then looked off in the direction Emily had been headed. He turned back to her and smiled.

"Are you Canadian?" he asked.

"No," Emily said. Had she not been exhausted, she might have detected the sarcasm.

"Then why are you headed north?"

Emily looked off in that direction, then started to cry. John

David grabbed his pack and slid down the embankment. He could see bright red scratches on her face where she had been raked by branches. Her jeans were soaked all the way up to her thighs and her sneakers were caked with thick black mud. Large clumps of her dark brown hair were matted against her face.

"I've been lost for hours," she admitted, sobbing. "I started up on that trail that goes to the pond over there," she said, pointing in the wrong direction, "and I left the trail to take some pictures on the other side of the pond. I thought I'd come around and get back on the trail, but I couldn't find it again."

She stopped crying abruptly, as if she'd swallowed something that had blocked her airway. She looked up at John David. He was wearing a long gray canvas coat and had a huge backpack at his side. His face was dirty, covered with soot, perhaps, or mud, she didn't know which. Maybe *he* was lost.

"What are *you* doing here?" she asked.

"You wouldn't want to know," John David said. He knew how Emily Davignon felt about hunting. Everyone did.

"Can you help me get back to the trail?" she asked.

"Well, I dunno, I'm kinda running behind."

Emily's faced dropped.

"I'm kidding. I'm *kidding*," he said. "Of course I'll help you. But I think it's too late for you to hike out tonight. It's twelve miles back to the road."

"Twelve miles?!"

"You're a lot more lost than you realize. You're going to have to spend the night."

"Where? Here?"

"Well, not *here*," John David said, pointing to the ground at his feet. "I have a cabin a couple of miles from here."

"I don't think I can make it that far," Emily said. "I'm so tired. I'm so cold."

"We'll make it," he said. His nonchalance was comforting.

John David turned his pack over and pulled out an extra pair of boots and heavy socks. "Size ten," he said, holding them up, "but they're a *dry* ten."

"Oh God, anything!"

Emily lifted one foot up onto the rock and began untying her sneaker. John David pulled a Sterno stove from his backpack and set it down on a flat stone.

"What are you doing?" Emily asked.

"I should make you something warm to drink."

John David took a little water out of his canteen and poured it into the bottom of the shallow pot. He watched Emily try to unlace her sneakers. Her fingers were so stiff that she appeared to have arthritis. He stepped closer to her and took her hands in his. The thin delicate fingers felt like sticks from the forest floor, cold and damp and nearly lifeless. She had worn mittens, but they too were wet. He took an odd-looking pair of mittens, made of canvas and leather with a single finger poking out the top, from his backpack and handed them to her. At first she declined, but then she realized that he hadn't been wearing them up to now and therefore wouldn't miss them.

John David carefully removed Emily's sneakers and socks and dried her feet with the cotton lining of his coat. They felt like stone. He held each one between his palms and blew his warm breath over them. Then he put the socks on for her and pulled them up over her calves.

Emily watched him as he laced the oversized boots. His hands were rough and cracked. They seemed impervious to the cold. He finished lacing the boots and then tied Emily's sneakers onto his backpack. When the water boiled he poured her a cup of tea.

The warmth of the cup radiated through her mittens. She sipped the tea slowly, holding it in her mouth to savor the heat. She even tried to swallow slowly.

"We'd better get going," he said after tying her sneakers to his backpack. "It can be a little tricky finding this place in the dark. Walked into a tree once."

Emily smiled and drained the rest of the tea in one swallow.

"You're going to be missed, aren't you?" he asked. "They'll be looking for you."

"Are you kidding?" she said, handing him the cup. "My father is having a stroke right now."

"Do you think the state police are already out looking for you?"

"No, but if I know my father, he'll call the National Guard and the Army Reserves if I'm not back by dark. But I didn't tell them I was coming out on the trails. He doesn't let me come out here by myself. Thinks I might get lost." Emily paused for a moment, then added, "Can you imagine?"

She expected him to say something patronizing, or sarcastic, and was surprised when he did neither. The light was beginning to fade and it cast a long shadow over his face. A handsome face, she thought, a kind face. His deep-set eyes were as dark as coal, so dark that she could not see the pupils. His face was sunburned, even in November. At that moment, watching John David put the tea cup back into his pack, she realized that her probable death, frightened, alone and cold, had been averted by an incredible stroke of luck. A wave of unspeakable gratitude came over her and she began to cry softly.

John David mistook her gratitude for fear. He looked up at her sitting on the rock and hugged her awkwardly. He'd never hugged a woman before. Hadn't even hugged his own mother in recent years, except grudgingly, at her insistence.

"Hey, c'mon. You're going to be okay," he said, patting her back. " I know this area like the back of my hand." He pulled a flashlight out of a pocket in his backpack. "You'll have to follow me single file. But I'll shine the light on the ground so you can see where you're going. You'll see. We'll be there in no time."

Emily slid down off the rock and started to follow him along the stream bed.

"Just be careful with those boots," he said.

Emily sniffled loudly and composed herself.

"They *are* a little big on me," she said.

"No, I meant don't get 'em wet," he said. "They cost me forty- seven dollars."

Then she heard him laugh softly, and she smiled at the unexpected humor.

They walked through a thick stand of black spruce. John David led the way like a pack horse, the huge backpack covering his torso. It must be heavy, Emily thought, judging by his labored movements. Where on earth was he coming from?

39

Everything she knew about him, which she now realized wasn't much, she had heard from Jack O'Neill. What did Jack call him? Daniel Boone? No, Dan'l Boone.

Several times they had to climb embankments, and each time he went ahead five feet at a time and extended his hand to pull her up. Sometimes he put his arm around her waist and hoisted her up to him. His hands felt like her father's old baseball glove that she had found up in the attic years ago. Each time he did something to help her she thanked him. The first time he said 'you're welcome,' but after that he only nodded. A single nod each time, a slow dip of the head, like a horse bobbing.

After nearly an hour they reached a clearing. From a distance, if anyone had been looking for them, they would have appeared as two tiny specks in a meadow. The light from the flashlight danced on the grass. John David stopped and looked at the evening sky. The silhouette of the spruce looked like sentries against the blue-black night. Few words had passed between Emily and John David over the past hour because it was difficult to talk while walking single file. Once they reached the open meadow Emily came up and stood beside John David.

"It's a beautiful night, isn't it?" John David said.

Emily looked up at the sky. The moon, nearly full, rose over the trees in front of them and cast a silvery hue upon the deep grass. Emily tried to agree, but she sounded unconvinced. Until that day she had considered herself as a naturalist, a child of nature. She read Thoreau and Emerson and Aldo Leopold. She argued with her father that hunting was morally wrong, the equivalent of killing our brothers and sisters. She wouldn't even go fishing with him. It all seemed so naive now. A child of nature indeed, she thought as they hiked through the damp forest. An *unwanted* child, perhaps.

Emily walked alongside John David through the meadow until they reached the hemlocks on the other side, then stepped in line behind him. The forest floor was covered with soft needles that muffled their footsteps. He was careful to hold branches so that they would not swing back and hit her, and he held the light downward, pointing backwards, so that it shown at Emily's feet.

"How can you see where you're going?"

"I can see just fine."

"Oh c'mon. In the dark!? I can't see a thing. I can't even see *you*." Then Emily recalled a story she had heard about John David tracking a deer in the dark. Her father had told it at dinner one night. He had heard about it from a woman who worked at the hospital, the daughter of a man who was nearly crippled. The woman's father had been there, had actually seen him do it. She had thought the story utter foolishness at the time, but now, following him blindly through the dark woods, it seemed quite obviously true.

Emily kept trudging along behind John David, but she was exhausted and was beginning to fall asleep even as they walked. Her feet barely came off the ground with each step, and several times she tripped over unseen roots. She felt the overwhelming urge to lie down on the ground and sleep.

"Can't we stop and rest for a moment?" she asked. "I just need to close my eyes for one little minute."

"No, we can't stop," John David said. He put his arm around her waist and held her up as they walked. Emily's head bobbed against his shoulder. A few minutes later he stopped and shined the light on something in front of him. A tiny flash of light shone back at them. Emily then realized that they were standing in front of his cabin and he was shining the flashlight on a padlock.

"It's locked?" she said, incredulous. "You lock your cabin?! Out here?!"

"You never know."

"What if I stumbled across this place after being lost all day and found it locked?

"You wouldn't stumble across it."

John David slid his backpack off and leaned it against the side of the cabin.

"Let me guess, you hide the key over the door," Emily said. Her voice was barely more than a sigh and she leaned against the cabin wall.

"Used to, but the raccoons found it and started having parties in here, so I had to move it. Now I hide it in the hollow of the tree we passed a minute ago." He opened the door and took Emily's hand. "Watch the step."

She felt the firm wooden floor beneath her feet and it surprised her. A *wooden* floor. In the dark she could not tell what the cabin was like, but a wooden floor meant that it was more than just a hut. She shuffled over a few steps so that John David could close the door. Then he moved over to the other side of the cabin. She heard him handling something metallic and the rasping of a match as he lit a Coleman lantern. The light spread forth and filled the room with a warm yellow glow. Emily looked around the cabin in awe. It was far more refined than she had expected. It was perhaps ten feet on a side, made of logs that had been stripped of their bark and made square so that they stacked neatly on top of each other. The roof was peaked in the center. There was a small square woodstove in the middle of one wall, a maple table with two chairs, a bunk bed and a footlocker.

"It's nothing special," John David said, watching her study the cabin. He held a chair for her and she sat down. Then he opened the door to the Franklin stove and placed a small stack of twigs inside. He lit them and a small flame quickly sprouted. John David went over to the woodbox in the corner and collected some larger sticks. One by one he placed them on the fire until it grew to fill the firebox.

He said, "I'm going to go down to the stream and get some water." He paused, then added, "You might want to ... it would be a good idea if you ..."

"What?!" Emily asked.

"You should probably take your wet clothes off and hang them over by the woodstove."

"And then what do I wear?"

"You can wrap up in one of the sleeping bags."

John David headed for the door with a large copper kettle. The stream was only one hundred yards away, but he wanted to give Emily enough time to remove her clothes in what little privacy the cabin afforded.

"I'll be back in ten minutes and make you something to eat." He closed the door behind him and she could hear his footsteps trudge off into the inky black night.

Emily removed her pants and hung them over a chair near the stove. She was freezing. She hesitated for a moment about taking off her underwear, but they too were wet from sitting on the ground and the thought of sleeping all night in wet underwear was more than even her modesty could bear. She removed her underwear and hung them discreetly inside one leg of her jeans where, she would later discover, they do not dry particularly well. She pulled her long gray sweatshirt down over her hips and, standing half-naked in the center of the cabin, looked around for the sleeping bag. There were two of them rolled up on the upper bunk. How convenient, she thought. This must be where Dan'l Boone brings all his dates. She unrolled one of the sleeping bags onto the lower bunk and climbed in. She thought, I'll lie here and pretend to be asleep and just keep one eye open. But the down-filled sleeping bag was so unlike the cheap quilted ones she remembered from Girl Scouts. This bag was soft and fluffy and the lining felt like silk. It was cold against her bare legs when she first slid into it, but within minutes it seemed to radiate heat. She became dizzy. The cabin began to sway like a canoe on an open lake. She felt herself slipping into the darkness, and the sensation was so foreign to her that she could not be certain it wasn't death. And by the time John David returned she was sound asleep, snoring, in fact, so loudly that several sparrows were frightened from the roof.

Chapter Five

The Adirondack Mountains. *The Adirondacks*, the name customarily contracted because the mountains, which are small by the standards of the Rockies or the Grand Tetons, are defined more by the wilderness that surrounds them than by geologic majesty. Mount Marcy, the tallest of the Adirondack peaks, rises only 5344 feet above sea level. A mile to the east is Mt. Haystack at 4960 feet. But between them lies Panther Gorge, a nearly impenetrable 2000 foot glacial cirque jammed with boulders and trees.

The Adirondacks comprise a vast expanse of wilderness nearly the size of Vermont, yet populated by so few people as to seem practically uninhabited. Early maps of the region referred to the great wilderness as Avacal, a name given to this unknown land in 1570 by Abraham Van Ortelius, the cartographer of Philip II of Spain. When the Dutch settlers and French trappers first entered New York in the 17th century, they traveled along the Champlain Valley to Canada and the Mohawk Valley to the Great Lakes, but they avoided the mountainous region that lay wedged in between. The mountains were covered with thick forests of pine and maple and spruce, and dense swamps hundreds of miles long. The soil was thin and rocky and did not support the growth of crops. Even the rival tribes of the Iroquois and Algonquin nations, who fought bloody battles for control of the fertile river valleys for centuries before the white men appeared, rarely ventured into the high peaks.

The Iroquois, led by the fierce Mohawks, overran the Hurons in the middle of the 17th century and ruled northern New York for most of the next one hundred years. They called the mountainous region *Couchsachrage*. According to local legend, the named 'Adirondack' was derived from the name the Mohawks gave to the Montagnais Indians. It is said that the name meant 'those who eat the bark of trees,' a name by which the Mohawks derided their weaker enemy whom they forced to survive in the inhospitable wilderness. But the Indian languages were spoken, not written, and it is therefore impossible to know

45

with certainty if the legend is accurate. Linguists have suggested that Adirondack may have been derived from the St. Lawrence Indian word meaning 'rock people,' or even the Mohawk word for 'white man.'

Although the origin of the name is something of a mystery, it is apparent that the Adirondacks experienced very little human history. The mountains that Samuel de Champlain gazed upon during his first foray into northern New York in 1609 were largely comprised of feldspar that had been formed fifteen miles below the surface of the earth one billion years ago. The upward doming that created the massive rocky peaks had been counteracted by a series of glaciers that, on four different occasions, completely covered the mountains. The receding glaciers carved out sharp ravines, crevices and cirques. Following the retreat of the last glacier 10,000 years ago a dense boreal forest arose and covered the land. So dense and forbidding was this forest that Lake Tear of the Clouds, the headwaters of the Hudson River, went undiscovered for more than two hundred years after Henry Hudson first sailed the lower reaches of the river.

The early explorers had little reason to enter the mountains because the lakes and rivers that stretched from Canada to Albany, and from there to the Great Lakes, were much easier to traverse. These waterways also gave the Hurons, who developed the birchbark canoe, a strategic advantage over the Mohawks, who carved their canoes out of logs. Logs, being rather cumbersome and having a tendency to sink, may have been the reason that the Mohawks preferred traveling on foot. They roved from their long houses west of present day Schenectady as far north as Montreal, but rarely went into the mountains.

On one such outing the Mohawks killed a young French nobleman named Sieur Chazy. Chazy was the nephew of the Marquis de Tracy, Lieutenant General of Canada and captain of the famous French regiment, Carignan-Salières. The French were the natural allies of the Hurons, who lived further north, as were the English and the Mohawks who lived near Fort Orange. The French had wanted to make peace with the Mohawks to provide them an in road to the south. The Marquis de Tracy hosted a grand council of peace and invited the powerful Mohawks to Montreal. During the ceremonies, he alluded to his nephew to illustrate how war brings suffering even to those who survive. But the Mohawk chief Aganata, who must have been caught up in the grandeur of the moment, boasted that 'This is the hand that split the head of that young man.'

The Marquis de Tracy was horror-struck. He stared at Aganata for several moments, barely able to believe what he had heard. Then he ordered his men to take Aganata outside and hang him immediately. The rest of the Mohawk party was sent home. But within a week the Marquis had assembled 1300 men and marched them south to the Mohawk River Valley. The Carignan-Salières raided the Mohawk villages and set fire to the longhouses. It was the first time in history that the mighty Mohawks had been so humiliated, and they never recovered from the defeat.

The ensuing one hundred years witnessed armies of increasing size and sophistication march through the Mohawk and Champlain valleys. The English and French built forts along the banks of the rivers and lakes and cleared roads to connect Fort Carrillion, Fort Miller, Fort William Henry, Fort Ann, and Fort Edward. The forts attracted farmers, wheelwrights and blacksmiths, who supplied the army with needed provisions. Settlements sprouted up and grew into villages with taverns, churches, gristmills, and schools. Stillwater, Sandy Hill, Wings Falls. The merchants had no interest in the political turmoil between the European powers and for a long while maintained neutrality. But the Indian tribes found it impossible to remain neutral. Both the French and English considered the Indians to be essential allies and demanded allegiances. The Mohawks sided with the English, the Hurons and Abenakis with the French. The alliances were disastrous for the Indians. After the British defeated the French and took control of New York, the Algonquin tribes were exiled to Canada. When the British were defeated by the colonial army twenty years later, the Iroquois were also forced to leave the country or relocate to reservations.

The Abenakis suffered greatly. Originally from Maine, they

had been forced westward by encroaching, and hostile, white seters. The Abenakis were skilled in hunting and trapping, but their westward exodus put them in conflict with the Mohawks, who fiercely protected their hunting grounds in northern New York. The Abenakis were poorly skilled in warfare and found it necessary to ally with the fierce Hurons for protection. They fought with the French under General Montcalm and stormed Fort William Henry, massacring hundreds of English men and women. When the British returned to crush the French, most of the Abenakis fled northward and have lived in Canada ever since. But a few remained in the Adirondacks, where they could hunt and trap in relative obscurity.

After the Revolutionary War the region entered into a period of steady growth. The timber industry grew rapidly in the middle of the nineteenth century. By 1870, more than two hundred million board feet of softwoods were being floated from the upper Hudson River to the saw mills in Glens Falls. Thirty years later the pine forests had been devastated and productivity fell to only 50 million board feet. The timber industry then turned its attention to other regions of the Adirondacks. Aided by the New York Central Railroad, which could carry hardwoods that could not be floated down rivers like softwoods, a sharp increase in the production of pulpwood began. In 1905 alone, more than 370 million board feet of hardwoods were taken. Lumber production declined precipitously thereafter as a result of this massive clear cutting. The once majestic Adirondack forest lay barren.

Following an amendment to the New York State Constitution that provided for the forest to remain 'forever wild,' the Adirondacks began a period of rebirth. By the time John David Marten was born in 1953, the great boreal forests had reappeared and game was once again plentiful. He hiked through the streams and valleys. He climbed all of the mountains within fifty miles. He came to know the yellow birch forests to the west, where deer were plentiful, and the spruce forests to the north that were ideal for trapping. This was the only forest he ever knew. But once, quite by chance, he came upon a two hundred-year-old white pine on the shores of a shallow pond. The tree had obviously been overlooked by the loggers and had managed to resist fungal diseases that decimated many others pines. Nearly six feet in diameter and straight as an arrow, it rose majestically over the surrounding forest. John David was so enamored of the tree's beauty that, despite being in a hurry to get back home before dark, he sat for a long while beneath its gentle branches and watched its shadow grow upon the still waters.

Chapter Six

Emily was only an infant when her real mother died. Susan Davignon had been working as a bank teller while her husband completed his surgical training at Mount Sinai Medical Center. Two men came into the bank that morning shortly after it opened. They were not seasoned criminals. They were young men, in their twenties, nervous, brandishing guns, shouting orders. The tellers knew how to handle robbery attempts. They had been taught to hand over the money and offer no resistance. No heroics. The liability of the patrons, they were told, was much greater than the money that would be stolen. So although her heart was racing, Susan did not consider herself to be in grave danger. The men were wearing stockings over their faces, which Susan Davignon thought made them look a little comical. She assumed the two men would take the money and run out of the building. The entire ordeal would probably be over in minutes.

One of the men held a gun at Susan and demanded the cash in her drawer. Had the gun been a typical revolver, which must be either cocked or the trigger pulled hard to discharge, Susan would never have died. But the young man had purchased a .45 caliber semiautomatic. Once a round is placed in the chamber, the gun is cocked. Some .45s have triggers that must be pulled hard. Others go off when the finger applies even the slightest pressure, a hair trigger. It is not possible to tell what kind of trigger a gun has simply by looking at it. Police officers practice with their handguns for hundreds of hours in order to know that feeling precisely. But the young man in the bank had purchased the gun only the day before. He did not understand the subtleties of the weapon. And he was nervous. Standing in the bank pointing the gun at Susan Davignon, mother of seven month old Emily Davignon, looking over his shoulder to see what his partner was doing. He testified in court, under the advice of his attorney, that the gun simply went off by accident. *By accident.* As if the presence of the gun in his hand at that moment were as capricious as a blowout on the freeway. The bullet struck Susan in the cheek and blew away the side of her face. In the confusion that followed, the screaming, the shouting, the bungled robbery, the aborted hostage attempt, the police cars and ambulances, Susan Davignon was rushed to the very hospital where her husband worked without anyone warning him that she was coming. The ambulance driver did not even get Susan's name.

The destructive force of a bullet is a product of its mass and the square of its velocity. Robert Davignon had learned in medical school that what a bullet lacked in mass, it more than made up in velocity. Such a tiny piece of lead, a bullet. If you threw it at someone who was wearing a winter coat they wouldn't even feel it. But at several thousand feet *per second*, it carried more destructive force than a moving car. Gunshot wounds were particularly fascinating training experiences for young surgeons. Robert would have loved to have been involved in the case that appeared at Mount Sinai one morning in early June, but it was far too serious for his level of training. Senior attending surgeons were already working on the woman when Robert arrived in the emergency room. There was such a crowd around her that he couldn't see much, so he went to the X-ray developing room to view the films that were being prepared.

"Did we get a name yet?" the technician asked as Robert entered the room. The technician was meticulous about labeling films properly. He hated these 'Jane Doe portraits.'

"Haven't heard," Robert said. He hadn't even known that the woman *was* anonymous.

Dr. Davignon reviewed the X-ray films in the same detached manner that he had reviewed hundreds of other films in his three years at Mount Sinai. The bullet had shattered the frontal and zygomatic bones. The left eye socket had collapsed. A nasty wound, he thought. Probably fatal. If she managed to survive, her face would be horribly disfigured.

"I'll check on the name," Robert said, turning to go back to the emergency room.

"Take the film with you!" the technician shouted. "They want it right away."

Robert reached for the X-ray. He noticed an odd metallic

shape on one side of the film. A piece of jewelry. An earring. The technician saw his glance.

"Yeah, I know what you're thinking," he said, "but it wasn't my fault. Her ear was such a mess that they didn't even know she was *wearing* an earring. Didn't show up until I developed the film. Kinda ruins the picture, don't you think?"

The earing was a tiny gold heart. The metal was impervious to X-rays, so it stood out perfectly against the gray, cloudy mass of bones and flesh. Robert stared at the earing for a long moment, then turned to look at the technician.

Robert heard himself say, "I gave my wife a set of earrings like that when we first started dating," but the words seemed to come from the other side of the room. The technician stared back at him but could not think of anything to say. Dr. Davignon instinctively looked down at the woman's face in the X-ray, but the image on the film did not show the features that made her Susan Davignon. The long brown hair, the cream-colored skin, the freckle on her left cheek. They were not evident in *this* photo.

"Jesus, doctor, it can't be," the technician blurted in disbelief, but Robert was already headed for the door.

For years afterward, Robert Davignon would awaken from a dream in which he relived the minutes that followed. The sounds in the emergency room were distant, like rolling thunder, and he could not comprehend the words that were being spoken. He pushed his way forward to the gurney, shouting something, words perhaps, or just noises. Susan's face was so swollen that he could not recognize her except by her hair. He followed the gurney to the operating room, which was located in the basement. He held her hand as they descended in the elevator and rushed down the long dark corridor, so deep underground.

He did not follow her into the operating room. The senior surgeons wisely refused. So Robert sat in the adjacent doctor's lounge and waited. Other residents came by to keep him company, but he could not tolerate their presence and asked them to leave him alone. He even turned out the light so that anyone walking by would think the room empty. Then the quiet descended upon him. He was alone.

The surgeons removed the bullet, what was left of it, but the damage to Susan's brain was extensive. It was obvious that, if she recovered at all, she would not be normal. That night Robert sat by her bed and looked at her face, now completely wrapped in gauze. Tubes remained in place to drain off fluid from her cranial cavity. He spoke to her. He told her that he was there, that he would always be there, he would help her recover. But she did not respond, and Robert Davignon knew in his heart that she never would. The bullet, in passing through her skull, had released all her memories, her affections, even her peeves, like air from a balloon. All that was left was the deflated remains of a woman whom that very morning had nursed their infant daughter.

Although Robert Davignon never admitted it to anyone, not even his second wife, who was Susan's best friend, he prayed that same night that she would die quickly.

And she did.

Chapter Seven

Robert Davignon finished his residency at Mount Sinai, but when it came time to look for a job he chose the tiny hospital in Henoga Valley, about as far removed from a city as one could get and still remain in North America. Robert's father was a surgeon in Providence and had dreamed that his son would join him in his practice. The two of them had talked about it many times, and up until Susan's death he had never even considered any other future.

"Bob, I know what you're going through," his father said after Robert broke the news that he had accepted a surgery position in upstate New York, "but running away isn't going to change anything. I lost your mother when you were about Emily's age. But I stayed right here."

"I don't want to raise Emily in a city," Robert answered. "I've seen enough." Robert hated doing this to his father. He could tell as soon as he'd broken the news that his father was crushed. The elder Davignon face flushed. He ran his fingers through his hair.

"You've seen enough of New York," he said. "Who hasn't? But come back here. Live in a nice neighborhood."

"Dad, I can't. It's the whole big city thing. I hate it. People aren't meant to live like that."

"How do they live up in the mountains? Log cabins and wood stoves. What kind of practice will you have up there? You'll be treating bear maulings and chain saw accidents?"

"Well, I'll do surgery and a little ER and some general practice."

"Good God," the elder Davignon said, shaking his head, "all these years of surgical training just to set broken fingers?"

"Look Dad. It won't be permanent. I'll just work up there for a couple of years. It'll give Emily a chance to grow up like a normal kid. I swear, as soon as Emily is older I'll come back to Rhode Island."

The elder Davignon nodded his head in resignation. He knew nothing he said would matter at this point. It was better to go along with it for a few years and hope for the best. He remembered the night Robert called with the news that Susan had been shot. Awfully hard to make sense of such a thing, someone yanking away your life like they were pulling an electric cord out of an outlet. Poor Robert, he thought, taking care of an infant daughter after losing Susan so abruptly. Good thing for him that Susan's friend Julia had stepped right in and offered to take care of Emily. Good thing that she and Robert hit it off and decided to get married. Seemed unlikely to Robert's father that little Emily ever suffered from lack of attention. As far as he could tell, Julia was the only mother Emily ever knew. The murder didn't affect *her*. Just Robert. Still, it bothered him so to watch this thing haunt his son. Was he throwing his life away? Throwing away a real career to become a country doctor, the kind that keep a little garden in the back of the house and picks a tomato for lunch between patients. The elder Davignon had a classmate like that. Billy Walker. IQ of 170 or something. Opened a practice in New Hampshire right after medical school and stayed there ever since. Even joined the volunteer fire company. He had seen Billy Walker at a college reunion a couple years ago. Billy drove up to the front of the hotel in a ten-year-old Studebaker, got out of the car wearing a ragged old sweater. God, what a character he had become. Told everybody a story about his grandson jumping off the dock and catching a fish in his bathing suit. Old geezer had everybody in stitches. That's what he knew of country doctors. They all became eccentric old men wearing sweaters.

But the elder Davignon had experienced much disappointment in his life. His own wife had died when Robert was still a young boy, and he had never remarried. He had learned how to accept disappointment, how to acknowledge it and treat it with respect. He went over to his desk and wrote out a blank check and gave it to Robert.

"Buy your family a nice house," he told him.

Julia first saw the house one June morning when there was yet mist on the lake. The grass leading from the house to the lake was up to the middle of her calves. She took her stockings off in the car and walked barefoot, against her husband's wishes, down to the lake. The dew on the grass was so cold that it made her feet ache. Emily was at her side and they were laughing like children. They pulled up stalks of grass and chewed on the stems and tried to talk like farmers. They walked down to the lake and waded in the frigid water. Robert could hear them squealing in the distance, and he thought, at that moment, not of the house, or the realtor standing next to him filling his ear with endless chatter, or even of his new job, but of how much he envied Julia's relationship with his daughter.

"Oh, Robert," she said, with Emily tugging at her hand and begging to return to the lake. "We have to buy this house. You can use the upstairs room for a library, a library that overlooks the lake. Just think of it."

"I don't know," said Robert. "It needs so much work."

"It'll be worth it. Look at Emily. She loves it here."

Emily fell in love with the big house on Raquette Lake immediately. The high ceilings with ornate cornices, the three oak staircases, the heavy doors that swung out to face the lake. Her mother sometimes left the doors open during summer to let in the breeze that came up from the lake. There were numerous small rooms and alcoves in which Emily could play, and the house was so large that her mother often had to search for her room by room.

Over the ensuing years, Emily's favorite room would become the attic, with its steep stairs climbing mysteriously from inside her bedroom closet. The attic, with its peaked roof and windows, so high above the ground that it made her dizzy to look down to the yard below. There was a turret at one end with four enormous windows, each facing a different compass point. On rainy days Emily sat in the turret and read her books, seated in an old stuffed chair that her mother had dragged up the stairs. There were crates full of old clothes and magazines, copies of *Life* and *National Geographic*. She found several pictures of her real mother, taken when she was a teenager, and one with Julia and Susan together, which she placed on an old end table. Emily also found an engraved silver hand mirror that she felt must have been left there on purpose. Perhaps left by a young girl, Emily imagined, a girl her own age who had moved because of a family tragedy, or left by an elderly woman who had owned it all her life and had no one to whom to bequeath it. She found a novel, *Wuthering Heights*, with the name 'Sarah P. Herresford' and the date '1892' inscribed in pencil inside the front cover. The letters were written in florid cursive. The 'S' and the 'P' had gently flowing French curves, and the 'H' was made with mirrored crescents. Did Sarah grow up in this house, Emily wondered? Did she read the Brontë sisters while sitting in this attic, in front of these windows? Over the summer Emily visited all the cemeteries in Henoga Valley to determine if Sarah had been buried locally. She checked the cemeteries behind the Methodist and Catholic churches on the other side of town, and although there were several belonging to the Herresford family, none of them had Sarah's name on it. And then one day more than a year later, quite by chance, she came upon Sarah's gravestone in a clump of sumacs on the western end of their vast property, down by the water's edge, near a stone wall that probably divided the property long ago. The area was densely overgrown, but Emily was looking for birds' nests and had wandered into the area. She would have missed the stone had she not stubbed her foot on it. It was small, shaped rather like a loaf of bread, with 'Sarah' inscribed in raised letters on the curved top. Emily knelt by the grave stone and stared in disbelief. She ran her hand over it and felt the roughness of the letters. *Sarah.* Had Emily given the matter much thought, she would have come to the conclusion that Sarah must be dead. Sarah had lived in the big house almost seventy years ago. How could she be still alive? Still, Emily could not stop herself from crying. Then, embarrassed, she got up and wiped the tears from her cheeks. *How stupid,* she thought, *crying over someone you never even knew and who'd been dead for God knows how long.* But she nevertheless returned the next day and cleared away the brush from Sarah's grave. On warm days she visited Sarah, sitting on the gravestone and reading, sometimes aloud, though in a hushed voice so that no one wandering by would hear her.

Emily's parents worried endlessly about her. *Invite someone over*, her mother would say. And Emily could be wonderfully animated, laughing and running around the house or taking friends out to the lake to look for turtles. Whenever she made a new friend, or 'reacquainted' herself with an old friend, she would devote all of her attention to that girl for weeks. But she inevitably tired of their company and their endless chatter about *boys*. And none of them ever shared her passion for books. If they read at all, they read girl adventures with insipid plots. No one she knew liked George Eliot or even Daphne du Maurier. She gave her precious Sarah P. Herresford copy of *Wuthering Heights* to Jennifer Baker the summer after seventh grade and had to ask six times to get it back. "I can't remember where I put it," Jennifer said, not bothering to hide the inescapable fact that she hadn't even looked at it. "Besides, we don't have to read it until high school. Why on earth would you waste your time on it now? In the summer? When there's so much else to do?"

And so it was not entirely surprising that *Sarah* became Emily's 'best friend.' She imagined a young girl much like herself, sitting alone in the turret of the great house, reading her books, walking down by the pond. There were times, particularly when the wind blew out of the north, that Emily imagined she could hear Sarah's voice. She was even convinced for a time that *she* was Sarah, reincarnated, but when she suggested this to her parents they became infuriated and banned her from the turret for several weeks. So she never mentioned it to them again, although she continued to believe it for many years.

Emily was eleven years old and had lived in the house on Raquette Lake for almost six years when she finally learned what had happened to Sarah. Julia Davignon had met a woman at the library, Mrs. Schaffer, who was president of the local historical society. Mrs. Schaffer had introduced herself to Julia, complimenting her on what a wonderful job she and her husband had done restoring the old Herresford house. Julia had been in a hurry to get back home before Emily's bus and didn't have time to talk to the woman right then, but invited her to visit the following day. Mrs. Schaffer and Julia were in the living room when Emily came home from school.

"Emily, come here," Julia shouted when she heard her daughter come in the back door. "There's someone here I want you to meet."

Emily joined them in the parlor and sat down on the sofa next to her mother. Mrs. Schaffer began telling them the history of the house and became so engrossed in the story that she did not stop talking even when Emily became upset and ran out of the room.

It was perhaps unusual that Emily had not heard the story earlier because Sarah's life was one of the more interesting historical anecdotes of Henoga Valley. Nearly everyone, it seemed, had heard at least *one* variation of the story. Young Sarah Herresford, whose wealthy father owned one the largest lumber companies in the Adirondacks, was only fifteen when she became 'involved' with a young man of Indian descent. Some said that the Indian, who worked for Sarah's father, was a full-blooded Abenaki, others said his heritage was so diluted by white blood as to be irrelevant to the story. But Sarah's father sent her to live with relatives in Georgia or Alabama to break up the budding romance. It apparently worked. The capricious Sarah not only got over the Indian, but she married into a wealthy family and had a son. Then her husband died, drowned, or was killed in a hunting accident, and Sarah returned to Henoga Valley with her three-year-old son. The Indian, still infatuated with the beautiful Sarah Herresford, but infuriated by her rebuffs, kidnapped the boy and disappeared into the mountains. What made the crime so heinous was that he took the boy right from the house and beat up Sarah's father, who tried to stop him, in the process.

What happened in the following days was often the subject of debate at the monthly meetings of the Henoga Valley Historical Society. A manhunt involving hundreds of local men and a dozen bloodhounds ensued, but the only sign of the boy ever discovered was his nightshirt, left in a heap a short distance from the house. Some members of the society believed that the Indian killed the boy out of spite, buried his little body in the mountains, and then crossed the border into Canada. Others believed that the Indian had been shot and killed, but the boy

60

was also killed by a stray bullet. This faction of the society theorized that search party engineered a cover-up of the fiasco to avoid the wrath of Sarah's father. Another small but growing faction of the historical society posited that the boy had been whisked away to the Abenaki reservation in Canada and raised there as an Indian.

The only point on which *all* members of the Henoga Valley Historical Society could agree was that a grief-stricken Sarah Herresford rowed out to the center of Raquette Lake the following day and drowned herself.

Chapter Eight

The panic that consumes a parent when a child is missing is glaringly primeval. A small child briefly lost in a department store incites a level of panic that reminds the observer of monkeys in the zoo. But when a child is truly missing, a feeling of dread comes over the parents, gripping them around the neck and chest, cutting off their breathing. They become irrational, wanting to run about in all directions searching, sniffing the air for the scent of their own. *Do something* they demand. *Do something!* Emily had been missing for several hours before the State Police found her parents' station wagon at the entrance to the state trail. It was almost nine o'clock at night.

"We've got men hiking up the trail right now," Sheriff Cooney told Dr. Davignon, "but if she's off the trail, we won't find her tonight."

"You've got to find her tonight," Julia screamed. "She can't survive out there in this weather."

"Now that depends," the trooper said. "If she's not hurt, she could be okay. Do you know if she brought matches or anything to keep warm."

"We didn't even know she was going," Dr. Davignon said. "I doubt she has a hat."

"Do you know where she might have been heading?" the sheriff asked. He'd been involved in several searches in his career, first as a state trooper, then as the sheriff of Hamilton County, the best-known being the man from Syracuse, lost almost seven years ago to the day, on the weekend after Thanksgiving. He remembered the man's poor wife, frantic, grief-stricken, waiting every day for news from the search party. She had come up from Syracuse to be near the search and spent every day at the State Police substation in neighboring Old Forge or out at the trail head where they'd found her husband's car. For the first four days there was nothing to report. No sign of the man. He'd gone up the Wall Mountain trail, which branched off into nearly a dozen different trails, and he left no note describing his plan. The search party couldn't just cover the

63

trails because the man wasn't likely to be lost *on* the trail. It was more likely he got lost off the trail, and in this vast wilderness it might have taken days to find the trail again. The sheriff didn't want to tell the woman that few people have the presence of mind needed to stay alive in the woods for a week in November. And the ones who do rarely get lost in the first place. They never did find the man. Some hikers found his backpack a year later about thirty miles north of the search area. No sign of the lost hiker, though. Sheriff Cooney couldn't help but think that the man was a fool, trying to push on when he was hopelessly lost. If he had just sat down and built a fire, they'd probably have found him in a day or two.

Julia said, "She takes pictures, nature pictures, for her paintings. We've warned her not to go up there alone ..."

"Forbidden her," Robert added.

"Yes, *forbidden* her," Julia added, but the tone of her voice suggested that only Robert held that conviction. "But I know she's done it before. I think she knows the trail."

"Anyone can get lost."

"What do we do now?" Robert asked.

"There's not much we can do," the sheriff said. "I've got men hiking the trail right now, but I can't really go *off* the trail 'til tomorrow. The state police will join in first thing in the morning and I got a helicopter coming over from the air force base in Plattsburgh. But it would help if we knew where she was heading."

"I can't imagine she'd leave the trail," Julia said.

"Not on purpose," Cooney said.

"You think she accidently got off the trail?" Robert asked.

"That's how it usually happens. They lose the trail and can't get back on it."

Julia said, "I'd feel a lot better if they'd keep searching throughout the night"

"I'll see what I can do, ma'am."

They saw the sheriff to the door and thanked him for coming to the house. Julia went to the kitchen table and sat down. She began to cry. Robert put his hands on her shoulders.

"I've always been afraid I'd lose her ... you know ... because ... I'm not ... we're not ..."

"Julia, please, let's not start this again."

"It's just that I feel ... I can't help but feel..."

"Julia ... *please*! I don't want to get into that discussion again. Not tonight."

They passed the night without sleeping a wink. Julia sat at the kitchen table and waited for the phone to ring, drinking cup after cup of tea. Around midnight, Robert put on his jacket and drove out to the trail head to check on the search party. He found several men huddled inside a large canvas tent, drinking coffee. They had nothing to tell him. He returned to the trail head at three o'clock and again at seven o'clock the next morning, but there was still nothing to report.

John David's cabin was nearly twelve miles northeast from the trail head. There was no chance that the search party would have found her there, even if they searched for months. But John David was afraid that they might run into the search party on the way back to the state trail and might have to explain that he had a cabin out here. The Department of Environmental Conservation would certainly make him tear it down. So he made other plans. He woke Emily at five o'clock and told her to get ready to leave.

"Why so early, for God's sake?" she asked. She was still half asleep.

"Because I want to get you back home before anyone finds you here."

"In your little 'love cabin?' Emily said. John David did not bother responding to her sarcasm. "Is that a problem? Them finding me here?"

"It would be for me. I don't want anyone to know about this cabin."

"Afraid they'll make you pay school taxes?"

"Afraid they'll make me tear it down."

"Who would care about a cabin way out here?" Emily asked. "It's hardly prime real estate."

"EnCon would. They don't like squatters."

John David had already been awake for almost an hour and

had boiled water for tea on a Coleman stove. He left the kettle on the Franklin stove to keep it warm. The cabin was filled with the warm steam and the window fogged over. Emily was astonished to see what appeared to be, and Emily wasn't sure at first, a loaf of home made bread on the table.

"Where'd that come from!?" she said pointing to the bread. She had fallen asleep the night before without anything to eat. She was so hungry that she almost climbed out of the sleeping bag. Then she remembered that she was half-naked.

"I made it," John David said.

"You made bread?" she asked. "You made a loaf of bread?!"

"I made it last night while you were asleep."

"I can't believe it," she said, her voice filled with laughter. "Homemade bread. I don't even get homemade bread at home."

John David explained that it was easier for him to store flour and yeast than to carry bread in each time he came out.. The cabin was remarkably well-stocked. John David had built a cupboard that was full of plastic containers. He also had Cream of Wheat if she preferred that. And raisins and nuts and rice. And powdered milk and coffee.

"You've got enough food to last the whole winter," Emily said. "Are you planning to move up here permanently?"

John David was trying to sound casual in responding to her, but in fact extremely proud of his ability to make bread in the woods. He was showing off, so he tried all the harder to make it look commonplace. He'd found little metal pans that acted like an oven when you cooked on a woodstove. He pretty much had the routine down pat. Whenever he came out to the cabin, he mixed the flour and yeast and let it rise overnight. During that time the stove would heat up. The next morning he'd throw the whole thing on the stove and have fresh bread in an hour. He cut several large slices and covered them with strawberry jam.

"Do you have any marmalade?" Emily asked, still in the sleeping bag.

John David went to the cupboard and started searching through one of the top shelves.

66

"Relax. I was just kidding," Emily said. But John David came back with a jar of marmalade and handed it to her.

"Dear God, you do have it!" Emily said, throwing her head back and laughing out loud. John David noticed the way deep lines formed beneath her cheeks and the way her lips pulled back from her teeth to form a straight line of upper lip. He never imagined having such company, someone as beautiful as Emily Davignon, sitting in this cabin, filling it with peals of honeyed laughter. He wanted it to last a little longer, so he made another pot of coffee and cooked some Cream of Wheat.

"Do you have any Whetena?" Emily joked. "I love Whetena."

"Nope. Makes you poop," John David said. "And the bathrooms out here ... being what they are ... this time of year ..."

"Gottcha," Emily said, nodding her head in exaggerated agreement.

John David had decided that they should not hike back toward the state trail, where they were sure to encounter the search party. They should instead hike further east, away from the searchers, then south toward Henoga Valley. He figured they would come out of the woods about a mile from Emily's house. Emily would explain that they spent the night in John David's *tent*, and the rest of the story would be the truth. Once she was found, the search party would stop looking and John David's cabin would be safe. He left the cabin long enough for Emily to get dressed and knocked when he returned, even though the ten minute absence was long enough for anybody to put on two articles of clothing. When he came back into the cabin she was sitting on the corner of the bunk. She watched as he cleared the table and placed everything back in its place.

When he turned, she stood up in front of him. John David was momentarily startled by how close she stood and instinctively stepped backward.

"I just wanted to say thank you for ... well, for *everything*." Emily reached up and held his shoulders and kissed him on the cheek. John David blushed so hard that he looked as if the blood vessels in his face were about to burst.

"I'm sorry," Emily said. "I didn't mean to embarrass you."

John David would have liked to have said that he wasn't embarrassed, that, in fact, her visit was the best thing that had ever happened to him, and he briefly imagined what the moment might have been like if he had actually embraced Emily in return. But while he was thinking the moment passed and Emily walked out of the cabin.

It was still an hour before sunrise when they passed again through the hemlock stand and began their long hike back to Henoga Valley. Both of them carried flashlights and the beams of light darted back and forth like antennae. They made their way slowly along the bank where the brush was less dense until they came to a small pond. The surface of the water was like obsidian.

"Is there any place on earth more beautiful than this?" Emily asked, looking at the crest of mountains that surrounded them. The silhouettes of red spruce looked like cathedral spires against the black horizon. A faint hint of sunlight was beginning to split the eastern sky. "Let's stop and watch the sun rise."

John David slid the heavy pack frame from his back and rested it against a tree. He sat on a large boulder and Emily climbed up next to him. She pulled her knees up under her chin and stared at the distant sky. They turned their flashlights off and in a few minutes their eyes became accustomed to the dark. Forms appeared as the blackness transformed into shades of blue and green and gray. Silhouettes of trees and rocks, branches sticking out of the pond, a small duck near the shore.

The first rays of the morning sun lifted the blanket of darkness and revealed the royal blue beneath it. Emily slid from the boulder and walked to the edge of the water. She stood motionless as a swath of alizarine slowly spread from the east, bathing the sky and pond, leaving only a jagged strip of black mountains in between. John David reached into his backpack for her camera, thinking that she might want to take a picture, but she held out her hand to stop him. The light struck the sides of clouds high above the mountains and refracted the light into infinite hues of orange and red and yellow. The tiny ripples on the surface of the water mixed the reds and black into thousands of delicate strokes. And then, suddenly, it was over. The great body of the sun appeared above the mountains and doused the pond in yellow light.

"Unbelievable," she said, unable at that moment to think of anything more reverent.

John David watched her for a moment. He noticed that she seemed to be wiping tears from her eyes and he could not help but chuckle.

"You think I'm pretty silly for getting emotional, don't you?"

"No, not at all. I can understand it. Sort of."

Emily turned to him and said, "Sometimes when I'm painting, when, for a moment, I see the world as it really is, when the colors are *here*, in my mind, I can't even stop to eat. I don't want to stop because I can't be sure I'll be able to see them again when I come back. And sometimes, when I'm busy with school and all that other stuff, I can't really see the world at all. All I see is homework and dinner, and the telephone and the radio and the television and newspapers and people talking, loudly, always trying to make a point or sell something, or just filling the air with *noise*. And then, out of nowhere, I'll see a maple leaf fall onto a puddle, and the mixture of colors, the red and orange and yellow on the black water, and I'll be hypnotized for minutes. Then I'll wake up and see other kids staring at me, and of course I'm embarrassed."

"But everybody knows you're a painter," John David said. "They expect you to be a little eccentric."

John David lifted his backpack to his shoulders and fastened the hip buckle.

"Tell me something," he said, "Why do you have blank spaces in some of your paintings?"

The question surprised Emily. She would not have imagined a boy like John David Marten would even notice her work, much less study it.

"It's supposed to represent the intrusion of man on nature," Emily replied after a moment. She took a cedar branch in her fingers and studied the needle pattern carefully. She even turned it over and examined the underside, as if the pattern of overlapping dendrites might contain secrets.

"Oh," John David said.

"But then what do *I* know about nature? Maybe I should shut up and let you tell me what it all means."

"What I have to say wouldn't be half as interesting."

"I'm not so sure about, Mr. Dan'l Boone." They looked at each other for a moment, then Emily said, "It's funny that we would go to the same school for so many years and not even know each other until now, out here, in the middle of the woods."

"Kinda...*unnatural?*" John David said, smiling.

"It's not that, it's just that ... well ..." Emily's voice trailed off. The separation of students had begun in the early grades, and Emily could not remember if she had ever spoken to John David before. She had scarcely taken notice of it and would never have imagined other kids felt slighted by the segregation.

The hike out of the woods took more than nine hours. The area was densely wooded, and more than once Emily wanted to question John David about where they were going. Was it possible that this dense wilderness was actually familiar to him? Had he passed through here before, or was he secretly reading a map? They crossed a stream several times, then climbed over a small hill. They followed a ravine for more than a mile and then, quite to Emily's surprise, they came out of the woods within several hundred yards of where John David had said they would.

"Wow! I can't believe it. We're right *here*," Emily said, looking up and down the highway.

"Didn't believe me?"

"You know what I mean. I can't believe anyone can do that. I'm very impressed," she said, slapping him on the backpack. John David shrugged his shoulders, as best one can with a fifty-pound backpack, as if to say 'no big deal.'

They had walked less that a few hundred yards when a county sheriff's car went by. Deputy Therrien was alone in the car. He locked up the brakes when he saw John David and Emily, and the tires screeched loudly on the pavement.

"It's a safe bet they've been looking for us," John David said.

The deputy jumped out of the car and ran over to them.

"What the hell's going on here?" he said. He sounded angry. "Miss Davignon ... You are Emily Davignon, aren't you?"

Emily nodded.

"Are you aware that your parents are looking for you?"

"I should hope so," Emily said.

The deputy looked at John David and the backpack.

"Were you *camping?*" he asked.

"*I* was," John David said, "but she wasn't."

"I was lost, for Chrissake!" Emily said. She could see that the deputy was confused. He looked to her like the kind of person who was always confused. "John David found me. Call it dumb luck."

"I beg your pardon?" John David said, pretending to be insulted.

"On my part," Emily added quickly.

The deputy ran back to the car and radioed the sheriff. Emily and John David crossed the road and waited behind the car. They could hear him saying, "Yeah, I got her right here. Yeah, she's okay. Dutch Marten's kid is with her. Don't ask me, she says she was lost."

John David looked at Emily.

"Looks like you got more problems now than you did when I found you," he said.

"I don't care. I mean, what the hell, I'm alive!"

"Yeah, but wait till the folks see the company you've been keeping."

"Oh, c'mon," Emily protested. "They're not like that." She knew it was a lie. Her folks *were* like that. There would be more questions about John David Marten than about being lost.

Within minutes there were a half dozen police cars from the sheriff's department and the State Police. The officers all seemed pretty angry. Were they upset that they didn't get a chance to find her, Emily wondered, or did they think she was lying?

Emily did all of the talking, and she kept it simple. She was taking pictures in the woods and got lost. John David found her and they spent the night in his tent. He led her out of the woods as soon as it was light enough to walk. John David was

71

impressed with her effortless lies. If she'd have told *him* that they slept in a tent, he might have believed his own memory faulty.

"Let me get this straight," the sheriff said. Cooney prided himself on having seen and heard just about everything. He'd been a state trooper for almost 24 years before retiring and running for the sheriff's job. So when he said he wanted to 'get something straight,' the implication was that he was hearing something he'd never heard before. And since he had heard everything before, this new thing must not be real. He was, as usual, annoyed that the state troopers were marching right in and taking over. His old colleagues. The hell with them, this was his jurisdiction now. He should be asking the questions.

"You're telling me that you went hiking yesterday, got lost miles from the trail, Mr. Marten found you, you spent the night in his tent, then you hiked out through God-knows-how-many miles of unmarked wilderness to end up in this spot."

"Yes," Emily said, "all except the part about 'God-knows-how- many miles.' I think ..." She paused to look at John David. "Fifteen miles?"

"Maybe a little less."

"Fourteen miles of wilderness."

Deputy Therrien grunted his disbelief. He'd hunted enough around here to know that you don't just hike through umpteen miles of this forest.

"Sounds like a lot of bullshit to me," he said just loud enough for most everyone to hear.

The sheriff looked at the deputy as if to say 'that's enough.' He'd been trying to make the deputies a little more professional since he was elected the previous year, but they often acted like a bunch of hicks. No wonder they didn't get any fuckin respect from the state police, he thought.

"Why didn't you just get back onto the state hiking trail?" Cooney asked, returning his attention to Emily. "You're four miles up the road from where she left the car. Wouldn't it have been shorter to go back there?"

"Don't be silly," Emily said. "I knew the car wouldn't be there when we got back. My father's probably been out looking for me since yesterday afternoon. The car's back home in the garage right now, isn't it."

"Your father called us around six," Cooney admitted. "He was pretty worried."

"Well, Dad's always worried, but I guess this time he had a right to be."

"All right," Sheriff Cooney said to his men, "let's wrap this up." He motioned for Emily and John David to get in the car, but John David begged off. He didn't want to go home by way of Emily's house. He'd just walk back home.

"Don't be stupid," Cooney said, "I'll have somebody give you a ride."

So John David accepted a ride with Deputy Therrien. He turned to say goodbye to Emily, but she was already climbing in the back seat of Cooney's car. She didn't even turn to wave as the car pulled out onto the main road. Had John David been the type of person to articulate his every thought, he might have said to himself 'that's gratitude for you.' But he was a man of few words, even unto himself. So he simply turned and lifted his backpack into the trunk of Deputy Therrien's car and climbed into the back seat.

Chapter Nine

Emily had plenty of time to prepare for her father's reaction. She'd thought about what she should say as she and John David hiked out of the woods and she was rehearsing it all again now, in the police car, riding down the long road. She had no intention of lying to her parents, except for the part about the cabin. She anticipated what they would say and rehearsed her answers. She knew her father would be relieved to see her, so he wouldn't be pissed now. Maybe later, but not right now. And her mother would be all teary and loving and smother her with affection, but later she'd have a million questions. Her parents didn't get any advance warning. The police car simply drove up to the house on Raquette Lake and stopped in the circular driveway, directly in front of the house. Emily's parents did not hear the car pull up. Emily got out of the car and walked in the front door.

"Mom, Dad? I'm home," she yelled, as if she'd just come home from a field trip.

She heard the scrapping of the kitchen chairs as they were pushed back from the table.

"Emily!?" her mother said, coming around the corner into the hallway. "*Emily!*" she repeated. "Oh thank God you're all right."

Sheriff Cooney was behind her and Robert Davignon went to thank him. It would be several seconds before Julia stopped hugging their daughter, so he figured he had a wait before it was his turn.

"I'd like to take credit for finding her," Sheriff Cooney said, "but the truth is, we found them out on Route 28."

"*Them?*" her father said.

"She was with some boy ... Marten."

"Emily?" her mother said, surprised. "Who's Martin? Martin who?"

"John David Marten," Emily said.

"What the hell is going on, Emily?!" her father asked. His voice rose with every word. "Were you ... *running away?*"

75

"*Dad*! C'mom. I wouldn't do something like that. I got lost in the woods."

"Am I missing something here?" her father asked. "How did you get lost with John David Marten?"

"I didn't get lost *with* him," Emily said. "I did it on my own. He found me. We stayed in his tent last night and hiked out this morning."

Julia Davignon looked at her daughter with a blank expression. Her mouth was slightly agape, and Emily reached over and placed her hand under her mother's chin to close it. Neither of her parents knew what to say because this was not a scenario they had envisioned.

"Dad, look, before you get into it, I'm sorry. All right? I'm sorry." Emily was sincere. She had never been the type to worry her parents needlessly. She had an aversion to trouble that children without siblings somehow master in order to escape their parents' scrutiny. "I got a little lost up off the state trail yesterday afternoon."

"How did you get lost," her father asked. "Why did you get lost? Do you mean to tell me you went hiking alone?"

"Yes I did," Emily answered. "Dad, I can't go up there with anybody else. I can't take pictures with somebody talking all the time."

"I'd go with you," her father said, "you know I would."

"Dad, you'd never have the time."

"Emily, what do you mean, exactly, when you say you were lost?" her mother asked. "You weren't really lost, were you?" She was nodding her head, begging agreement. Emily did not respond. She looked down at her boots, John David's boots. "Emily?" her mother repeated.

So Emily recounted, in remarkable detail, how she'd been lost for hours, how she'd been trapped in a swamp and stumbled over knolls, how the trees had whipped her face. Yes, they could see that. The crimson welts were still on her cheeks. Emily removed her hat and her dirty matted hair fell into her face. Emily continued with her description of the ordeal, but her mother just stood there in disbelief, tears running down her cheeks, unable to comprehend the words. Here was her daughter speaking calmly about a situation that seemed hardly trivial. Lost. In the *Adirondacks*. She had heard about people being lost, and not all of them being found. Seemed to happen about every other year. Wasn't there a man from New York City, no, Philadelphia, who went hiking on his own two or three years ago and was never seen again?

"I don't mean to butt in, folks," Sheriff Cooney said, "but I think you're one lucky young lady." He wanted to say his goodbye. He didn't know this family at all and he wasn't convinced that the girl hadn't concocted the whole story. "In the future I'd be careful going in there alone."

Emily wanted to say, did in fact say, in her mind, 'No shit.' But Emily was well-bred, as her mother would say, and given to only more subtle forms of sarcasm. And she knew she'd been a fool. Now her father, the great hunter, slayer of deer and bear, spoke with primeval authority.

"Emily, no one in their right mind, *no one*, goes into the woods alone. I've been hunting for years around here and I can't tell you the number of times I've almost been lost."

"So what's the point, Dad? You'd die with company?"

"No, the point is ... the point is you just don't do it. If you get lost in the woods, two heads are better than one."

"Some of my friends have two heads and both of them are up their butts."

"Well then maybe you shouldn't be going up there in the first place if you can't be responsible." Robert Davignon was angry now, and he always became more authoritative when he was mad. Emily hated it when he got this way. He sounded so ... parental. She leaned over and pulled off the boots. She placed them by the back door.

"Who is this boy who found you?" her mother asked. "Do I know him?"

"He's a classmate. John David Marten."

"Dutch Marten's son," her father said. "You know who I mean."

"Oh," Julia said. Her voice sounded disappointed.

"What do you mean, 'Oh'?" Emily asked.

77

"I don't mean anything, dear. I've just heard that Dutch is, well, *rough*."

"Well John David isn't anything like him. He isn't rough."

"Sure, tell that to Frank Tomecki," her father added. "I treated him for a concussion after he got in a fight with John in the schoolyard. I never saw a face so smashed up. The kid looked like he'd been kicked by a horse, for Chrissake."

"Frank was a bully and got what he deserved and everybody knows that."

"Was everything all right," her mother asked, wanting to get back to discussing the woods. "What did he do?"

"Well, let's see," Emily said. This was the part she'd rehearsed. "He gave me a pair of boots, he gave me his gloves, he gave me a hat. Then he fed me, gave me his sleeping bag, and led me out of the woods. He was a perfect gentleman."

"How did he find you?" Julia asked.

"I don't know. I was lost for a long time. It was almost dark and I was starting to panic. Then all of a sudden I looked up and there he was. Just standing there, kinda watching me, I guess."

"I'll bet he followed you."

"That thought crossed my mind, but I think he would have dressed better if he intended to molest me in the woods."

"Emily!" her mother shouted. "Don't even talk like that."

"And don't think for a minute that it doesn't happen," her father added. "Even here."

"Dad, he was hunting or trapping or something. He had a backpack that was loaded with something furry. I didn't want to know what it was. It must have weighed a hundred pounds."

"Probably a body," her father added.

"Robert, don't you think we owe this young man a debt of gratitude? Let's call him up right now and thank him."

"No, Mom, don't." Emily had her hand on her mother's arm. "He doesn't want you to call him. I think you'd embarrass him."

"Well, we have to do something appropriate. Maybe I should bake him some cookies and you could take them into school."

Emily laughed out loud. Her father loved that laugh, so

deep, so masculine, so unlikely a sound to come out of her little body. "Of course, cookies. The universal symbol of gratitude. Do you think we should check Emily Post to find out what kind of cookies are appropriate for saving someone's life?"

"Emily, stop being so sarcastic," her father said. "We've been frantic wondering what might have happened to you. We had no idea where you were. And I don't appreciate your sarcasm."

Emily apologized and said it was because she was tired, which was not entirely true. Emily was sarcastic even when well-rested. "If you don't mind, I'm going to take a bath and then take a nap." She kissed her parents on the cheeks and left them standing at the kitchen table.

Julia walked over to the kitchen door where Emily had left the boots. She picked them up and examined them. They were covered with mud and ...what ... grease? She scrubbed them with a stiff brush and then cleaned off the grease with a strong detergent, not knowing that John David greased his boots to make them waterproof. When she was done, she placed the boots on a radiator to dry. She went down to Emily's room and tapped on the door. There was no answer. She pushed the door open and walked in. Emily was asleep in her bed, her back to the door. Julia looked around the room, which was so much like Emily, so reflective of her personality. There were paintings everywhere, and several of them were piled on her desk. Julia sat on the edge of the bed and ran her fingers gently through Emily's hair.

"God, you had us so worried," she whispered.

Emily turned over and faced her mother.

"I don't know what happened. One minute I was walking around the pond taking pictures and the next I was hopelessly lost. It was like it wasn't really happening to me. It was like I was watching someone else get lost in a movie. Then, all of a sudden, the sun was going down and I was in the middle of nowhere." Julia ran her fingers over the scratches on Emily's face as she spoke. "That's when I realized it was really happening ... to me. I was wet and cold and I knew I was in big trouble."

"Did John David build you a fire?"

"Yeah, he ... look, Mom, if I tell you something, will you promise not to repeat it?" She was sitting up on one arm now.

"Well of course, Em," her mother said. Julia was certain there had to be more to the story than she had heard, but she was expecting her daughter to say that she had done it intentionally.

"Not even Dad? You won't tell Dad?"

"Emily, you know I don't like keeping secrets from your father. Maybe you'd better not tell me."

"Okay," Emily said and laid her head back on the pillow. She knew her mother would never be able to walk out of the room without knowing what had really happened.

"You know I hate it when you do this to me," Julia said.

"Do what?"

"Manipulate me. Am I such an easy mark? Why don't you manipulate your father this way?"

"He's unmanipulatable."

"Maybe *I* should be."

"Oh, c'mon Mom. You were born to be manipulated."

"All right," Julia conceded. "I promise. Under duress."

"I didn't stay in a tent." Julia felt a rise in her throat. "John David has a cabin in the woods. In the middle of the deepest forest."

"Was this whole thing ... planned?" Julia asked, trying to be delicate.

"No! I was really lost. But he said I'd never make it in the condition I was in. It was something like twelve miles back to the car. So he took me ... *in the dark* ... to a cabin. I slept in a sleeping bag on a bunk bed and he made me a loaf of bread for breakfast." Emily was laughing now. "A loaf of bread. Can you imagine?"

Julia could not imagine any such thing. She'd heard stories about John David Marten. Who hadn't? Henoga Valley was a pretty small town and everyone either knew, or knew of, everyone else. When somebody shot a deer, pretty soon everyone in the Barkeater Coffee Shop and Gift Store had heard the story, and then their spouses, and then it became common knowledge. It was pretty sad if you didn't find out about it until

80

a week later. It meant you were really out of touch. So when guys like Mac Driscoll, who weighed pretty close to 300 pounds, started bragging about shooting deer, the rumors about John David doing everything but skinning the animals for them weren't far behind. Still, Julia wasn't sure she knew who John David Marten was. She couldn't picture his face. And now he was baking bread, in the woods, for her daughter.

"Why can't I tell your father about this?" Julia asked. "There's nothing wrong with it?"

"He said he's not supposed to have a cabin on state property. EnCon would make him take it down."

"How would they find it?"

"He'd just rather they didn't even *know* about it. Then there's no chance they'll find it."

Julia was still a little confused. "So, how about your wet clothes? How did you dry them?"

"He went out of the cabin. I got undressed and hung them by the woodstove. Then I got into the sleeping bag. In the morning they were dry. All except my sneakers."

"Woodstove? How could he have a woodstove so far into the woods?"

"You know, I never asked him that. After I got used to the cabin being there, the rest of it seemed pretty logical. Same way that he got the doors and windows in there, I suppose."

It was beginning to rain, a cold rain, mixed with sleet and snow. It tapped against the window next to Emily's bed. Julia instinctively pulled the blankets up and tucked them around her daughter's neck. Little Emily. So petite, like Susan had been. Tiny body, big heart. She pulled the shade three quarters down and closed the door on her way out.

Chapter Ten

John David Marten and John Masterson O'Neill. A couple of Johns born not three weeks from each other in Henoga Valley Hospital in the summer of 1953. Each was named after a relative, John David for his father and his father before him, Jack for an uncle who had died many years earlier, tragically, at the age of seven. The boys began playing together before they learned to walk, each mother babysitting for the other whenever they needed to run errands. The boys spent so much time at each other's house that they began to call each other's mother Mom O'Neill and Mom Marten. Not so with the fathers, particularly Dutch Marten. Jack stayed out of the way of John David's father and would never have felt comfortable calling him 'Dad.' And since John David rarely referred to his *own* father as Dad, he felt uncomfortable calling anyone by that name. By the time the boys were twelve years old they had slept at each other's house a thousand times, on several occasions without one or both of the mothers being notified. The two boys were so seldom apart that people were surprised to see one without the other, and might even inquire about it.

Out of necessity, the boys' names evolved so that they could be distinguished one from the other. John Marten became John David, and with time the names fused into a single 'JunDavid'. John O'Neill became Johnny and then 'Jack' upon reaching adolescence. A couple of Johns quite unlike one another, yet the best of friends. Both were remarkable athletes in their own ways, John David in sheer strength, Jack in quickness and finesse. Jack was tall and sinewy, with cobalt blue eyes and auburn hair. He had been an outstanding pitcher in Little League and then became the cornerstone of the high school team. John David continued to play baseball in high school, but he never mastered the sport. He would drop a routine fly ball and then make a diving catch on the next play. Not that anyone came to watch him shag fly balls. They came in anticipation of a towering home run, a 'tree shot,' in reference to the stand of white spruce 380 feet dead away in centerfield. There was no fence at the high school field, so the ball remained in play no matter how far you hit it. But outfielders wouldn't suffer the humiliation of searching for a baseball in the thick stand of spruce, so they didn't bother to chase fly balls into the woods. A 'tree shot' therefore meant that the batter could take a leisurely jog around the bases and bask in the adulation of the cheering crowd. In the 62-year history of the high school baseball team, John David was the only boy from any school ever to reach those trees, and he'd done it 23 times by the end of his senior year. So while Jack O'Neill led the team in batting average (mostly singles and doubles, nothing memorable) and pitching, and was named most valuable player three years in a row, John David Marten hit home runs that little kids talked about years later. The attention bestowed upon John David angered Jack, for couldn't they see that he was a lousy outfielder?

"Have you ever hit a *triple*?" Jack asked once, his voiced tinged with sarcasm, when John David crossed home plate after a solo homer.

"Nah," John David replied after a moment, as if he was trying to remember. "I'm not fast enough."

The two boys were not only inseparable, they were also the de facto leaders of a large group of younger boys who lived on the western end of Henoga Valley. There were two O'Neill children, Jack and his younger brother Bobby, the Massillo brothers, Frank and Tony, who were the same ages as Jack and Bobby, and John David's younger brother Stephen. These three families, along with the four Miller brothers Chris, Eddy, Ralph, and Joey, each one year apart, and the three Henderson boys, occupied the dead end known as Foundry Road. John David's sister, Eva, was the only girl on the entire street, which may have had something to do with her utter disdain of boys as she grew older. Although several of the boys were as old as Jack and John David, only the Johns picked sides for games of baseball or kickball. They were the ones who organized fishing trips to Beaver Pond and hikes to the top of Boreas Mountain.

A group of children that large takes on a personality of its own and in some way this particular group came to be associated, in their younger days, with fire. Particularly the

84

Miller family. Both of their parents smoked and each of the children invariably had a pack of matches, just in case they were called upon to light something. The two fire companies had been called to the old barn behind their house no fewer than eleven times, and it was a testament to speed at which those fire companies responded that the building stood for as long as it did. The barn was an abandoned outbuilding that Mr. Miller had threatened to tear down a number of times, coinciding, for the most part, with visits from those fire companies. On rainy days all of the boys would gather in the barn and climb up into the loft to play Tony Chestnut, a game in which a jackknife is flipped in succession from a foot, knee, sternum, and forehead. Mrs. Miller was an exceptionally patient woman, as one would have to be to tolerate a dozen or more children in her yard at one time. On so many occasions one of the children, usually Joey, would run up to the house to announce an emergency. Mrs. Miller had instructed all of the children that, under these circumstances, only *one* child was to speak, in a calm voice, and to present all of the facts.

On one of those occasions, Joey Miller ran up to the house and found his mother in the bathroom with the door locked.

"What is it, Joey?" she asked, though the door.

"I don't want to alarm you," he said. "But Ralphy is locked in a trunk and he only has a few more minutes to live."

Mrs. Miller calmly found a hammer and a screwdriver in the basement and walked down the barn. She found the rest of the boys banging on the sides of the trunk and shouting to Ralph, who apparently had not responded for several minutes. She wedged the screwdriver behind the brass lockplate and smashed it open with two perfectly aimed blows. Ralph was decidedly cyanotic and took several minutes to even remember where he was.

"Ralphy," she said to the still groggy boy, "do you know how to spell 'oxygen?'"

Ralphy nodded, although I suspected that if he'd been in a spelling bee at that particular moment he would have been eliminated.

"Do you know where it's found?" she asked, holding his shoulders and speaking in a gentle voice. He nodded again.

"And why our bodies need it?" she continued. Again, he nodded. His color was a little better by this time and a smile came to his face.

"Then what the hell are you doing locked in a trunk where there isn't any?" she shouted and stormed off to the house.

You couldn't help but be impressed with Mrs. Miller, who faced each emergency with the stoicism of a gunslinger. On each of the occasions that the barn mysteriously caught fire, she calmly dialed the volunteer fire company and wrote out a check for a $25 contribution, which she handed to the fire chief when they were finished. She didn't have to pay them. She didn't have to serve them iced tea, either.

The fires that were started in the old barn were ignited from a wide variety of materials in a series of experiments performed over a span of four or five years under the direction of Chris Miller. He had earned, although no one could remember how, the nickname 'Firemeister' on account of the scientific approach he took to the arson. Wood shavings, twigs, bark, paper, leaves, pencils, a radiator hose and the elastic waistband from a pair of Haines briefs were just a few of the items that the Chris Miller had tested over the years for flammability. The adults in the neighborhood just called it 'playing with matches.' They could never appreciate Chris for the artist that he was. Once, during a Boy Scouts meeting, the scoutmaster planned a fire building contest in which the various groups raced to build a fire big enough to burn through a piece of rope strung ten inches above the fire pits. Chris accomplished the feat in 53 seconds, which remains a record in Troop 23 to this day.

During the summer of 1964, when Jack and John David were only eleven years old, Chris undertook the last of his uncontrolled experiments to determine if a magnifying glass could ignite a two-by-four. Chris had lit many things on fire with his magnifying glass, but it was common knowledge among the boys that a fresh two-by-four could not be set afire with a magnifying glass. Nevertheless, Chris had calculated that it could work if the board were soaked in gasoline before the beam of light was focused onto it. Like many great scientists, he performed this experiment alone. He knelt over the gasoline-doused lumber and skillfully focused the sunlight from the doorway into a single spot. Chris proved his theory in short order. Unfortunately, he had been careless pouring the gasoline and it had spilled over a large area of the old wooden floor. He compounded that mistake by leaving the gas can with its accordion spout only six inches away. It must have been divine serendipity that Jack O'Neill entered a door on the opposite side of the barn at precisely the same moment that Chris arrived at the flash point of gasoline. In an instant a ten-foot circle around Chris Miller was engulfed in flames. He stood up with a quizzical look on his face, as if to say, *My clothes are on fire!* Jack dashed across the room, through the first layer of flames, and lifted Chris Miller under one arm. Jack was much bigger than Chris and carried him out of the building like he was a stuffed toy. He threw Chris into the tall grass and pounded on him until the flames were extinguished.

Joey Miller was sitting on the swing set when his flaming brother appeared at the barn door. He ran to the house and found his mother doing laundry. The sight of his brother engulfed in flames so frightened him that he choked on the words.

"Oh, for heaven's sake, Joey," she said. "Just spit it out." She was scrubbing the collar of a shirt with a toothbrush and didn't even look up.

"Chris is on fir ..." he blurted out.

"What do you mean, he's on fur?" she asked.

"*Fire!*" Joey said, correcting her.

Mrs. Miller flew out of the house with a blanket and raced down to the barn. She reached the boys just as the can of gasoline inside the barn exploded. Bright yellow flames shot out of the doors and windows. Jack had already snuffed out Chris' clothing and the two of them were sitting on the grass like spectators at a bonfire. But they were scared. Chris had some nasty looking blisters forming already and his hair was completely gone. Jack had second and third degree burns on his hands, arms and chest. The two of them would share a hospital ward for six days (Chris would stay for more than three weeks), but at the moment they just sat there in silence and stared up at Mrs. Miller. She looked at them and then looked at the barn. Then she looked at them again. All of them, including Mrs. Miller, were so shocked that they could not speak. It would be several hours before she would fully understand what had happened, that if Jack had not walked through that door at that precise instant, her son would have been identifiable only from dental records. She sat down next to them and gently touched Chris' head. Then she began to cry.

Jack looked over at Mrs. Miller. He wanted to say something, but he was afraid she would erupt in anger. It was impossible to tell how much anger she might be suppressing.

"You know, little buddy," he said after they had all been silent for several minutes. "You'll never be able to top *this* one."

Chris and Mrs. Miller looked up at him with identical quizzical stares. What was he getting at, they wondered? It seemed inappropriate to make a joke at a time like this.

"I think it's time for the firemeister to retire," he added in a voice that showed a depth of compassion that was unusual in someone so young.

Chapter Eleven

The news of the brutal murder of Jack O'Neill swept through Henoga Valley like a firestorm. It was early June of 1971, only weeks before he was to have graduated from high school. He had accepted a full academic scholarship to Union College and he had hoped to play varsity baseball in the fall. The fact that his body was found a little after 4:00 a.m. with a single knife wound to the chest made people gasp when they heard about it. This was not the kind of news they pondered for long. As soon as one person heard this incredible story they called someone else, and kept calling until they found someone who hadn't already heard. By ten o'clock that morning, there was no one left to call, so neighbors gathered in their kitchens and discussed the details of the case over coffee. At first everyone assumed that he must have been killed by a transient. An act so heinous could not have been committed by anyone they knew, and they knew everyone. But by the middle of the afternoon a second rumor, equally stunning, raced through the village. John David Marten was missing, reported to have run off into the woods in the middle of the night. With a full backpack.

"Do you know where he was headed," Sheriff Cooney asked Mrs. Marten. The sheriff had come to her house at a little after seven in the morning, walking across the yard from the O'Neill's house.

"I never know," Diana said. "Not exactly."

She led the sheriff and his deputy into the kitchen and stood near the sink with her arms folded in front of her. She began rubbing her forearms nervously. Not many people knew of the murder at that point, so Diana received the shocking news at the same moment she heard that her son was a suspect. She was trying to put the facts together in her own mind and didn't like doing it in front of the police. She sat down at the table and began to sob. She cried as much for Jack, whom she had loved, as she did for the boy she could not believe capable of murder. Sheriff Cooney believed that her grief was an admission of guilt.

"What time did he leave?" Cooney asked.

"Around ... four, I think," Diana said, lying. It had been closer to two o'clock. It struck her as odd, but then she had grown accustomed to John David's odd behavior. He had not seemed desperate, not like she imagined a murderer would be. She would not have even known that he was gone if she hadn't gotten up to go to the bathroom last night and heard him downstairs. But now the mere fact that he had left in the middle of the night implicated him as nothing else could. His leaving at two o'clock made him appear much guiltier that four o'clock would, so she added the two hours. But Sheriff Cooney already knew that he had identified the murderer. He just needed to uncover the motive. And, of course, find the suspect.

"You can't be certain?" he asked.

"I didn't check the clock when I got up."

There was at that moment the sound of footsteps in the hall and Dutch Marten walked into the kitchen. He was barefoot, wearing a T shirt and a pair of jeans.

"What the hell's going on here?" he asked, rubbing the top of his head. He looked at the sheriff and assumed that the police wanted to talk to him. "Shit, I wasn't even drinking last night."

"This isn't about you, Dutch," the sheriff said. "It's about your son. He's wanted for questioning in the murder of Jack O'Neill."

Sheriff Cooney always tried to sound official when handling matters like this, but he did it poorly. These were Jack's neighbors and his first concern should have been to break the news gently. But Cooney worked hard at acting like he thought a sheriff should and saying things in a manner worthy of a high ranking elected official.

"What the hell? Jack?!" Dutch said, his mouth hanging open in disbelief. "Jack O'Neill is dead?!"

"Stabbed last night. His body was found at four-thirty this morning in the little park down by the river."

"Damn," Dutch whispered. "I can't believe it." Then he added, "Why do you think John David would have anything to do with it? They were best friends."

"They were seen together last night, around ten. They had been in a fight."

90

"If John David got in a fight with Jack, he wouldn't use a knife," Dutch said with a little pride in his voice. It did not go unnoticed by Sheriff Cooney. He knew of Dutch's reputation for bar room fighting. "And I don't think he even carried a knife. You know, in *town*."

"Look," Sheriff Cooney said, "we don't know who did what. There's a good chance your son had nothing to do with this. But we have to talk with him." Cooney paused for a moment. "But you say he left in the middle of the night."

"We're not going to answer any more questions without talking to a lawyer," Dutch Marten said, waving his hands. He'd had plenty of experience in this area, having been indicted, though never convicted, of killing a man behind the Tahawus Hotel twenty-two years ago. Sheriff Cooney remembered the case. He'd been with the State Police back then. Dutch Marten had gotten into a fight with the man that night inside the Tahawus Hotel. The bartender had called the police and they told Marten to leave. Someone remembered the other guy going out back to take a leak, which these guys did whenever the one-stall bathroom was occupied. He never returned. And since he wasn't with anyone, no one cared much that he didn't return. It was quite possible that, in his rather drunken state, he could have peed too close to the ravine and fallen down the embankment, hitting his head on the way down. It had been cold that night, so he wouldn't have lasted long if he'd been unconscious. In all fairness, there wasn't any evidence to link Dutch Marten to the dead man, but his smug answers to police clearly showed how much he enjoyed hearing of the man's death.

"You realize, of course," Sheriff Cooney added, "that your unwillingness to help us find him means we will have to start up a search right away. And we will have to consider him armed and dangerous."

Diana looked up from the table for the first time since her husband had come into the room. The gentle curves of her face were gone, replaced with the sharp angular lines of raw panic. That wasn't a search he was describing, she thought. It was a hunt. They were going to hunt down her son.

"What are you talking about?!" she asked, rising from the

table, her eyes darting between her husband, the sheriff, and the deputy standing in the kitchen doorway. "Dutch?! What is he saying?"

"Mrs. Marten," Cooney said. "Your son is our prime suspect right now. Not for any particular reason, not because of any physical evidence. Just the circumstances. I wouldn't be doing my job if I did not initiate an immediate search for a suspect who has obviously fled in the middle of the night and now has a four to six hour lead on me." The sheriff looked at her and then Dutch. "I'd rather not be forced to do this."

"You don't even know that he's done anything!" Diana Marten screamed. She brushed back the hair from her brow with both hands. "He goes into the woods all the time. Even in the middle of the night! Ask anyone. Maybe he did get into a fight with Jack and was upset and decided to go off for a little while. I don't know. But you can't just go after him with guns and hunt him down. Something could happen."

The sheriff motioned to the deputy, who went out onto the porch. The sheriff offered his apologies. There was nothing he could do, he told them. He was just doing his job. He would take every precaution to prevent an accident. Then he turned and headed for the door. It was then that Dutch Marten spoke and, for the first time in his life, his words showed that he had not only observed, but actually studied, his remarkable son.

"Sheriff Cooney," he said, his voice subdued. "You won't find him in those woods."

The sheriff stopped with one hand still on the kitchen door. He looked at Dutch Marten, expecting him to say that John David didn't go into the woods, that he was hiding somewhere. Maybe with friends. But Dutch meant that the sheriff simply would not be able to *find* his son.

"He's not just a kid with a backpack," Dutch said. "You remember how he found that girl that was lost. If he's desperate and you're following him, he might turn on you. He could end up hunting *you*."

Goddam Dutch Marten, Cooney thought, just like him to make a threat. Sonofabitch never did know when to shut up.

But there wasn't time to argue, so Sheriff Cooney merely nodded as if to thank Dutch for the warning.

But as soon as he was out on the porch, he turned to his deputy and told him to 'get the dogs.'

Chapter Twelve

Dutch Marten knew a lot more about his son's prowess in the woods than he was willing to admit to Sheriff Cooney. Dutch had been hearing stories about John David down at the River House and the Tahawus Hotel for years. Dutch usually pretended to know something about these events, like Mac Discoll's deer being shot through the heart with an arrow, the shaft buried up to the feathers. He told everyone that he'd taught his son a few things, gave him pointers now and then. Dutch was careful not to brag. *Hell, the kid's a lot better than I ever was*, he'd say. *But I make sure he practices. I don't want him wounding no deer.* Poor Dutch. He hadn't even known his son *owned* a hunting bow. He had no idea where John David would have bought it, or where he kept it.

When John David was fourteen years old Dutch Marten decided to follow him into the woods and find out where he went. Maybe find out if the rumor about him having a log cabin in the woods was true. So he gave his son a half hour lead one day in early December and then started tracking him. There was a light cover of snow on the ground and Dutch figured it would be easy to follow the boy. But he followed John David's tracks for several hours without ever catching sight of him. The tracks led up the west side of Sugarloaf Mountain, down the narrow ravine on the north side, and across a swampy area to an old abandoned road. He was getting tired and had almost given up when he heard someone shout, "Why the hell you followin' me, Dutch?"

Dutch Marten looked up and saw Bill McKeever standing fifty yards in front of him dressed in his red plaid hunting clothes. McKeever had been hunting this land for years, but his knees were bad and he had a difficult time getting around in the woods. McKeever was seventy-two years old. He wasn't likely to shoot many more deer. He parked his Jeep up on the old abandoned logging road about twice a week during hunting season and then wandered around for a while. He'd go down into the swamp, hoping to flush a buck, but usually he just scared up rabbits. He couldn't go up into the deeper woods or climb the hills to where the deer took refuge in the day. He was afraid one of his knees would give out and then he'd be stuck up there. But it didn't much matter. He had grown up on a tiny farm off this old logging road. He just liked being out in the woods because it reminded him of his youth, of cool October mornings with wet leaves on the ground, of the rustle of autumn wind in the oaks.

"How long you been following me?" McKeever asked.

Dutch mumbled something, then turned and looked in the direction from which he'd come. He knew Bill McKeever didn't start out from Dutch's back yard, where he had picked up his son's trail. And he'd only followed one set of footprints. He turned and stared at Bill in disbelief. Then it dawned on him. John David had somehow led him onto Bill McKeever's trail. Dutch hadn't noticed the change in footprints. John David must have watched him go by, wandering off on the wrong trail. *That son of a bitch,* Dutch said under his breath.

"Hope to hell I didn't mess up your huntin'," Dutch said apologetically.

"Hell no," McKeever said. "He popped the clip out of his rifle and placed it in his coat pocket. "I never see nothing anyways."

"Me neither," Dutch said. Then he laughed, adding, "That's why I don't carry a gun."

McKeever laughed, too.

"You sure are a long way from your house," McKeever said. "You want a ride back? Got the Jeep up the road."

Dutch accepted McKeever's offer and they walked back to the Jeep. On the way home they stopped in the River House for a couple of beers.

"If I hunted like I drank," McKeever said to Dutch as the bartender set down a couple of drafts, "there wouldn't be no game left for that boy of yours."

Dutch smiled, but the mention of John David reminded him how pissed he was at the smart ass.

"Did that boy of yours ever tell you 'bout the time we tracked a wounded deer in the dark?" McKeever said, wiping beer foam onto his coat sleeve.

Dutch Marten shook his head.

"Well it was the damnedst thing I ever saw," McKeever said. "Little over a year ago. I was out in the swamp where we was today and your boy come out of the woods. We was talking for a moment, then all of a sudden he holds up his hand. I said, 'What is it?' He says, *Four points.* Well, shit, it was nearly dark. I couldn't see a damn thing. So he tells me where to point the gun." Bill gently nudged Dutch Marten's arm. "He even moved the barrel a little bit. Then he told me to shoot. So I shot. Still couldn't see for shit. So I asked him, 'Did I get him?' John David said *He's wounded.* So we go over to the spot where the deer fell, maybe a hundred fifty yards away. I don't see a deer, but John David starts feeling the leaves, touchin' them with his fingers and tasting them. I said, 'Whatcha doing?' He says *There's blood here. You got em.* I said, 'What do we do now? Can't track him in the dark.' He says *sure we can.* So we tracked that deer for maybe a quarter mile, in the dark, with John David smelling the air and tasting the leaves like he was a bluetick. Well, don't you know that we come across the deer, shot right through the neck. God- damnedst thing I ever saw."

Bill McKeever paused for a moment, then he added, "John David never said anything to you about it?"

"No, he didn't mention it to me," Dutch said. "But he's never been one to brag."

"Well I never told anybody about it 'cause afterward I got to thinking that maybe John David had already shot the deer, and the rest of what happened he just made up to look like *I* shot it. Don't know why he'd do a thing like that. And he was only carrying a .220. Hardly big enough to kill a deer, I wouldn't think, unless you shot it just right."

Dutch Marten nodded and drained the beer from his mug. His own son. Bill McKeever knew him better than *he* did. He thought of John David in the woods, watching him walk on past. Neither one of them would, of course, mention it.

Dutch told this story to his wife after the sheriff left. Diana listened, stone-faced.

"But what would they do if they *did* find him?" she asked, after Dutch had finished.

"You really don't get it, do you?" he said. "They aren't *going* to find him."

Chapter Thirteen

The events that followed the murder of Jack O'Neill and the disappearance of John David Marten so overwhelmed Diana Marten that she became ill. By Saturday evening, television crews from Albany, Utica, Syracuse, Buffalo and Plattsburgh had arrived and set up camera trucks along Main Street. Dozens of newspaper reporters came from as far away as Pittsburgh and Cleveland. They feasted on this story like young pups on a nipple, greedily pouncing on every word. *Honor Student Murdered by Best Friend* one headline read. *Manhunt to Begin in Adirondack Wilderness.* A group of reporters had camped out in front of the Martens' house, forcing Diana to draw all of the shades. She walked around the house from room to room, drumming her fingers against her teeth. She felt trapped, as if the mob outside were there to get *her*. When the evening news showed Sheriff Cooney walking down the steps of County Building, explaining to the reporter that they would have to track down the suspect with bloodhounds and that this might take two or three days, Diana threw up on her coffee table.

Dutch didn't feel trapped by the reporters. He walked outside and told them that if any one of them so much as stepped on the grass he'd kick the living shit out of them. For once Diana was almost thankful for her husband's violent nature, although he only convinced them that they were in the right place. An acorn doesn't fall far from the tree. If John David was anything like his father, he was big, loud, and violent.

Late Saturday evening a second piece of information was deliberately released to the reporters by a sheriff's deputy. Mark Therrien was off-duty and dressed in civilian clothes when he went down to the River House to look for a reporter. His information wasn't going to jeopardize the case, and the media was going to find out about it sooner or later, he decided. He'd better cash in tonight.

Therrien ordered a beer at the bar and listened to two men sitting nearby, discussing the case. One of them said that he had heard that the boys had been drinking. God, they were so misinformed, Therrien thought. They had to be reporters from out of town, because all the locals knew that Dutch Marten's son didn't drink. Therrien picked up his beer and walked to the other side of the bar. The place was packed with people he'd never seen before. He wandered into the back room where two young men were playing pool. One of them was a big, fat kid, who Therrien knew to be something of a loudmouth. The other was tall and skinny, with long greasy hair pulled back in a ponytail. They were talking loud enough to be heard by all of the reporters sitting nearby.

"I don't know what happened down by the river," the skinny kid said, referring to the park where the murder was apparently committed. "Nobody does. But I will tell you one thing. Ain't no *posse* gonna find John David Marten in them woods." He didn't even look up from the pool table. He lined up the two ball in the side pocket. An easy shot normally, but he missed rather badly.

"What about the dogs?" a reporter asked. "I've heard they're tracking him with dogs."

"*A* dog," the fat kid said, correcting him. Then he added, laughing, "One dog. On a leash. I'll give anybody in the room four-to-one the dog is dead by tomorrow."

"John Marten will kill the dog?!" another reporter asked. He had walked over to the pool table, oblivious to the fact that he was in the way.

Both of the men nodded in agreement.

"Guarantee it," the fat kid said.

The boys were enjoying the attention. It wasn't often they were asked their opinions. Certainly not down at Millers sawmill, where they both had worked since graduating from high school several years earlier. All day long they hauled fourteen foot logs and placed them on the conveyors. It wasn't the kind of job that required a lot of opinions. But on this particular night they were experts. It wouldn't last long. No one was going to ask either of them what they thought about the legal case against John David Marten. But tonight, these hungry reporters were starving for information about the suspect, and they were the only suppliers. They tried to appear nonchalant. It made them seem so much more authoritative. Yeah, they knew a thing or two about dogs and guns. And the woods.

"How will he kill the dog? Shoot it? Won't the State Police shoot back at him?"

"When Marten shoots the dog, they won't see him. They'll be too busy running for cover. And then John David will sneak off."

"How far can he go?" someone asked. "Won't they find him sooner or later?"

"There's only two roads north of here for the next hundred miles or so. There's several thousand square miles of lakes and woods, nothing else. John David knows it all. Every square inch. You'd need ten thousand troopers to cover that area. Maybe a hundred thousand."

"How do you know that Marten is good enough to shoot the dog and not one of the men?" another reporter asked. Therrien recognized him as one of the two men who'd been sitting at the bar a few minutes ago. He must have heard the commotion and decided to join in.

"John David's been hunting since he was maybe seven or eight," the skinny kid said. "Alone. I know for a fact that he shot a black bear when he was twelve because he was underage and he called up my brother to tag it for him. My brother went and tagged it, only it was hardly bleeding. Tiny little bullet hole right between the eyes. 'What'd you shoot this with?' my brother asked him. John David says a .220."

The significance of this observation was lost on the reporters, none of whom was an expert in firearms. There was a brief silence while they jotted down notes, then somebody asked *What's a .220?*

"It's a woodchuck rifle," the skinny kid said.

"You mean, like a .22?"

Both of the kids laughed.

"No, not exactly," the fat one said. "*Nobody* could kill a bear with a .22. The lead is about the same size as a .22, but there's more powder. Still, it ain't no bear rifle. You'd have to be in the bear's face to kill it with a .220."

"Was he?"

101

"Nobody knows. John David's always been real vague about his hunting. But go ask Don Higgins at the gun shop how many beaver and mink and muskrat pelts John David brought in last year. Hundreds, I'll bet."

"Can I get your name?" one of the reporters asked.

"Why?" the kid asked. He was naturally suspicious.

"Just for my records. I won't use it in a story unless I get your permission."

"Shit, I don't mind you using my name," the fat kid said. "Frank Tomecki."

"Are you a friend of John David Marten?"

"Yeah. I know him pretty good. We was friends back in high school."

"Do you think he killed Jack O'Neill?"

Tomecki paused for a minute.

"It's *possible*," he said, then added, rather quietly, "but I dunno."

Deputy Therrien caught the eye of one of the reporters and motioned for him to meet him outside. The reporter had asked most of the good questions, so Therrien assumed he must be one of the better ones. A few minutes later they were sitting in the deputy's pickup truck.

"Who do you write for?" Therrien asked.

"The Albany *Times Union*," the reporter said. He stuck out his hand and shook Therrien's. "Thomas P. Sawyer."

"Any rela .."

"None whatsoever. My father was a high school English teacher and he thought the name was cute. But enough about me. Let's talk about you."

"I want a thousand bucks for the real story," Therrien said.

"How do I know you have the real story?" Sawyer asked. "The one I heard in there was pretty good, and it didn't cost me a cent."

"That stuff you heard in there doesn't have anything to do with the case. I'm a deputy with the County Sheriff's office. I have what you need for a real story."

"Go on. Tell me a little more."

"A thousand bucks. Up front. You get the whole thing."

"A thousand bucks is a lot of money. I don't carry that kind of money."

"You've got it back in the motel, I'll bet," Therrien said.

"Okay. Let's suppose I *can* give you a grand. What kind of story are we talking about?"

"How about Jack O'Neill being accused of rape two days ago?"

"Okay, you got my interest," the reporter said, excited. If he'd been interested in haggling over the price, he'd just blown it. But he wasn't interested in haggling. He was the reporter, not the accountant. Let them back in Albany worry about the finances. "Rape?! Who?!"

"First the money."

The reporter actually had more than a thousand bucks on him. It was advance money for the motel and meals and gas. He didn't like carrying it with him, but there wasn't a safe in the motel. Now he was glad he had it on him. It was only nine o'clock. If this panned out, he could call in another story by midnight.

"I've got five hundred on me," Sawyer said. "How's that for a down payment?"

Therrien took the money and stuffed in awkwardly into his pants pocket.

"On Thursday night a local girl came into the Sheriff's office with her parents. She claimed Jack O'Neill tried to rape her."

"*Attempted* rape," the reporter said, "not rape."

"Not much difference in a small town like this."

"Was O'Neill booked on that charge?" Sawyer asked.

"No. The girl couldn't prove anything. She didn't have any bruises, least not on her face. No witnesses, nothing. Couldn't even prove it *was* attempted rape. The sheriff told them that there was no way the District Attorney would prosecute a case against a 'good kid' without something more to go on."

"Did he even question O'Neill?" Sawyer asked.

"I don't think so. He told the parents that if they tried to prosecute, everyone would find out about it. He asked them if that was what they wanted. After all, it was only an attempted rape. Not the real thing. Maybe the boy thought he could, you

103

know, go a little further. Cooney asked the girl if she gave him any reason to think so. Man, you shoulda seen the girl's father when he said that. Jesus, his face got so red I thought he was going to explode. But he didn't say anything. He just grabbed his daughter's arm and walked out."

"Who was the girl?"

"I can't tell you her name. This is a real small town and there were only four of us on duty that night. I don't think anyone else knows about it."

"Do you think the father could have killed Jack O'Neill?"

"No, not a chance. He's a doctor."

"What's this got to do with John David Marten?"

"That I don't know. But last fall, around Thanksgiving, the same girl got lost hiking in the woods. She went up into the mountains west of town to take pictures. When she didn't return by dark, her parents called us. They didn't know she went into the woods by herself. We figured that out when we found her car by one of the trail heads. We searched the woods that night and the next day without finding a trace of her. Then she appeared in the afternoon with John David Marten, out on Route 28. She said she was lost and that Marten found her. Personally, I think there was something going on between them."

"Can you verify that?"

"Verify what? Finding them together on Route 28? Sure I can. *I* found them. They were acting all cool and everything when I picked them up. I think the whole story about her being lost is a crock. The rumor going around is that John David has a secret cabin in the woods. No one has ever seen it. But I heard from my girlfriend, who heard it from someone who says she heard it from the girl's *mother*, that the girl and John David stayed in the cabin the night that he 'found' her."

The reporter thought for a minute. Then he said, "But the official story is that John David found her in the woods. She was lost and he was called in to track her down?"

"No, he didn't track her down. He was out there on his own. They just ran into each other."

Therrien thought about the two stories that were emerging. One was a simple love triangle, which everybody has heard a thousand times, but which was nevertheless a pretty good story. But the other story involved a backwoodsman who rescues a girl in the woods. Then his best friend tries to rape her. The woodsman steps in again to avenge her. There was something wonderfully primeval about it. It was unquestionably the better story.

"So who was this girl that John David Marten would kill his best friend over?" Sawyer asked.

"Hey man, I could lose my job if they find out that I leaked this information."

"I'll cover for you. I know how to make these things sound like they came out of the beauty parlor. Trust me."

"We don't have a beauty parlor in this town." Therrien said.

"Then I'll say I heard it down at the gas station. You have a gas station, don't you?"

"Look, you got enough. You don't need to know who the girl is."

"Is she pretty? Just tell me that much."

"Yeah, she's a looker," Therrien said.

The story that appeared Sunday morning in the *Times Union* caused a horde of reporters to descend on Henoga Valley like locust. Sawyer's byline said that Jack O'Neill had been accused of attempting to rape the daughter of a local physician. Although the editors of the *Times Union* withheld her name, everyone in Henoga Valley knew it was Emily Davignon. Dr. Emerson was the only other doctor for a hundred miles. He also had a daughter, but she was only five years old. Jack wouldn't have tried to rape *her*. The story also reported how John David rescued the girl months before, saving her from a probable death during a cold rainy weekend in November. By Monday evening television crews from New Jersey, Long Island and Pennsylvania had rented every motel room from Blue Mountain Lake to Lake Placid. And more crews had arrived on Tuesday afternoon.

The story of the two best friends and the girl that came between them was certainly compelling enough, but it was actually the news coverage on Sunday evening of a State Police dog handler and his wounded bloodhound that sent the media into frenzy.

105

Sheriff Cooney had called in a dozen State Troopers and one bloodhound to begin tracking John David on Saturday afternoon from the last place he'd been seen, his own backyard. John David had a good ten- hour lead on them. Cooney would rather have waited until Sunday to give himself more time to prepare. He needed to coordinate the drop off of tents and food by helicopter so that they could stay on John David's trail. He needed to organize the fresh search teams and the additional dogs needed to stay after him and wear him down. But he couldn't wait. Cooney figured John David would head through the woods, then maybe hitch a ride with some trucker on a remote stretch of highway up north. Then they'd be searching the whole goddam country, and Cooney wanted to catch him right here in Hamilton County.

The dog had no problem picking up John David's scent. It led them almost due west, up the steep eastern slope of Raquette River Mountain. That son of a bitch thinks he's so goddam smart, Cooney thought. Take us up steep terrain and tire us out. Well, he isn't so goddam smart. It's a lot easier to follow than to lead. We'll just keep on him until he breaks. Two days, two weeks. Hell, they did this for almost a month when that nut case killer got loose down around Speculator. They would drop supplies and tents so that they could spend the night wherever they ended up. And someone would follow them to pick up the gear from the last campsite. When one of them got tired, the helicopter would lift him out and send in someone else. Same with a dog. No point in using three. One at a time was enough. It was really great fun, Cooney had to admit. Kind of like the raccoon hunting he used to do with his old man when they owned black and tans, except these bloodhounds had better noses. A bloodhound could tell if you'd gone by in a *car*. No creature on earth could disguise their scent enough to fool a bloodhound.

It turned out that John David apparently had no intention of fooling the bloodhound. It seemed odd to the dog's handler, a young trooper named Cronin, that the scent was so strong. Usually a bloodhound tracks by trial and error. If the dog begins to lose the scent, it moves in another direction until the scent becomes stronger. Back and forth, finding and losing it, a metronome of a nose. But John David's trail seemed obvious. The dog simply walked in a nearly straight line from John David's back yard, through a heavily wooded ravine, then up Raquette River Mountain. Kid's not doing such a good job, the sheriff thought. The sweat was pouring off the sheriff's brow and his shirt was soaked through. He was a big man, weighed almost three hundred pounds. He wasn't used to this kind of hiking. But the handler was. He was up ahead holding the bloodhound with a leash, shouting words of encouragement. Several of the younger troopers were with him, but the less fit stayed back with Sheriff Cooney. Several of them wondered if they'd be practicing their CPR skills on the sheriff before nightfall.

Sheriff Cooney had stopped to sit on a rock ledge when he heard the loud wail of the bloodhound. He jumped to his feet. Other troopers began shouting up ahead, but he couldn't make out what they were saying through the trees. He and the troopers with him ran ahead up the steep incline as fast as they could go. The hound continued to wail. The poor animal sounded like someone was beating it with a stick. The other troopers were still shouting. No gunfire yet, the sheriff thought. What the hell's going on?

He arrived on the scene to find several troopers standing in a loose circle with the dog handler in the middle. The dog was now sitting quietly at his side, licking its paw.

"What the hell's going on up here?!" the sheriff bellowed.

The bloodhound, which had briefly settled down, leapt to its feet again and starting wailing. The handler tried to calm the dog down, but he had all he could to keep her from running away. The dog leapt into the air like it was being stung by hornets. Then the sheriff noticed the steel leghold trap on the dog's right front paw.

"That bastard's setting *traps*," Cooney shouted in disbelief. He suddenly realized why the trail had been so easy for the dogs to find. Marten *wanted* them to follow him to this narrow place between two boulders, where the dog was certain to step in the trap.

"Can you believe this crap?" the trooper in charge said, disgusted. The trooper was Sergeant Payne, a ten-year veteran. He was a tall man, six-foot-four, with dark hair and a neatly trimmed moustache. Perfect physical specimen. Ran five and a half miles a day, lifted weights, went to the practice range three times a week. Twice decorated for outstanding service.

"Get that thing off him, for Chrissake," Cooney shouted to Cronin.

"He tried," Sergeant Payne said. His voice dripped contempt. He didn't need the sheriff telling him what to do, pointing out the *obvious*. Fat old man was only slowing them down. "The dog bit him when he tried to touch his paw."

"Well, *muzzle* the goddam dog and then take the trap off."

Sergeant Payne looked at the sheriff. If he thought this was all going to be wrapped up in a couple of days, he's wrong, Payne thought. As soon as the dog stepped in the trap, he realized they were in for a long haul. They could bring in another dog, but they couldn't land a helicopter on this heavily wooded mountain. There wasn't an open meadow anywhere nearby. They'd have to start over. And who's to say there weren't *more* traps. John David would be leading them through densely wooded areas and setting traps every few miles. Then when the dog stepped in one of them, they'd have to stop everything and decide what to do next. Each delay would give John David more time to escape.

"Well, we got two choices," Payne said. "We can send some men out after him, without a dog. Or we can go get another dog."

"Let's just get another dog in here," Cooney said.

"Oh? Do *you* want to go over there and try to take the trap off that dog's paw?" the trooper asked. "We better set up a ring around this area before we lose him."

"A ring around *what* area?" Cooney said. "We've got the highways covered as best we can. But we don't have enough men to search these woods without a dog. Can't be done. *Cannot* be done."

Trooper Cronin had finally calmed his dog and was able, with the help of two other troopers, to remove the trap. One of the troopers brought it over to Cooney and Sergeant Payne.

"How's the dog?" Payne asked, fearing the worst.

"Not bad, surprisingly," the trooper said. "Look at this," he said, holding up the trap. "Duct tape on the jaws."

Sergeant Payne took the trap from the handler and examined it. A thin layer of duct tape had been applied to the steel jaws of the trap.

"Looks like he wanted to hurt the dog as little as possible," the handler added. "The foot may be broken. I can't tell. She won't let me examine it. But the tape kept the trap from cutting her foot."

"Give me a break," Cooney said. "Like I'm supposed to have sympathy for a guy who kills his best friend but doesn't want to hurt a dog." Cooney had made the mistake of letting the reporter from the *Times Union* tag along. He looked over and saw Sawyer writing furiously. "Don't make him out to be some kind of saint," Cooney added, pointing to the reporter, "cause he ain't. Believe me." He turned back to the dog handler. "Any chance she can continue?"

"No way, sir. Even if she could walk, which is doubtful, I don't think she'd follow *that* scent."

"Goddam it," Cooney said, slapping his thigh. He stood on the rock and surveyed the area. He wondered if the kid was watching them, getting a good laugh.

"Let's make a stretcher for the dog," Sergeant Payne said, walking away from the sheriff. He took out the walkie-talkie and told the base they were coming back. Then he told the trooper on the other end to call the governor and order the National Guard to saturate all roads surrounding Henoga Valley. Desperate move, he admitted to himself. Not a chance in hell they'd find him walking along a road. And in the darkness he could cross anywhere, and then he'd be gone for good. He'd have to get a second dog in here and pick up the scent. The area was too big to search, even if they gave him ten thousand men.

It was with no small measure of ignominy that Hamilton County Sheriff Cooney and Sergeant Payne of the New York

109

State Police appeared on the Albany and Plattsburgh news late Saturday night to explain why the manhunt was temporarily stalled. Sergeant Payne tried to explain how the bloodhound had been injured by a trap deliberately set by the accused murderer. He wanted to paint Marten as the most sinister of criminals, one who would stoop to wounding a dog. However, the television reporter and many of the newspaper reporters had been feasting for hours on local stories of John David Marten's prowess in the wilderness. The stories invariably were tinged with a little pride. Not that anyone was condoning what had happened. No one could figure out how one friend could kill another. But the murder and the manhunt were two separate things in their minds. They simply could not help boasting about John David, and perhaps adding to the stories a little bit. So the bear that John David shot was 'around 800 pounds' and the deer that he tracked for Bill McKeever in the dark was found 'two-three' miles from where they shot it.

"Would it be fair to say that John David Marten has outwitted the sheriff's office and the State Police?" the television reporter asked. The reporter was so enthused by the manhunt that her emotions and bias were obvious.

"This isn't a case of *wits*, ma'am," the sheriff answered gruffly. "We'll track him down if it takes all summer."

"At what point will you give up?"

"Let's cross that bridge when we get to it," Payne said.

"Sheriff Cooney," the reporter asked, "can you comment on the rumor that Jack O'Neill was accused of attempted rape two nights before he was murdered?"

Cooney was caught off guard, and it showed on the camera. "I can't comment on rumors," he said.

"But wasn't a complaint filed in your office last Wednesday," the reporter continued. "A complaint specifically accusing Jack O'Neill of attempted rape?"

"I can't comment on that at this time," he answered. Which, on television, sounded like an unequivocal 'yes.'

The broadcast, showing an obviously frustrated State Trooper and local sheriff, was subsequently broadcast by affiliate stations across the country on Sunday. By Monday,

110

people from as far away as Seattle knew the details of the manhunt and the fact that, despite the presence of 150 state troopers, John David Marten had not even been sighted.

"The sonofabitch has disappeared," Sheriff Cooney said, slamming his office door the next morning. "And this whole fuckin media thing has gotten totally out of control."

His nine deputies, the dispatcher, and the office staff were all packed into the second floor office. Cooney was afraid to talk anywhere else for fear that somebody could hear him.

"There have been too many leaks to the press, and I want it stopped," he said. "I don't know which one of you is responsible and to be perfectly honest I don't give a shit. But if anything else is said about the investigation, I'll fire every one of you and hire a whole new staff."

"Sir?" Officer Therrien said. "There's a rumor going around that John David Marten has a cabin in the woods."

"I've heard that one," Cooney said. His voice said tell me something I don't know.

"But the rumor I heard was that he took the Davignon girl there the night he found her in the woods."

Sheriff Cooney looked up with a little more interest.

"Who told you this?" he asked.

"My girlfriend. She said she heard it from the girl's mother. I heard it before all this happened. Months ago."

Therrien watched as the sheriff nodded his approval.

"And one other thing," Therrien added. "Marten wasn't carrying a tent when I found him on the road that day. So either he left the tent in the woods, or they stayed in the cabin. I figure the girl could tell us where the cabin is."

The sheriff followed up on his deputy's advice. This was a good lead, Cooney thought. He liked Deputy Therrien. Ambitious kid. He'd go places. Some of his other men just rode around in the cruisers and put in their time, but Therrien put in the extra effort. Cooney was thinking maybe he ought to promote the deputy as he pulled into the Davignon's driveway. It was Monday afternoon, but the doctor's car was in the driveway. Cooney was embarrassed that someone had leaked

111

the attempted rape story. Probably one of the secretaries. Christ, they talk about everything but their bowel movements.

Julia Davignon let Sheriff Cooney in. He explained that he wanted to ask her daughter a few questions.

"Is this absolutely necessary, sheriff?"

"I'm afraid it is," he answered. "We've heard a rumor that your daughter stayed in a cabin with John David Marten the night she was lost in the woods. I'd like to ask her about it."

Cooney was glad Mrs. Davignon had answered the door. He didn't think he'd get much out of Emily. What he really wanted to see was Mrs. Davignon's reaction. After all, *she* was the one who supposedly leaked the story about the cabin. It worked. Julia Davignon's face reddened. She led the sheriff into the living room, where Emily was resting on a couch.

"Emily?" her mother said, "Sheriff Cooney would like to ask you some questions about the night you were lost in the woods." Emily nodded and sat up. She looked exhausted.

"Emily, that night you were lost in the woods, back in November, did John David Marten take you to a cabin?"

Emily glanced at her mother ever so slightly, then immediately hated herself for being so gullible. Sheriff Cooney noticed the glance and figured he had his answer.

"We slept in a tent," she answered.

"But John David wasn't carrying a tent when we picked you up on the highway the next day."

"No, we left it in the woods. With the sleeping bags. It was too much to carry. John David said he'd return later to get them."

"The sleeping *bags*? More than one?"

"Yes. He had two of them?"

"Why would he have *two* sleeping bags if he was alone? Do you think he was expecting company?"

Had Emily not just awakened she would not have been so easily caught off guard. But she recovered quickly. "It wasn't a little pup tent. It was one of those big canvas things. It was like ... six feet tall. He had a cot and a propane stove, a couple of sleeping bags and a blanket. I think the tent had been there for quite awhile."

112

The sheriff nodded. A sliver of doubt entered his mind. That could be true, he thought. A cabin tent. That would make sense. John David could set one of those up and use it for months at a time. Emily sensed that she was beginning to lead him off the track, so she poured it on.

"I guess you could call it a cabin," she admitted. Her voice sounded so sincere that even her mother started to believe her. "But I don't think I can be of much help telling you where it was. After all, I *was* lost."

"True. But you did walk out with him."

"Do you want me to describe the trees?"

"You wouldn't be protecting him just a little, now would you?" Cooney asked. "Maybe John David came to your rescue a second time?"

"Compared to you," Julia said, beginning to shout, "I'd have to say yes."

Cooney did not take offence. He was used to this behavior. People don't like being questioned, particularly about a murder. If they acted normal, if they were at all polite, he became suspicious.

The sheriff felt sorry for Emily, a lot more than he showed. He had two daughters of his own, grown now, both of them out of college. If either of them had been raped by a man, he'd have killed the guy with a baseball bat. He sometimes wished he had an option like that, wished that a judge would just give him a court order that read something like 'go over there and beat the shit out of this sex offender.' Just once he'd like to be instructed to give someone a taste of his own medicine. Big 200 pound guys who came home drunk and then slapped their 120-pound wives around. He wouldn't even assign it to a deputy. He'd do it himself. Once, years ago, when he was a young man with the state troopers, he'd been radioed on a domestic violence call. These were normally assigned to the county sheriff's office, but they were short-staffed and the house was less than a quarter mile from Cooney. It was not State Police policy to send a single trooper on these calls, but rural Herkimer and Hamilton Counties were simply too big to be covered by the few troopers assigned to them. So Cooney went alone.

113

New York State Troopers pride themselves on their training. They are the consummate professionals. They hide their emotions behind a cool, almost nonchalant exterior. They remain polite at all times, even calling you 'sir' while they are pinning your head to the blacktop with their boots. Cooney was proud to have earned an appointment at the academy. He heard the shouting as he approached the house from the driveway. Then a woman screamed. Cooney went onto the porch and let the screen door slam behind him. He banged on the door. A man in his forties with a black stubbly beard and a bloodstained tee shirt appeared at the door. He saw Trooper Cooney, then immediately started shouting more obscenities at his wife. He could hear a child crying in the background.

"Sir, please open the door," Cooney said in a loud voice. He heard what sounded like the man slapping the woman. She was hysterical. "Open the door, *sir*!" Cooney repeated. Still the man did not reappear at the door. Cooney could have smashed the window and reached inside for the lock. But instead, he kicked the door with his size 14 shoe. The lock on the door, which was brand new, was stronger than the hinges, so instead of the door swinging open, it spun around and landed near the refrigerator. Cooney saw the child, a three-year-old boy, his bare skin dark red from his neck to his feet. Cooney later discovered that the father had placed the child in a scalding tub of water because he had shit in his pants. The boy was suffering from a bout of diarrhea. But the father had been alone at the time, and the inconvenience of it all infuriated him. The woman had run to the store to get more beer for her husband. She was terrified of him and only beer kept him from killing her. She often hoped he'd get drunk enough to pass out. The woman loved her son and tried to protect him as much as she could. She rarely let him near the man. But in the ten minutes she was gone, he'd stripped the kid of his clothes and dunked him in a scalding tub.

"Get the fuck outta my house," the man shouted at Cooney. He was standing over the woman with a flat skittle in his right hand.

"Help us!" the woman pleaded. Her face was covered in blood from the blows. Cooney was so enraged that he could feel the veins throbbing in his neck.   But his voice remained impassive.

"Sir, you're under arrest."

The man charged at Cooney, swinging the pan.   Cooney ducked and grabbed the man's arm after he missed and, with his other hand, grabbed the back of the man's head.   With one seamless motion he threw the man's face into the door jam.   His head bounced off it like a football and blood immediately spurted from his mouth and nose.   The man swung again with his free arm, catching Cooney on the right side of his head.   Cooney had boxed in the Navy and was used to being hit.   He barely felt the blow.   He swung the man around and backed him up a little, giving him room to charge again.   When he did, Cooney lifted him off the porch floor and threw him through the screen door.   The man landed on the sidewalk in front of the house.   The neighbors were out now, down by the street.   They watched the man get to his feet, dazed but still raging.   They saw Cooney come down the porch stairs seemingly as calm as a man going out for a walk.

"Don't get up," they heard Cooney say to the man on the sidewalk.   "I'll need you to lay face down so that I can put on the handcuffs."   It was their testimony that Cooney was cool and professional at all times that helped save his job with the State Police.   That and the testimony of the dead man's wife, who convinced the board of inquiry that her husband intended to kill *someone* that day and she was grateful to Cooney that it hadn't been her.   The man had rushed Cooney when he reached the last of the porch stairs and grabbed him around the chest, thinking, one might guess, that he would wrestle the six-foot four, 240-pound trooper to the ground.   He was much shorter than Cooney.   The top of his head only reached Cooney's chin.   Cooney placed both of his hands on the man's forehead.   He'd planned to push the man's head back and break his grip, but he was simply and truthfully unaware of his own strength, which was formidable even under ordinary circumstances.   Cooney wrenched the man's head back with such force that his neck snapped at the base of the skull.   He died instantly, dropping to the ground like wet towel.

Trooper Cooney had been investigated and later cleared of using excessive force. Though his record remained exemplary throughout his career with the State Police, he often felt he was overlooked for promotions. It may have had something to do with the fact that he later married the woman whose husband he killed, but he doubted that. He hadn't even *known* her before that day, had never set eyes on her before. Still, it made his superiors uneasy, and they were perhaps less likely to consider him for promotion.

Cooney stood in the living room of Dr. Davignon's house and looked at Emily. He understood what she felt. He'd heard enough about that from his wife. He had *wanted* to do something when she came into the office with her father. He would have been willing to go out to Jack O'Neill's house and haul the kid in. He'd have done it in an instant. But he felt obliged to explain to them that, under the circumstances, not much was likely to happen to him. All he had to do was deny it. Hell, even if he admitted hitting her, he'd have gotten some kind of slap on the wrist. Emily wasn't hurt badly enough to make a big case.

Cooney said, "You and Jack O'Neill were ... going steady? Is that right?"

"Not exactly," Emily answered. "I don't believe in 'going steady.' But I wasn't going out on dates with anyone else, either, if that's what you mean."

"So, did *John David* consider this relationship 'going steady?'"

"Yes, I suppose he did."

"But you were also spending a lot of time with John David Marten."

"Not really," Emily said. Then shrugging her shoulders, she changed her mind. "Well, I don't know. Maybe."

"Was there anything between you and John David?"

Emily looked up at the sheriff. Her expression was quizzical, like she'd been asked to compare eastern religions and hadn't had time to prepare an answer.

"I've gone to school with John David since kindergarten, but I never got to know him until the time he found me in the woods.

116

I would have thought ... *before* ... that he was some kind of animal. But after I got to know him, I found out we actually had a lot in common, and he became, well, sort of my best friend. He wouldn't say much, but he listened like no one else I've ever known. Really listened. He could quote anything I'd ever said. Even offhand remarks, things that I wouldn't even remember saying. And when he did say something, it always seemed to be the right thing. Who wouldn't want a friend like that?"

"Was Jack O'Neill jealous?"

"Oh yeah. Big time. Jack and I didn't have lunch together. Different periods. But he'd make these sarcastic remarks like 'what did John David have to say today?' Like he cared what John David had to say. You know what I think? I think Jack was jealous of what everybody *else* would think."

"Emily, I have to know something else. Did Jack rape you?" He was playing a hunch. Kids don't kill each other for no reason. It happens in the cities, over racism, or drugs, or gangs. But not up here in the Adirondacks. Not between friends. Something else had to be going on. Something was missing.

Emily nodded and tears welled up in her eyes.

"Don't you think you should have told me that on Tuesday night?" the sheriff asked, his voice rising slightly, in anger.

Dr. Davignon had entered the room in the middle of the discussion and had been listening quietly. He noticed that his daughter was getting upset again, so he interceded.

"Sheriff Cooney," he said, taking him by the arm. "Emily had better rest now."

The doctor led him out of the living room to the back door. Out of earshot, he explained to the sheriff how Julia had gotten a call from Emily that night. Emily was in the parking lot of the old train station on the western edge of town. Julia should have taken her right to the hospital, but she didn't want to spring this on Robert at the hospital, considering how he'd found out about the murder of his first wife. So they went home. And while Julia had been on the phone trying to reach Robert, Emily went upstairs and took a shower, washing away the semen needed for evidence. It was Robert who had decided that they wouldn't have a chance calling it rape.

117

"I wish you'd have let me decide that," Cooney said.

"Sheriff, I saw a lot of these cases in New York. A guy like Jack O'Neill *never* gets convicted."

The sheriff knew that Dr. Davignon was correct. It would have been impossible to convict a well-liked athlete like Jack O'Neill unless Emily had been beaten up. Can't tell rape from consent without a black eye, he thought. He looked at Emily's father and tried to think of something to say. But even if he had come up with something, it wouldn't have mattered because the doctor was already closing the door.

Chapter Fourteen

No one could remember how it came to be that Jack O'Neill and Emily Davignon started dating at the end of their junior year in high school. They had always appeared to be the worst of enemies, but then one day there they were, walking together down the hallway. Even the teachers stared in disbelief. Jack had been out with just about every pretty girl in the class and even flirted with the less attractive ones. But Emily had always been his goal, made all the more desirable because she showed not the slightest interest in him. Or anyone, for that matter. As far as Jack knew, Emily Davignon had never gone out on a date with anyone.

Jack O'Neill assumed, perhaps correctly, that every girl in the school was at least a little attracted to him. He believed that they liked his nonchalance and admired his self-confidence. It was during a history class that Jack finally realized Emily Davignon did not harbor any such feelings, and he therefore attempted a different approach.

They had been discussing the causes of the Civil War, and Jack argued that slavery wasn't the issue, it was 'states' rights.' Jack had read an article in *American Heritage* about the Emancipation Proclamation and how Lincoln only wrote it as a threat to end the war.

"He didn't care about ending slavery, " Jack said. "He just wanted to end the war. He said he'd do anything to uphold the union, even if it meant upholding slavery. The real issue was whether the individual states had the right to determine their own course."

"That's such bullshit!" Emily said, waving her hand as if to shoo him away. "The only *right* the south was interested in was the right to own slaves."

The teacher, Mr. Dunleavey, admonished Emily for her language. She ignored him.

Jack O'Neill said, "Do you think anyone but a handful of radical abolitionists actually cared about the slaves? Personally, I think history was rewritten to make the Civil War this great battle between right and wrong, but at the time it was just a struggle to see who was boss."

"*All* moral causes are started by a handful of radicals," Emily countered. Her face was flushed with anger. "At the time of the American Revolution only a handful of people knew what democracy was all about. And civil rights, do you think its about blacks wanting to ride at the front of the bus? Do you think women's liberation is about women wanting to open their own car doors?"

"No," Jack said. He held a finger up to his chin, pretending to be pensive. "I thought women's liberation was about not wanting to wear bras."

He smiled at Emily as the boys in the class erupted in laughter, but Emily was undaunted by such a sophomoric rebuttal.

"No, Jack. Women's lib is about not being subservient to a man strictly because of his Y chromosome and his ability to pee without sitting."

Then all of the girls in the class laughed, and several of them applauded.

"But that's another issue," Emily said. "We should get back on track. Everyone knew what the Civil War was about, just like everyone knows what civil rights and women's rights are about. You see, Jacky boy, that's why Jefferson could say 'we hold these truths to be self-evident,' because he knew that people like you and King George III, with football score IQs, would understand. Human rights are *self evident*. That means you don't have to explain them."

Emily paused to look around the room. Everyone was staring at her, including Jack and Mr. Dunleavey. Their heads were tilted slightly, as if to listen more closely, or perhaps merely to reflect their bewilderment. Some mouths were slightly agape. I've gone too far again, she whispered, and then closed the open book on her desk.

"We should probably continue this discussion after the scarecrow visits Oz and gets a brain." Emily said, putting her book away. The bell rang to mark the end of the period.

Mr. Dunleavey stood to the side of the classroom, leaning on the radiator. He was in his late thirties and had been teaching in Henoga Valley for fifteen years. He had spent years trying to encourage debate in the classroom without much success. Now that he was successful, he felt oddly uncomfortable. The debates he had imagined were supposed to be friendly and encourage the students to think for themselves, but Jack and Emily always seemed to zero in on the most emotional issues. Jack was happy to argue either side of a cause and he'd use a variety of tactics to win. Like making fun of someone to break their train of thought, or quoting an article that he'd read, regardless of whether he was quoting it accurately. He'd insert a joke to make everyone laugh, knowing that it is human nature to side with someone who makes you feel good. The kid would make a good lawyer, Dunleavey thought. Emily Davignon, on the other hand, cared so deeply about everything. Maybe too deeply. She could not be made to take the opposing side, or even tolerate an opinion she considered unethical or uninformed. She argued like a summer thunderstorm, a great whir of words and emotions. She was not above heavy-handed sarcasm and would ridicule without mercy an opponent's lack of sophistication. She had long ago terrorized the entire class, and there was no one left to argue with her but Jack O'Neill.

The rest of the class loved their outbursts. What fun, what entertainment. They were a little larger than life, so it was like having movie stars in your own high school. Who hadn't heard about the arguments, the jokes, the barbs? Boys in other classes would seek out Jack in the lunch room to hear first hand what Emily had said that day in class. In contrast, Emily ate her lunch on the stairs behind the gym and read a book, never bothering to look up when someone passed by.

It was after the argument on slavery that Jack realized how much Emily cared about things, even slavery. He found it hard to understand. Henoga Valley didn't even have any black families and slavery was just history. He excused himself from his friends as they headed for gym class and found Emily on the stairs.

"Hey, how about a truce?" he said.

Emily looked up from her book and saw Jack O'Neill

standing at the bottom of the stairwell. She stopped chewing for a moment and listened to see if there was more. But Jack didn't say anything else. He started to walk away.

"Wait!" Emily said.

She stood up and walked down to the bottom stair. She brushed the bread crumbs from her lips, then stuck out her hand. Jack shook it.

"Look," he said, "I know you're probably not interested, but would you ... consider ... going to a movie with me? Or something?"

"You mean a date? Are you asking me to go out on a date?" Emily sounded sarcastic, but in fact she was surprised. She knew why she didn't get any dates. She knew the boys were intimidated by her. But she had always been a little surprised that they didn't even bother to ask.

"Uh, yeah," Jack said.

Emily shifted her weight to lean on the railing. Jack's eyes glanced to the curve of her hips, now accentuated by her position.

"I don't have any experience with this dating thing," Emily said, not in the least self-conscious. Her voice was softer than it had been in class. "You'll have to explain exactly how it works. Do you pick me up and bring me flowers? And hold the door and pay for the movie?"

"More or less," Jack said. Then, chuckling, he added, "Probably less when it comes to the flowers, but certainly the movie. And I'll take care of all the doors."

"Well then, I suppose I should be gracious and accept the terms of your surrender." Emily turned and walked back up the stairs.

"*Surrender?!*" Jack shouted after her. "I didn't say anything about a *surrender*. I said a *truce*."

"What's the difference?" Emily asked. But her eyes had already returned to her book, which meant she didn't care to hear the answer.

Emily's parents were obviously pleased when Emily announced at the dinner table later that evening that she had a date. They had long worried that she was destined to become a tortured artist. But Emily surprised them. She appeared to enjoy the idea of going out on a date. She even acted like a teenager. She laughed out loud when Jack showed up with a bouquet of carnations.

"I figured I might as well make it an unconditional surrender," he said.

"I could learn to like this dating thing," Emily said, taking the flowers into the kitchen.

Jack stayed by the front door. He'd never been in the Davignon's house. Hardwood floors, oak moldings, velvet drapes. Everything looked so expensive. No one over on his end of town had a house like this.

Emily's parents came in from the parlor to greet their daughter's first date. Emily's father asked him about school and what he was going to do after he graduated.

"I'm applying to some Ivy League schools, Dartmouth and Harvard, and Siena, Union, a few others. I guess I'll go wherever I get the best deal."

Dr. Davignon nodded and seemed to approve.

"You must have pretty good grades," he said.

"Well ... *yeah*. Emily and I are sort of ...like ... competing ... for valedictorian."

Jack seemed a little disappointed that Dr. Davignon didn't already know this. Didn't Emily think enough of him to even mention the competition?

In fact, Emily had never mentioned to her parents that *she* was in the running for class valedictorian. Her parents knew that her grades were excellent and that was good enough for them. They never thought to ask about her ranking.

"Isn't that something," Dr. Davignon said. "Julia, did you know that?" he shouted.

Julia had gone to help Emily put the flowers in water. She poked her head out from the kitchen.

"Know what?" she asked.

"That Emily and Jack here are ranked one and two in the class?"

"No," Julia said, genuinely surprised. "I didn't. Emily, how come you've never said anything?"

123

Emily came into the dining room with the vase full of flowers and placed them on the table.

"This is the first I've heard about it," she said. "Who decides such things."

"It's just based on your average," Jack said awkwardly. "It's just a number."

Emily walked over and stood in front of him with her hands tucked in the back pockets of her jeans.

"So what's your average?" she asked.

"96.5"

"And mine?"

"96.6"

"How is it that you know *my* average?" she asked. She did not seem angry.

"Mrs. Van Dorn in the office told me. It's no big deal. It's just like, keeping score. I mean, how would you know how you were doing if you didn't keep score."

"How long have you been keeping score?"

"Since freshman year."

Julia Davignon came over with Emily's coat.

"Emily, dear," she said. "Don't argue. Just go out and have some fun. It doesn't matter who's first and who's second. You're both so very bright."

"Forget it," Emily said. She turned and headed back to the kitchen. "I can't go out tonight. I've got to go study so I can build up my lead."

"*Emily*," they said in unison. The sound of her parents' voices mixed with Jack's was so comical that she turned and started to laugh at them. Jack was shrugging his shoulders and mouthing the words 'I'm sorry' and her mother was practically begging.

"Okay, okay, I'll go," she said, throwing her hands into the air. "You're all so pathetic. But I guess I have a big enough lead to take a night off."

Jack was nervous walking Emily to the car. He dreaded the possibility, now more likely than ever, that the evening might turn into one long argument. But she surprised him by putting her arm in his at the movie theater, and by flicking popcorn at a man and woman kissing several rows in front of them. And after the movie they walked down Main Street to the Barkeater Coffee Shop and Emily allowed Jack to hold her hand. Some of their classmates saw them having coffee together and were obviously surprised. But Emily remained uncharacteristically pleasant.

"I have to confess something," Jack said. They were sitting in a corner booth drinking coffee. "I've been in love with you since the fourth grade."

"Really?" Emily said, unconvinced. "The fourth grade."

"Yeah. When you did that thing with your eyelids." Emily had sat directly in front of Jack and was annoyed by his constant chatter. So she had turned around once to tell him to shut up and get serious. With both of her eyelids inverted.

"Hardly the basis for love," Emily said. "Why haven't you asked me out before now?"

"I did. Several times."

"You did? I don't remember?"

"Well, maybe I didn't word it clearly enough. Anyway, I figured you hated me."

"I did, but I might have gone out with you anyway. It's not like there's anything on television on the one station in Henoga Valley."

"Wow," Jack said, checking his watch. "You've gone two hours and ... twenty-seven ... minutes without resorting to sarcasm. Is this a personal best?"

"No, I went a whole day once," Emily said, sipping her coffee. "But I had the flu."

She smiled at Jack and propped her chin on her hand.

"And you don't seem like you've been pining away for me for the last seven years," she added.

"I have been, I swear," Jack said. "This gaiety thing is all an act. I keep my pining inside."

"I see," Emily said. "So what do you want to talk about?"

Her question sounded like an interview.

"How about something that we can *agree* on?" Jack said.

"Favorite book?" Emily asked.

"*The Great Gatsby,*" Jack said, lying. It sounded better than his real favorite, *The Godfather.*

125

"*Ada,*" Emily countered with a frown. "How about favorite movie?"

"*The Dirty Dozen,*" Jack said. He couldn't even think of a movie that Emily might like.

"*Splendor in the Grass.* How about your favorite poem?"

"I don't have a favorite poem," Jack said. He never even read poetry.

"Neither do I. It would be too hard to choose."

"Let me ask one," Jack said. "What's your favorite sport?"

"Bullfighting."

"*Bullfighting?!*"

"Yes. I root for the bull. It's like hunting would be if the deer hunted back. Imagine a herd of bucks attacking a group of hunters who are drinking coffee in a parking lot."

"It's a good thing evolution has been kind to us," Jack said.

"So, Jack," Emily said, moving onto the next subject, "How would you summarize yourself. What's important to you?"

"Viet Nam, pollution, human rights, civil rights, women's rights." He looked at her from slightly different directions, trying to determine if he was getting a reaction. This *was* an interview. "You'll tell me when I'm scoring points, won't you?"

"I'll tell you if you sound sincere."

"I don't think I've ever been sincere. Contrite, perhaps, but never sincere. I'm too young for sincerity."

Jennifer Baker walked into the Barkeater with her boyfriend. Jennifer claimed to be Emily's closest friend when, in fact, Emily didn't make many friends because she had so little patience. Jennifer's theatrics grated on her, but Emily tolerated them in small doses.

"Emily?!" Jennifer said, walking over to their booth. Her mouth hung open in exaggerated surprise. "*The* Emily Davignon is out in public?" Jennifer took Emily's hand and dropped down on one knee. "Milady."

Emily turned to Jack and motioned with her eyes. This is what I have to put up with.

"Emily, I'd like you to meet Brad," Jennifer said, stepping aside to introduce her enormous boyfriend. "You don't know him. He just moved here last year. Isn't he just the biggest teddy bear you ever saw?"

Emily looked up at the goliath. He seemed to have a rather small head for such a large body, and it occurred to Emily that perhaps his head had been transplanted from a much smaller being of questionable lineage.

"Are you sure he's fully evolved?" she asked.

"Oh, don't mind her, Brad," Jennifer said in mock anger. "She's such a bitch. But once you get to know her ... well, she'll still be a bitch, but you won't mind it as much. Can we join you?"

Jennifer didn't wait to be invited. She sat down next to Emily and pushed her further into the booth.

"This is so *exciting!*" Jennifer said. "I can't believe you two are finally going out on a date." She turned to Jack. "And *you!* You'd better be nice to my friend here. She's the sensitive type."

"Sensitive?!" Jack said. "Jen, it's like going out with the dean of college admissions."

"Oh, everybody reads her wrong," Jennifer said. Then turning to Emily, she added, "I'm the only one who knows what a sweet little thing you are. "Course, you *do* go out of your way to hide it."

They sat together in the booth for another forty-five minutes, but moments afterward Emily could not remember a word that was said. She watched the three of them talk as if she was concealed behind a secret mirror. Jennifer loved to talk and could fill the air with a mind-numbing avalanche of words. She laughed and told jokes and greeted everyone who entered the Barkeater, even the elderly farmers who came in for a late night cup of coffee. She went from one subject to the next effortlessly. Jack engaged her in this conversation and laughed heartily at her jokes, though later he admitted to Emily that Jennifer drove him nuts.

"Then why do you put up with her?" Emily asked after Jennifer and Brad had left.

"Just being polite," he answered.

"You're always 'polite,' aren't you?"

127

"Now you're going to tell me there's something wrong with being polite?"

"No, of course not. I guess it's that sincerity thing?"

"So what do you do when you see Mrs. Parente in a new dress?"

"I try to avoid looking directly at her," Emily said. Mrs. Parente was the tenth grade English teacher. She was five feet, two inches tall and weighed 320 pounds. But she sewed her own dresses out of brightly colored fabrics that hung straight from her shoulders. Jack could not help but think she looked like a hot air balloon. But every morning he would stop by her classroom, open the door, and say 'tonight, in the park, ten- thirty?' Mrs. Parente would slap him, or throw an eraser, and say something about being a married woman. And Jack would whisper for her to leave her old man, just for the one night. All this in front of her class. Mrs. Parente would usually have some difficulty regaining control of her class, but in fifteen years of teaching she had never been as popular as she was now that Jack O'Neill was there to tease her.

"Would it *kill* you to throw her a little compliment? Tell her she looks nice? I mean, okay, so deep down she knows I'm lying. But on a day-to-day basis, nobody wants to look deep down. Do you think she wants me to tell her the truth? No. She *wants* to hear the lie. And she wants everyone else to tell her lies, too. The truth just isn't all that it's cracked up to be."

"I don't want to hear lies," Emily said.

"Of course *you* don't," Jack snapped. "You don't need them. You've got great looks, a perfect body, you're an A student. The truth is just fine with you. But for most people, the truth hurts. They're not too bright, or maybe they've got bad skin. So where's the harm in lying to them? Just let them grab a little of the spotlight."

Jack's ability to create a bond with everyone he met fascinated Emily. He knew every student by name, even the freshmen, and he wanted them to know him. He had something to say to every teacher, a comment about their favorite baseball team, the stock market, or cars. He knew some small detail about everyone in school, thereby creating a bond that made

128

everyone seem special. Emily remembered him popping his head into the home economics classroom and shouting to Mrs. Fifield that yarn was on sale at Woolworth's. The class erupted in laughter, but Mrs. Fifield was an avid knitter and she thanked him for telling her. Did he really care about them at all? Or was it all just a game? And if it was a game, how could he do it so well for so long?

"How do you keep it in check?" Emily asked.

"What do you mean?"

"Doesn't it ever get out of control? The lying?"

Jack just shook his head out of frustration. She always makes things difficult, he thought.

Jack O'Neill also had a wonderful gift of self-confidence. He believed that he could will himself to make a jump shot from the top of the key when the game was hanging by one point, to strike out a batter with the bases loaded, to predict that he would have the highest score of the SAT exam, and then do each these things with aplomb. He always chuckled as he said these things, a guttural snicker that made his shoulders twitch, as if these feats were trifling.

"This is going to be a slaughter," he would say, laughing, at the start of every basketball game, "a travesty." Once, after he scored a breakaway lay up in close game, he ran down the sidelines doing a little dance step, swinging his arms to hype up the Henoga Valley crowd. This was an away game and the hometown crowd became infuriated. What a showoff, what a hot dog, they said, disgusted. The guard for the other team brought the ball right up the middle to challenge Jack, more interested in revenge than in scoring. But Jack stripped the ball from him and threw a behind the back pass to Frank Massillo on the break, and Henoga Valley took off on a fourth quarter 16-2 run.

At the end of their senior year in high school, Jack's varsity baseball team played, for the first time in its history, in the varsity baseball sectional championship game against the team from Wells. Both teams were undefeated. The pitcher for Wells was a six-foot-four inch, 225 pound left-hander named 'Big Boy' Noonan, who threw the ball around 90 miles per hour. No

129

curves, no sliders, not even a change-up. Just a blazing fastball that nobody could hit. It was up to Jack O'Neill, who was pitching for Henoga Valley, to hold them off until somebody got lucky. Jack, who normally threw only about a quarter of his pitches as curve balls because of the strain it put on his arm, threw more than seventy percent curve balls against Wells. Twisting his arm furiously inning after inning, keeping the ball away from the batters. He matched Big Boy Noonan inning for inning, with neither side able to advance a runner beyond first base. Noonan walked only two batters in seven innings. Jack walked only one. He threw seven and a half innings of no-hit ball before the Wells shortstop hit a little fly ball that dropped between the left-fielder and the third baseman. Jack was furious. He threw two inside corner fast balls to the next batter and retired him with a curve that caught him lunging for the outside corner of the plate.

In the dugout after every inning, Jack rubbed his arm. The curve balls were putting an enormous strain on his elbow. But Jack knew he couldn't throw fast enough to keep them from hitting, and couldn't afford to let Wells score a couple of runs. Nobody on his team was hitting Big Boy Noonan. A two run lead would seal the game, so he kept throwing the curve.

Henoga Valley eventually won the game 1-0 in the tenth inning. Although the entire team owed Jack an enormous debt of gratitude for his heroic pitching, it was John David's game-winning double with a man on second that ignited their emotions, and they carried *him* off the field into the frenzied crowd.

It was the only time in his life that Jack did not enjoy winning. He sat on the bench in the dugout and loosened the laces on his cleats. He remembered only the groan that arose from the Henoga Valley crowd when he struck out, just before John David came up to bat for the last time. Of course the crowd had groaned every time anyone had struck out, but this was different. They were disappointed in *him*. Jack sat alone in the dugout after the game and put his cleats in his bag. He could hear the cheering of the crowd behind him.

The next morning he stared at the picture of John David on

the front page of the sports section. There he was, John David Marten being carried off the field. Of course, the paper mentioned the one-hitter pitching duel between Big Boy Noonan and Jack O'Neill, but it was John David who was the hero of the game. And it was amidst this self-pity that he did not notice that it was Emily Davignon, who had never before even attended a baseball game, who came to the dugout and congratulated him on the victory.

Chapter Fifteen

With each passing day the manhunt for John David Marten grew both in the number of searchers and the number of reporters. By the end of the first week an additional 100 national guardsmen had been added to the search. They had barricaded Routes 28 and 30, stopping every vehicle that entered and exited the region. This quickly became an enormous task because traffic had increased dramatically following the reports of the murder. Dozens of troopers combed the wilderness north of Henoga Valley, but they had no idea what they were looking for. Some of them half expected to see him bolt from behind trees, like a deer flushed from its hiding place. But after they had heard some of the stories of how John David Marten had stalked a wounded deer for six miles in the dark, *over solid rock*, they began to doubt they'd ever spot him.

A second bloodhound had been brought in days ago to pick up John David's trail where the other dog left off. Two troopers with sticks walked several yards in front of the dogs to set off any traps that might be in the way. They followed his trail down the north side of Moose Mountain and up along a steep ravine. Several leghold traps had been set along this run, but the troopers found all of them. They came to an area where the wet sides of the oak leaves laying on the ground were showing. One of the troopers recognized that the leaves had been overturned recently, which explained why they weren't dry like all the others in the area. Two of the troopers went ahead of the dog with their sticks, poking at the wet leaves. They were getting very good at this. They were beginning to feel like real trackers and they could envision reporters questioning them about the manhunt. They would explain that you had to notice the little things, like overturned leaves and scuff marks in the dirt. They did not, however, notice the strand of rope that led from the area to a log, hanging over the edge of a steep embankment. They did not see the rope because it was buried beneath a layer of leaves, each of which had been carefully replaced with the dry side facing upward. The rope was secured by three tiny saplings approximately ten inches apart, each cut off two inches from the ground. In between the saplings was a small stick, attached to two of the saplings by perfectly carved notches. When one of the troopers, who was carefully walking around the wet leaves, accidently stepped in the middle of the rope, it popped loose from its mooring and wrapped around his ankle. The log at the other end of the rope was hanging down a ravine, propped on two small stakes and secured by a series of small knots along the way. When the trooper sprung the rope from the saplings, it set off a chain reaction and none of the remaining knots could keep the log from rolling down the steep ravine. The trooper was yanked from his feet and dragged down the side of the ravine like he'd been harnessed to a raging bear. When they found him at the bottom of the slope, he was unconscious, his leg dislocated at the hip, his left arm broken in two places. The manhunt was delayed by more than four hours while they brought in a helicopter to airlift the injured trooper.

They debated unleashing the bloodhound and letting him chase down John David Marten, but they quickly rejected the idea. There wasn't much doubt in anyone's mind that Marten could kill the dog. So they continued with the hound on a leash, leading the six troopers and two deputies from the sheriff's office. It was exhaustingly slow work. The dog had no trouble finding the trail, but he could only travel as fast as the men behind him. And Marten was leading them through nearly impenetrable woods. They crossed a blowdown, where hundreds of trees had been knocked down years before by an enormous summer storm. But the swamps were the biggest problems. John David apparently knew these swamps, knew how to hop from one clump of grass to the next. The troopers were up to their knees in mud, and it was anyone's guess where John David Marten was leading them. He seemed to be crisscrossing the vast wilderness north of Henoga Valley.

They left the swamp and crossed a narrow stream. The men had a tough time keeping their footing on the slippery rocks. The dog bounded through the water and up the other embankment, which John David had measured precisely. A double-spring steel jaw trap was set two feet from the water, and it slammed shut on the bloodhound's left paw. There was no duct tape on this trap. The poor dog jumped in the air and fell over backward into the stream. It began howling and thrashing around in the water, blinded by the searing pain.

"Aw ... *shit*! Not again," the handler said. "Goddam it. God fuckin dammit."

The handler was trying to hold the dog down, but he lost his footing and fell into the stream. The poor dog had never experienced anything like this. The handler finally got a muzzle on the dog and two troopers held it down while the handler released the trap. He had to stand on the springs to release them. The dog's foot was clearly broken. So by the end of the first week they had abandoned the idea of using dogs to track him down.

Sheriff Cooney had been given the name of a man who was supposed to be an expert tracker. He was said to be part Abenaki Indian and lived in a log cabin up north, somewhere beyond Big Moose. The sheriff had put the piece of paper with the man's name and address in his wallet almost a week ago, but he'd been thinking about the last few days. Local residents were getting upset with the searches out on Route 28. Traffic had been backed up all week, probably for nothing. It was clear that John David wasn't trying to hitch a ride out of town. Cooney decided to keep up the searches for another week, just for the sake of appearances. Those reporters would be all over him about giving up if he pulled the road blocks now.

Cooney and Deputy Therrien drove up to Big Moose on Sunday, one week after the search had been started. Sheriff Cooney sat in the passenger's seat and talked the whole way up to Big Moose. He considered Therrien his student and lectured him on points of law enforcement. Therrien hated these lectures, hated answering his rhetorical questions, but he wanted the promotions. So he kissed the old man's butt.

"Any luck finding the knife?" Therrien asked.

"State Police have thirty men searching the fields and the river. I can't believe they haven't come up with anything. You know what I think? I think Marten would have done something like sticking the blade into the ground and stepping on it."

"Metal detectors haven't picked up anything yet?"

"Nothing. I can't figure it out."

"Would he have kept it on him?" Therrien asked.

"Most of the time an assailant gets rid of the weapon as soon as possible. If you're caught with the murder weapon on you, you're nailed. But John David might think differently. He kills O'Neill at night ... maybe figures no one's around to see him. Might as well make the weapon disappear altogether."

They came to a roadblock and Therrien turned on the dome light. They nodded to the state troopers as the drove past a line of cars.

"This is a waste of time," Cooney said. "They aren't going to find this kid in a car."

They drove in silence for a few miles.

Cooney said, "I hope this Indian is the real thing, not some guy with feathers doing the war dance."

"I'm pretty sure he's for real," Therrien said. "They say he's the best outfitter in the Adirondacks."

"Yeah, well what does it take to guide a bunch of city boys through the woods?"

Michael Sabelle was reported to be part Abenaki Indian, descended from a tribe of Indians that originated in Maine and migrated to the Mohawk and Champlain valleys in the 18th century. Sabelle was born around the turn of the century and grew up on the Abenaki Reservation in Canada. He moved to the Adirondacks in the early 1930s, when the logging industry still cut trees in the winter and floated them to the mills during the spring thaws. It was a dangerous business. The logs were piled onto a pond that had a sluicegate. When the spring flooding began, the sluicegate was opened and the 14 foot logs began their 50-mile journey along the upper Hudson River to Glens Falls. Sabelle was an oarsman, whose job was to row a fourteen-foot jamboat out to a logjam with two pikemen, who would jump out of the boat and climb over the logs, prying them apart. As soon as the logs began to break up, the pikemen had to jump into the jamboat. Then their lives depended on the skill of the oarsman, who had to get them to shore before they were crushed. The jamboat was pointed in the bow and stern, so it could move in either direction and Sabelle's skill in the boat was legendary. He could row a boat forward as fast as most men could row in reverse, and in six years on the logging teams, no one had ever been killed on his boat.

Once, in the spring of 1938, one of the pikemen on Sabelle's team fell into the river just as the logjam was breaking up. Sabelle took off straight down the middle of the river, chasing the pikeman's bobbing head. A fully clothed logger didn't have much chance in the swollen Hudson River. The 400 pound logs slammed against each other crushed anything caught in between. The pikeman in the stern of the boat was yelling to Sabelle to get them the hell out of the river, but Sabelle ignored him. He kept his eyes trained on the bobbing head of the pikeman, even as the first of the logs were catching up to the boat. Sabelle rowed with ferocious intensity. He could see the pikeman's face, his eyes fixed on the boat. There was no look of panic on the man's face, just concentration. He knew that his life depended on getting a hand on the boat as soon as Sabelle maneuvered close enough. Then it would be up to Sabelle to outrace the logs. There would be only one chance. Anyone not out of the river in the next couple of minutes would be crushed by the logs.

Sabelle caught up to the pikeman in less than a minute, which seemed like an eternity in the water. But the first of the logs had already caught up to the boat and the three of them were surrounded. The pikeman in the stern was keeping the logs away from the boat, which worked as long as they did not hit anything. If they hit a rock or became trapped by a wedged log up ahead, the logs coming behind them would crush the boat in a matter of seconds.

Everyone in the logging camp traded stories about boats getting trapped in the middle of the river. The boat was supposed to get to the bank before the logs built up speed. Once they got going, it was nearly impossible to outrun them. And once you were surrounded, you couldn't get over to the bank. The pikeman in the stern of Michael Sabelle's boat pushed the logs away from the side where the other pikeman was holding on. Then Sabelle tucked the oars into the boat and grabbed the downed pikeman's belt with both hands. With a single motion he lifted the man into the boat. Then he grabbed the oars and started rowing again. He was rowing with short strokes, more for steering than for speed. He didn't dare leave the oars in the water for fear they'd be snapped off by the logs. But without oars, they didn't have a chance.

The boat picked up speed as they headed down the river. Some of the logs had already passed them and they were now nearly surrounded. The men did not speak. They concentrated on their instincts. The pikeman who had fallen into the water was now kneeling in the center of the boat, trying to maintain balance. Michael Sabelle took both oars out of their locks. They had become useless for steering because they just hit other logs. He handed one of the oars to the pikeman in the middle of the boat and with the other climbed forward into the bow. They were traveling at least twenty miles per hour now and the boat was bouncing over the rocks just beneath the surface. Up ahead a log rose out of the water like a serpent, one end apparently wedged between the rocks. Sabelle instinctively stuck his oar off the left side of the boat and edge the bow away from the jutting log, which they missed by inches. They were steering the boat like a canoe, trying to avoid the plumes of water that marked the rocks beneath the surface. Suddenly another log lifted the boat from below and threatened to capsize it, but the pikeman in the middle threw his body to the opposite side and stabilized it.

They were approaching the most treacherous stretch of the upper Hudson, near North Creek. Sabelle knew that log jams formed here every year because huge boulders rose out of the river. Sabelle steered the jamboat to the inside of the approaching bend. The logs would naturally head to the outside of the bend, thrown that way by the centrifugal force of the swirling water. With both oars of the left side of the boat, the men veered toward the eastern bank. The boated rocketed toward the boulders near the shore. Sabelle ordered everyone to the back of the boat so that the bow would be elevated and they braced for the collision. The boat hit the first boulder without even touching the bow. It became airborne for a brief moment and turned onto its side, then landed in a shower of splinters as it hit a broad flat rock on the water's edge. Sabelle and one of the pikemen were knocked unconscious, but the other pikeman, the one who had fallen into the water, was barely scratched. He scrambled to his feet and looked around in disbelief. The shattered hull of the boat was strewn about and one piece dangled from a branch high overhead. The other loggers were running down the riverbank to help them, shouting as they barreled through the woods. They dragged the two men off the rocks and propped them up against a tree until they came around.

The story of the rescue on the river was told many times over the years, and always with great admiration for the skill of the Indian Sabelle. What they never mentioned, what they never admitted, was that there was not a man among them who would have done the same for Sabelle had *he* been the one in the water. They had never trusted Sabelle. When money was discovered to be missing after a poker game, Sabelle was the first one they suspected even though he never played cards with them. All of these things Michael Sabelle kept in his heart. And it was therefore with great suspicion that he greeted the sheriff of Hamilton County when he approached Michael Sabelle's cabin.

"Afternoon," Sheriff Cooney said, getting out of the car. Cooney moved slowly. His knees were sore from all the hiking. Gotta lose some weight, he thought. Gotta get back down to 265, like he promised his wife.

The Indian sat on the cabin porch. A wooden sign with 'Sabelle Outfitters' hung from the roof. He didn't really need the sign. Anybody coming this far out had to know where they were going or they'd have turned around miles before. Sabelle was one of the few successful outfitters in the area, hiring out to hunting and fishing parties that came up from Connecticut, New York and New Jersey. The back of his property dropped off to Clear Lake, from which they would canoe ten miles north into the vast wilderness. A lot of Canadians hired Michael Sabelle because he spoke French. He was the guide you hired if you really wanted to get away from civilization.

"Are you Sabelle?" the sheriff asked.

The Indian looked up and nodded. His shoulder-length black hair was pulled back into a small ponytail under a Yankees' baseball cap.

Doesn't look any more like an Indian than I do, Cooney thought.

Sabelle stepped off the porch and met the men in the gravel driveway. Cooney introduced Deputy Therrien and they all shook hands. Cooney asked if Sabelle was familiar with the murder in Henoga Valley, and the Indian nodded again.

"I'll get right to the point, Mr. Sabelle," Cooney said. "We've been trying to track down this kid without much luck. We sent in two dogs and he got both of them with steel jaw traps."

The Indian seemed to chuckle. He made no noise, but his head bobbed a few times and he smiled.

"We'd like to hire you to help us track him down," the sheriff said.

"How many men do you have in the woods now?" Sabelle asked.

"About a hundred and fifty."

"Then it can't be done," Sabelle answered quickly.

"What do you mean?" Therrien asked.

Cooney held up his hand to quiet him. Goddam deputy didn't seem to know it was his job to stand there and *listen*.

"A hundred men walking through the woods are going to cover up the trail," Sabelle said.

"What if we take the men out and you start all over?" Cooney asked. "In time, maybe you'd be able to find a new trail."

"In time, perhaps. But then what would I do if I did I find him? I'm too old to take him into custody. I don't think I'd want to shoot him, neither."

"We'd send someone with you," Cooney said. "All you'd have to do is find him for us. You could do that much for us, couldn't you?"

Sabelle shook his head.

"I don't think an Indian tracking a white man would go over well around here, especially when a lot of people are probably hoping the kid gets away."

"The kid's wanted for *murder*," Cooney said.

"Didn't the guy he killed rape a girl?"

"Look, it wouldn't matter if he killed Lee Harvey Oswald," the sheriff growled. "I'd still have to bring him in."

Sabelle nodded again. He never completely understood the white man's law. It sometimes seemed that justice didn't have a lot of common sense to it. But he had learned long ago not to argue with these laws because it only made them more confusing.

"I'm sorry I can't help you," Sabelle said. "It's just not the kind of hunting I'm used to. But if you ever need to track down a black bear, or even a wolf, come back and see me. I'd be glad to give you a hand."

He offered his hand, which Sheriff Cooney shook, but Deputy Therrien had already turned back toward the car. Sabelle stood in the driveway and watched as the car turned around on the gravel road and drove away slowly. When the car was gone from his sight, Sabelle thought of John David Marten, who from this very shore had paddled silently into the Adirondack Mountains two nights earlier, and he permitted himself a rare laugh.

Chapter Sixteen

Sheriff Cooney knew that there had to have been some romantic involvement between Emily Davignon and John David Marten, even if none of their classmates would admit it. Cooney's deputies had interviewed most of the senior class by Sunday afternoon, but no one had suggested that they were anything more than friends. But Emily had, in fact, secretly taken long trips into the woods with John David Marten and had spent several nights in his cabin. Only her mother had known. Emily's father, who would never have allowed her to go, wasn't consulted, so the trips always occurred when he was either out of town or working overnight at the hospital. Julia had permitted Emily to go because she believed her when she said that she was safe with John David, and that he alone could show her the real Adirondacks.

In February of 1971, with more than two feet of snow on the ground, John David and Emily snowshoed to his cabin for the first time since she had been lost. John David taught her how to read the topographic map and use the compass. He showed her how to find her bearings by the shapes of the hills. There was an incredible simplicity to it all. Emily watched in fascination as John David sketched from memory the silhouettes of a dozen mountains and described particular spruce trees that gave a mountain its distinctive profile.

"If anybody cut down a single tree, I'd be lost," he joked.

The wilderness was much less terrifying than the previous time Emily had been there. They walked along the stream bank where John David had found her. Emily paused for a moment to sit on the rock where he had removed her wet socks and warmed her feet. The stream was lined on both sides with balsam and spruce, their branches laden with a heavy blanket of fresh snow.

"This place is a lot more beautiful when you're not freezing to death," she said, clicking the shutter of her camera.

They continued along the stream bank to the stand of hemlocks until they reached the cabin. They unpacked their backpacks and built a fire in the stove and placed a large kettle of water on to boil. Then they ate their lunches and hiked across the frozen marshes to Lost Creek. John David watched in fascination as Emily sketched the stream, the snow-covered branches, and tufts of grass blowing in the wind. She laid on her stomach to photograph an ice-encrusted rock.

That night they sat at the kitchen table and ate homemade bread with butter and jam, and soup made with rice and freeze-dried chicken and vegetables. The stove had been burning for hours and the cabin was so warm that Emily stripped down to her long johns. Her wet clothes were drying by the stove.

"I appreciate your not killing anything to make the soup," Emily said.

"I gave them the day off."

"I can't believe how good it tastes," Emily said. "It's the bread, I think. Is this the kind of food you eat when you're out here alone?"

John David thought for a moment and then said, "For the most part."

"What's the ... *strangest* thing you ever ate?"

"Beaver," John David answered, this time without hesitating.

"Oh! That's disgusting!" Emily had her hand over her mouth. "I can't believe you'd eat a beaver."

"They're not bad, really."

"What do they taste like? And don't tell me 'chicken.'"

"Oh, hell no," John David said with a little laugh. "They don't taste *anything* like chicken. Anybody that tells you beaver tastes like chicken hasn't had beaver."

"Well then, what does it taste like?"

John David thought for a moment, then he said, "Muskrat, sort of. Only sweeter."

Emily threw back her head and laughed, a hearty baritone that surprised John David. The sinews of her neck stretched from the white long johns. Her hair fell from her shoulders and bounced against the back of the chair and when she lowered her eyes once again and brought them to rest on John David, he saw a smile that he hadn't known before. The tiny mouth drew back into a perfect bow and her eyes shown like agate. The smile and the sweetness of her voice burned in his chest, and he felt weak.

144

"You're a pisser," Emily said, her laughter tailing off into a giggle. "Muskrat." She lifted the bowl to her lips and drank the warm soup.

"Why do you do this?" Emily asked, spooning out the last drop of soup from her bowl.

"Do what?"

"Live like this. Out here in the woods, all alone. Don't you like company?"

"Sure I do," John David said. "I like people. Some of them, anyway. Not all, but some."

"I don't," Emily said. "They're boring."

There passed between them a moment of silence in which John David assumed that he, too, must be boring. Emily seemed to realize this.

"But not you," she added. "You're not boring. But the rest of the boys in school talk about football or baseball like it's some kind of religion. And they talk about girls like *they* are the sport. And the girls aren't any better. They talk about boys as if their sole reason for living is to find one. But you can bet they'll spend the next fifty years complaining about the one they do find."

"I suppose you find everybody boring because you're so smart. I've always admired that about you. I remember when we were in second grade together. I sat right behind you. You used to raise your hand with your arm perfectly straight and the fingers together. You never waved like the other kids when you knew the answer. You kinda ... saluted. Mrs. Bradt asked if anyone knew who James Monroe was, and your hand went up with the fingers together and said he was the fourth President of the United States. I was so amazed. I didn't even know he *was* a president, much less the fourth."

"Actually, he was the fifth. Madison was the fourth." Emily roared with laughter. "Guess Mrs. Bradt didn't know either."

Emily noticed that John David was laughing just as hard.

"Can you rattle them off, just like that? In order?"

"Washington, Adams, Jefferson, Madison, Monroe, the other Adams, Jackson, Van Buren, Harrison, Tyler, Polk, Taylor, Fillmore ... Pierce ... Buchanan, Lincoln, Johnson, Grant, Hayes,

145

Garfield, Arthur, Cleveland, another Harrison, Cleveland again, McKinley, Roosevelt, Taft, Wilson, Harding, Coolidge, Hoover, Roosevelt, Truman, Eisenhower, Kennedy, Johnson and Nixon."

"That's amazing," John David said, giving her an ovation. "How can you remember all of them?"

"It's easy. I made an anagram. Their initials mean 'What a joy, me, Mary and Jane Van Buren helped Tyler pick the first paper back library journals, going happily/gladly after Catholic Hospital Children's Magazine, Readers Treasure, World Health Catalogue, Home Repairs, Time, and Eskimo Kids Junior Newsletter."

"Eskimo Kids Junior Newsletter? How do you remember *that?*"

"Yeah, I know it's pretty lame. Long anagrams tend to get weak near the end."

John David took a sip of tea and rested the cup on the corner of the table. "You like to learn things, don't you? It's fun for you."

Emily nodded.

"School's always been such a chore for me," he said. "I never understand why you study things like algebra. It always felt like I was playing a game for somebody else. Maybe I would feel differently if I met somebody who actually used it."

Emily said, "But you're very smart. I didn't realize it until I saw how you've memorized the silhouettes of the mountains."

"I learned that trick from an Indian I met when I was nine years old. He lived by himself up north and we met in the woods. I was hiking alone, like you were last fall, and I got a little lost."

"*You?! You got lost?*" Emily was out of her chair, leaning over the table.

"Hey, I was only nine years old."

"I don't believe it," Emily said, sitting back down. "The great John David Marten's been lost, too. Oh, it *kills* me not to be able to tell my father about this one. What happened?"

"It was when I was first starting to set traps. I came out this way in early November and got a little disoriented. I started heading north instead of south. Then, all of a sudden, there he

146

was, standing on the other side of the stream, in the trees. He scared the hell out of me."

"What did you do?"

"Nothing. I just stood there staring at him."

"What did *he* do?"

"He asked if I was lost? I said, 'No, I'm just heading home.'"

"Then what?"

John David smiled. "He asked if I was Canadian?"

Emily bolted out of her chair and hopped onto John David's lap, straddling the chair.

"You used that line on me!" she shouted, slapping him playfully. The presence of her breasts so close to his face made him blush.

"I like this color on you," she said. Then, seeing how painfully embarrassed he was, she climbed off his lap.

"So, tell me about the Indian," she said, settling back into her chair. "I didn't know there were any still around here."

"He's an Abenaki. His tribe moved to Canada after the Revolution. The Abenakis were better hunters and trappers than the other tribes, but they were chased out of New York by the Mohawks. A few of them stayed around in the Adirondacks and became guides."

"What revolution?" Emily asked, thinking that this Indian had been involved in a local uprising. But instantly she remembered that most of the New York State Indians had sided with the English during the American Revolution and were forced to leave afterward. "Oh, *that* Revolution."

"The Abenakis lived in Canada for the next hundred years or so, but Sabelle came back to the Adirondacks as a lumberjack, then became a guide about twenty-five years ago. He never married. He sort of adopted me and taught me how to hunt and trap, how to skin a muskrat in less than a minute, so your hands don't freeze."

"How can you stand to skin the animals? It's so barbaric."

"They're not alive when I do it."

"I should hope not, but it's still barbaric. What even gives you the right to kill them?"

"It's not *illegal*," John David protested.

"I know it's not illegal. I'm saying it's unethical."

But John David did not seem to have an opinion on ethics. He wasn't even sure what they were. So Emily used the recent reintroduction of the wolf into the Adirondacks as an example.

"A lot of people are upset about it. They say man and wolf can't live together. Can you imagine?" she said. "The wolf belongs here. The wolf lived in the Adirondacks long before man was here."

"So did the Indians. Nobody seems to want them back."

"Well, if man and wolf can't coexist, I think that man should be the one to leave."

John David did not argue the point. He wasn't even sure what the argument was, or what side he should be on. But then the next day they actually saw a wolf. Emily and John David had been standing at the edge of a grove of spruce trees overlooking a meadow. A small herd of whitetail deer, numbering perhaps twenty, were grazing on the tufts of grass that poked through the snow. Emily held a pair of binoculars to her face and watched the deer in fascination. They looked up every once in awhile and turned their ears like radar, trying to pick up the sounds of predators. Emily had watched for several minutes, then began scanning the open meadow. Suddenly her eye caught the dark profile of a wolf. Even at the distance of nearly one hundred yards she could see the danger in its eyes. The wolf was low to the ground, invisible to the herd. It seemed to crawl on its belly, patiently inching closer to his prey.

"John David!" she whispered.

"I see them," he whispered back.

"Them?" she asked.

"Five of them," he said. "Maybe more."

Emily took the binoculars away from her face. John David pointed out the four wolves that she hadn't seen. The other four were spread out on the opposite side of the meadow from the one she had seen. Emily studied each of them with the glasses. They were laying in the snow, not creeping forward like the other one. They must be the ambush, she thought. Suddenly all of the deer had their heads raised and the lone wolf from the west charged the group. The distance between them was more than thirty yards. In the summer the wolf would not have been able to catch the deer, which are much faster and able to leap eight feet in the air. But in the heavy snow, the deer, with its arrow-like hooves, was at a disadvantage. They leapfrogged through the deep snow. The wolf, with its broad, flat paws did not sink as deep. It quickly made up the thirty yards. The herd might have escaped into the woods were it not for the four other wolves waiting at the other end of the meadow. They sprang forward as the herd approached. The deer turned and headed north. It was only twenty yards to the woods, where the snow was not deep. The wolves seemed to make a collective decision. They did not each chase a separate deer. They picked the slowest, a yearling trailing behind its mother. It was still small and moved slowly through the drifts. One of the wolves grabbed it by the hind flank, and the yearling squealed in terror. It bucked and kicked, trying to free itself from the wolf's jaws. It pawed at the snow with its front hooves as if it could drag itself to safety. A second wolf grabbed the other hind leg, and the two of them engage in a tug of war. The deer's hind legs were yanked in opposite directions. Emily could see the fear in the yearling's eyes. She heard it bleat and squeal. A third wolf lunged at the deer's belly and tore out a huge chunk of flesh. My God, Emily thought, they are going to eat it alive.

"Do something!" Emily shouted. "Use your gun!"

John David raised the rifle and fired. The bullet struck the deer between the eyes and it died instantly. The sound of the small bore rifle was muffled by the snow and the trees, and the wolves did not even hear it. The yearling collapsed and the wolves tore into it, tearing away hunks of flesh and hide and gulping them down whole. Emily stood in horror as they looked up with their snouts covered in the steaming blood.

"You dumb sonofabitch," she shouted. "I meant the *wolves*."

"I knew what you meant," John David answered.

"Why didn't you shoot *them*?"

John David looked at her with a puzzled, slightly angry expression.

"It's against the law to shoot wolves."

"Not when they're torturing deer!"

"What did you think wolves would eat? Berries?"

"No! But they were torturing the deer."

"They weren't torturing it. That's how they hunt."

They were both quiet for several minutes. They watched as the wolves tore at the carcass of the deer. At times they yanked so hard that the deer's head popped up into the air, as if it was still alive. Emily could hear the wolves' low growl as they gorged themselves on the fresh kill.

"It's not always pretty," John David said, turning to her, "but it's usually quick."

Emily did not respond. She looked angry.

John David said, "Someday one of these wolves will make the mistake of coming down out of the mountains and dragging off a little kid. Then people will go crazy and shoot every wolf within a hundred miles. That's *our* nature."

"Well I can tell *you* weren't in favor of reintroducing them."

"I don't get into those kinds of arguments," John David said. He yanked back the bolt on his rifle and a single empty shell spun out of the chamber and landed in the snow.

John David and Emily never spoke of hunting again. They came back to the cabin in March and in April, and for the last time in May, before the blackflies came out. Each trip was something new to Emily. In March the ground was wet with melting snow. John David had tapped several maple trees over the spring vacation and together they boiled down the sap over an open fire outside the cabin. The next morning they made pancakes and Emily spoke for nearly twenty minutes about the syrup, describing its flavor, its aftertaste and its color. She was fascinated how something as simple as tree fluids could be transformed into a thing of sublime beauty. In April John David took her to a sunny grove of budding maples, where the ground was covered with thousands of white trillium. The sight took Emily's breath away. And that night John David listened as Emily spoke of gardens of nature and their ethereal beauty, how the white birch sprang forth with delicate verdure, laying it gently over the cold, dead earth. John David watched her as she spoke, noticing how her hands rose and fell with the words, like water tumbling over rocks in the stream. Her full lips formed each word with care and her voice was like a song.

"Have you ever read Walt Whitman?" Emily asked.

John David shook his head no.

So on the next trip, in May, she carried in her backpack a brand- new copy of *Leaves of Grass* and gave it to him as a gift. John David held the book in his hands and leafed through the pages, but his movements were awkward. Emily reached over and took the book from him.

"Let me read you something," she said, and for the next hour she read without stopping, looking up now and then to direct the verse.

> *Alone far in the wilds and mountains I hunt,*
> *Wandering amazed at my own lightness and glee,*
> *In the late afternoon choosing a safe spot to pass the*
> *night,*
> *Kindling a fire and broiling a fresh-kill'd game,*
> *Falling asleep on the gather'd leaves with my dog and*
> *gun by my side.*

And later that night Emily awoke to the sound of wolves.

"Do you hear that, she whispered?" But there was no answer. "John David?"

She was frightened. She climbed out of her sleeping bag and felt around on the top bunk in the dark. John David wasn't there. Could he be out in the woods taking a leak, she wondered? Emily wrapped her sleeping bag around her and shuffled over to the door. She pulled it open and leaned out into the darkness.

"Where are you headed?" a voice said.

Emily jumped.

"God, you scared me!" she said.

"Sorry."

"What are you doing out there?" she asked.

"Come over here. I'll show you."

"I haven't got my shoes on," Emily protested.

She heard John David walk toward the cabin. He lifted her

151

into his arms and carried her, still wrapped in the sleeping bag, out to the clearing. Directly above them was a canopy of stars so numerous that they seemed to fill every inch of the sky.

"My God," Emily whispered in awe. "It's beautiful."

They stayed in the clearing for a long time. John David stood motionless, like one of the trees, holding her as if she were but a bundle of asters. The air was filled with the earth's vital humors, the scent of wet pines and hemlocks, the murmur of a distant stream. The tips of the trees swayed gently against the speckled night. Drugged by the beauty that surrounded her, Emily forgot that she was in John David's arms until she felt his lips press against hers. The kiss, in utter darkness, surprised her, for it seemed to come from the sky itself.

Chapter Seventeen

Jack O'Neill was buried in the tiny cemetery behind the St. Margaret Mary's Church one week before graduation. Every one of his classmates attended the funeral, everyone except John David Marten and Emily Davignon. The newspaper photographers were made to stand outside the wrought iron gate that surrounded the old cemetery, but the pictures they took with their telephoto lenses appeared in newspapers as far away as Houston and San Diego. The photos showed classmates holding onto each other for support, unable to comprehend a tragedy of this proportion. Jack O'Neill, with his effortless charm and quick smile, had been the most popular boy in his class. Everyone seemed to think of him as their closest friend.

Diana and Dutch Marten had attended the wake. As awkward as it was, as much as they hated the way the sea of people parted to let them through and then whispered about them from behind, they knew they had to be there. Diana had loved Jack like he was her own boy and grieved the loss as much as her own son's disappearance. She remembered how Jack had been so much more sociable than her own boys. He would carry on conversations with Diana while waiting for John David. He would help clear the table after dinner, even, on occasion, when he had merely shown up as they were finishing. And if they were not yet finished, he would pull up a chair from the kitchen and sit down with them. Diana would offer him a piece of cake for desert, and Jack would say 'Oh no, really, I can't' even as he held out his plate. It became a ritual between them and sometimes Diana would say it for him to save time. Once, when Jack came over to the house early one morning and caught Diana crying at the kitchen table, she quickly wiped her eyes and tried to compose herself. He put his arm around her and kissed her on the cheek, which surprised her because John David had stopped kissing when he was six years old.

The rumor that Jack O'Neill had tried to rape Emily was widely circulated by the time of his funeral. Then, less than a week later, everyone had heard the new rumor that she *had* been raped. How it came to be that new version spread so quickly when only Emily and her parents knew about it is a mystery, but it may not be possible to harbor a secret of that magnitude in a small town. Perhaps the wind carries the whispers, or the birds in the trees speak at night.

Of course, not everyone believed the story. Why would Jack O'Neill do such a thing, they whispered? He didn't need to resort to force when so many girls were willing. And hadn't Emily Davignon antagonized him on purpose? Didn't she *like* to stir up trouble?

And then Emily Davignon appeared at the wake minutes before it was to end. She walked in the door amidst the stares and whispers. She looked straight ahead and walked to the casket. Several people were nearby, relatives apparently, from out of town. Someone motioned for them to move aside and let her through. She went to the front of the room and knelt beside the bronze casket. There were pictures inside, snapshots placed there by classmates, and they cluttered Jack's chest. He looked like a river boat gambler who'd been shot at the card table. Emily reached into her sweater pocket and removed something, which everyone in the room strained to see while pretending *not* to look. Was it his class ring? Some gift he had given her? She placed it along side the body rather than on top. Those who went to view the body one final time tried to determine what Emily had placed in the casket, but no one figured it out. Emily got up from the casket and spoke briefly to Jack parents. Everyone watched as Mrs. O'Neill gave Emily a long hug, and they wondered what it was that Emily whispered into the woman's ear.

She said, in a voice so delicate and fragile, like a leaf falling from a tree, "This is all my fault."

Chapter Eighteen

At its peak, the manhunt for John David Marten involved eleven hundred men. State troopers set up road blocks and searched cars on all major highways in upstate New York. The forests were combed by teams of National guardsmen that assembled every morning in parking lots on the edge of town. Pictures of John David were posted in grocery stores, gas stations, post offices and tollbooths throughout the state, although many of the posters were stolen by children and tourists. Reporters rented every motel room from the town of Alder Creek to Blue Mountain Lake. With each week they asked the question, how long can he elude them? Two weeks? Three? *Four?* Surely he could not elude a search of this magnitude for four weeks. Unless he was already gone.

The summer of 1971 changed Henoga Valley forever. What had once been a quiet little village known only for its record-breaking winter cold suddenly became a tourist attraction. The manhunt brought throngs of tourists from Glens Falls, Albany, Utica and Syracuse. Hiking was forbidden during the manhunt, so the tourists contented themselves with souvenir shops and ice cream stands. They had no greater purpose than to walk the streets and breathe the clean air. Oh, how sweet, they said, how beautiful. Love to buy a piece of land and build a cabin up here.

The tourists continued to pour into Henoga Valley all summer. Merchants on Main Street were at first reluctant to stock up on souvenirs, afraid that it would end as soon as John David was caught. But as the weeks passed they became more daring and ordered large stocks of souvenirs, like pieces of spruce cut like French carrots that said 'Welcome to Henoga Valley' or 'A Little Piece of Heaven from the Adirondacks.' They couldn't keep their stores stocked. They'd call up their vendors, frantic, as if they were supplying sand bags to a town in danger of flooding. Gotta have it by *Tuesday* they'd shout into the phone. Their wives would look at them liked they'd just come back from a sex change operation. Their husbands, whom they had known for so long. They'd never seen them act like this before.

Sawyer was alone among the reporters in believing from the beginning that they would never find John David Marten. While the other reporters continued to follow the State Police and the National Guard, Sawyer busied himself with interviewing the townsfolk. The real story, he decided, wasn't the capture of John David Marten, but whatever it was that drove him to kill his best friend. Only jealousy or revenge could drive a man to so heinous an act. He sifted through the details of the story. Emily was in the middle of it all, that much was certain. Did she have sex with both of them, he wondered? None of the girls in town had the slightest idea what was going on in her social life. Jack, for all his alleged faults, must have been a real gentleman. There were no kiss-and-tell stories there. And then there was John David, who apparently said so little to anyone that it was difficult to decide what was real about him. Everything that had been written about Marten was from someone else's point of view. John David the easy-going baseball player who could suddenly unleash tremendous power. John David the hunter, whose exploits were obvious fiction, but which he printed anyway because they made such excellent copy. But the people who really knew him, his family, Jack O'Neill, and maybe Emily, weren't talking.

By the end of August Sawyer had exhausted the journalistic possibilities. The manhunt had long since become boring. They hadn't uncovered even a trace of him. He had truly vanished. Everyone had an opinion of where he might have gone. Wyoming, Canada, Hudson Bay. Someone even suggested that he had escaped to Australia. These were uninformed opinions, based largely on where *they* would have gone. But one thing was certain. John David Marten was no longer in the Adirondack Mountains.

Sawyer pressed on with his investigation of what had happened before the murder. Emily's parents would not allow Sawyer or any other reporter to talk to their daughter, but Sawyer persisted. He called their house. He followed Dr. Davignon to the hospital, once even feigning a sprained ankle in hopes of being able to talk to him about Emily. Finally, Dr. Davignon obtained a court order that prevented him from talking to them. So he tracked down other leads. He interviewed Dr. Emerson, who had signed the death certificate. The boy hadn't put up a struggle, Dr. Emerson told him. There were no knife wounds to the upper arms, suggesting that he probably didn't see the attack coming. He was probably killed by someone he knew, and trusted.

Sawyer continued to call Deputy Therrien periodically for new information on the case, but the deputy was no longer willing to talk. He was still angry about the article in which Sawyer reported that Jack O'Neill had raped the daughter of a physician days before his murder. Therrien had been chewed out by the sheriff over that one, even though the sheriff could not prove he was the one who had leaked the information. But Sawyer begged and promised another $200, and Therrien finally provided a photocopy of the autopsy report. The cause of death was a single knife wound in the chest that severed the aorta from the heart.

Near the end of August Sawyer decided to give the Martens one last try. He'd stayed away from them up until this point because he had been warned that Dutch Marten was unpredictable. Sawyer was a good reporter and not one to shy away from an unpleasant situation. He'd even been punched in the face on one occasion. But it was the way people said it, *unpredictable,* a long rolling of the syllables while they looked away, that had unnerved him. And of course, Sawyer was worried how Dutch Marten might react to the story he had written about the death of the man outside the Tahawus Hotel twenty years ago.

Sawyer walked up onto the porch of the Marten house on a Sunday morning. The house was plain, a simple clapboard of faded peach with gray trim. There was a large porch on the front that wrapped halfway around the house. Impatiens, begonias and irises were planted everywhere, which surprised him. He had expected the place to be more run down. Eva opened the front door just as Sawyer reached the top stair of the porch. She looked surprised to see him and immediately shouted something to her mother. Diana appeared at the door behind her.

"Can I help you?" Diana asked, ever polite. She still could not bring herself to say 'get off my porch' to a complete stranger.

"I'd like to think so," Sawyer said. He held out his hand. "I'm from the *Times Union* in Albany and I was hoping you could answer a few questions."

"No ... I don't think so," Diana said, closing the screen door.

Sawyer stepped forward to protest.

"Please," he said, "just a minute of your time. Please?"

Sawyer pressed his hand against the door, preventing Diana from closing it all the way. He did not see the movement by the window, the sudden flash of color moving toward the front door. A moment later Dutch Marten burst past his wife and grabbed Sawyer by the throat with one of his powerful hands. His grip was like a leather belt drawn taut around Sawyer's neck. Dutch backed the reporter out onto the porch and up against the wall. Although the men were of nearly the same height, Dutch seemed much taller. Sawyer had both of his hands around Dutch's wrist, but his instincts told him that he should not put up a struggle to break Marten's grip. Instead, he stood motionless like a mouse trapped in the jaws of a cat, waiting, hoping, to be released. Yet Marten was choking him, and in a moment he would surely lose consciousness.

"Did you forget to call ahead and *ask* to talk to my wife?" Dutch said between clenched teeth.

Sawyer shook his head as best he could.

"Well let me tell you something you little fuck," Dutch hissed. "The next time you come up on my porch without an invitation, I'm going to shove my 12-gauge Remington up your ass and blow your fuckin liver right out your fuckin nose."

Marten released his grip and Sawyer dropped to his knees, gasping for air. He crawled toward the stairs on his hands and knees. Dutch followed him until he reached the edge of the porch. Then he kicked Sawyer in the ass, knocking him down the steps.

"You know, you should be grateful it's Sunday," Dutch said

158

to the reporter sprawled at the foot of the steps. "My wife doesn't let me kill people on Sunday."

Diana Marten was so distraught over the events of that summer that she grew pale and gaunt. Day after day she saw Peggy O'Neill in the huge yard that separated their houses. They had never been close friends, but they had always been cordial and never hesitated to call on each other for favors. They did not, however, confide in each other. Diana never talked about Dutch and his drinking in front of Peggy. Peggy O'Neill, with her perfect husband and his perfect job and their perfect children, was perhaps a little embarrassed by her neighbor's domestic troubles. Diana admired the way Peggy spoke up at school board meetings and the way that she organized the PTA and school trips. So although they had never been close friends, they had always been friendly. Now they could not bear to talk to each other. They could only look at each other momentarily when passing in the yards lest they stop and be forced to confront the reality that the boys whom they had loved and shared were now gone. Does your loss compare to mine, they might ask? Do you feel the guilt for what has happened?

And then one day Diana was in the garden pinching back the geraniums and saw Peggy O'Neill come out of the house. It was Labor Day weekend, but no one in Henoga Valley had planned any parties. Everyone, it seemed, was worn out. Diana saw Peggy walk to her car and their eyes met. They looked at each other briefly, Diana kneeling by her flowers, Peggy standing by the open door of her car. Diana raised her hand to wave, and Peggy did likewise. Then Diana returned her gaze to the ground, to the flowers in front of her, lest her shame rest to long on her neighbor. She clipped a brown and withered flower from one of the geraniums so that the new shoots would blossom. She would do this again next week, and every week thereafter until the frost came and killed the plants. Diana began to cry. She had not cried for weeks and had hoped that the sickness of grief, the wrenching pain of sorrow, was over. She had prayed for the relief of numbness and emptiness, but it did not come. Her chin dropped to her chest and the tears began once again to flow freely down her cheeks. Her arms hung limp by her side and her shoulders sank low. She leaned forward and pressed her hands against the grass to keep from losing her balance. The earth seemed to reach up and take hold of her, drawing her down into the cool, damp soil. The pain gripped her chest once again. The pain. Only the earth promised her respite. She felt her strength seep from her bones, her muscle, and her blood, and her face nearly touched the ground. Her long hair fell about her like a shroud and deep sobs welled up in her chest. That, too, the earth swallowed, gluttonous for the warmth of her grief. And then the other woman was beside her, standing over her. Peggy O'Neill. Her lips trembled in grief and her eyes poured forth a well of tears. She knelt down on the grass beside Diana and placed her arm around her, and the women cried together in unabashed sorrow.

Part II

161

Chapter Nineteen

Emily Davignon's presence in the freshman class of Brown University in the fall of 1971 was as much a surprise to her as it was to her parents. Emily had graduated as salutatorian of her high school class, losing to Jack O'Neill by 0.001 points, but she did not attend graduation ceremonies. It was the only time in the history of Henoga Valley High School that neither the valedictory nor the salutatory addresses were given.

Emily had debated for almost a year about which college to attend. Her grandfather promised to pay her tuition and buy her a car if she came to Brown University in Providence, which was only a few blocks from his house on Hope Street. But Emily had her heart set on Boston University. Boston seemed so attractive, a *real* city. Then she received a letter from Brown offering her a complete scholarship with room and board. She hadn't expected a scholarship, being the only child of a surgeon, even a country surgeon. She sort of wished that she hadn't gotten the scholarship because that made the decision that much more difficult, but her parents agreed to let her go to Boston in spite of the cost. So she sent the letter of commitment to Boston University in April and had to change her mind in late August when she discovered that she was pregnant.

"Is there anything left that can happen?" her father said when Emily told him in the office. They were alone. Emily wasn't certain that she was pregnant, but she had missed two periods and she wanted him to perform the blood test on her.

"Have you told your mother?" he asked.

"No. I thought I'd wait until I was sure. I started feeling sick a few weeks ago, but I thought... you know ... with everything that's happened these last few weeks, maybe it was nerves or something. I'm hoping that it's leukemia so I can just die."

Her father sat her down in a chair next to his desk. He had patients visit him here in his office and it was fully equipped. He opened a drawer and removed a tourniquet and a vacutainer. He tied the tourniquet around his daughter's arm and watched the vein swell with blood.

"A little pinch," he said as he slid the needle into her arm.

The blood test came back positive. Dr. Davignon spoke to Emily at the kitchen table when Julia was out grocery shopping. Emily nodded in agreement when her father broke the news. Her father reached across the table and held her hand.

"Emily," he said, after an awkward silence, "I'd like to suggest something to you and I don't want you to ... *react* ... right away." Emily looked up at him, puzzled. "I have several colleagues, out of town, who could perform an abortion. If that's what you want to do. You don't even have to tell your mother. No one will ever find out about it."

Emily stared at her father in disbelief. Abortion was illegal. A doctor could lose his license for performing one. She realized at that moment how little she knew of her own father. He had always been a mysterious figure, the surgeon, practitioner of ancient rituals of the body, but a man who had never even spoken to her about sex. Now, from his lips came the word 'abortion,' spoken in hushed tones, a secret that they alone were to share. Had *he* performed abortions as favors for these men, on their daughters?

"You can't bring a baby into the world fathered by a rape," her father said.

Emily looked down at the table and studied her hands.

"It wouldn't be fair to you or the baby," he added. "You're going away to college."

"Dad, it might not be Jack's baby," Emily said.

Dr. Davignon straightened up in his chair. It was clear he hadn't thought of that possibility. He slapped his hands upon his face and let out a single, muffled 'Oh shit.' Then he rubbed his face a few times, as if washing away the haze of ignorance, and brushed back his hair with both hands.

"I've been trying very hard not to pry into your private life," he said. "Your mother said I was stifling you ..."

"It might be John David's," Emily offered.

Her father stared at her, confused.

"Did Jack know about John David?"

Emily looked down at the floor and nodded.

"Don't you have ... any idea, which one?" her father asked.

"Dad. I only did it once."

"Not counting the rape."

"*Of course not counting the rape,*" she said. The tears welled up in her eyes. "How could you say something like that?"

"I'm sorry. I'm just confused. It just that ... well, two months ago you were this reclusive girl who hardly dated and now you're pregnant and the father is either dead or a fugitive. Things are moving a little too fast for me."

"Welcome to the club," Emily whispered.

"What do *you* think you should do?" her father asked.

"I was thinking about Brown. Maybe I could go there and live with Pépé. That way I could have the baby and still go to school."

"You mean, raise the baby there?"

"Where else?"

"I think it's time to involve your mother," he said. He hadn't even grasped the idea of Emily having the baby. "I'm not very good at these kinds of details."

Julia Davignon's response to the news was not any better than Robert's. She immediately started to cry.

"We could raise the baby here, I suppose," she finally said.

"Here?! Are you kidding, Mom? *This* baby, in *this* town?"

Her mother nodded in agreement. Of course not, she thought. How silly to have entertained the idea.

They made phone calls to Brown University and to Robert's father. Brown accepted her into the freshman class, even though it was supposedly months after the commitment deadline. And they still offered her the scholarship. Emily was dumbfounded. Had she not been such an outstanding student, she might have suspected that her grandfather had given Brown University the entire sum of the scholarship. But she had so many things on her mind that it never occurred to her.

Emily's grandfather owned an enormous old mansion on the east side of Providence, a few blocks from Brown University. It had originally been built by a wealthy shipping magnate during the latter half of the eighteenth century. The house had been meticulously restored by Emily's grandfather over a period of forty years. There were eight bedrooms, four bathrooms, a library, a grand ballroom, and several parlors and sitting rooms. Emily had spent weeks at a time there in the summers while she was growing up. She loved the pool and the gardens and the quiet tree- lined street. When Emily and her parents pulled into the circular drive in a U-Haul truck in late August, they found the driveway partially blocked by pickup trucks and a dumpster. Emily's grandfather rushed to greet them.

"What's going on here?" Robert asked his father, barely out of the truck.

"Just some minor renovations," Pépé said with a wave of his hand. "Where's my girl?" He gave Emily a long hug, rubbing her back. "Come here and see what we're doing."

There were carpenters all over the house. Emily's grandfather had added a separate entrance at the side of the house that opened into the south wing. In the living room he built a circular staircase that climbed to the bedrooms on the second floor. In one corner was a dozen wallpaper books. They had to move out of the way to let three men carrying a porcelain sink into the kitchen. Emily and her mother climbed the stairs to the second floor to look at the nursery. While they were gone, Robert and his father wandered through the downstairs rooms.

"Dad, this is really ..." Robert voice trailed off. He was at a loss for words.

"I figured she'd get tired of me pretty quick if I didn't give her some privacy."

"Are you sure you are up to this?" Robert asked.

"Yes, yes," the elder Davignon said. "I missed all this fatherhood stuff the first time around. Anyway, it'll be easy. I can hire a nanny to do all the hard work."

"This might not work out, you know," Robert said. "With the baby, I mean."

"She'll be fine."

They unpacked Emily's belongings, the books, her art supplies, her overstuffed chair, which looked much shabbier in the brightly lit rooms of Pépé's house than it had back in the attic

166

on Raquette Lake. Emily's father disappeared for a few hours and when he returned he was driving a bright red Camaro. He presented it to Emily as a graduation present. She thanked him, but secretly wished he had bought her something more practical, like a Jeep.

Emily's first year at Brown went by so fast that she would later have difficulty remembering it in detail. She followed a strict regimen, waking up a six o'clock each morning, attending classes, studying afternoons in the library, and then home in the evenings. She gave her phone number to no one. Boys around campus introduced themselves to the beautiful stranger and tried desperately to strike conversations, but she always seemed to be in a hurry. She often accepted their names, it's a pleasure to meet you, without offering hers in return. Even in the library she rebuffed conversations, stifling them with rules of etiquette. She became known by the red Camaro, *as* the red Camaro, which pulled up outside buildings minutes before classes and left as soon as they were over.

Emily Davignon would not return to Henoga Valley even once during her first two years at college. Providence became her new home, her only home. Her parents called at least once a week and they drove down to Providence for her birthdays and most of the major holidays. They inquired enthusiastically about her classes, they always asked if she was making new friends, they even asked how the car was running, but they remained conspicuously indifferent about her pregnancy.

"Of *course* I'll come down and stay with you when you have the baby, Em" Julia had said. "How could you think I wouldn't?" They were alone in Emily's apartment, sitting at the kitchen table after the Thanksgiving dinner during Emily's freshman year. Her father was watching a football game with Pépé in the other part of the house.

"It's just that you haven't offered."

"Well, I assumed you *knew*," Julia said, but she never sounded less convincing. Her own mother, for whom sincerity had always been so effortless, now sounded like a bad actress.

"I know you and Dad want me to put the baby up for adoption, but I can't think about that right now."

167

"Emily, you *have* to decide before you have the baby. You can't keep it for a couple of weeks and expect to be able to give it away. You'd be too attached. If you're going to do it, you have to give it up right away. It's the only way."

"Then I'd have to say 'no.'"

"Emily," Julia said, stroking her daughter's hair, "don't you realize what this could do to the rest of your life? Don't you understand the implications? It would be difficult enough if this were just a child out of wedlock, but the child of a rapist?"

"Maybe John David was the father."

"Is that any better? You didn't love *him* either."

"How do you know I didn't love him?" Emily asked.

"Well, you never brought him to the house. You never went out on a date with him."

Which was true. Emily could not have imagined going out on a date with John David Marten. Where would they have gone? What would they have done? It was hard for her to imagine John David sitting in a movie theater holding hands, and harder still to imagine him going to a dance. The only way she could picture him was in the forest, by a stream or beneath the outstretched boughs of the hemlocks.

"I don't know what I felt for John David," Emily said. "It was so ... different. *He* was so different. When we were together, in the woods, it was beautiful. It was like heaven. It was just ..."

Emily's voice tailed off. She knew that she couldn't describe so new and unfamiliar an emotion. The warmth that emanated from deep within her heart and washed away her sarcasm, her anger, her distrust of the opposite sex. John David had never wanted anything from her. He was simple and forthright in most everything, except perhaps, *his* own feelings. And although he had never actually said so, Emily knew that he had loved her.

Emily had thought about John David every day since he disappeared into the woods. At first, during the early stages of the manhunt, she pictured him running like a hunted animal. But when she heard that he had set traps for the dogs, she realized that he wasn't scared at all. She imagined him living in the cabin by the stream. It seemed so utterly possible. Couldn't he live out there, she reasoned, and grow crops during the summer and hunt deer in the winter? Couldn't he trap animals for skins to keep him warm? She indulged herself in these thoughts even while she knew that he probably was working at a lumberyard or on a construction site, far from Henoga Valley and out of his element. A wild animal in a zoo.

"It's just that I'm afraid that life is going to be so hard for you and your baby." Julia said. The words snapped Emily from her daydream.

"Hard?! This is hard?!" Emily asked, holding her hands up to display her apartment. "Living in a mansion with a pool." Emily laughed. She pretended to pick up the phone to make a desperate call home. "Mom, help. What do I do? I can't find the corkscrew and wine is growing tepid."

"You're so much tougher than I was at your age," Julia said, unable to hide her amusement. "I suppose you'll handle it like you have everything else. But what about the baby? What if he or she isn't as strong as you are? What if the kids in the neighborhood find out that the baby was born out of rape? You know how cruel kids can be. At least if he grew up with new parents he could start over. He wouldn't have this rape thing hanging over his head. Unless, of course, you don't plan to tell him."

"Don't be ridiculous. Of course I'll tell him. Or her. He'd find out sooner or later anyway."

"Still," Julia said with a sigh, "*I* wouldn't want to grow up knowing my father raped my mother, or that my father killed the man who raped my mother." Julia's head bobbed back and forth to emphasize the point.

Emily got up from the table and stood by the counter. The tears welled in her eyes and ran down her cheeks. Her hand went to her mouth to stifle a cry. She wasn't going to cry about the murder anymore. That was the past. The future was she and the baby.

"I don't know if I hate Jack for raping me, or if I hate myself for allowing things to get out of hand," she said. "I knew he was jealous of John David. I *knew* it. I should have just ended my

169

relationship with Jack before I got interested in John David, but I didn't *know* that I was interested in John David. How can you know something like that? At first we were just friends. He would take me into the woods and help me take pictures. I never in a million years thought I'd fall in love with him. He was a hunter, and I hated hunting. But then, somewhere along the line, I don't know exactly when, I started to see him a little differently. In school he always seemed so out of place. But out in the woods he was different. He was beautiful and graceful."

"You can't blame yourself for being raped, Emily. It's not your fault."

Emily folded her arms across her chest. She nodded, as if in agreement.

"You know," Emily said, trying to draw an analogy, "I once saw a pack of wolves kill a deer, one of those times when I went with John David. It was a fawn. The mother was helpless to save it, so she ran away. All of the deer in the herd ran away and left the fawn to be killed. I was so sick I threw up." Emily trembled as she spoke. "I guess I thought the wolves would be less vicious, or the deer more courageous, like Bambi or something. But John David said that they behave the only way they know. The deer is the deer and the wolf is the wolf. They don't make moral decisions. It's just biology to them."

"But people *do* make decisions," her mother argued. "Jack didn't have to rape you. John David didn't have to take revenge."

"I know, I know. It's just that, up until I got involved with Jack, everybody in Henoga Valley loved him. And he and John David were best friends. You saw what it was like at his wake. Nobody *hated* him. Now Jack's made out to be some kind of monster. But if I hadn't gone out with him, he probably would have turned out to be someone. And John David wouldn't have turned into a fugitive murderer. So what is it about me that I can bring out this kind of ... *evil* ... in a man?"

"Emily!" Julia shouted. She jumped from her chair and ran over to her daughter. She put her arms around her, but Emily's arms remained folded. "Don't talk like that! You didn't bring out anything that wasn't already there. They're the ones who did something wrong, not you."

"Don't you get it, Mom? I ruined their lives as much as they ruined mine. Probably more."

Julia didn't have any answers for her daughter. Were all of these things that happened in life just random events in nature, no more under our control than an attack by wolves? Bad luck or good luck, all just a matter of where you happened to be when the wolves struck? Julia could not believe it. She had grown up in Catholic schools, where you were taught to exert complete dominance over evil. Guilt was the engine that drove the whole system, counterbalancing things that were fun, which was just about everything. That seemed to explain her own life, and maybe the lives of everyone she touched.

Julia Davignon had been with her daughter in the delivery room, and in spite of the thirty hours of labor, she had quite obviously not been excited about the new little baby. Emily could almost see the words *rape child* in her eyes.

"You don't have to be so put off, Mom," Emily said later. "After all, it might not be Jack's baby."

"Yes, well," was all Julia could say, not placated by the possibility that the child was merely illegitimate. She looked upon the baby with a forlorn expression, like it was a cat born with a severe defect, and perhaps better off put to sleep.

Emily disappeared from the Brown University campus during the spring semester and some of her classmates wondered if she had dropped out of college. She reappeared in the fall, but by then she was no longer *pretending* to be busy. She had a full academic schedule and a baby to care for, though she could safely guess that no one knew of the latter because she hadn't started showing until after Christmas.

It was naive of Emily to think that she could attend Brown University for four years without anyone discovering who she was, without anyone linking her to the story that had been splashed over so many newspapers. But Emily believed that people would forget her momentary celebrity, like they had the lone girl who survived the Richard Speck murder spree or the driver of the President Kennedy's car in Dallas. Certainly the

171

people back home wouldn't forget, but she hoped that in time it would become vague in everyone else's mind. That never happened, largely because in the spring of 1973, Sawyer published a book entitled *An Adirondack Life - The Legend of J.D. Marten*, and Emily instantly regained the notoriety that she had been hoping to lose.

Sawyer had tried to contact her several times while conducting his research, so Emily should have known that a book was imminent. Yet she was genuinely surprised to see it in the college bookstore. The book was on a display table and the words 'Marten' and 'Adirondack' seemed to leap out at her. She trembled as she paid the cashier for the book and she started reading it before she got out of the store. So much of the book was absolute fiction. Things like John David tracking a wounded deer for six miles over wooded terrain, in the dark. John David killing a raging bear with a .22 caliber rifle. John David tracking Emily and rescuing her in the wilderness. But the most disconcerting was simply the way in which Sawyer referred to John David as 'J.D. Marten.' Emily could not recall *anyone* calling him by his initials. Jack O'Neill was portrayed as someone who practically stalked Emily throughout high school, wanting her because she was equally as smart and beautiful as he. Each piece of the story seemed vaguely accurate, but it was in its entirety completely false. Yet Sawyer's version of the story would come to be regarded as the truth, and even those close to Jack and John David would eventually remember the story the way it appeared in *An Adirondack Life*.

There was only one detail Sawyer got entirely correct. He concluded the book with an epilogue in which he revealed that Emily Davignon had become pregnant, either as a result of being raped by Jack O'Neill or by her secret lover, J.D. Marten, and that she was now a college student raising the child alone. Sawyer didn't mention the gender of the child or that Emily went to Brown University, but somehow everyone at the school knew it was her.

Emily had agonized over naming the baby, and did, in fact, put it off until the infant was three days old. Emily heard her parents whisper in the hall outside her hospital room that she was

172

rejecting the child, refusing to even give it the most basic mien of existence.

"She can't love it," she heard her mother say.

And although Emily did not bother arguing with them, she knew that she loved the baby the moment she saw it. She studied her little face as she nursed and later undressed her completely in order to examine her tiny arms and legs. Such a perfect creature, Emily thought. So undeserving of her sordid heritage. And so Emily simply disavowed the existence of *any* father and named the little girl Danielle.

Chapter Twenty

The first time Emily realized that everyone at Brown University knew who she was occurred when she walked into a field biology class the week before Christmas. Sawyer's book had sold out in the college bookstore. Everyone knew the victim went to Brown.

'That's *her*,' someone whispered. Several boys were standing on the building steps.

Emily turned sharply, as if her cloak of anonymity, now torn, had been her only clothing.

"And just who am I?" she asked, her face red with anger.

"You're ... that girl in the book," one of them stammered. He backed away slightly.

"What book would that be?"

"You know. The one about the murder."

"And were you able to read it all by yourself or did someone help you with the big words?"

"All by myself."

Emily motioned for him and his friends to move closer.

"Your parents are paying a fortune for you to come here," she whispered. "You should at least be reading the *real* Tom Sawyer."

Emily continued to live a sheltered life. She left the house on Hope Street early in the morning and returned around noon to have lunch with Danielle. She attended classes again in the afternoon and occasionally in the evening, but otherwise, she stayed at home. She never studied in the Brown library like the other students. Instead, Pépé came over every night around seven o'clock and watched Danielle while Emily did her work.

"She's a little fussy," Emily would say, ritually, though in fact Danielle was remarkably good natured.

"Well, maybe if I rocked her while you study," her grandfather would say.

Emily usually had the baby ready for bed by this time, and her grandfather would take the wrapped bundle to the overstuffed rocker in the living room and rock her to sleep.

Emily would go up to her grandfather's library. After an hour or so, Emily would come back and check on them, invariably finding them fast asleep. She'd lift Danielle gently out of Pépé's arms and place her in the crib, but she'd let her Pépé sleep. Some time later, he'd wake up and shake his head to clear the cobwebs.

"I must have fallen asleep," he'd say night after night. Then he would get up from the chair and kiss Emily goodnight.

Pépé Davignon quickly became a doting grandfather. Every morning, even in the winter, he bundled up Danielle and took her for a long walk in the stroller. If Danielle minded going out in cold January air or sweltering July afternoons, she never showed it. They took long walks all the way down Hope Street to Wickenden, then over to the little Portuguese bakery in Fox Point. They usually walked around the Brown University campus and then down to the water at India Point, where they sat on the rocks and ate Portuguese sweetbread from the local bakery.

Pépéépé Davignon developed a close relationship with his granddaughter during the next few years. Emily appreciated this relationship because her own father remained aloof. Her parents' visits were becoming less frequent, the phone calls less newsworthy. They asked about Danielle, but always in a noticeably offhand way. And when they did visit, they seemed to study Danielle. Emily once heard her father say *Well, it's impossible to tell because she looks like Emily* just as Emily was entering the room. Her parents had been sitting on adjacent corners of matching sofas in the parlor. They looked up as she entered the room and her mother blushed.

"Does it make that much difference to you?" Emily asked. "Are you going to hold it against her for the rest of her life?"

"Oh, Emily, it's not *that*," her mother said. "It's just that, naturally, we were curious."

"Well, you can stop being curious. She doesn't have a father. She doesn't *need* a father."

The conversation would go no further. Emily became irritated whenever someone alluded to Danielle's father. What were they thinking, she wondered? Would it really matter if it

176

was John David or Jack? Emily had noticed for the past three years the way the boys looked at her in class. She noticed the stares of the other women who took their babies for walks in the park, women who must have known who she was. They had read Sawyer's book, no doubt, and would later tell their friends that they saw *her* in the park, with the baby. Did they think that Danielle was somehow imprinted with either the violence or the love of her conception?

The elusive Emily Davignon, who had not been out on a single date since she entered Brown University three years earlier, was now increasingly wary cf all men. Professors who made comments in class, singling her out for an opinion on *Roe* vs. *Wade,* and teaching assistants who felt compelled to take certain liberties with her, touching her arm to make a point, or patting her hand. They approached her in so many ways. Outside of the classroom, in the student union, in front of the library, brazenly accosting her and asking, or demanding, a date.

"I don't even know you," she said to a young man who had struck up a conversation and then, quite unexpectedly, asked her to have dinner with him. She was standing outside the registrar's office waiting to add a course. Their conversation had been casual up until that point. Then, out of nowhere came 'the request.'

"But, hey, you can *get* to know me," he said.

"I don't date," Emily said curtly.

"How can you not date?" he asked. "Everybody dates." He thought for a moment and then added. "Hey, you aren't a lesbian, are you?"

"No," Emily said. The urge to throw a sarcastic answer at him overcame her, but she swallowed the words and simply looked away. If only men were taught at an early age to accept 'no' graciously, she thought.

"Hey, I'm sorry. I didn't mean anything."

"I'm certain you didn't," she answered, then added, "... couldn't."

But Emily Davignon was not the same student she had been in high school. She no longer engaged other students in debates and she never challenged her professors' opinions, regardless of

177

how absurd they seemed. She sat quietly in the back of all her classes, entering late and leaving as soon as the lecture was over. She never expressed her opinions. She was, in fact, so unobtrusive that several of her professors could not remember her when Sawyer's book was published. The only time anyone could remember her speaking in class was during a lecture by Dr. Haney. Haney taught Introduction to Sociology, a lower level course whose subject matter bored everyone, including the professor himself. He digressed into the subject of his own book, *The Sociology of Sports*, at the slightest provocation.

"Sports are the modern equivalent of war," Dr. Haney said. "They fulfill the need in man to compete, to *conquer* something."

Dr. Haney was much more animated when he lectured on sports or war than he was when discussing anything else. It was rumored that he had tried out for the Boston Red Sox and had played on the Red Sox AA farm team in Rhode Island for a few seasons. Dr. Haney researched the social causes and consequences of war. It was therefore not surprising that he should combine these interests into a treatise whose premise, if not always believable, was certainly more entertaining than his lectures on male bonding.

"The symbolism in football is so obvious that it's hardly worth commenting on," Haney said, though he nevertheless spent twenty minutes listing the analogies between football and battlefield tactics. Flanking maneuvers, enemy territory, aerial attacks. "The blitz in football has nothing to do with 'lightening,' as the German implies, but to the 'lightening attack' of the German blitzkrieg. Soccer, too, has the elements of battlefield tactics, whereas basketball is a metaphorical rumble between rival gangs. Hockey, on the other hand, *is* a rumble, with scoring added to break up the monotony of the violence. And boxing ... well, boxing is no metaphor, either."

"What about tennis?" someone asked. Students delighted in trying to think of a sport that could not be associated with some form of warfare.

"Fencing," Dr. Haney replied. "Tennis players are merely the modern equivalent of two individuals with sabers."

"Bowling?" someone else shouted.

"Grenadiers," Haney said, "lobbing bombs at the enemy. And what do we call it when you knock down all the pins? A strike."

"Billiards!"

"That's a *game*, not a sport," Dr. Haney said, waving off the student. "It's not a sport unless there's danger. You don't need *violence* to make it a sport, but at the very least there has to be some risk of pain, even if it's only a sore arm. But violence in sports doesn't contribute to violence in society, it just serves as a legitimate outlet for a natural human behavior ... the desire to fight."

Not surprising, many of the students disagreed. The desire to fight is learned, they argued. Babies don't fight.

"The hell they don't," Dr. Haney scoffed. He loved to rebuke the anti-violence faction. "Just put a toy between two toddlers and watch them go at each other. They'll fight to the death."

"What about *baseball?*" Emily asked.

Dr. Haney paused and studied her for a moment. She had never before spoken in his class.

"Ah, *baseball*," the professor said, clearly pleased that someone would think of the national pastime. "Not an obvious correlation, is there?"

Dr. Haney walked slowly in front of the class, his hand on his chin. He paused to allow his question to sink in.

"Baseball is the only sport that doesn't seem to fit the mold," he said. "Offense and defense are not equally represented on the field, not that they are in war, either. But it doesn't even *look* like war." He paused again, seeming to ponder this analogy. "But that's because baseball represents the sublime battle of man against the odds. It is the one team sport in which the offense is an individual effort. The batter is outnumbered *nine to one* when he walks to the plate. The chances of him getting on base are only about one in four. So late in the game, if your team is down by four or five runs, the situation becomes statistically hopeless. Statistically hopeless, but never *futile*. It is when the game looks hopeless that baseball takes on mythic proportions. The lone

179

batter facing the horde. You walk to the plate alone. If you strike out, you accept defeat for the whole team. If you hit the ball, you alone keep the dream of victory alive."

Dr. Haney paused again and looked out over the class. He could tell from the looks on their faces which of the students had played sports in high school.

"And if you are lucky enough to hit a home run when the game is on the line, the trot around the bases becomes a metaphorical victory march through enemy territory. It is a sublime moment. The hopes of the masses fulfilled by a single individual against overwhelming odds. It's the closest we will ever get to the thrill of battle without having to die for it."

Emily appeared ready to ask another question. Dr. Haney looked at her in anticipation, but she fell silent.

Emily was in her senior year in college when she finally accepted a date, a dinner date, with a young man in her creative writing class. He was a prelaw student by the name of Mark Welton. They had been sitting next to each other since the beginning of the spring semester, now several weeks old. He was only a few inches taller than the petite Emily Davignon, with sandy brown hair and a pale complexion. He seemed impervious to Emily's moods, which might one day be dark and sullen, the next engaging and witty. And, unlike most guys, he could not be turned away with an insult. Emily knew little about him except that he was from a small town in Maine that she'd never heard of. She assumed he knew who she was. She assumed everyone knew. But weeks went by and he never once mentioned *An Adirondack Life*, and that alone was enough to endear him to her.

Mark came to pick her up at the house on Hope Street driving an old red Volkswagen.

"This is where you live?" he said, staring up at the tall white pillars from the driveway.

"It's my grandfather's house," Emily said. She had come out to meet him in the driveway.

"Does he know you're going out with me?"

"No. Would he worry if he did?"

180

"If I lived in a house like that I wouldn't let my granddaughter go out with a guy driving a car like mine."

Mark held open the car door, which Emily viewed as a sign of chivalry, but which turned out to be a matter of necessity since he alone knew how to close the door. Then they drove to a Greek restaurant on Benefit Street, which was packed with college students, some of whom appeared to recognize Emily.

"Why are you taking 'creative writing' if you're going into law?" Emily asked.

"Creative writing should be very useful in law school, you know, like when I have to defend someone who commits murder in front of 37 witnesses. Besides, if I don't get into law school, maybe I can earn a living as a writer of sleazy novels."

"What's your GPA?"

"2.2"

"Ooh," Emily said with a pained expression. "Better get working on a novel."

"Only kidding. Actually it's around 3.7."

"So what kind of writing do you want to do?" Emily asked

He did not answer right away.

"What? Poetry, short stories?" Emily asked.

"I'm not really a writer, as in 'one who actually writes,' to be honest."

"What kind of writer are you ... actually?"

"The kind that *thinks* about writing but never seems to get anything done because he's addicted to *Star Trek*."

"I see. So, have you ever written ... anything?"

"My masterpiece is a book report that I wrote in the eighth grade on *Last of the Mohicans*. Got an A⁺. Seven pages long, which was about three pages more than I'd actually read in the book. *That's* creative writing."

"Did you at least cite 'Monarch Notes' as a reference?"

"Not really. I couldn't muster the ambition to read *that*."

"Just for the sake of discussion," Emily said, "have you ever heard of intellectual integrity?"

"Yes, I have," Mark said, stuffing a Greek salad into his mouth. "It's an ancient Greek philosophy having absolutely no identifiable purpose. Look what it did for Socrates."

181

"Well at least he's remembered."

"Genghis Khan is remembered. Kubla Khan is remembered. Nancy Khan is remembered. You don't need intellectual integrity to be remembered."

"Who is Nancy Khan?" Emily asked.

"She starred with Dick Van Dyke in *Robin Crusoe, USN*. If I had been Dickie Boy I would have stayed on the island with that little minx."

"That was Nancy *Kwan*, you nitwit," Emily said, and they both laughed.

"What about you?" Mark asked with food in his mouth. "What kind of writing do you do?"

"I don't," she said. "But I paint a little."

"Hey, no kidding? My parents own an art gallery."

"Why am I finding that hard to believe?"

"Hey, you'd like them. They're real artsy-fartsy. They only watch PBS and listen to National Public Radio and they read authors like Wallace Stegner and talk about him at dinner. And they talk about the wine, too, before they drink it, and they never shout or get excited. I was so embarrassed by them as a kid I told all my friends that I was adopted and that my real father was in prison."

"What kind of gallery do they have?" Emily asked.

"It's one of those bogus summer tourist galleries. I call it the weight-loss clinic for wallets."

"You don't strike me as an art critic."

"I'm not, believe me. But I do know when somebody is being taken. The higher the price tag, the better everyone thinks it is. I've begged my parents to let *me* paint something and put it in the gallery with a $10,000 price tag on it. Of course, they won't let me. They know it would sell and then they would have to admit that I was right."

"Do you mind my asking why you went to college?" Emily asked.

"Just to put off being an adult for another four years. I hoping to find myself, at least that's what I tell my old man. I haven't the slightest idea what that means."

"You're just trying to impress me, I can tell."

182

"No, I'm not. I know I can't impress you," Mark said. "You're way out of my league. But the way I see it, if the *other* girls on campus see me with you, they'll be so impressed they'll be dying to go out with me. You're like a first-class upgrade ticket for my ego."

"God, you're such a liar," Emily said, putting her fork down. It almost sounded like a compliment. "And you don't even feel self- conscious about it."

"I'm not a liar. Don't ever call me a liar. Telling the truth is my one and only virtue."

"And you really think I'm beautiful?" Emily asked, laughing.

"A face that could launch ships," Mark answered quickly. "And, might I add, at the risk of being impertinent, a body that could stop traffic."

His unabashed adoration, or his feigned adoration, filled Emily with a sense of appreciation. It had been a long time since she felt 'loved' by anyone but her daughter and her grandfather. It felt good to hear Mark say these things, even if he was lying.

They finished their dinners and went for a walk down Benefit Street. The fall air was cool and they held each other close as they walked. Emily wore a long wool coat and she pulled the collar up around her neck. A full moon broke from behind the clouds and she looked up and smiled. A full moon always reminded her of the meadow she had crossed with John David Marten after he found her in the woods. It had been about this time of year, a night much like this one, now four years distant in her memory. For a moment her mind drifted back to that Adirondack meadow. She could smell the wet grass and the hemlocks. She could hear the soft rustle of the wind. She could see John David's silhouette moving slowly, methodically, silently, through the meadow.

"I should be getting back," Emily finally said.

"Really? It's still early. Gramps can put himself to bed, can't he?"

"Yes, of course. It's not him. It's just that I have ..." Emily paused for a moment and the silence grew in size. "... a small child at home."

183

"You have a kid?!" Mark said.

"Yes."

"Holy shit. How old?"

"Three years." Then after a moment, she asked, "Are you surprised?"

"Well, *yeah*. Are you surprised that I'm surprised?"

"Well, *no*," Emily said, imitating his inflection.

Emily did not want to explain the circumstances. She said that the child's father was someone she had known in high school. She tried to gauge Mark's reaction, but in the back of her mind she heard her mother saying 'boys don't want to date girls with babies.'

"Is he ... you know, the father, still in the picture?" Mark asked after they had gotten back into his car.

"No."

"Does he know about the baby?"

"No."

It was a short drive back to Emily's house. Emily got out of the car and asked Mark if he wanted to come in for a cup of tea. He seemed to think about it for a moment before declining the offer.

"I'd better not," he said. "It's getting kind of late."

"Well, then, good night," Emily said. She showed no disappointment. She had long ago given up on ever being disappointed. "And thanks for dinner."

Emily watched Mark's car drive away and then let herself in the side door. Pépé was asleep in the recliner with Danielle sprawled out on his lap. She carried Danielle to the crib and then came back downstairs.

"So, how was your date?" Pépé asked, dragging himself slowly from the chair. He looked particularly stiff, or perhaps his legs had fallen asleep from the weight of his great-granddaughter.

"All right, I suppose," Emily said. "Until he found out about Danielle. Or should I say 'the baby.' He never asked if it was a girl or a boy. He just wanted to know about the father."

184

"That's the male dog syndrome," Pépé said. "He's just checking to see who else is peeing on the hydrants. What did you tell him?"

"Nothing. He doesn't seem to have heard about it." Then Emily laughed. "Of course, he *is* from Maine."

"I think they have newspapers up there," Pépé said. "He'll put two and two together sooner or later."

Emily filled her tea kettle and nodded her agreement.

"How was Danielle tonight?" Emily asked.

"She was a little angel. We played hide-and-seek and she hid in the L.L. Bean bag. It actually took me awhile to find her. Then I carried her around the house in it. You should have seen her. Her little head was sticking out the top and she was holding on to the straps, laughing. I just hope my back isn't sore in the morning."

Emily came over and gave her grandfather a kiss on the cheek.

"You're so good to her," Emily said. "I hope you know how much I appreciate all that you do for us."

"I'm the lucky one," he said.

"I just wish Mom and Dad were half as happy."

"It's different with them," Pépé said, waving his hand as if shooing away a fly. "They're too close to it. But they'll come around in time. Parents always do."

"I hope so, " Emily said. "I can understand Dad being like this. He's always been so rigid. But Mom has always been able to go along with things."

"Yeah, but she probably envisioned you getting married in a white gown."

"So, I spoiled her plans for a wedding?"

"Yeah, I suppose you did," Pépé said, tapping her forearm, "but don't pick at a sore or it will never heal."

Mark was already seated when Emily entered the room for their next writing class. He smiled at her as she took the seat next to him. Ten minutes later he handed her a folded piece of paper. She carefully unfolded it and read the note that said 'My parents want to see your paintings.'

"Get out of here!" Emily hissed.

185

"I tease you not. They want to see them."

"But I haven't painted anything since high school."

"What do you have to lose?" he said.

Emily had nothing to lose, so she and Mark drove up to the town of Windsor the following weekend with Emily's paintings packed neatly in the trunk of her car. Mark had come to the house and helped her take them out of the attic and wrap each one in brown paper. He had even played with Danielle, holding up her pigtails and pretending that they were handlebars on a motorcycle while running around the backyard.

Mark's parents raved about the paintings of Adirondack leaves, ponds, drops of water falling off hemlock needles. They especially loved the one of John David walking through the mountain meadow at night. They took them all on consignment and arranged a personal showing for later that spring.

Emily was shocked. She hadn't painted anything new since she'd gone off to college. She had always intended to take up painting again when Danielle was a little older, but this visit to the art gallery really fired her up. The Weltons had seemed so excited about her work.

It was several weeks before Emily returned to Windsor. Mark's parents had scheduled a showing for the last week in April, less than a month before her graduation from Brown. Mark and Emily drove up in her car on a Friday afternoon and arrived in time for dinner.

Mrs. Welton greeted her at the door of their impeccable white Victorian house and showed her to the guest room. When Emily came down for dinner, Mark and his parents were already seated at the table. They all stood up to greet her.

"You'll be pleased to know we already have several buyers for your paintings," Mr. Welton said while the salad was being passed around. "Of course, we told them that they couldn't possibly buy anything until the showing. We wouldn't want you to have a grand opening without any paintings."

"How many?" Emily asked.

"Seven," Mrs. Welton said, obviously pleased.

"Seven?!"

186

"Can you believe it?" Mr. Welton said. "I've doubled the prices for the show."

"How much are you asking?"

"From $800 to $7,000."

"Seven thousand dollars?!"

Emily could not believe what she was hearing. She never would have imagined her paintings selling for that kind of money. A hundred dollars would have been asking too much. These were paintings she'd done in *high school*. No high school artist was ever worth that kind of money. Emily was so unnerved by the news that she could not eat her dinner.

The four of them drove down to the gallery after dinner. Emily walked slowly through the exhibit, as if viewing the work of some other artist. She hadn't looked at them in a long time, and there was a certain freshness to them. The paintings had been mounted in ornate Victorian wooden frames, giving them an air of maturity. They looked as if they had been painted long ago. Emily decided that the Weltons must have done this to cover up her youth.

There were nearly fifty paintings in the show. Emily wandered from room to room, examining each of the paintings. Mark had started to walk with her, but when he noticed the distant gaze in her eyes, he decided to let her continue by herself. There was a painting of a red oak leaf floating on the blue black surface of a pond and another of a tuft of grass sprouting between two lichen-covered rocks. She remembered sitting on the side of Panther Mountain, sketching the rocks with a number three pencil. It had been one of the first times she had realized that taking pictures of her subjects wasn't enough. Sketching them had forced her to spend more time with them, to examine them more fully.

It bothered Emily to see price tags on the paintings, little white cards with a number written in perfect calligraphy placed in the lower left hand corner. $500. $900. $2,500. Emily wondered how Mark's parents had arrived at these prices. Were they indicative of the work's relative quality, or merely its size? Wouldn't it be more appropriate, Emily wondered, to let people offer whatever they felt a painting was worth?

She wandered into a larger room and saw the painting of John David Marten on the wall directly across from the doorway. Emily had painted it in the weeks following her ordeal in the woods. It showed John David's silhouette in a meadow with tall spruce trees rising out of the background. She had painted it with only two colors, blue and black, which she had mixed in different hues to capture the meadow during the final moments of dusk.

Staring at the picture she could see John David once again, walking in front of her through the wet meadow. The air was cold, near freezing. She had never felt so tired in her life. Exhausted, maybe even near death. She had wanted only to lie down in the wet grass, to curl up like an animal and go to sleep. But John David had forced her to walk on through to the other side of the meadow, through the spruce and hemlocks, to the shelter of the tiny cabin.

Emily's eyes drifted to the lower left hand corner of the painting and the tiny white tag. $7,000. Her heart began to pound furiously. Emily's natural distrust of people suddenly welled up. Was all of this a set- up, she wondered? Were they exploiting the connection to Sawyer's novel? Emily looked around the room. The Weltons were still in the foyer, out of sight. She looked for some clues that might confirm or allay her fears, but it was all beginning to make sense. Seven thousand dollars for a painting by a high school student? Not likely, unless the subject was *J.D. Marten*. Emily saw a cardboard box near the door filled with copies of the program. On the cover of the program was a picture of Emily Davignon, with the words 'An Adirondack Artist' written in Chaucer typeface. On the inside cover was her biographical sketch, including her prominent role in Sawyer's *An Adirondack Life*.

Emily felt nauseous. She dropped the program back into the box and walked back slowly through the rooms. She needed time to calm down before she faced the Weltons. If she had been in familiar surroundings, she might have stormed out of the building. But she was a long way from home and didn't want to leave now, in the middle of the night. She tried to control her breathing, which was coming now in short, hard pants. How could I let myself be taken in, she wondered? How could I let down my guard? She walked around the rooms for several more minutes until she calmed down.

"What do you think, Emily?" Mrs. Welton asked when Emily returned to the foyer.

"It's all very nice," Emily said quietly. "You've done a wonderful job. But if you don't mind, I'm awfully tired."

"Mark can take you back to the house," Mr. Welton said. "I just have a few final preparations to take care of around here. We'll see you first thing in the morning?"

Emily nodded and said goodnight. She thanked them once again for setting everything up. Then she followed Mark out to the car.

"It's going to be a beautiful day tomorrow," Mark said as they walked across the parking lot. "A great day for an opening."

Emily did not respond, but later, as they were driving back to the house, she asked, "So, how long have you known who I am?"

"What do you mean?" Mark said.

"You *know* what I mean. How long did it take for you to figure out that I am the girl in *An Adirondack Life?*"

Mark paused for a long moment before responding. Emily waited patiently for his reply.

"After you told me about your kid," Mark said. "I sort of put two and two together."

"And you went out and read the book, I suppose."

"Well, yeah."

"So, is this 'showing' for real, or is this just taking advantage of an opportunity? Am I the circus attraction tomorrow?"

"Emily, it's nothing like that," Mark said. "They wouldn't have a showing if your paintings weren't really good. No one spends thousands of dollars on junk."

"No one spends thousands of dollars on paintings by high schoolers, either."

"Listen Emily. You have name recognition. You can't deny that unless you're going to change your name. A lot of painters take twenty years to gain that kind of recognition."

189

"I never thought of it that way," Emily said. Her sarcasm boiled to the surface. "Only a lawyer would think of rape as a career move."

"Oww. That hurt. I can't believe you'd say something like that to me. I've always avoided this topic, for your sake."

"And I can't believe you didn't tell me what I was getting into."

Mark apologized for his omissions. He explained that he hadn't known how to discuss this kind of thing. He hadn't meant to hurt her. Emily accepted the apology, not so much because he sounded sincere, which he didn't, which he never did, but because she decided it no longer mattered. She had been hiding from her past for four years and it hadn't done her any good.

The showing the next day was, Emily later admitted to a gloating Mark Welton, one of the most wonderful days of her life. The gallery was packed and so many people asked her to autograph the program that Mr. Welton had to set up a table in the corner of one of the rooms. The gallery became a mass of confusion, with a long line of patrons extending out the front door. Everyone raved about the paintings. And everyone, it seemed, bought them. Forty-three paintings in all were adorned with little yellow tags with the word 'sold' written in red ink. Nearly ninety-thousand dollars worth of art. The amount was staggering, even to the Weltons.

When the show finally ended, Emily walked through the rooms to view the paintings one last time. The following day the Weltons would start shipping them to the various addresses people had written in the ledger and her work would vanish. She had never before sold a single painting, and now most of them were gone. It felt as if strangers had come and bid for her child.

The painting of John David with the $7,000 price tag had been sold. It was an enormous painting, three feet high and almost five feet in width. It wasn't the kind of painting that would look good in any room.

"Who bought this one?" she asked.

Mrs. Welton got out the ledger and showed it to Emily. Emily scanned the names and addresses of the buyers. They had come from all over the east coast, and a few from California as well. She had to go back to the painting of John David to find the identifying number, then ran her finger down the column until she found it in the ledger. Thomas Sawyer.

"Was he here today?" Emily asked.

"He came in last night," Mrs. Welton said. "He didn't want to ... *upset* you ... on your big day."

"How thoughtful of him," Emily said. "But he wouldn't have upset me. After all, what would I be without him. I wouldn't even exist." Emily sounded so earnest that Mrs. Welton did not notice the sarcasm.

There was one man left in the gallery when the show ended. He came over to Emily and introduced himself as Geoffrey Neiswender, art critic for *Time* magazine. He was a handsome man, short, with a neatly trimmed beard. He handed her his business card.

"Is that your real name?" Emily asked. "Geoffrey?"

"My parents spelled it with *J,* but then they were Bohemians. But enough about me. Do you mind answering a few questions?"

Emily shook her head, but she was dumbfounded.

"This ... show ... was quite impressive," he said. "A most unusual occurrence, don't you agree?"

Again Emily shook her head.

"You *are* capable of speech, Ms. Davignon, are you not?"

"Yes, yes, or course. I'm sorry. It's just that you caught me off guard."

Neiswender took her by the elbow and led her through the gallery. The Weltons followed closely, beaming.

"A most unusual display," Neiswender said. "Tell me, with whom did you study?"

"No one, really," Emily answered. "Not formally. I painted these when I was in high school."

"Yes, I wondered about that," Neiswender said, stroking his beard. He was standing in front of the John David painting. "Tell me about this one."

Emily studied him for a moment. He isn't here as an art critic, she thought. He's here for the show.

191

"I suppose you've read the book," Emily said.

Neiswender looked at her with a hint of disdain. A smile came to his face.

"Of course I read the book," he said. "Why else would I have come? Why else would anyone have come?"

"I'm sorry you came all this way just to make fun of me," Emily replied. "But I'm as surprised at all this attention as you are. If you ask me, anyone who pays several thousand dollars for a painting by a high school student is nuts and shouldn't be trusted with money."

Neiswender studied her again for a moment.

"You are so wonderfully unpretentious," he finally concluded, touching her arm. "It's *so* refreshing."

He motioned for her to turn toward the painting.

"But I didn't travel any distance to get here. I have a home in the area and so I thought I stop by. To be honest, I wasn't prepared for this little showing of yours. I'm still not sure what to make of it." He looked at the painting of John David. "This is ... well, brilliant. If it's what I think it is."

"What do you think it is?" Emily asked.

"No, no," Neiswwender said, wagging his finger. "You explain it to me. I want you to tell me what all of these paintings are about. What motivates a child to paint like this?"

And so Emily explained, in a voice that she did not quite recognize as her own, how she had experimented with lacquers and pigments of her own made from crushed oak leaves and birch, and extracts of sumac berries, to make the water reflect light as if from the depth of an Adirondack pond. At first it had been a simple technical problem, she explained, to create something both opaque and transparent. This painting, she said, presented different depths to sky and the water, blue fading into black, both of them being swallowed up by the forest as night approached. She was fascinated by water, she told him. The streams and the rivers and lakes were what give the Adirondacks their defining characteristic, what brings them to life. Yet the water is not itself a living thing. Emily found herself revealing details that she had never articulated, perhaps never fully understood, until the moment the words escaped from her lips.

Emily continued speaking for more than an hour. A torrent of words and emotions, some of which were so new and barely formed that they sounded like mere grunts. The water, the water pulls you down, sucking life, creating life, reflecting life, and the mountains ... the wilderness, so loving and gentle, but then so cruel and uncaring. And in the end, and all you can do is accept it. Don't the mountains swallow us up, all of us, sooner or later? We try to be different, above it, better than the animals, but were not really. We're no more civilized than wolves.

Neiswender listened and stroked his little beard, but he said nothing the entire time. Emily could not gauge his reaction to everything she said, could not, in fact, remember everything she had said to him. She had painted in silence for so long, never describing her emotions to even her parents. In the review published several weeks later, Neiswender lauded Emily Davignon for her unpretentious simplicity and unabashed love of nature. He described her style as 'the Hudson River School writ small' and a 'study of nature on the microscopic scale.'

The painting of John David Marten covered half the page.

The dean of the college called Emily after reading the review in *Time* magazine. The public relations benefit of her presence in the graduating class had not been lost on him, even though he had not the slightest idea who she was. He knew he had to act quickly. In another two weeks she would be gone. Would she be interested in addressing the graduating class at the commencement, he asked?

Emily declined. She could not think of anything to offer the graduating class, she explained. Her life was not an example for anyone else. Her experiences, both good and bad, did not translate well into generalities. But the dean persisted, and rumors abounded on campus that the mysterious Emily Davignon, the girl in the red Camaro, was going to speak at commencement. She began receiving phone calls from different groups on campus, groups that thought they might have common interests. A spokeswoman for the Equal Rights Amendment asked her to use the commencement as a forum urging voters to approve the amendment. Another caller asked her to speak out

193

for gun control. Yet another asked her to promote the environment.

"We would like you to be a spokeswoman against the Roe vs. Wade decision," one caller said. When Emily hesitated, the caller became more persistent. "You, of all people, should feel strongly about abortion. Where would your daughter be if abortion had been legal when you got pregnant?"

"The same place she is now," Emily said, upset. "In bed."

"But then you do understand the sanctity of life," the caller said. "You need to get that message across. It's your responsibility as a celebrity."

But Emily declined politely and appeared at graduation with her parents, her grandfather and her daughter. She did not take the stage and deliver a speech on the environment, or abortion, or the equal rights amendment. She stood in line with the other students arranged in alphabetical order and filed into the field house waving to the crowd. Her parents were proud of her, proud of the article in *Time* magazine. They told her how everyone back in Henoga Valley was talking about Emily Davignon, the famous artist. The library wanted to place some of her paintings on display and could she find some to donate?

As the students were lining up to enter the field house, several young women whom Emily did not recognize approached her and asked her to autograph their commencement programs. Then others came, dozens at a time, and the orderly line broke into an entropic mass. Strangers, mostly women her own age, some of them with tears in their eyes, gave her hugs and patted her on the back, as if they had grown up together and been friends for years. And afterward, Emily wished she could have known who they were.

Chapter Twenty-One

Julia sank into a prolonged state of depression shortly after Emily gave birth to Danielle. Her daughter was gone. Her innocent little baby, whom she had raised from infancy and loved as if she were her own flesh, was now the mother of a child conceived in rape, or sired by an animal that had escaped into the woods like a wolf. And Julia felt that *she* was to blame, that she alone had welcomed this evil into their lives.

Julia Behrens met Emily's mother, Susan Harkins, when they were freshmen at Plattsburgh College in 1948. They came from different parts of the state, Julia from Glens Falls, a small town near the Vermont border, and Susan from Poughkeepsie. They were thrown together as roommates by the lottery system that was used for all new students. They seemed at first an unlikely match. Julia stood five feet nine inches tall with angular shoulders and long dark hair. She was striking, a young woman whom everyone noticed at the crowded parties they later attended. Susan was barely five feet two inches tall, with sandy brown hair and skin that tanned ever so lightly. Their personalities were equally disparate. Julia was shy and nervous, and prone to fits of passion and despair. Susan was carefree and self-confident. Julia majored in nursing and Susan in teaching, and they shared a dormitory room in MacDonough Hall for four years.

They decided, or rather Susan decided and Julia acquiesced, that they would move to New York City together after graduation and get a taste of the big city.

They found a small two bedroom apartment on the lower West Side, two upstate girls who had never seen anything like Manhattan. Julia got a job at Mount Sinai right away, but Susan had difficulty finding a teaching job. The year was 1952 and a lot of servicemen had come back from the war and gone to college. They had filled up all of the available teaching positions in the city, and schools felt obligated to give them preference. Susan was offered a teaching job in a Catholic school, but it did not pay enough for her to stay in Manhattan, so she accepted a better paying job at a bank.

Susan met Robert Davignon on her third day on the job. He walked into the bank wearing his surgical scrubs under his jacket. There was blood on the front of the gown.

"Oh my God!" she said, backing away instinctively. "You've been hurt!"

Robert quickly closed his jacket over the gown. Residents weren't supposed to wear their surgical scrubs out of the hospital, particularly with blood on them. He would be severely reprimanded by the Chief of Surgery if he were caught. But he had to make a deposit in his checking account and there wasn't time to change before the bank closed.

"Hey, don't worry," Robert whispered, "I'm a doctor. I just need to make a deposit." He slid the money across the counter.

Susan was unnerved by the sight of blood. She had cut her head open as a child and received fifteen stitches, but not before she saw her own face covered with blood. She had been deathly afraid of blood ever since. That fear, she would later explain to the angry young surgical resident, was the reason she made a mistake on his deposit, leaving off the last zero. With the matter cleared up, and Robert realizing that *he* had been partly to blame, he invited Susan to dinner. And six months later, they were married.

All of them considered it a stroke of luck that a studio apartment became available in the building three weeks before the wedding. At first, Robert had argued that he and Susan could not afford a two-bedroom apartment. As a resident, he was earning less than the nurses, although he received free room and board at the hospital. But if he moved out of the hospital dormitory, his salary wouldn't go very far. But Susan hated the idea of moving to another building, away from Julia. So Robert moved his things in with Susan and Julia took the studio apartment at the end of the hall.

The three of them spent a great deal of time together. Julia worked the night shift at Mount Sinai Hospital and Susan worked days at the bank, so they ate dinner together every evening. Robert joined them on his days off, and he often walked home with Julia after being on-call during the night. It seemed only natural, on these occasions, that Julia and Robert ate breakfast together in Robert's apartment.

Susan could not have guessed that Julia was also in love with her husband, and Julia did everything she could to hide the fact for more than a year. They were all such good friends. If Susan had by chance walked into her apartment and found Robert and Julia sitting on her bed, clothed, she would not have been jealous. She would have made an innocent joke about Julia being careful not to get pregnant. And so she did not know, could not have known, how Julia felt each time she was alone with Robert Davignon. She did not know that Julia had studied his every movement, the way that he tapped his fingers on the table when he was anxious to get to the hospital, the way that he rubbed both arms when he was telling something less than the complete truth. Susan did not realize that her best friend noticed the way that the hairs on Robert's wrist lay in whorls, and that he stirred his coffee counterclockwise.

Once, when Julia and Robert were having breakfast alone, Robert went into the bedroom to change. He came out of the bedroom without a shirt, and Julia felt her nipples become erect. She had to cover herself by crossing her arms lest they show through her thin cotton uniform.

Robert, for his part, was equally attracted to the tall, statuesque Julia, with her long legs and full breasts. He found it nearly impossible to keep his eyes from drifting downward to that magnificent chest.

Once, when he and Julia were having breakfast at the apartment, they had a discussion about a radical mastectomy case he had assisted the day before. Robert said playfully that it was a shame to resect a breast nearly as perfect as Julia's. And Julia had blushed. The three of them had always been able to talk about anything, including sex. Susan and Robert often made sexual innuendos and Julia always told the latest dirty joke she had heard on the hospital floor. It was easy to pretend in this manner, when they were all together, but it was harder for Julia to hide her attraction for Robert when they were alone.

197

Julia got up from the table and grabbed her purse from the back of the chair.

"I'd better go," she said and headed for the door.

"*Julia.* I'm sorry," Robert said, getting up quickly from the table. "You know how it is, we kid around so much, all of us. I wasn't thinking. Honest, I didn't mean anything."

Julia was standing at the door with her hand on the door knob.

"It's okay, Robert, really. I didn't take offense."

"Then why are you leaving? You didn't even finish your coffee."

"I shouldn't be here," Julia said, "you know ... when Susan isn't."

"Is that what you're thinking?" Robert said. "Nothing's going to happen, I swear. You know me. I'm all talk. I thought we were just having fun. You don't have to worry about me."

"It's not you I'm worried about," Julia said, looking directly into his eyes. "It's *me.*"

And then, impulsively, she kissed him full on the lips.

Robert looked at her slightly puzzled. He was not an impulsive man and quite certain that he loved Susan, as certain as a man can be about these things. But most men must actively resist the primal urge to mate with every attractive woman and expand their claim on the genetic pool, and while Robert may not have been impulsive, he was not particularly strong-willed either. He reached out and pulled Julia back into his embrace and kissed her. Her hands went up to his face and caressed his neck. Without saying a word, Robert lifted Julia into his arms and carried her to the couch. He tore into her blouse with hungry hands, ripping off one of the buttons. He loosened her bra strap and made a hissing sound when her large firm breasts fell into his hands. He was kneeling on the floor in front of her now, between her legs, kissing her breasts and sucking on her nipples. Her chest heaved and he felt her ribs press against his hands. He tore off her skirt and panties and entered her in unbridled lust. Julia let out a gasp of virginal pain and held onto his arms while he thrust at her body. Finally, he arched his back and let out several long, deep groans and collapsed onto her chest.

For several minutes afterward, Julia lay perfectly still. Her legs were still wrapped around Robert's waist and his head lay between her breasts. Looking over his shoulder she could see the entire apartment, the coffee cups on the table, the coat tree by the door, the pictures Susan had bought at flea markets and hung in a chaotic manner on every wall. A pair of socks lay drying on the radiator.

What will we say to each other now? Julia wondered. She was still breathing hard, whether from passion or fear, she did not know. There was little chance that Susan would come home and find them. But the fear was nonetheless strong and made her slightly nauseous.

Robert moved first. He lifted himself upright, still kneeling between her legs, and looked down to where their hips were joined. He was still inside her and the sight of her supine body, her large breast standing fully upright, her muscular thighs pressed against his pelvis, excited him again. He began to move his hips back and forth slowly, lifting Julia from the couch with his hands beneath her back. Having already emptied his lust into her, he was now capable of greater patience. Julia felt the rhythmic movement of his lovemaking. His hands slid from her back to her buttocks. His chest heaved and his head swayed from side to side. She felt herself breathing harder. She began to groan. Robert reached down and lifted her legs up so that her knees were touching his chest. Julia let go of his arms and placed her hands on the couch to brace herself. And although she could not remember having cried out, Robert's hand came up and covered her mouth when they erupted in their passion.

"Oh, Julia," was all Robert could say when it was over. But Julia could think of nothing to reply.

Robert pulled away from her and stood up awkwardly. There were red spots on each of his knees from the carpet and he massaged them with his hands.

"Do you want to use the bathroom first?" he said.

Julia shook her head no. Such a strange thing to say, she thought, right after making love. As if it were just another bodily function.

When Robert came out of the bathroom Julia was dressed

and standing by the kitchen table. She fidgeted with the blouse where the button was missing. He walked over to her and kissed her gently on the lips. She looked into his eyes, expecting him to say something that might explain why they had done this. *He* was the experienced one, and a doctor. Surely he would know what force drove them to this madness. Surely he would know what to say at a time like this. But Robert said nothing.

"I'd better be going," she said, this time with more certainty.

Robert merely nodded.

Julia returned to her apartment down the hall and filled the bathtub with hot water. She slid under the water up to her neck and gently rubbed the insides of her thighs. Her legs ached and her skin was raw. She had been a virgin and hadn't known fully what to expect. Susan hadn't given her the details about lovemaking. She might have joked about it, but the real event was far too private. Julia's body was still trembling with fear of their act, their secret.

She did not feel guilty for having seduced her best friend's husband. She knew that she had given in willingly. The fact that neither one of them even mentioned Susan was what bothered her now. She had expected Robert to say something like, 'we have to keep this from Susan' or 'this will have to be our little secret,' but he had said nothing of the kind. And how would he act the next time the three of them were together, or the next time he and Julia were alone?

Julia avoided Susan and Robert for the next two days, which was not an uncommonly long period of time for them to go without seeing one another. Robert ran into her on the surgical recovery floor, but he was entirely professional, except for the nearly imperceptible way in which his eyes lingered on her. Julia's greatest fear was that she would be suddenly overcome with guilt in Susan's presence and break down. That, she decided, had to be avoided at all costs.

All of Julia's fretting, it turned out, was for naught. Susan was completely unsuspecting, consumed, as she was, with her own news.

"I'm pregnant!" she exclaimed to Julia less than a week later.

"You are?! Susan, I'm so happy for you. For you *both*."
Julia gave her a big hug. "Have you told Robert yet?"

"No, not yet. He's been on call for the last two days. I
haven't even seen him. I should have waited and told him first,
but I just couldn't wait any longer. I had to tell somebody."

"He'll be so excited."

"I'm not so sure," Susan said.

"What do you mean? Robert wants children, doesn't he?"

"Yes, of course, but not now. He doesn't make enough
money to support us yet. He wanted to wait until he finished his
residency."

"So, what will you do?"

"I *have* to work," Susan said. "We can't make it on his
salary. Do you think you can help me out?"

"What do you mean?"

"Well, I was thinking, maybe you could babysit
sometimes?"

Julia was thrilled to be asked.

"Of course I can babysit! I get home at 7:30. I can take the
baby from then until you get home at 3:30."

"But will that give you enough time to sleep?"

"Plenty."

The excitement of the pregnancy swept away all of the
anxiety that Julia had been feeling. She had been certain that
Susan would detect the affair the moment they were all together,
that she would see the illicit act playing like a movie within the
vitreous humor of Julia's eyes. But they were laughing and
hugging and so fully engaged in their emotions that the secret
was simply pushed beneath the surface, where it would forever
consort with the other privities.

Nothing more was said between Robert and Julia about the
affair. It was easy for the three of them to be together because
Susan and her swollen belly were always the center of attention.
Susan lolling on the sofa in the evening reading a book, rubbing
her abdomen slowly with one hand. Susan lifting up her shirt on
an almost daily basis to show them the taut skin and inverted
naval.

"Look at these breasts!" Susan said one evening, cupping

201

one in each hand. She was then in the fourth month of her pregnancy. The three of them were playing cards at the kitchen table. "Can you believe the size of these things?"

"They're impressive, dear," Robert said, still sorting his newly dealt hand.

"You bet they are," Susan said. "Now you won't have to lust after Julia's."

The remark was made with the same innocence that Susan had used hundreds of times before, but the words caught Julia off guard and she blushed. Her eyes darted over to Robert. Was she testing us, Julia wondered?

Robert thought to himself *Don't panic, Julia. She doesn't mean anything by it.* He was aware that Julia had glanced toward him, but he kept his eyes on the cards. Carefully, he moved the Jack of diamonds three places to the right. Then, with the cards arranged in apparent, if not actual, order, he placed them face down on the table.

"Well, I don't know about *that*," he said, smiling. "I need the two of you to stand side by side with your shirts off before I can make a final decision."

Susan slapped him playfully on the arm and he pulled back with a chuckle. Only Julia, whose heart was racing and on whose forehead tiny beads of sweat had formed, showed any sign of the turmoil that had momentarily surfaced.

For Julia, too, was pregnant, and only Robert knew.

She had never been sick a day in her life. Never missed a day of school, high school or college. And then one day she was vomiting her guts out and dragging herself around, exhausted.

"Don't worry, it's probably not the flu," the head nurse said sarcastically when Julia called to say that she couldn't come to work. "You're probably just pregnant."

The horror of the revelation came to Julia in a private doctor's office. She could have arranged the blood work at the hospital, but someone was bound to know her. So she found a kindly general practitioner several blocks away.

"Judging by the lack of a wedding ring, I assume you're not pleased with this news," the doctor said. He was a pleasant man, in his late fifties. There were pictures of his wife and family on the walls along side his diplomas.

Julia could not respond at first, but after a long moment, she said, "How could it have happened? I've only ..." She paused and searched for the appropriate word, "... been with a man once. Well, I mean, he *did* it twice, but it was only one occasion."

"It only takes one occasion, Miss Behrens," the doctor said. "But I'm sure you knew that, being a nurse."

Julia nodded in agreement. Of course she knew that, not that they had taught it in nursing school. The doctor meant that a nurse would have learned about it on the hospital floor, from the other nurses, where they received their real education. Still, Julia would never have believed it possible. Pregnant? After just one time? My God, she thought, how is it that the world isn't overrun with babies?

Julia cornered Robert at the hospital two nights later to tell him the news. Robert could see that she was in a panic. He assumed it was something at home because he hadn't been there in three days.

"What is it, Julia?" Robert said. They were standing at the end of a long dimly-lit corridor, far from the eager ears of the hospital staff.

Julia stood in front of him with her chin on her chest, playing with her fingers. Looking down, Robert could see that she had bitten the skin off the side of her thumbnail.

"Julia?" he repeated. This time his voice was a whisper.

"I'm pregnant," she said, so quietly that Robert almost had to ask her to repeat it.

"Oh, shit," he hissed.

"What are *you* worried about? *I'm* the one who's pregnant."

"Yeah, yeah, I know. But I assumed you were telling me because I'm the father."

"Of course you're the father," she said harshly. She looked up at his face and her expression softened. "Robert, what do I do?"

"Geez, I don't know," he answered, rubbing his forehead. "Let me think about this for a day or two."

Julia nodded. She turned and started to walk down the hall.

The hallway was empty and the lights had been dimmed. Julia had only taken a few steps when she felt Robert's hand grab her arm.

"I suppose it goes without saying ... that we can't let Susan know about this?"

Julia again nodded but did not say anything. Tears welled up in her eyes. Robert put his arms around her and drew her close to his chest.

"Julia, I'm sorry," he said.

Sorry for what? she wondered. For having sex with me? For getting me in trouble? Or is it just one of those things that men say when they can't think of anything appropriate?

A week later Robert was in her apartment. They spoke in hushed tones just inside the door. He had asked around, discreetly, and found a doctor. The doctor had lost his medical license over a malpractice case several years ago and now made a living performing abortions. He would undoubtedly go to prison if he got caught, but that wasn't likely to happen. Certain city officials already knew about him; had, in fact, employed his services on more than one occasion. They would continue to look the other way as long as he remained utterly discreet and nothing went wrong. More than one member of the Mount Sinai nursing staff had been to him, Robert said.

"An abortion?" Julia could hardly say it, a word not meant to be spoken aloud. She had never even heard of one until she was in college, where it was mentioned in reference to a girl who had not returned to the dormitory after Christmas break.

"Julia, we don't have a lot of options right now."

"Yes, I know. Of course ..." she said. Her voice trailed off as if she were losing her train of thought.

"I can have someone take you there and spend the night with you afterward," Robert said, "just to make sure there are no complications?"

Julia looked at him, surprised.

"Can't you take me there?"

"No, no ... *I* can't. If I was seen going in there, I could lose my license."

And so Julia went alone to the three-story house on a side

street in Brooklyn. The taxi driver offered to circle the neighborhood and pick her up in half an hour. Julia was surprised that he seemed to know why she was being dropped off at this address and how long she would be, but she intuitively accepted his offer without further discussion.

Julia was met at the side door by a stern-looking woman in her late forties. She was short with muscular arms, and she guided Julia to a changing room without saying more than a dozen words. There wasn't much that needed to be said. There were no forms to fill out and no history to be taken. Just the payment, fifty dollars, in cash, which the woman tucked into the large apron pocket.

Julia changed into a gown that the woman provided and was wheeled into the surgical area, which at one time had been a kitchen. The 'doctor' came in and washed his hands in the sink. Julia thought for a moment about engaging him in conversation. She wanted to tell him that she was a nurse and allude to their common bond in the practice of medicine. Then she remembered that Robert said the doctor had lost his license. He probably wouldn't care, she thought. She was right, The doctor wasn't interested in hearing that she wasn't like all the others who came to him. He didn't want to know if she was a housewife with too many children in a small, two bedroom apartment, or a politician's mistress, or a common whore. The origin of the pregnancy didn't really matter to him. He was only concerned with its termination.

The doctor had once been an excellent surgeon and he performed the abortion with remarkable alacrity. A heavy cotton towel was placed in Julia's mouth and fastened behind her neck to prevent any screams from escaping to the street below. Her hands were strapped to the sides of the gurney. The doctor never asked her name. Never, in fact, even looked at her face. To his credit, he cautioned her that there would be some pain and that he would do his best to keep it at a minimum. He inserted a smooth metal rod into her cervix and scraped the sides of her uterus with a series of firm circular motions. He paused whenever Julia writhed in pain, then resumed as soon as she relaxed. The entire procedure took only minutes.

205

The woman came in and cleaned her up after the procedure was over, then gave Julia some verbal instructions about what to do over the next forty-eight hours. If anything went wrong, the woman said, Julia was to go to a hospital. Under no circumstances should she return to this house. Then she guided Julia down the back stairs to the alley where the taxi had parked. The door was already opened. Julia returned to her apartment doubled over in the back seat of the car with excruciating abdominal cramps, like angry fists inside her bowels, ripping and tearing at her organs.

And all of their lives resumed.

Julia went back to the hospital after the long weekend. Robert worked even longer hours at the hospital, sometimes home for less than ten hours in a week. Susan got up every morning and went to the bank. If Robert had initially been worried that Julia would break down, his fears were soon allayed. She never again mentioned, even in private, the affair or the abortion. And she never again engaged in any of the playful sexual jokes.

"God, she's turning into a prude," Susan said to Robert the night after they had played cards.

"I hadn't noticed," Robert said. He climbed into bed and pulled the covers up to his chest.

"No, really. I'm beginning to worry about her. She's not herself."

"She's fine. Don't worry about her."

Susan climbed into bed and slid over next to Robert. She laid her head on his chest and he stroked her hair.

"You know what I think it is," Susan said. "I think it's *you.*"

Robert's body tensed.

"What do you mean?" he asked.

"I think she wants to find someone like you. Handsome, fun to be around, someone who is smart, but not bossy. A guy you can trust. It's not easy to find a man like that. I just got lucky."

Robert patted her gently on the shoulder.

"I think she's got a crush on you," Susan said.

"Don't be ridiculous," Robert answered.

"No, I'm serious. I can tell." Susan sat up a little in bed.

"Hey, I'm not jealous. I think it's kind of cute, kind of flattering. I mean, if anything ever happened to me, I'd want you to marry her."

Robert started to make a joke, something like 'sure, I'll put her on the list.' But he was unable to form the sentence clearly in his own mind, and he did not want to accidentally say something wrong. Words, once beyond the confines of the lips, are capable of spontaneously rearranging into something never intended. Robert knew he was capable of changing a sentence like 'that would hardly seem fair to you' into 'our unseemly affair would be hard on you.' So he prudently decided not to respond. He pretended to breathe more deeply, as if falling asleep. Susan knew that after years on the surgical service, he was likely to fall asleep as soon as the lights went out. She would not suspect that he was still awake.

Susan leaned on her elbow and stared at him in the dark. The street light shone through the window shade and bathed him in a dim, silvery sheen. The hairs on his chest were faintly illuminated and his skin glistened. He laid perfectly still, except for the rhythmic breathing. He was, in fact, falling asleep. In another moment he would no longer be pretending. And then, just before he actually fell asleep, he thought he heard her say, in a voice barely above a whisper, "but not before then."

But of course he dared not ask her what, if anything, she meant.

207

Chapter Twenty-Two

Emily's showing at the Welton's art gallery and the review that appeared in *Time* magazine left her in an unusual predicament. Her work was suddenly in great demand, and she had none to display. Of the original forty-eight paintings shown at the Welton's art gallery, forty-six of them were sold either that day and or in the weeks that followed. When the Sierra Club offered to make a nature calendar from her paintings, she had to refer them to some of the individuals who had bought them. But she was excited by the prospect of painting again.

Emily spent the entire summer at the *Ocean House,* located in the little village of Watch Hill, Rhode Island. The hotel had been built on a bluff overlooking the ocean during the Civil War. It was the last of the grand hotels to survive in Watch Hill. The others had been destroyed by fires or hurricanes decades before. The hotel opened each year in June and closed shortly after Labor Day. It filled each summer with an odd assortment of people, many of them wealthy, all of them with a penchant for nostalgia. Some were old enough to remember the *Ocean House* of their youth, with the black servants in tuxedos and white gloves. They returned to the *Ocean House* to remember an earlier, more elegant, time.

Emily chose a suite of rooms on the fourth floor that were decorated with an odd collection of Victorian and Edwardian antiques. A mahogany poster bed and a near-matching dresser, an oak bed in the smaller bedroom, and several tables, lowboys, and an uncomfortable sofa. The floor was covered with an old wool rug, now badly worn in the center. From her window Emily could, on a clear day, make out the faint outline of Block Island and Montauk Point. When she opened the windows, the room filled with the scent of salt-spray roses blooming on the dunes below and she could hear the distant rasp of the surf and see the beach grass rattling like sabers in the breeze.

Emily and Danielle were common sights on the dunes that summer. Emily immediately began photographing the plants on the dunes and in the salt marshes. Many were unfamiliar to her, so Emily went to the library for books to help identify the silverweed, marsh elders, and a dozen species of rushes and fleabanes. She brought her drawing pad with her and sat on a blanket on the dunes, sketching the plants from different angles.

Danielle loved the ocean, and though she was yet only three years old, she was remarkably strong. Emily knew that Danielle could never sit still with her while she sketched, so she allowed her to wander a short distance down the beach, but always within sight. Don't go near the water, Emily warned every morning as Danielle wandered down the beach to chase the sandpipers.

The only other person on the beach early in the morning was the *Ocean House* lifeguard, Jake. Jake didn't go on duty until nine o'clock, but he showed up every morning at eight and ran from the *Ocean House* to the Charlestown breachway. Jake had run in several Boston marathons and was perpetually in training. The first time he saw Danielle on the beach he stopped, wondering what a child would be doing all alone on the beach. He looked around and saw Emily on the dune. She waved to him and shouted that everything was 'okay,' so Jake continued his run. Every morning thereafter he would run by and wave to the two of them.

Danielle stopped playing whenever Jake ran by, then watched him until he was out of sight. Finally one day she shouted to him *What are you running away from?* Jake was on his return from the breachway, so he stopped to talk with her.

"I'm not running away from anything," Jake said, laughing. "I just like to run."

"Can I run with you?" Danielle asked.

Jake smiled at her.

"I don't know," he said. "You're kind of little."

But Danielle pleaded and begged, and Jake agreed to take her with him the next morning.

"Are you sure it's not too much trouble?" Emily asked.

"No, not at all," Jake said. He winked at Emily. "We probably won't go very far."

To his surprise, Danielle ran all the way to the breachway.

"You want to take a rest?" Jake asked as they approached the rocks.

"Why?" Danielle asked. "Are you tired?"

So they ran all the way back to the *Ocean House*. And every morning for the rest of the summer, Jake and Danielle ran to the Charlestown breachway and back. Danielle loved to run, and even on rainy mornings she pleaded with her mother to let her go down to the beach. At first she ran like a typical three year old, with short little steps and flailing arms. But Jake encouraged her to take longer strides and to loosen her arms, and she quickly picked up his style. She had incredible stamina for a child, and Jake marveled at the fact that she was barely winded after their half-hour runs.

Danielle took a nap every day in the late afternoon, curled up on the big mahogany bed, and then she and her mother went to the dining hall at 6:30. They had a table by the windows overlooking the ocean. Emily refused the high chair, preferring instead to kneel on her chair. At least twice a week, Mark or Pépé joined them for dinner, and afterward they walked down to shops on the main street and let Danielle ride the antique carousel. They kept up this routine for weeks, until it seemed natural, as if they had lived there all their lives. No one in this little village seemed to notice them.

Emily painted in the parlor of her hotel suite. Starting over was far more difficult than she had imagined. She experimented with her paints to produce the hues she wanted, but she was unable to find the right textures. The oil paints were too glossy and reflected too much light for the soft, muted tones of the plants that grew in the marshes and dunes. And the water was of a different consistency from that of the Adirondack ponds. Perhaps the salt refracted the water differently, she concluded, or the soft sandy bottom did not absorb the light like the leaf-strewn ponds of the Adirondacks. The techniques she had labored to develop, the tiny brush strokes, the layers of clear enamel to retain the deepened tones, now seemed inadequate in the blinding sunlight of the Atlantic coast.

Emily packed away her oil paints after several frustrating weeks and began to experiment with water colors. The delicate faded hues gave the impression of bright sunlight, although she found that shading was exceeding difficult to accomplish with

211

these anemic pigments. Still she painted every morning from before sunrise until a hungry little Danielle came padding into the parlor around eight o'clock. After only a few weeks she began to produce paintings of silverweed and pimpernel that were, she decided, not entirely embarrassing. And then several weeks later she concluded that they were terribly mediocre, and destroyed them.

"Hey, give yourself a little time," Mark said that night at dinner. "After all, this is a whole new medium for you."

Emily nodded in agreement, mostly to avoid a discussion about art, of which Mark knew only a few words. Medium. Texture. Strokes. It had surprised her that Mark hadn't acquired any real interest in art despite growing up in a gallery. He couldn't tell a Monet from a monad. But she enjoyed his company and his unique ability to discuss any subject without coming to an opinion uniquely his own.

"Who'd you find for a babysitter?" Mark asked, deliberately changing the subject.

"One of the waitresses," Emily said. "She gets off at nine."

"Great. Wanna go drinking?"

"And then go driving real fast on a winding road?" Emily said sarcastically.

"Either that or see a movie." Mark leaned over the table to whisper in Emily's ear. "Or we could go for a walk on the beach and do some sand wrestling."

"I'd rather crawl naked in a snake pit."

"Oh, God, the symbolism," he said, excitedly, still chewing his food. "I've got to get that thought out of my head or I won't be able to finish dinner."

The baby sitter was a waitress named Myra who had served Emily and Danielle breakfast and dinner every day since they had arrived at the *Ocean House*. She was a tall girl, younger than Emily, with long straight red hair and a broad freckled face. Guests at the hotel had reserved tables and consequently had the same waitress until they checked out. Myra was stricken with the beautiful Danielle. She brought her little treats from the kitchen, hard-boiled eggs, cupcakes, tapioca pudding, even things that could not be found on the menu, and lingered at

212

Danielle's table even when other customers were trying to get her attention. She had offered several times, sometimes almost pleading, to babysit if Emily needed a break, and was obviously thrilled when finally offered the opportunity.

Emily had wanted to put Danielle to bed before Myra arrived, but she decided that it would be cruel to deny the poor girl the company of her daughter. So Emily and Mark took Danielle for a walk to the old carousel near the beach and let her ride until it closed.

"She's a remarkable child," Mark said, watching her ride the horses. Danielle leaned over to grab the brass rings from the metal chute. "So easy-going. So untroubled. Does she ever ask about her father?"

"Not as often as you do," Emily said. They had discussed this before on several occasions, and it always annoyed her.

"I'm sorry," Mark said apologetically. "It's just that you look at her and have to wonder which one was her father. Doesn't it bother her, doesn't it bother *you*, not knowing?"

"What would it change, at this point?"

"You wouldn't feel different if you knew the father was Jack and not J.D.? Or vice-versa?"

"I didn't say that. I meant that it wouldn't change who Danielle *is*."

"Well, *of course* it wouldn't. I just meant that, well, if it was me, I'd want to know."

"Maybe I do"

"Really? You know?"

"Mark," Emily said, holding her hands up, "can we drop this subject? Danielle doesn't have a father. It's as simple as that. She received more DNA from lunch today than her father gave her, but that doesn't make lettuce or tuna her parent. Passing on DNA doesn't make you a father."

And so they never again spoke of Danielle's father.

Except once.

Early one morning in August, Myra came to the table at breakfast and whispered something in Emily's ear. Emily and Myra had become close friends over the summer. Myra had finally confided to Emily that she'd had an abortion two years

213

earlier, and that seeing Emily with Danielle filled her with an unspeakable longing. She often sat with them at breakfast if her other tables weren't busy. She joined them on the beach in the morning and took Danielle for walks to the carousel in the afternoon if Emily had errands to run. Myra handed Emily a supermarket tabloid and pointed to a title printed in the lower lefthand corner that said, **Adirondack Artist Knows Identity of Daughter's Dad.** Emily's face went pale. She leaned on the table and held her head in her hands.

"I just thought you should know about it," Myra said apologetically. "I don't read these papers, not very often, but I was getting some milk at the Stop 'n Shop and it was right there."

Emily's face suddenly flushed. She grabbed the paper and opened it to the article which, though typically vague, stated that Emily Davignon, the celebrated Adirondack artist and perhaps the most famous rape victim in the country, knew the identity of her daughter's father. The source was not, of course, disclosed. But Emily knew it had to have been Mark.

"That son of a bitch," Emily whispered. "And I *trusted* him."

Emily said nothing about the article for several days. No one in Watch Hill would ever say anything to her about it. They were too discreet. But the reporters started to call the hotel and then began to show up in town. Mr. Banker, the owner of the *Ocean House*, refused them access to the hotel. But one of them approached Emily early in the morning as she and Dani were walking on the beach. He must have been waiting for her back in the dunes, for all of a sudden he was there, beside her, on what had been moments before an empty stretch of sand. Leave me alone, will you? I have nothing to say. *Can you tell me why you can't disclose his identity?* I'm not going to tell you anything. *Why you need to keep it a secret?* It's none of your business. *Did J.D. Marten know you were pregnant when he killed Jack O'Neill?* My daughter is here, Emily said, pleading. You're asking me these questions in front of my daughter.

Emily started to walk faster, but the reporter kept up with her.

"What does it take to get rid of you?" Emily asked, frustrated.

The reporter would have continued to hound Emily if Jake had not appeared on the beach to start his morning run. Instead of jogging off down the beach, he stepped in front of the reporter and began shadow boxing. Left jabs, hooks, his feet dancing in the sand, always moving in front of the reporter.

"What are you *doing?*" the reporter finally said. But Jake did not answer until Emily was safely back at the *Ocean House*, at which point he stopped boxing and implored the reporter to 'have a nice day.'

The sanctity of the *Ocean House* was ruined, and Emily checked out of the hotel the following day. That morning they awoke before dawn and hiked several miles down the beach. Emily studied her daughter as she walked on the hard packed sand, her body held erect, her muscles already taut. The waves came up and splashed at her ankles, and though the water was frigid, Danielle did not flinch. The wind blew her thick hair back from her neck and caressed her finely muscled shoulders.

And Emily did not show the least sign of anger when Mark Welton called to have dinner with her the evening before. He joined her at the table in the *Ocean House* restaurant. They talked for almost a half-hour before Emily mentioned that a reporter had approached them on the beach that day and started asking questions about Danielle's father.

"Can you imagine? Coming right up to us on the beach?" Emily did not sound angry.

"What exactly did he want to know?"

"Just what you've always wanted to know, who Danielle's father is."

"Bastard. It's none of his business."

"Exactly. Of course, the fact that someone told the *Enquirer* that I knew the identity of Danielle's father probably piqued his interest."

"What are you talking about?"

"There was this little article in the *Enquirer* that said I knew who the father was. Where on earth would they *get* such an idea?"

215

"Don't look at me."

"But, Mark, *you* are the only one I have ever mentioned it to."

"Yeah, but I wouldn't tell any of your little secrets."

"That's what I thought. I always felt I could trust you in spite of your absolute lack of character. But then I got to thinking about how I met you in that creative writing class and I decided to call one of your friends from the fraternity. I won't say which one, and he's certainly not one of your best friends. To my surprise, he told me that you had been trying to think of a way to meet me for almost a year before that class. But I distinctly remember you saying that you didn't figure out who I was until after I told you about Danielle. So I figure that you've been lying all along and you'll continue to lie when I ask you how much the *Enquirer* paid you for that information."

Mark stopped chewing his food.

"Hey, lying is not one of my vices."

Emily had been calm and dispassionate up until this point. She did not want to create a scene in the *Ocean House*, whose patrons were rather elderly and probably prided themselves on self-control.

"You probably don't even know what the word means," she shouted. "You knew who I was and you wanted to get your parents to sell my paintings. Our whole relationship is a lie."

"Oh, don't be so high and mighty," Mark snapped. "I helped make you famous. Thanks to *me* you got a full page review in *Time* magazine. But left to your own devices you'd still be squirreled away in your grandfather's house with your paintings stored up in the attic."

"You tricked me."

"It was for your own good."

"Deceit is never 'good.'"

"Oh, c'mom, Emily," Mark said. "If I had said, 'Hi, my name's Mark Welton. My parents own an art gallery and would like to exhibit the artwork of the most famous rape victim in America,' do you really think I would have had a chance?"

"No, of course not."

"That's right. So I had to take a different approach, and

you're certainly not hurting because of it. Okay, so I mentioned to a reporter that you knew which of the two guys was the father and I made a few bucks out of the deal. I don't see what's the big deal. I never said *who* it was."

Emily's face reddened and the veins in her neck throbbed. She picked up a large handful of oily greens from her salad bowl and threw it at Mark.

"Jesus, Em," Mark said, wiping the salad off his pants. The salad dressing left stains on his pants. Emily picked up another handful of salad and threw it across the table.

"Christ almighty, Em! Get a grip, will ya?!" Mark shouted. He looked around the room and laughed nervously. Everyone in the *Ocean House* restaurant was staring at them. Even the waitresses had stopped serving. "C'mon, Emily," he said. "Let's just calm down."

"Mark, there isn't a creature in the forest that can stand the smell of a skunk."

"What the hell does *that* have to do with anything?" Mark said, brushing away bits of salad.

"Just leave," Emily said. "Just go away and leave me alone."

Mark opened his mouth to say something, then stopped. Then he tossed his napkin onto the chair and walked out.

Mark Welton was still mulling the skunk analogy as he walked through the lobby of the hotel and onto the veranda. *What the hell did she mean by that? She sells a few paintings and now she talks like she's Mother Earth.* Moments later he would come to understand Emily's choice of metaphor. But while yet on the *Ocean House* porch, where the air smelled of salt spray and freshly mowed grass, Mark was simply unaware that Jake had carried a dead skunk wrapped in a plastic bag and placed it in the backseat of Mark's unlocked Volkswagen.

Chapter Twenty-Three

The manhunt for John David Marten never officially ended back in 1971, now seven years past, but the roadblocks gradually disappeared and the search parties stopped forming at the edge of town. For awhile, a holdup at the IGA store on Route 28 captured everyone's attention, and when they returned to the subject of John David Marten it was with considerably less fervor. The entire search had been anticlimactic. Maybe someday he'd be picked up on a street in Buffalo or in a bus station in Utica. That's how these things were usually resolved, if they ever were resolved. He was probably living somewhere far away under a new name, and if he stayed out of trouble, if he were never again fingerprinted, he could avoid the police for the rest of his life.

John David Marten fascinated the tourists who drove to Henoga Valley from downstate. They were less repulsed by the murder of Jack O'Neill than local residents because they didn't know the victim. The murder had philosophical quality to it, like the debate over capital punishment. John David Marten had killed a rapist. He had taken it upon himself to deliver the sentence of death to his best friend for a crime committed against a defenseless woman. He had acted on principles, however primitive. It was the feral nature of the act, one young man killing another on the edge of civilization, that fascinated people. This murder, this revenge, was nature at its purest.

Although the store owners in Henoga Valley would never have admitted it, many of them hoped that John David Marten would never be found. He was the best thing that ever happened to Henoga Valley. Commercial survival in the Adirondacks had always been tenuous if you weren't located in one of the bigger towns, like Lake Placid or Saranac Lake. Stores in Henoga Valley had come and gone on a regular basis until the summer of 1971, when they suddenly made unimaginable profits. The Tahawus Hotel, hardly more than a brothel for thirty years, briefly had legitimate customers that summer, even if they were just reporters looking for a place to stay. But as the summer turned to fall and the manhunt fizzled, the prospects for the tourist business coming back the next year started to fade. Business leaders debated what it would take to bring them back. The summer of 1972 confirmed their fears as business dropped off by seventy percent. But the publication of Sawyer's book in the spring of 1973 presented a second chance, and no one, it seems, overlooked it. T shirts with *An Adirondack Life* appeared in all of the stores. Then more shirts, with *Adirondack Lives* and *An Adirondack Lifer*, the latter showing a man behind bars made of pine boughs. Barkeater hats, with a visor made of birch bark laminated over cork, were so popular that no one could keep up with the demand.

Sawyer's book had another, somewhat unexpected effect. It spawned the rumor that John David Marten lived in the forests beyond Henoga Valley. Over the next few years the number of J.D. Marten sightings grew until it seemed that just about everyone had spotted him. Young children, who often played in the woods near their houses, reported seeing him on a regular basis. The more cynical of the townsfolk thought that the rumors were propagated by the store owners, for Marten was still the town's only real tourist attraction. *You're entering J.D. Marten Country*, a sign said on the outskirts of the village. *Come back often.*

Not everyone in Henoga Valley was proud of the notoriety. The whole J.D. Marten business had a tawdry air about it, some people complained. J.D. Marten was a murderer and should not be a role model for our children. What message were they taking from this affair? The Town Board listened to their complaints and nodded in agreement, but nothing ever came of it.

The publication of *An Adirondack Life* devastated the O'Neill family. Sawyer could not have made J.D. Marten into an Adirondack legend without vilifying Jack O'Neill. The more Henoga Valley depended on J.D. Marten, the more despicable it made Jack. Most of Jack's friends from high school had graduated and were no longer around to defend his reputation. The O'Neills and the Martens, after living next door for more than twenty years, no longer felt comfortable even noticing one another. And then one day a moving van pulled up in front of the O'Neill house. Diana Marten was shocked. There hadn't even been a *For Sale* sign in front. She ran next door to ask Peggy where they were going, but the only ones there were the movers. The O'Neills had left in the middle of the night, saying goodbye to no one. Diana later discovered that they had moved to Florida, and although she got their forwarding address from the Post Office and wrote them several long letters, she never heard from them again.

It was nearly seven years after Jack's death that the murder weapon finally turned up. Sheriff Cooney was driving through Henoga Valley with Deputy Therrien on his way to a drug prevention talk at the high school in April of 1978. He hated giving these talks. The kids wouldn't listen to a fat old man telling them that drugs were dangerous. He knew they were laughing at him. These were the same kids who went out to the swimming hole on the Raquette River and jumped out of a tree thirty feet up. They weren't afraid of danger. Cooney was toying with the idea of maybe just telling them, sure, drugs make you feel wonderful, but then you wake up and realize that ten years of your life have gone by and you thought it had been just a really cool party. But some of the parents would hear it the wrong way. They would hear the part where the sheriff said 'drugs make you feel wonderful' and he'd get fifty phone calls. So he decided to stick to the same old message.

Deputy Therrien turned the car down the road by the school. Cooney checked his watch and saw that they were twenty minutes early. The ladies in the school cafeteria would give him a cup of coffee. As they neared the park where Jack O'Neill was killed, the sheriff looked out the window. He could see the park bench near where the body had been found. Poor sonofabitch, Cooney thought, the kid's body lying there on the bench. Knife wound in the chest. But other than that, hardly a mark on the boy.

Sheriff Cooney heard the sound of a chain saw. He looked beyond the bench to an old sugar maple. A storm the night before had taken down a huge branch that made up half the tree, leaving the other half in an awkward arc. They'll probably take

221

the whole tree down now, Cooney thought. Just as well. The tree was in pretty bad shape.

The tree had been damaged in another storm many years ago that left a gaping hole in the middle of it, eight or so feet above the ground. New branches had sprouted from the old wound and made up the two halves of the tree. The wound grew over, but a large hole had remained in the middle. Kids would drag the park bench over to the tree and climb up to sit in the crotch of the tree. He remembered more than one occasion having to send over a deputy because some kid got his leg stuck in that hole. The vision of a small child stuck in the crotch of the tree sparked a revelation.

"Stop the car!" Cooney shouted.

Therrien pulled over to the curb and Cooney got out and walked over to the tree. A man with a chain saw was already cutting up the huge limb on the ground. He saw the sheriff coming and turned off the saw.

"The hollow tree!" the sheriff said. "Why the hell didn't I think of it? He could have dropped the knife in the hollow tree."

"Who?" Therrien asked. "What are we talking about?"

"Marten. We couldn't find the knife in the river because he never threw it in the river." Cooney was standing in front of the park bench. The man with the chain saw came over to listen. "He stabs O'Neill right here," Cooney said, acting out the murder. "Then he walks fifteen feet over to the tree, reaches up, and drops the knife into the hole." Cooney looked at the man with the chain saw. "You taking the whole tree down?" he asked. The man nodded. Cooney pointed to the trunk. "Mind starting right here?"

The man made several cuts into the standing truck. The wood inside was gray and weathered, and stuffed with leaves that had been collecting over the years. But the knife was there, perfectly intact, its stainless steel blade no worse for the wear. Cooney removed it carefully, thinking that perhaps there might still be fingerprints, or even blood, somewhere on it. Therrien went back to the car for a plastic bag.

"Very smart, J.D.," Cooney intoned as he dropped the knife into the plastic bag. "Very, very clever."

Sheriff Cooney had grown fond of J.D. Marten over the years and often spoke to him in this manner. He had never known the kid personally. Marten was now in his mid-twenties, and Sheriff Cooney couldn't be certain that he would be able to recognize him if they passed each other on the street. He had come to admire Marten's style. It was difficult now after seven years to distinguish between myth and reality, but the manhunt had taught him that, out there in the woods, J.D. Marten was in his element. The way that he neutralized the bloodhounds was brilliant. Marten understood exactly what the dogs would do and then used it to his advantage. He did the same thing with the men who tracked him. He knew they'd circle something obvious, as if one angle was better than the other, and in doing so they would step into a more concealed trap. Cooney might have felt less admiration for J.D. Marten had the sheriff not survived the failed manhunt with his reputation intact. But everyone believed that it wasn't a matter of Cooney or the State Police being incompetent. The vastness of the Adirondack wilderness simply favored J.D. Marten. They wanted to believe that no one could have found him. And Cooney had been reelected by a large margin.

Cooney studied the knife in his office later that day. The cheap imitation of a Buck folding knife was the first solid piece of evidence in seven years. He held it in his hand and turned it over, studying it from every angle. If only it could tell what it knew. But the knife had yielded little evidence. There were no fingerprints and no blood, both of them presumably washed away by the rain and snow that had fallen into the hollow tree trunk over the years. But the shape of the blade clearly matched the description from the autopsy report, and that would be important in court.

In court. Cooney chuckled to himself. Like he'd ever see J.D. Marten in court. Maybe they'd get lucky someday and Marten would get pulled over for a broken tail light in Boise or Bozeman. The cop would run a check on him, maybe print him and bingo, everything would fall into place. It was all up to luck now.

Cooney dropped the knife back into the plastic bag and

drove off to The Backpacker, a small general store that supplied most of the hunting gear in the village. He had known the owner, Joe Phelps, for years. Joe had an encyclopedic knowledge of hunting and camping gear. He claimed to know every fishing reel and every rifle ever made. He said you could tell a lot about a man by the equipment he carried into the woods. Phelps was attending a customer when Cooney walked in, but he waved to the sheriff. Cooney walked over to the case of knives. Phelps had more than two dozen of them, ranging in price from a few bucks to fifty bucks. The sheriff was leaning on the glass counter studying them when Joe finally came up and slapped him on the back.

"Take one," Joe said. "On the house."

Cooney laughed. Everybody knew Joe Phelps was tighter than a dog's ass. He hadn't had a sale in twenty years, but you had to admire his sense of humor.

"Relax, Joe. I'm not looking for a handout." Cooney pulled the knife in the plastic bag out of his pocket. "You ever see one of these?"

"Yeah, I used to sell them. Not back here. Up at the front counter. They aren't real knives, if you know what I mean."

"Do you still have any?" the sheriff asked.

"Maybe in a box somewhere," Joe said, shaking his head. "I don't sell them anymore. They were too cheap. People kept bringing them back. Look, it's got a stainless steel blade. You can't even sharpen it."

Joe looked at the sheriff, who was once again studying the knife.

"Why are you interested in a cheap knife?" Joe asked.

"Because it was used to kill Jack O'Neill seven years ago."

"No kidding!" Joe said. "Where did you find it?"

Sheriff Cooney explained cutting down the tree and finding the knife a few feet from the murder scene.

"Did you sell one of these to J.D. Marten?" Cooney asked

"*John David?!* Not likely. John David was very particular about his equipment. He wouldn't have touched a knife like that. I sold him a .22 Marlin once. He must have been 11 or 12 at the time, but he knew everything about the gun before he walked in the store. I had to order the one that he wanted." Joe emphasized his point by jabbing his finger against the glass case.

"Maybe he bought the knife just for the purpose of killing Jack O'Neill. You don't need a forty-dollar knife to kill someone."

"Maybe," Joe said, shrugging his shoulders. "But *I* didn't sell it to him. Believe me, I'd have remembered John David buying a cheap knife."

"Could anybody else have sold it to him?" the sheriff asked.

"Well, you can ask around," Joe said. "It would have to have been Mrs. Wright or Larry Powles. But, by Jesus, don't expect them to remember something that happened seven years ago. I doubt either one of them could remember what they had for breakfast."

The sheriff nevertheless questioned the two employees. Mrs. Wright didn't seem to understand his question. She thought the sheriff was asking about kitchen knives. Larry Powles rambled on for three or four minutes about everything he had sold during the past two weeks, but the sheriff noticed Joe Phelps standing behind Larry and tapping his own temple and circling his ear with his pointer finger. Even if they claimed to have sold John David a knife, they were not what you'd call credible witnesses.

"What about receipts?" Cooney asked Phelps. "Don't you have copies of those little handwritten receipts that you give?"

"I do," Joe said. "But if the customer paid cash, it wouldn't have any name on it. I just write 'cash.' What good would a receipt made out to 'cash' be?"

"Is it possible that someone else in town sells these knives?" Cooney asked.

"I'm sure. The Agway, probably."

Later that evening, sitting in his recliner and drinking a bottle of beer, Cooney thought how much easier this would have been if he weren't asking about a knife seven years after the murder. Knives in these parts of the Adirondacks are as common as dinnerware. No one was going to remember anything about a particular knife after seven years.

Quite suddenly a wave of panic overcame the sheriff. He

225

jumped out of the chair and began pacing around the room. What if the knife *didn't* belong to John David, he thought? What if he didn't even commit the murder? What if he just wanted to make it look like he did? The sheriff began pacing faster and swearing to himself. His wife heard him from the kitchen and came out to see what was going on. She recognized the pacing. It meant he was going over the details of a case and shouldn't be disturbed. She turned around without saying a word and went back into the kitchen.

Sheriff Cooney was angry with himself and his face turned red. He didn't say aloud what he was thinking, just the swear words. Swearing released pressure from his brain, so about every fifteen seconds another 'shit' or 'god dammit' would escape from his lips. Neither the sheriff nor the State Police had ever considered looking for another suspect. The manhunt and the investigation had centered around this one kid because John David had all but issued a confession by running away. Why else would he have run off like that without even saying goodbye to his family? People would have thought the sheriff was nuts if he had been looking for other suspects instead of chasing John David. But now, seven years later, the sheriff was struck by the possibility that John David had run off to divert the attention from the real killer. And the only person he could possibly be covering up for was Emily Davignon.

Whatever the circumstances might have been back then, John David would probably have had to act quickly. If Emily had killed Jack and John David had realized there was nothing he could do to save him, he might have told Emily to go home while he ran off into the woods. As long as John David was never found, he would remain the only suspect and Emily would be off the hook.

Sheriff Cooney knew from experience that it was possible to conjure up a hundred different scenarios in a criminal case. He had to be careful not to let his imagination get the better of his judgement. The only thing that really mattered was the evidence. The problem was that he was asking these questions seven years too late. It was going to be hard to piece the story together now. If he started asking around about where Emily was that night, pretty soon everyone would know that he thought she was a suspect. They would probably think the sheriff was just trying to generate a little publicity for himself.

Sheriff Cooney set up an appointment with Dr. Emerson to review the autopsy of Jack O'Neill. He was careful to tell Dr. Emerson's secretary that this was a routine procedure, that he was just tying up loose ends. He didn't want the secretary telling everyone that something was going on with the old J.D. Marten case.

"This *is* a surprise," Dr. Emerson said, entering the office with a thick chart in his hand. Cooney had been waiting for him and he started to get up from his chair. Dr. Emerson waved for him to sit back down.

"I just wanted to ask you some more questions," Cooney said, "about things I may have overlooked the first time around."

Dr. Emerson sat behind his large oak desk and opened the file. It had been a long time since he had looked at the file. Being a criminal case, the file was filled with grisly photographs of the body and the wounds. Dr. Emerson opened the large manilla envelope and started leafing through the 8" by 10" color glossies.

"I'm sure you'll recall, Sheriff, that the knife wound was immediately fatal," Dr. Emerson said. He handed Cooney a photo showing the upper half of Jack's body. The photo had been taken with the body on the gurney in the morgue. The skin was an ashen gray, a sickly color, devoid of its vital humors, except the single laceration, which still appeared bright red. "The wound could not have been worse if it had struck the heart directly, which, by the way, it did not. People sometimes survive knife wounds to the heart, *if* the knife is left in until they get to the hospital. The knife itself prevents some of the blood from escaping. But the knife actually missed the heart and severed the aorta. He died instantaneously. It's quite possible that he never even knew what happened."

"Isn't it odd that he didn't show any signs of struggle?" Cooney said.

"Yes, it is. But I thought we went over that point. He was probably killed by someone he knew. Or someone snuck up on

227

him and he never saw it coming, which is unusual if the victim is awake."

"Just for the sake of discussion, what would we have seen if he had tried to defend himself?"

Dr. Emerson leaned over and showed Cooney photographs of Jack's arms and fists. "Something here, I would guess," the doctor said. "Bruises on the arms, some lacerations. Abrasions on the knuckles where he struck his attacker. Jack was a good athlete. He would have put up a terrific struggle if he had seen it coming."

"So you can't find anything out of the ordinary," Cooney asked. "Nothing to suggest he tried to fight back."

"No, not that I recall," Dr. Emerson said, looking down at the photos. He continued to shift through them, then seemed to notice something. He put the photos down and picked up the written autopsy report. "Well, I take that back. There was one thing that was odd." He slid a photo of Jack's face over to the sheriff. "There was a mild abrasion on his face. No cuts, just a contusion."

The sheriff stared at the photo but couldn't find what the doctor was describing.

"That's the problem with photos," Dr. Emerson said. "That's why we take notes." He found the passage where he had dictated a description of the abrasion. "A large contusion on the left cheek, measuring five inches by seven inches and suggestive of a hand print."

The sheriff held up his own hand to estimates its size.

"That's a pretty big hand," Cooney said.

"Yes, I suppose. Does it surprise you?"

"No, I suppose not," Cooney said. "But if John David slapped Jack before he stabbed him, how could Jack have been surprised? How could he have been stabbed without putting up a fight?"

Dr. Emerson was still looking at the picture.

"I hadn't given it much thought," he said. "To be honest, I never even looked at this report after I wrote it. It never went to the DA, I suppose because we didn't have a suspect in custody."

"Let me ask you this, doctor. Do you think that maybe John David didn't kill Jack?"

Dr. Emerson looked surprised. For a moment he did not answer.

"I don't know how to answer that, Sheriff," he said finally. "I'm not a forensic pathologist, I just serve as the county coroner because I have a medical license. There are people who are trained to do this sort of work, who can answer those kinds of questions."

"Do you think they can answer these questions now, seven years after the fact?"

"I really don't know. But I assure you, I wasn't trying to hide anything." Dr. Emerson was visibly nervous.

"Don't worry, Doc. I don't think anyone bungled the case. I'm just wondering if we weren't led astray on purpose."

Cooney removed the knife from his coat pocket and opened the blade to show the doctor. He explained where he had discovered it.

"The blade looks like a perfect fit," Dr. Emerson said. "I won't be able to say for sure until I do the precise measurements, but that's certainly close."

"The problem is that John David never bought cheap equipment like this knife. He left Emily Davignon's house around four o'clock and the murder occurred around midnight. If he didn't already own a knife like this one, he would have had to buy one. And the stores all closed at five. He would have had no more than forty-five minutes to buy a knife."

"Seems like plenty of time," the doctor said, obviously confused.

"Not really. He would have had to buy it at either The Backpacker or the Agway just before five o'clock. Joe Phelps says he's sure John David didn't buy it there and the Agway closed that day at noon for inventory."

"You don't think he could have bought it days before?" Dr. Emerson asked.

"Could have," Cooney said, "but then it would have had to have been premeditated. John David didn't even know about the rape until four o'clock that afternoon. It doesn't add up."

229

Dr. Emerson scratched his forehead.

"Well, *I'm* baffled," he said. "You can see why I'm not a detective." The doctor was a busy man and he was about to conclude that there was little more he could do to help the sheriff. He rose and extended his hand to the sheriff. "Now, if you'll excuse me," he said. "I still have to make rounds. But feel free to review the file and I'll tell my secretary to make copies of anything you need."

Dr. Emerson headed for the door, but Cooney's voice followed him.

"You wouldn't happen to remember where Dr. Davignon was that night, would you?"

"Well, yes. He was here at the hospital," the doctor said. "We take turns on call. It was his night."

"Did he have to *be* here?"

"No, he didn't have to, but he usually came in on his night. But he just had to be in phone contact."

But the hospital records Cooney later reviewed showed that Dr. Davignon had reported to work at seven o'clock that evening and had not signed himself out until the next morning.

Chapter Twenty-Four

It was at the age of ten that Danielle Davignon first expressed a desire to play Little League baseball. Danielle, or Dani, as she now insisted on being called, was eating breakfast with her mother and Pépé. It was Pépé who verbalized the request. Emily looked up from her coffee and eyed first Dani, then her grandfather. She knew that Pépé had been practicing with Dani in the backyard, and had lately been taking her over to the baseball field and throwing batting practice to her off the mound, which was no small feat for a man of 74. Dani stared into her bowl of Fruit Loops, a treat allowed only on Saturday mornings, and waited for her mother's response.

Emily was not fond of sports. She had never agreed with Dr. Haney and imputed organized sports of cultivating aggression in boys. Sports are the remnants of warrior societies, she argued with her grandfather, symbolic of death and dying on the battlefield. They prepare men for war. Boys crashing into each other on the hockey rink or the football field, or legally attempting to kill one another in the boxing ring. The goal was always to crush the enemy, to *humiliate* them. Dani had heard these arguments but did not understand a word of it. Death and dying? How could the one thing that made her feel alive represent death? There were times, sitting in a classroom on a hot afternoon, or in church on Sunday, that Dani was overcome with the urge to free herself from stockings and suede pumps, of her cotton dress and even her slip, and run down the street and onto the park trails. Run like a deer, jumping over low- lying branches and up onto boulders, to scout the terrain like a lynx, and dive into a pool of water and swim like an otter, diving deep until her lungs ached. She loved the feel of a baseball glove on her hand, loved the smell of oil rubbed lovingly into the leather until it was so supple that it became an extension of her own flesh. She loved to dive into the dirt to grab a line drive, like a cat pouncing on a field mouse.

Emily took a sip of coffee and glanced at the two of them. She knew they had planned this together, perhaps discussing it for hours. Dani liked to watch baseball games sitting on her great-grandfather's lap, although she was now too big to sit on the old man for more than a few minutes. She knew how the game was played, the nuances of pitching high and inside or low and away. She knew batting averages, pitching records, the standing of each team in the National and American Leagues. How long had the two of them discussed this, Emily wondered? What argument had they concocted?

"Baseball?" Emily said. "Why *baseball?*"

It was, of course, a rhetorical question. Dani looked at her mother and tried to think of a reply.

"Why baseball?" Pépé intoned. "Why Honus Wagner? Why Babe Ruth and Lou Gehrig? Why DiMaggio and Ted Williams? If it hadn't been for baseball, they would have been bartenders and insurance agents."

"They were all baseball players, I assume," Emily said.

"*Mom! Yes!*" Dani said, horrified. They were the founding fathers and their descendants, as important in their own way as Washington and Lincoln. How could her mother not know who they were?

Emily, in fact, only pretended not to recognize the names. She studied her daughter, who was sitting with her elbows propped on the table, chewing a large mouthful of cereal. After a moment, Emily nodded her agreement.

Dani bounded out of her chair and high-fived Pépé, then went around the side of the table to hug her mother.

"Thanks, Mom. Really, it'll be cool."

"Oh yes, I'm sure." Emily said, her voice lacking enthusiasm.

"She's really very good," Pépé added.

"Good?" Dani said, stopping to question her great-grandfather's assessment.

"All right, *outstanding.*"

"When are tryouts?" Emily asked.

"About forty-five minutes from now." Dani said. She had already run off to her room to get her glove. "Don't worry, Pépé will take me," she yelled from down the hall.

Emily looked at her grandfather.

"*Baseball*," she said, with an air of amused disgust.

Dani strode across the Fox Point Little League field to a group of men and boys sitting on a set of wooden bleachers. An older man with a clipboard in his hand was writing down the names of the boys and another man in a cheap blue windbreaker was handing out registration cards. Dani walked up to the man and, after waiting patiently for several minutes, stuck out her hand for one of the cards. The old man looked at her kindly.

"Hey, there missy, softball sign-ups were *yesterday*."

"I don't want to play *softball*," Dani said. "I want to play baseball."

Several of the boys snickered. Some of them laughed aloud. There had only been one girl in the history of the Fox Point Little League, and she hadn't lasted the whole season. Every time she came to bat the first pitch came in high and inside and the poor thing thought someone was trying to take her face off. Her parents had complained, but they were told that throwing a baseball isn't a science, kid's lose control from time to time, someone gets hit by a pitch every game. It's part of the game, they were told.

The old man with the clipboard had been through this before. He had daughters of his own, now grown up with daughters of *their* own. He looked down at Dani and touched the side of her face gently.

"Sure you can play," he said. "But are you sure you *want* to play with this ugly bunch of brutes."

"They're not so ugly," Dani said, looking them over. "A couple of them aren't half-bad looking." A chorus of 'oohs' went up in the crowd and several of the boys slapped each other on the arm.

The kids lined up in two straight lines, one at shortstop and the other at second base. They took ground balls from two of the younger coaches, and each kid was supposed to stay at the front of the line fielding balls until they missed one. Then they went to the back of the line and waited for their turn. Dani was eighth in her line. She had started out in third place, but five boys butted in front of her. The coaches hit the first ball right at the kid, then successive balls became more difficult to catch. None

233

of the boys in front of Dani was able to catch more than three, although one of the kids in the other line caught five. Dani easily caught the first four balls, including one that she had to backhand. Then all eyes were on her, and the other coach stopped hitting to his line of boys.

The coach hit a hard one-hop to Dani's left, which she blocked with her body. Then he hit two more to her right. The last one almost got past her, but Dani made a diving catch. Then he drove a hard line drive directly at her, purposely trying to intimidate her. Dani nonchalantly caught it with one hand and gave him a melodramatic look of boredom.

"*Two* hands, Dani," Pépé yelled from the stands. "Don't get ..."

He stopped before shouting 'cocky' because his instincts told him that he might get an unwanted reaction from the boys. After several more hard grounders, the coach hit a high fly ball to centerfield in a tacit admission that he couldn't get a ball past her on the ground. But Dani took off on a dead run and caught that one over her shoulder.

"She ain't half-bad," the old man said, laughing.

Dani was the third pick by the Tigers and joined a group of boys who had already played together for three years. Most of the other kids were from the Italian neighborhood of Federal Hill or Portuguese neighborhood of Fox Point, but the catcher was a black kid named Chris Tubb. Chris was a big kid, and in spite of the undeniable racial tension, nobody picked on 'Tubby.'

The kids appeared to tolerate having Dani on their team, even though they paid very little attention to her. She even heard some of them say, when they didn't realize she was nearby, that she wouldn't last long in the league anyway.

"I can't believe we got a *girl* on our team," Vince Antonucci said in the dugout just before the start of the opening game. He was twelve years old and played first base. He hadn't said anything about Dani playing with them throughout spring practice, but a friend of his on the other team had made a kissy face during the national anthem, and that really pissed him off. Vince took baseball seriously. He was going to play for the Red

Sox some day. And this girly stuff just for the sake of equality made him feel like nobody else took it as seriously as he did.

"Don't let him get to you," Tubby said. "He said the same thing last year about having a *black* kid on the team."

But Dani *did* take him seriously. Vince was the teammate she wanted most to impress. He had initiated the ritual of slapping gloves as a way of congratulating each other at the end of an inning. He always ignored Dani's glove, in spite of the fact that over the first six games she had fielded 23 ground balls without an error. On one occasion a grounder was hit hard back to the pitcher. The ball careened off his shin and rolled halfway to first base. Dani reached it before the pitcher could recover, but there was no time for her to turn and throw the runner out. So she picked up the ball and in one seamless motion fired it behind her back to Vince. They got the runner out by half a step. The crowd was so thrilled that they pounded the bleachers with their feet. Vince and Dani stared at each other for a moment, expressionless. Dani did not beg for approval, and Vince did not offer it. Embarrassed, Dani turned and jogged back to her position.

Dani had not looked forward to playing against the Cubs because their pitcher was a tall lanky kid by the name of Joaquim LaPorta. Everyone called him Wacko. Wacko had bragged that there wouldn't be any more girls in the Fox Point league after the Tigers played the Cubs. Each time Dani came to bat Wacko threw the first pitch right at her. Pépé had warned her not to cry even if she got hit. She *was* hit by a pitch in the second inning. The ball was thrown hard and Dani spun away, taking it in the middle of her back. She tried not to cry as she trotted down to first base. But a double to right field by Tubby scored Dani, and that turned out to be the only run of the game.

Dani's back was still sore when she was called in to pitch in the bottom of the sixth inning. Dani was only the fourth best pitcher on the team, but the coach was saving his other pitchers for a game two days later against the best team in the league. Dani got the first two batters out on grounders. Then Wacko came to bat. Dani called time out and waved Tubby and Vince to the mound. The third basemen, the shortstop and the second basemen also came because they didn't want to be left out. Dani included them in the conference, but she really only needed the two biggest kids on the team.

"I'm going to throw the first pitch at his ear," Dani whispered. Vince nodded in agreement. Retaliation was important in baseball. He respected Dani for that. "He won't charge the mound, 'cause he knows I owe him one. He'll be expecting it, and he'll get out of the way. But then I'm going to throw a second one at him, and a third, if I have to."

"Jesus, Dani," Vince said, "he'll go nuts. We don't call him Wacko for nothing."

"That's why I need you guys. You have to cut him off before he gets to me."

Dani's first pitch came in high and inside and Wacko just leaned back a little to get out of the way. He had expected the brushback and he laughed. But Wacko obviously didn't expect a second beanball, because he had to drop flat on his back in the middle of his swing to avoid getting clocked. Wacko got up and brushed the dirt off his butt.

"You missed a little," Dani said. Wacko spit toward the mound.

Dani threw another pitch at Wacko's face and once again he had to buckle at the knees to get out of the way. This time he jumped to his feet and bolted toward the mound. But Vince was already blocking his path and Tubby was right behind him. Wacko paused for a moment and by then the home plate umpire caught up to them and told everyone to 'calm down and play baseball or I'm going to call the game right now and don't think I can't do it cause I can.'

"I'll show Wacko back to the plate, sir," Tubby said. He grabbed Wacko by the arm to lead him, but Wacko yanked his arm away.

"If she throws another beanball at me I'm going to throw the bat at her," he said.

"But then I would have to kick your face in," Vince said calmly, "and I don't want to get blood on my new cleats."

The umpire told them all to shut up and play ball. On the way back to the plate, Tubby said to Wacko, "I tried to talk her out of it, you know. But she got really pissed when you hit her back there in the second. She said she doesn't care if you get on base. She just wants to hit you back. Hey, did I tell you her father killed someone once? He did it with a rock or something."

Emily sat in the stands with her grandfather and watched her daughter play baseball. It was obvious, even from a distance, how much Dani loved the game. When she was playing second base, she spit on the ground before each pitch, like a wild animal marking her territory. This is my den and this is my litter. Don't even think of touching them. But she was pitching now, the lioness on the hunt.

Emily hadn't attended Little League games when she was a child. Girls weren't allowed to play in those days and she didn't have any brothers. But she had seen Jack O'Neill and John David Marten play in high school. She remembered the game Henoga Valley played against Wells for the sectional championship back in her senior year of high school. Everyone had gone to the game, which had been played over in the neutral field of North Creek so that neither team had an advantage. Even if you didn't follow baseball, and Emily certainly counted herself in that group, you couldn't help but get caught up in the excitement of the day. They had all but canceled classes because everyone was too excited to even think about schoolwork. Busloads of students poured out onto the parking lot in North Creek. Cars parked all over the school grounds and lining the roads. The crowd was so large that Emily and Jennifer Baker had to climb up on the roof of a storage shed just to see the field.

Emily hadn't recognized any of the Henoga Valley players. They looked so much older in their clean gray and maroon cotton uniforms and their neat caps pulled low over their brows. They seemed to glide across the field as they ran to their positions. They threw the ball to one another with such agility that the catching and throwing appeared to be a single fluid motion. Who were these boys, she thought? Certainly not the awkward guys she saw every day in the halls of Henoga Valley High School. Was that Chris Miller on second base? Chris Miller, who sat next to her in social studies and picked his nose

237

all through the tenth grade regents exam, rolling his boogers into little balls and flicking them subconsciously onto the floor. Was it the *same* Chris Miller, now at second base catching practice grounders and flicking them to first base? Emily remembered the sudden wave of fear that overcame her when the first Wells batter drove Jack O'Neill's second pitch deep to centerfield, and then the relief she felt, and the embarrassment for feeling relieved, when John David Marten jogged twenty yards to his left and caught the ball with one hand. She remembered how John David ran a few more steps after he caught the ball, as if he were a large truck that had to decelerate slowly, when in fact it was just to show the other team how casual the play was. Then he turned and threw the ball in a long arc to the second baseman and jogged with his head down back to his position. Emily marveled at the simple beauty of the game, the fact that someone could judge the flight path of a small round object and snag it out of the air.

Emily was still in this nostalgic stupor when Dani threw a low and inside pitch to Wacko LaPorta got him to pop up to Vince. She heard the crowd yell and saw the players converge on the mound, and her first thought was that Dani had been injured. Had Dani been struck by the ball? That didn't seem possible, because two of the bigger boys, the first baseman and the catcher, had hoisted her on their shoulders and were carrying her off the field. And Dani was making an awful spectacle of herself by waving her glove wildly and hooting at the top of her lungs.

Chapter Twenty-Five

It was later that same summer of 1982 that Emily and Danielle piled suitcases and sleeping bags, a three-man tent and all of Emily's art supplies into the back of Emily's brand new Ford Bronco and drove up to Henoga Valley. When Emily first mentioned coming up for a visit, Julia could not believe what she had heard and asked her daughter to repeat it. Emily had not been back to Henoga Valley since she left for college more than a decade earlier. Julia had stopped inviting Emily to come back and visit because she always had an excuse not to come. It had become an embarrassment to both of them. And then Emily simply mentioned it over the phone, that she wanted to bring Dani up for a month in the summer, and Pépé, too, if she could get him to go.

The three of them left early on a Saturday morning after Dani's last baseball game. It was the fourth of July weekend and they were afraid of the traffic, so they left Providence at five in the morning with Dani asleep in the back seat. Emily was afraid to let Pépé drive. He was getting too old, so she drove the whole way. They took the Massachusetts Turnpike to the Northway, then got off and followed Route 28 up into the Adirondacks. Dani woke up as they got off the highway and insisted on rolling down all the windows so that the car filled with the cool mountain air, fragrant with the scent of black spruce and pine needles. She bounced from side to side in the back seat like a young puppy. The trees, the rivers, and the mountains were so magnificent to Dani, who was accustomed to the flat and rather expressionless Rhode Island. When Emily pulled off the road at a rest stop, Dani bounded out of the car and ran down to the shallow, boulder-strewn river. Within seconds she had her sneakers off and was wading in the icy waters.

As they drove deeper and deeper into the mountains, Dani became even more excited. She couldn't wait to see her grandparents' house and play in the pond out back. She had heard about the pond, how it was cut off from the lake only 30 yards away, like an offspring, and had now grown up to be so different. The glacial Raquette Lake was carved out of rock, deep and cold and crystal clear. The pond was shallow and muddy, warm, reedy, and teeming with life. And so much more interesting to the young Emily Davignon, as it would be to her daughter.

At first the ride seemed like so much fun, a summer outing to the mountains to get away from the city. But as they drove deeper into the mountains, Emily became increasingly anxious. The sight of the rocky cliffs and the black spruce made her pulse quicken. The blood vessels pounded in her ears and her hands became so sweaty that she repeatedly had to wipe them on her jeans. The roads seemed too narrow, so that cars in the other lane appeared to be coming right at her. Several times she had to yank the steering wheel over to avoid someone in the middle of the road, and she could hear the awful rumble of the tires on the gravel shoulders. The wind that had seemed so refreshing suddenly turned cold. It blasted through the open windows and stung her face. Emily wanted to roll up her window but dared not hold the steering wheel with just one hand lest the wind grab the car at that moment and dash it against the rocks. She knew this mountain wind and how full it was of prankish spirits.

But Dani did not hear the spirits. Or she heard only their playful laughter and mistook it for the innocence of other children. The wind played with her hair, blowing in all around her face. Dani leaned her head out the window to breathe in the air in huge gulps, unable to fill her lungs quite enough. She pointed out the birch trees growing on rock ledges and drowned lands with blue black water. Oh, thanks, Mom, she said, over and over from the back seat of the Bronco. Thank you for taking us up here. This is going to be the best vacation ever. And by the time they pulled into the driveway Dani's excitement had reached such a fever that she ran around the yard and down to the pond, twice, before even giving her grandparents their hugs.

"Mom. Can I set up the tent and sleep down by the pond!?" Dani begged, her bare legs already covered in mud.

"Dani! We just got here. You haven't even been in the house yet. C'mom, you have plenty of time to sleep out. But not tonight."

But Dani was off again, running down to the pond. She waded through the cattails until the water came up the cuff of her shorts and leaned down to examine the tiny minnows that darted away from her. Emily could see her from the driveway, reaching into the water and scooped it up in her hand to examine it up close.

"It's so good to have you back here, Emily," Julia said as they stood alone in the driveway. "It's been so long."

"Yes, it has," Emily said. For ten years she had heard almost nothing of Henoga Valley. Even when her parents had visited Rhode Island, Emily had not shown much interest in news from her hometown. But now that she was back, it was hard to avoid a little reminiscing.

"Jennifer Baker called last night," Julia said. "She'd like to get together with you sometime. She has a little girl, too, a few years younger than Dani."

A slightly pained expression came to Emily's face.

"She was married to someone she met in college, but she's divorced now. She moved back to Henoga Valley two years ago, after her father got sick. I really think she'd like to see you."

"Can't I just hide out here and avoid everyone?"

"I suppose."

"Who knows that I'm home?"

"Well, Jennifer knows. I couldn't lie when she asked about you. And she always asks about you."

"So now that Jennifer knows, everybody else does, too."

"People don't talk much about it anymore, Em," Julia said.

It amused Emily to hear the murder referred to as 'it.' But that was how her mother always referred to Jack's death and John David's escape. It.

"You don't hear from Jack's family, do you?"

"No, never. No one has since they moved away."

"And what about the Martens?"

"Eva moved away, to Denver, I think. John David's little brother joined the Navy after high school. I don't know much more about him."

"Have they ever heard from John David?"

241

"Dutch Marten says they haven't. But maybe he can't say anything. Of course, there are rumors that John David still lives in the mountains, and it seems that just about everyone has seen him at one time or another."

"Yeah, I'm sure."

"Some people say that Mr. Phelps starts a rumor whenever the hiking business is slow. It's so crass."

Emily nodded her head.

"Mac Driscoll heard from a trucker friend that John David works for a logging company out in Oregon. It's hard to know what's true anymore."

Dani fell asleep early on the couch, so Emily put her to bed and went for a drive. There had been some trepidation in her parents' faces when she left, but she assured them she was fine. I'm just going to drive around for awhile and see what had changed, she told them. She drove around the lake and back through the village from the south side. She slowed down and coasted past the park where Jack was killed. She noticed that the old maple tree was gone. Then she drove to the high school and parked near the gymnasium. She followed the path behind the school toward the knoll overlooking the track and baseball field. Nestled among the white birch was a large boulder. She remembered how she used to sit there and read years ago, and how she could barely see the Henoga Valley teams down below. Her view from this clump of trees had been obstructed and she often had not been able to tell which team was at bat. But she remembered how, from time to time, she had heard the crack of the bat and the cheers from the crowd on the sidelines.

As she approached the knoll, Emily noticed a plaque on the boulder. It was made of bronze, and the words *Ondama Field* were printed in large block letters. Beneath the name, in much smaller print, it said 'judge not, that ye be not judged.' There was no dedication date on the plaque and no indication of who had placed it there.

And then Emily drove to Jennifer's old house to get her address from her parents. But Jennifer was there and greeted her on the porch with a long hug. When they broke away there were tears in Jennifer's eyes. She wiped her face with the palms of her hands and they sat down on the wicker settee.

"Never thought I'd see *you* again," Jennifer said.

"Never thought I'd be back," Emily whispered.

"Was it hard, coming back here after all this time? After all that's happened?"

"Yes," Emily said, "it was very hard. But looking back, everything seems like it was hard. It's like my life ended right here. I don't think I've really been alive ever since. Even my painting. I've been doing ocean scenes and salt marshes for six years now, but it's like someone else is holding the brush. I haven't really loved to paint since I left the Adirondacks."

Jennifer looked at Emily, who sat slightly hunched. She reached over and brushed the hair from the side of her face.

Emily looked up at Jennifer and said, "And then one day I watched Dani play baseball, and I saw how passionate she was about the game. That's when I started to wonder, where did *my* passion go?"

Jennifer could think of nothing to say, and they were silent for a moment. A large June bug crashed into the porch screens and beat its wings furiously. Jennifer got up from the settee and knocked the insect off the screen.

"I hate those things," Jennifer said. "They're disgusting."

The evening air returned to silence.

"Em, I'm not going to ask you anything about, you know, ... what happened, because I don't want to know anymore. I used to want to know, but not anymore."

A tear rolled down Emily's cheek. Yes, she thought, sometimes it's best not to know.

"Who put the plaque up at the high school field?" Emily asked, wiping away the tear.

"It just showed up there about eight years ago. No one noticed it until the fall, but they think it had been there for a couple of months by then. At first there was a lot of controversy over whether it was 'appropriate.' But the school board finally decided to leave it alone and the name just caught on."

And for the next week Emily appeared in town more than she had even when she lived in Henoga Valley. Everyone

243

greeted her warmly. *We're so happy to see you, Emily. It's been such a long time. And look at your little girl, she's so beautiful.* But of course they could not help trying to decide who she looked like. Emily graciously accepted their greetings. She pretended not to notice the stares of tactless people who drove by in cars and slowed down to stare at Emily and Danielle. She did not raise her voice in anger or shoot back an angry glare. Instead, she buried every trace of contempt and bitterness deep within her heart and became as serene as the morning water on Raquette Lake.

And if Emily knew who the father was, she never told anyone.

Chapter Twenty-Six

Emily and Danielle did not leave the Adirondack Mountains at the end of summer. Both of them knew within a week that this was their home. Emily set up her easel one evening down by the pond and began painting cattails. With the first stroke of her paintbrush, spirits came out of the water and held her wrist, gently teasing mellifluous veins of color onto the canvas. A breeze came up from the lake and greeted the tiny white hairs on her arm.

Danielle loved Raquette Lake, the little muddy pond, the overgrown fields down by the stone fence. She began making friends immediately. Her new friends, of course, asked her about her father. Was he the dead guy, or the other guy, they asked innocently? But Dani wasn't offended by the questions. She didn't have a father, but many of the other kids lived with only one parent so it didn't seem unusual. Dani begged her mother to buy a house in Henoga Valley.

"But are you sure you want to live *here*?" Emily asked one night. She was tucking Dani into bed after a long day of swimming. "In Henoga Valley? We could buy a house over in Essex or Elizabethtown, or up in Lake Placid."

"But we don't know anybody there," Dani said. She was lying on her stomach and Emily was rubbing her back.

"But *everybody* knows you here. Won't it bother you that people are always looking at you?"

"The kids here don't care. They think it's kinda cool."

Emily pulled the sheets up to Dani's neck and turned off the light on the night stand.

"Hey, Mom?" Dani asked as her mother was going out the door.

"Yes, dear?"

"How come you can't tell me who my father is?"

Emily had told her daughter about the 'attack' and murder several times, always in the gentlest of terms. People make mistakes, she had said. Even good people.

"Somehow, you appeared out of all that. Something good

245

from something bad. Something beautiful from something ugly." She leaned over and kissed her daughter on the top of the head. "Your father is some good spirit, I suppose."

And that was as much of an answer as Dani ever got. It was not particularly satisfying to a ten-year old. Certainly not very tangible. But her mother never wavered from the story. Her father was a spirit from the mountains. A good spirit. A kind spirit.

But unfortunately for Danielle Davignon, not one with whom she could play baseball.

Chapter Twenty-Seven

Those of us who were still young and innocent in 1971 were suddenly made to believe that there existed in the world a wellspring of dangerous forces that could be unleashed at any time. How was it possible, we wondered, that two boys who had always been the best of friends, could set upon one another like wolves? And then the O'Neills packed up and left in the middle of the night and no one ever heard from them again. It was as if they never even existed. We didn't even have a chance to say goodbye to Bobby O'Neill and we wondered if he even *knew* he was moving. Maybe they just woke him up in the middle of the night and told him to get in the car. The fabric that held our lives together had been torn.

Our childhood was over. We no longer had heroes.

But in time we began to see that Jack O'Neill and John David Marten were like explorers who performed wondrous feats, but at great expense. Where everyone else was content to grow up, get a job and settle down, and die slowly over many years, Jack and John David devoured life and died of gluttony. No one ever saw them grow old, no one had to sit next to them in a dingy bar and listen to stories of how good a baseball player they were in their day. John David and Jack's virtues and faults were writ large on the community, like the letters on a tombstone. Their lives had meaning, however tragic.

But the disappearance of an eleven-year old girl during the summer of 1986 had no such meaning. She had been on vacation with her family on Caitlin Lake and simply vanished late one afternoon in July. It would be several days before the girl's parents would discover the truth about what had happened, that the young girl had *not*, as everyone assumed at the time, just wandered off.

Caitlin Lake lay on the border of Hamilton and Essex Counties. The sheriff of Essex County was a young man named Armand Fleury, nicknamed Army as a child and made all the more fitting by a stint with the Green Berets in Viet Nam. He had been decorated for bravery in battle and won election as the county sheriff in a wave of patriotism that followed Ronald Reagan's presidential bid. Fleury turned out to be a capable sheriff, but he had no experience in conducting searches. He didn't want to waste any time learning, so he called in the State Police and Sheriff Cooney from the neighboring Hamilton County.

"We only have about two hours of daylight left," Sheriff Fleury said after thanking the various teams that had assembled at the missing girl's cottage. "We need to get organized. The kid's name is Luisa Ianucci. The family is from Brooklyn. Her parents have three other children, ages three to twelve. Luisa was last seen around four o'clock, when she went outside. The other kids stayed in the house to watch a video. They called her for dinner around 5:15, so she wasn't gone more then an hour, hour-and-a-half at the most. The kid has no health problems, but it's supposed to get down to the high fifties tonight."

Sheriff Fleury handed out copies of the kid's photograph.

"We don't have much to go on," Fleury said. "The parents and some people in nearby camps have already searched the woods near the lake, so it might be hard to pick up a trail."

Fleury stepped to one side and motioned to Sheriff Cooney.

"I've decided to turn over the coordination of this search to Sheriff Cooney from Hamilton County. He has a lot more experience in conducting searches. Many of you already know him. Those of you who don't can introduce yourselves later."

Cooney stepped forward. He followed Fleury around the circle, handing out topographic maps of the area. He spoke to them as he went.

"The girl is eleven years old, so she's not your typical lost child. But she's from Brooklyn and has never even been camping before. She's stronger than a little kid, so in a panic she could cover a lot more ground. The area to the east has one large mountain that forms a bowl around an area of one square mile. There's a small river to the north. She'll probably stay on flat ground and not cross the river, so she should be in the bowl. If she's *lost*. We haven't ruled out a kidnappinging, but it doesn't seem likely. The only road through the area runs in front of the house and the girl's father was on the front porch reading when she disappeared. The parents are pretty sure she was out in the back by the little pond."

Cooney instructed the men to set up a line that surrounded the bowl and work toward the middle. The teams quickly scattered and disappeared into the woods. Each of the men carried flashlights and their flickering lights could be seen for several hours after the sun went down. The search continued until ten o'clock that night without finding a trace of the girl. Cooney had made a phone call to the State Police for a bloodhound, and the dog and its handler arrived from around nine o'clock. Cooney recognized the trooper as the one he had worked with years ago on the Marten manhunt.

"Cronin, isn't it?" Cooney said, shaking his hand. "Still working with the dogs, huh?"

"Beats people most days," he said. Trooper Cronin had been a dog handler for the State Police for almost fifteen years now. His name had appeared in Sawyer's book, and that small measure of fame had maintained his interest in dogs ever since. Cooney handed the trooper a pair of the child's pajamas.

"I won't be going with you on this one," Cooney said with a little chuckle. The sheriff was sixty-three years old and would not have made it far in the woods. "But Sheriff Fleury should be able to keep up with you."

"As long as we don't run into leghold traps, right sheriff?" Cronin said.

"That son of a bitch," Cooney said. But Cronin noticed a hint of affection in the sheriff's voice.

"That son of a bitch," Cronin echoed.

The men were in a good mood. They assumed the search would be over in twenty-four hours. But things went wrong. The dog could not seem to pick up the girl's scent. The dog was led around the area for hours, but it never picked up her trail. It might have been that the long bath she had taken minutes before she disappeared covered her scent. Perhaps it had been the presence of so many other people who tramped through the area in the hours following her disappearance. But Trooper Cronin and the bloodhound wandered back and forth along the eastern shore of the lake all evening without picking up the trail.

249

Mr. Ianucci himself went into Newcomb and pleaded with the local volunteer fire company to recruit a larger search party. Over the next two days they covered every square foot of the bowl on the east side of Caitlin Lake and then expanded the search to the north and to the east.

But all to no avail. Because by the time anyone figured out what had really happened, it was, unfortunately, too late.

Chapter Twenty-Eight

Luisa Ianucci had been playing by the tiny pond in the woods behind her cottage and had not even noticed the man until she turned and saw him standing over her. He was odd-looking, hardly taller than her twelve-year old brother, but muscular. He smiled at her but said nothing. Luisa's first impulse was that she had done something wrong. Perhaps she was playing on someone else's property. Maybe she had picked a flower that wasn't supposed to be picked. But he said nothing. She stood up slowly and looked around. There was no one else in the woods. She looked to the cottage and thought about screaming for help, but that seemed so rude. This man hadn't done anything to her. Luisa's senses sharpened. She could hear the wind rustle the leaves in the poplar beside her. She could smell the man's musty perspiration. In the instant that Luisa began to run the man pounced on her. He placed one hand over her mouth and lifted her around the waist and took off on a slow run into the woods. Luisa kicked and struggled, but the man was strong and she quickly tired. After several minutes he stopped and put her down. He kept a hand around her mouth. Without saying a word he pulled a roll of duct tape out of his shirt and wrapped it around her mouth. Then he bound her hands and feet and threw her over his shoulder.

Luisa's mind went numb with panic. She was totally helpless. The man seemed to be following a trail so narrow that it disappeared behind them and they raced off deeper and deeper into the forest. Her stomach hurt from being slung over his shoulder and her hands and ankles stung from the tape. It was hard to breathe with her mouth taped shut. The man carried her for almost thirty minutes before stopping to rest.

"I can't believe I got her," the man whispered. He rubbed his hands through his hair, which was greasy and poorly cut. He avoided looking at the little girl's eyes. "I can't believe I did it," he repeated with obvious satisfaction.

Luisa Ianucci was small for her age and looked no more than seven or eight years old. She had thick black hair that hung straight to her delicate shoulders. Her hands and feet were exceptionally small. But she lived in the tough Bensonhurst section of Brooklyn and had plenty of experience with bullies. They would pretend not to see her at the bus stop and then bump into her and grab her ass. Or follow her home from school, walking ten yards behind and taunting her with sexual jokes. Her older brother was also quite small and therefore not able to offer any protection, so she had learned how to get by on her own. She had learned that, under no circumstances, should you cry in front of them. It only makes them more excited. Always act bored by their antics. But something told her this man was different. She had heard about kids being snatched for no reason. She had seen their pictures on milk cartons and wondered how their parents could possibly hope to find them using a picture that was years old.

Luisa turned to her side and struggled to a sitting position. Her hands and feet were still bound with duct tape, so she wrapped her hands around her knees for balance. She looked up at the man with her best placid expression, but he still avoided her eyes. He seemed nervous, like a kid who had stolen a bike or something. *Maybe he hasn't thought this thing out all the way.* He was breathing hard from having carried her for more than a mile. His Marlboro T-shirt was soaked with perspiration and the red logo was pasted to his chest. Luisa motioned to the tape covering her mouth. The man looked around to make sure they were alone before taking the tape off. He left her feet and hands bound.

"You got a cigarette?" Luisa asked coolly.

The man looked at her startled, as if surprised she was even capable of speech. He slowly took a crumpled pack out of his T-shirt pocket and lit one for her. He was looking at her now, studying her face. She had smoked cigarettes a few times before. Everybody in her neighborhood had. But she was a 'good girl,' and good girls were defined, at least at her age, as those who didn't smoke. Luisa was careful to take only a small puff and blew out a stream of smoke.

"You should switch to Newports," Luisa said. "They taste way better."

"Your parents know you smoke?" the man asked. His voice was low and slurred.

"Hell, no," Luisa said. She never swore, but she knew how to do it. She'd heard enough on the streets back home, where everyone swore. "They'd kill me. They don't let me do shit."

"Guess they wouldn't be too keen on you running away with me, now would they?" the man sneered.

Luisa took another drag on the cigarette.

"No. I ran away last year and they grounded me for six friggin' months afterward."

"*You* ran away from home?" the man asked, obviously surprised.

"Well, not *really*," Luisa said. "I mean, I just went to a friend's house for two days to get away from them. They're such assholes. They never let me do anything."

Luisa watched the man light his own cigarette. He was squatting down now to get a better look at her. Luisa's heart pounded in her little chest, but she tried to act calm. Her parents weren't rich, so she knew this guy didn't grab her for the ransom money. She was in danger. He was going to kill her.

"So, what's your story?" Luisa asked. "Is this how you meet chicks?" She knew it was risky to engage him in a conversation, but she had given herself up to gut instinct. She had decided to pretend that she hated her parents and was willing to run away with him. Her accent became more Brooklyn, more Italian.

The man was embarrassed by the question and refused to acknowledge it. *Got something here*, Luisa thought.

"Hey, look, I didn't mean nothing by it," she said apologetically.

He stood up and dropped his cigarette and ground it in with his sneaker. He sniffled once, as if hc had a runny nose. But it was a dry sniffle. A nervous habit. *He's almost as scared as I am,* Luisa thought.

"Let's go," he said curtly. He grabbed her by the hands and yanked her to her feet.

"I *can* walk, you know," Luisa said.

The man stared at her for a moment, trying to judge her

253

intentions. Luisa had already decided that he probably wasn't too bright. Something about his eyes, which did not focus completely. And his hair, disheveled and poorly cut. His voice was oddly muffled, as if he did not truly speak the language. But his instincts were another matter. You couldn't predict what someone's instincts were by observing them for just a few minutes. She had to be careful.

"You gonna try to run away?" he asked.

"From you or from home?" Luisa asked.

"From me."

Luisa flicked her cigarette the way she'd seen older girls do on the street corner.

"Better step on that," she said to the man, motioning to the smoldering butt. "And I won't run away from you as long as you're good to me."

The man took out a knife and cut the tape that bound Luisa's ankles. He had intended to rape her and hide the body in a shallow grave. But he liked her. She was kinda funny and she seemed to like him. Girls never talked to him like this, they only made fun of him. It was almost like he was helping her get away from her parents. He could understand that. He never liked his own parents, who always picked on him for being stupid. Dumber than a bucket of shit, his father said. The man decided to cut the tape that bound the girl's wrists.

"Let's get outta here," Luisa said, rubbing her hands. "Which way?"

"This way," the man said, leading her up over a small ridge. Luisa couldn't believe that he was letting her walk behind him. *God, he is stupid. Isn't he worried that I'll run?* The man seemed to be following a trail, but Luisa couldn't see it. She figured that she would get one good chance to run and she couldn't waste it. It was better to go along with him for days, even weeks, if she had to. She just couldn't make a mistake.

And so it was that Luisa followed the man over a steep ridge down to a stream on the other side, several miles from her cottage and far beyond the search area. The man had set up a cheap tent and it looked as if he might have been camping there for several days. Luisa wasn't sure how long he intended to stay, but she didn't like the idea. As long as they were here she would never have a chance to run from him. She was a city girl. She needed a street or a road to make her move. This was definitely *his* territory.

"Shouldn't we keep on moving?"

"Keep on moving?" the man said. "It's getting late."

"Well don't you have a car or something? I mean, like, where are we going? We're not going to get anywhere on foot."

"I can't bring a car into the *woods*," he said, obviously delighted in knowing something that she apparently did not.

"Jesus," Luisa said. "I wait all my fucking life for someone to come along and get me out of this miserable life, and you show up on *foot*."

"Hey, I gotta car," the man said defensively.

"Well, when can we get it?"

"In the morning," the man said, uncertainly. He had paused before answering her, and it worried her. "I got it hidden along the old logging road that nobody uses anymore."

Luisa asked the man to build a fire, but he refused.

"What do think I am, stupid?" he said. "They'll be looking for a fire."

"Sorry. I was just cold."

It was beginning to get dark and Luisa was afraid of the dark, even in Brooklyn. But out here in the forest, it would get *really* dark. She knew this guy intended to rape her. She was surprised he hadn't done it already. Instinctively she knew that he was afraid of women. That's why he kidnapped a girl, she thought. *The older I act, the better my chances are.*

"Got another cigarette?" Luisa asked.

The man handed her another Marlboro and struck his lighter for her.

"Really, Newports. Ever try menthol?"

"Newports is for girls," he said.

"What's your name?" she asked. He looked at her but didn't respond. "Doesn't matter," Luisa added, "as long as you have a car."

The man told Luisa to sleep in the tent and she went without arguing. She laid down on top of his cheap sleeping bag, not daring to get inside it. It smelled of perspiration and the stench nearly gagged her. Luisa laid awake, expecting the man to enter the tent at any moment. She had to pee, but with great difficulty she managed to hold off until day break.

The sun rose the next morning and filled the tent with orange light. Luisa was surprised to find that she had fallen asleep, and even more surprised that nothing had happened. She crawled out of the tent and saw the man asleep on the ground several feet away. Luisa walked a few yards into the woods and relieved herself. As she was pulling up her shorts, she debated making a run for it. The man was asleep. If she managed to get even a hundred yards away she could hide and he wouldn't be able to find her. *But then what? How long can I hide? Where do I go?* She was as afraid of the forest as she was of the man.

"Hey, watcha got for breakfast?" Luisa asked, returning to the campsite.

The man was startled by Luisa's voice and jumped to his feet. He pulled a can of Spam from his backpack and handed it to her.

"Spam. My favorite."

Luisa opened the can while the man packed up his tent. He stuffed the sleeping bag into the backpack and tied the tent to the top. Luisa handed him the half-eaten Spam.

"I saved you some," she said.

He took the can from her and tossed it into the trees.

"Let's go," he said, giving her a shove.

The kidnapping hadn't gone anything like the man had thought it would. He lived with his parents about two miles down the road from Luisa's camp. He'd never left home and was only intermittently employed, so he had a great deal of time on his hands. He'd never been in any kind of trouble before, but he wanted a girl. This girl. He had seen her at the State Beach in her black one-piece bathing suit, as smooth and shimmering as skin itself. She was so beautiful, the most beautiful thing he had ever seen. He told himself that kidnapping her wouldn't be like taking someone from town, someone that his parents might know. He hiked up through the woods to spy on her for several days, hoping to see her naked. He had seen movies about people who lived in cities and they always got naked. And then she was right *there*, alone, right in front of him. He decided to just take her. He imagined he would grab her, take her deep into the woods and have sex with her, then hide the body somewhere. No one would ever find out.

He was now thinking that he had to get rid of her soon. He hadn't planned to keep her this long. Just do it to her in the woods and get back home. Somehow she had talked him into running away with her. But then he got to thinking while she was sleeping in the tent. Once he got back to the car, he'd be out on the main roads with a kidnapped girl. There would be roadblocks everywhere. He wouldn't get far. It wouldn't work. He had to do it. He had to kill her. *Just do it and get it over with,* he told himself all morning long. *Just get it over with.*

Luisa and the man reached a clearing at the top of the small hill. The man took out a cigarette and lit one for each of them.

"I can't take you no farther," the man said. He sounded apologetic.

"What do you mean?" Luisa asked, even though she knew what he meant.

"I like you and all," he said. "But I ... you know, I can't take you back. If they find me with you, I'll go to jail."

"I could say it was *my* idea," Luisa said. She tried to sound casual, but her lips quivered. "I could say I ran away with you."

"Yeah, like they're gonna believe *that* story," the man said.

"Well, you can just ... let me go, can't you?" Luisa stammered. "I'll ... I'll say I got lost. They'll believe me. I can lie real good." Tears welled up in her eyes and her voiced cracked. Her accent disappeared."

"I won't say anything, I *promise*," she sobbed.

But Luisa's fear excited the man. It gave him courage. He dropped his cigarette and grabbed her by one arm. Luisa jumped to her feet and tried to pull away. The man grabbed her T-shirt with his other hand and yanked it over her head. Luisa tried to cover her tiny breasts.

"I won't let you suffer," he said. "I promise. I'll kill you real quick."

But suddenly the man's legs buckled and he fell to the

ground, writhing in pain. Luisa looked down and saw an arrow buried deep in the man's thigh. She gasped, but she was too shocked to move. Then she regained her senses and started to run, but the man lunged and grabbed her by the ankle, hauling her back toward him. He pulled her body on top of himself for protection. Then he reached for the hunting knife strapped to his belt and held it to her throat.

"I'll kill her!" he threatened, shouting at the trees. "I'll kill her right here. I'm gonna cut her fuckin' throat!"

No one answered his threats.

The man dragged Luisa to the base of a large maple tree so that he could sit upright, always keeping her body in front of his. For the next several minutes the two of them lay together on the ground. Luisa sobbed uncontrollably, and every time she moved the man pulled the knife tighter against her throat. Several times he tried to pull the arrow out of his leg, but each time he bellowed in agony.

"You got to the count of five to come out," the man finally shouted. "I mean it. At the count of five, I'm gonna cut her throat."

Luisa turned her head to one side to protect her throat from the knife, and at that moment she heard what sounded like a B flat plucked on her cello. It was followed by a whistling sound. A second arrow flew by her cheek and struck the man in the chest with a hollow thud. His grip immediately loosened and Luisa rolled away. She stood up and screamed in horror, and her feet danced on the ground as if she were running in place. She watched the man paw at the arrow for several seconds until his body went still.

Luisa waited for several moments, expecting someone to come out of the woods. Although she was still in shock from nearly being struck by the arrow, she was nevertheless self-conscious about her bare chest. She found her T-shirt and pulled it over her head, her chest still heaving from the sobs. After a few minutes she stopped crying and looked around the edge of the clearing, still waiting for her rescuer to appear. But the forest was again nearly silent, except for the rustling of the leaves. Perhaps they're waiting to make sure he's dead, she thought.

She looked back at the man lying against the tree. His chest was now covered with blood.

"You got 'em," she yelled. "I think ... I think he's dead!"

There was no answer.

"What am I supposed I *do?*" Luisa screamed angrily into the trees. "Why won't you help me?!"

The silence frightened her. Perhaps the arrow had been fired by this man's partner, she thought, and now *he* was after her. She started to run down the hillside in a panic. *Why is this happening?* she asked herself as she jumped over logs and plowed through the dense brush, clawing and flailing. She began to pray, to the god she hadn't spoken with in a long time, but who now seemed to be her only hope. *Oh God, please don't let them kill me. Please don't let them. Please.*

Luisa ran until her lungs ached, then she slowed to a walk. She turned in a slow circle, looking at the stoney ridge and the trees that surrounded her. There was no one there. She was utterly alone. She began to wonder if she had dreamed the kidnapping. *Maybe I picked a flower whose oily residue made me hallucinate,* she thought.

She wandered through the forest for several hours, stopping occasionally to call for help. But her throat became sore and she had to stop yelling. Her path was finally stopped by a wide marsh. Luisa was so thirsty that she scooped up the murky water and sucked it out of her cupped hands. Then she splashed the cool water on her sunburned face. With her fingers she probed the welts raised on her arms and legs by the branches.

And then it began to grow dark. The sun had already dipped behind the tallest trees and long shadows quickly spread across the ground. Luisa's T-shirt was soaked with perspiration, and in the shadows she began to feel cold.

Just before dark a faint light appeared, flickering in the distance. At first she wasn't sure that it was a light. It danced among the trees like a red leaf. She stumbled onward, groping through the branches, yelling for help. As she got closer she could see that the light was a campfire. Luisa yelled, but no one answered. When she finally stumbled into the little clearing where the fire burned in a shallow pit, she found no one there.

Just the fire and a light woolen blanket. She wrapped herself in the blanket and sat cross-legged before the fire.

A metal pot rested on the rocks surrounding the fire pit. Luisa reached over and removed the lid. The pot was filled nearly to the brim with cooked rice. Steam rose from the pot and ran along her arm. This must be somebody's campsite, she thought, but the absence of a tent seemed odd to her. She noticed a pile of wood stacked nearby. Firewood. There was enough to last the entire night. Luisa decided to go ahead and eat the rice. If anyone came back, she would explain to them that she had been kidnapped and was starving. Surely they would not blame her for eating their rice.

When the rice was gone, Luisa dragged a stone over to the fire pit and sat on it, wrapping the blanket around her. The forest had grown dark and Luisa feared that wild animals were lurking beyond the flickering shadows, so she piled logs on the fire until the flame grew to a height of several feet. With her head resting on her knees, she stared into the fire for more than an hour.

Finally she rose to her feet and gathered the blanket around her shoulders. She looked to the sky above. Thousands of stars dotted the moonless sky, and the fire cast a reddish glow upon the arboreal spires above her. It reminded Luisa of a cathedral in Italy that her grandmother had shown her in a book. She had been married in the basilica many years earlier and often said, in her thick accent, that she wished only to live long enough to see Luisa married at the same altar. Luisa stared at the sky until her neck hurt.

God?

But if God was listening, he did not reply.

"Thank you!" she shouted at the top of her lungs, knowing that he would be watching.

Chapter Twenty-Nine

The five years that followed Emily Davignon's return to Henoga Valley were the most productive of her life. Emily and Dani packed up the Bronco nearly every weekend and went camping in the woods, where Emily would set up her easel and paint while Dani hiked the nearby trials, or canoed the rivers, or swam in the lakes. The entire summer, from the day Dani got out of school to the time she returned to classes in September, was spent on the back roads and trails. They slept in tents and cooked on camp stoves wherever they went, always avoiding motels and campgrounds. Emily returned to painting with oils and acrylics and once again began to experiment with natural pigments, which she extracted from hundreds of plants with acetone and xylene. She renewed her interest in the mountain waters. She painted Adirondack bogs with unusual patterns of colors, jonquil, damson, civette, that seem to dance beneath the surface like spirits.

Emily's camping trips were periodically interrupted by art shows in Lake George and Blue Mountain Lake, and the two of them often showed up dressed in torn jeans and flannel shirts, smelling distinctly like campfire. But this eccentricity only made Emily all the more popular. People flocked to the shows and waited patiently to get her autograph.

Geoffrey Neiswender, who had introduced Emily Davignon to the public in *Time* magazine, hailed her return to the Hudson River School. *There is an air of elegance about these paintings, an expression of reverence for nature that fills even this city dweller with emotion, the way the earliest settlers, indeed, even the Indians, must have felt when they first saw these great forests.*

A single painting of Lake Tear of the Clouds, the tiny pond near the summit of Mount Marcy that forms the headwaters of the Hudson River, was sold in an auction in New York City in 1985 for $62,000.

She received hundreds of requests to endorse her own line of hiking apparel. She received offers from companies wanting to create an Adirondack perfume, calendars, posters, and camping gear, all of which she politely refused.

She bought a small log cabin cottage on the north shore of Raquette Lake and surrounded it with an immense perennial garden. For many months of the year she and Danielle were quite comfortable in the secluded cabin, but with each passing year her fame grew and it became increasingly difficult to maintain anonymity. In the summer, tourists with cameras slung around their necks hiked along the road looking for her house and on more than one occasion she found someone in her garden picking flowers. And it was therefore much easier for them to simply travel all summer long and leave the cabin in the hands of a caretaker.

Emily and Danielle were camping off a remote trail near Lake Colvin when the girl from Brooklyn disappeared, and they did not hear of the incident until they returned to Henoga Valley four days later. By that time, Luisa Ianucci had already been reunited with her family. Emily was surprised by all the traffic and television vans in Newcomb when she drove through on her way home, but she didn't bother to buy a paper or ask anyone what had happened. Emily heard from her mother about the unsuccessful search for the missing girl, who turned up days later on a remote logging road. And how, at first, no one had believed the girl's story that she had been kidnapped. But then they found the body of a man pinned to a tree with an arrow exactly as the girl had described, and there was little choice but to accept her improbable tale.

"Well, *who* killed the kidnapper?" Emily asked, thinking she had missed something in the story.

"Nobody knows," Julia said. "The girl didn't actually see anybody."

Emily sat on end of the wicker sofa on her mother's back porch with a confused expression on her face.

"Everyone's saying it was J.D. Marten," Julia said. "I thought you should know about it. You know, in case the TV reporters come around again."

"Oh, c'mon, it can't be," Emily said, incredulous.

"Well, I agree. It's probably some vigilante from over in

Newcomb who didn't want to deal with the law. But you know the reporters are going to come around asking more questions."

"I already saw them," Emily said. "They're all over the place."

"Yes, that's why I was thinking that maybe you ought to go down to Rhode Island and see Pépé for a couple of weeks. Just get away from this place until it blows over."

Emily nodded. It would be nice to see Pépé again. She hadn't been back to Providence more than a couple of times since she moved to Henoga Valley.

"No," she said finally, shaking her head. "I don't want to run anymore. If they come, they come."

And, of course, they came.

For a week it was just like the summer of 1971. Hundreds of reporters poured into Newcomb to cover the fantastic story of the little girl's rescue from a kidnapper. The nature of the rescue was so incredible that the identity of the kidnapper became of little concern. Some thirty-five year old loser who lived with his elderly parents. Quiet kind of guy, really kept to himself, everyone said. No one seemed to know him well. A few of the papers made it clear that the identity of the man, and they *assumed* it was a man, who had killed the kidnapper was not known. There were a great many hunters in the Adirondacks. There were plenty of men in Essex County who were experienced with a bow and good enough to place an arrow into a two-inch circle from seventy-five feet. But none of them could imagine shooting at a man who was holding a girl in front of him.

"The thing about an arrow," said Joe Phelps, appearing on the evening news, "is that the smallest branch will change its direction. It had to have been a perfect shot or he could have killed the girl."

Which, in fact, it was. The State Police investigators later determined, based on the angle at which the second arrow struck the kidnapper, that the person who shot it had been standing in a tree at the other side of the clearing. And when they climbed several trees in the area, they found a large maple in which several small branches had been broken off to provide an open view of the clearing. He was practically on top of them.

"Classic hunting technique," Sheriff Cooney told the reporters later in the week. "A lot of guys use it. It was a pretty easy shot. It doesn't mean a thing." Cooney refused to speculate on the possibility that J.D. Marten had fired the arrow.

"Are you going to try to track down the man who did it?" one newspaper reporter from Buffalo asked.

"That'll be up to Sheriff Fleury," Cooney said. "This county isn't my jurisdiction."

Cooney was standing outside the Essex County Sheriff's office getting ready to head back home. Sheriff Fleury and the State Police had asked him to stay on for a few days after the girl was found because of his experience with J.D. Marten. So he listened to the girl's story and had studied the photos of the kidnapper with an arrow in his chest. Cooney immediately understood what had happened, though he did not let on to the reporters.

"Whoever killed the girl's kidnapper knew exactly where they were headed," he told the other investigators. "He knew that they were going to walk into that clearing. That's not something your average hunter can do. This was the work of a real pro."

The most startling pieces of evidence were the arrows taken from the man's body. Cooney and Fleury had been present during the autopsy and examined the arrows on a metal table in the back of the room.

"Christ, you ever see anything like these?" Fleury asked.

"Never," Cooney replied, holding one of them up.

The arrow was hand made, with a flint arrowhead, not the kind you could buy in a sporting goods store. The shaft was made of maple rubbed as smooth as marble. The arrowhead itself was small, no more than an inch wide and an inch-and-a-half long. The feathers looked like they were from a blue-jay. A State Police investigator was also present and Cooney handed the arrow to him.

"Looks like it was made by an Indian," the investigator said. "I didn't know anybody still knew how to make these things."

"What about J.D. Marten," Fleury asked.

"Marten usually hunted with a rifle, as far as I know. But there was some talk years ago about him being pretty good with a bow and arrow."

The sheriff ran his thumb over the arrowhead. The sharp edge cut into his skin. He studied the thin strips of rawhide that were wound tightly around the shaft to hold the arrowhead in place. He examined the length of the arrow and noticed that it was perfectly straight. He then held the two arrows side by side. They were perfect matches.

"They're goddam works of art," he pronounced. He looked up at the two men next to him. "You guys are going to have your hands full with the media as it is. I suggest you keep quiet about the arrows."

Fleury and the State Trooper nodded in agreement.

Several months later Sheriff Cooney received a three-page report from a professor of Native American Culture at Union College in Schenectady. Each of the Algonquin and Iroquois tribes in New York State had distinctive arrows, the report said, although many descriptions were inaccurate. The arrows were most likely of Mohawk origin, the professor concluded. The report was forwarded to Cooney by Sheriff Fleury, who had penned the words *be prepared for an Indian uprising* on the bottom of the last page.

The description of the arrows and the report by the Union College professor would remain a secret for many years. Nevertheless, the kidnapping and the rescue of the little girl were the biggest topics of discussion in the Adirondacks for the remainder of the summer. The reporters interviewed Emily Davignon, who politely told them that she had not heard from John David Marten at any time in the past fifteen years and had no opinion on the likelihood that he had killed the kidnapper. Several wilderness experts appeared on television talk shows to discuss how a man like J.D. Marten might survive in the wilderness for fifteen years, although in the end they all concluded that it seemed like an impossibly long time.

265

Yet everyone who heard the story of arrows flying from the forest and striking with supernatural accuracy came to the same conclusion, the only logical conclusion. *John David Marten.*

Except Danielle Davignon, who whispered to no one but herself, *Dad.*

Chapter Thirty

Danielle Davignon. At the age of fourteen already eight inches taller than her mother, with long, sinewy arms and muscular legs, and thick chocolate-colored hair that hung to the middle of her back. She swam across Raquette Lake and back on the morning of her fourteenth birthday just so the day might be 'memorable, and during a three-week period that summer she climbed all of the 46 Adirondack high peaks. She dominated girls' sports, playing varsity basketball her freshman year at Henoga Valley High School and leading the team in scoring and rebounding. She so intimidated other teams that her mere presence in the 'lane' often forced shooting errors. In the spring she starred on the boys track team, having already broken both the 1600 and 3200 meter records in eighth grade, and she was to remain undefeated throughout high school.

It was not possible to look at her magnificent body and read of her incredible feats without wondering who her father was. The opinions, voiced in kitchens around Henoga Valley, were evenly divided between those who believed her father to be Jack O'Neill and those who favored J.D. Marten. Her tall, powerful body bore a decided resemblance to John David's, but her blue eyes were distinctly Jack's. Some even questioned if *both* of them could have been her father, but that theory was met by derision from those who knew it to be genetically impossible.

As a child growing up in Providence, Dani had showed little interest in knowing who her father was. Pépé had been her father for those first ten years, rocking her to sleep, attending all of the school functions and Little League games, taking her for walks. But since moving to Henoga Valley, the question of her parentage had become more difficult to avoid. While most of the girls in school avoided the subject, at least in her presence, every now and then one of them would let a remark slip. And the mere mention of the word 'rape' twisted her stomach into a knot. In a manner that is comprehensible to only a child, Danielle came to believe that she could decide this issue for herself. And so it was not surprising that she chose the legendary J. D. Marten, a man who could walk though fifty miles of Adirondack wilderness without a map and kill a bear with a woodchuck rifle. A man whose life was the subject of a book Danielle had read dozens of times.

Like many people in Henoga Valley, Danielle had always assumed that her father had fled the Adirondacks. The rumors of his being sighted in the woods near Henoga Valley were patent lies, for if he were half the woodsman he was purported to be, he wouldn't have been seen by so many people. Dani liked to think of him the way her mother had taught her, as a spirit that resided in the mountains. She could be with her father simply by walking down to the lake or into the woods behind her house. She felt his presence in the water when she swam across the lake. She pretended that the wind was his kiss and the cool water his touch. But she never told her friends about him, because believing that J.D. Marten roamed the forest was a child's game, like believing in Paul Bunyan and his blue ox.

It was a great concern to Emily that her daughter became obsessed with her father after the kidnapping in Newcomb. She was alarmed when Dani set up an archery target in the back yard and began practicing for hours every afternoon. And she was concerned with how little time she spent sleeping in the house. Dani preferred the tent to her own bedroom. At first she had merely set it up in the backyard, but gradually moved it to the edge of the woods, then into the woods. Until finally, the tent was not within shouting distance of the house.

"Dani, I really don't like you sleeping out there all alone," her mother said. They had just unloaded the car after having spent three days in the woods north of Tupper Lake.

"C'mon, Mom! You don't mind me sleeping in the woods when you're out there painting."

"You're not *alone* then."

Dani gave her mother the 'look.' One hand on her jutted hip, her eyes lowered.

"Like *you* might be able to protect me?" Dani said.

"It's not safe to be out there alone. It makes me very nervous."

268

"And I suppose that's how you felt when you went hiking by yourself and got lost?" Dani said, emphasizing every third word.

Emily laughed because she knew she couldn't win this argument. Danielle was far more adept at reading maps and judging distances than she was, and Emily had long ago given up that responsibility to her daughter.

"The woods were a lot safer when I was your age," Emily said feebly.

"Looks like they're pretty safe now," Dani said.

"And what do you mean by ...?"

"Now that Dad is patrolling them." Dani said things like this to see if she could get a reaction from her mother.

"Even mountain spirits can't be everywhere," Emily said.

The more time Dani spent alone in the forest, the more she came to believe that her father would one night appear at her campsite and sit next to her by the fire. She envisioned the scene hundreds of times. He was tall and dark, and dressed in buckskins. He was clean-shaven because Dani hated beards, but his hair reached his shoulders. He used to carry a rifle, though recent incarnations carried a bow and quiver instead. He never spoke. At times, though, alone in front of a campfire, Dani spoke to *him,* in a strong, clear voice, not the least concerned that boys from school might have followed her into the woods and were listening to her ranting. She told her father how she was still undefeated in track, though other schools were now sending three and four runners to box her in. She spoke of how grateful everyone was for his having saved the little girl over in Newcomb. And how proud *she* was of him. But she never pleaded with him to show his face. To do so would have seemed disrespectful and immature, and she was no longer a child.

In the mornings Dani would climb from her sleeping bag and hike around the outskirts of her campsite, looking for a sign that her father had been there the night before. There was, of course, no such sign, which Dani accepted as further evidence of her father's legendary skill. Certainly a man as clever as J.D. Marten would not leave a trail that a fourteen-year old girl could find.

She took to hiking further into the woods alone. She had

long ago covered all of the state hiking trials with her mother, but she knew they were not part of the real wilderness. J.D. Marten would no more follow a path worn to bedrock by city dwellers than he would pitch a tent in a parking lot. And so, armed with map and compass, she began to leave the trails and wander off into the deep woods. She traced all of her hikes in blue pencil on the topographic sheets. She even followed, more or less, the path her mother took when she got lost as a teenager, and stood on the spot where J.D. Marten changed her mother's wet socks. She found the meadow they had crossed in the waning hours of daylight, the subject of one of her mother's more famous paintings.

"You found that meadow?" Emily asked after her daughter had returned from an entire weekend in the woods.

Danielle shook her head and described it in detail. The tall grasses growing over what must have once been a pond ringed by black spruce and hemlock. Danielle could see the excitement in her mother's face as she described it.

The next day Emily followed her remarkable daughter to the meadow to see it for herself. They entered the clearing early in the afternoon after hiking since seven o'clock in the morning. The bright sunshine shone through the trees as they approached and they quickened their pace.

"This is it!" Emily said when they walked out into the tall grass. It was the first time she had seen it in fifteen years, and although she had returned to John David's cabin with him several times, they had never come by way of the meadow. She immediately thought of the cabin. It wasn't far, not more than ten minutes away. Across the meadow, through the stand of hemlocks to the stream. But she had never even told Danielle of its existence. She debated crossing the meadow. What if the cabin was still there? What if, by some incredible chance, John David was there? She looked at her daughter, who was utterly unsuspecting. Even Sawyer's book never mentioned a cabin. The cabin was a rumor only the Sheriff and his staff had believed, and one that Emily had effectively squelched.

Dani was saying something about how she wanted her mother to do another painting of the meadow with her father in it, like the one she had seen in the old issue of *Time* magazine. But Emily was not paying attention. Her heart was pounding and the blood throbbing in her ears drowned out the other sounds. *Go on. Cross the meadow* she heard herself say.

And so they started across the meadow to the woods on the far side. Emily led the way and Dani followed her path in dry grass.

"Where are we going?" Dani asked. She was uncomfortable letting her mother lead in the woods.

"Just follow me," Emily answered. "I know where I'm going."

They reached the stand of hemlocks and walked on until they came to a stream. They followed it a short way until Emily gained her bearings.

"Over this way," she said and pointed to a small rise. Just behind the trees they found the cabin.

"Whoa!" Dani said. "What's this?!"

"This is a cabin," Emily said, stalling. She hadn't yet decided what to say.

"Yesss .." Dani drawled. "I can see that. And how did you know it was here?"

"That's a long story," Emily said, reaching for the door. She noticed the lock had been removed. "It's not locked," she said, disappointed.

"Why would it be?" Dani said. "No one could ever find it out here?"

"It's just that he always kept it locked."

"He?"

"John David."

"Oh, so *that's* it. This is *his* cabin."

Emily didn't know what to expect when she opened the door, but the possibility of finding it empty had not crossed her mind. The bunks were still there, stripped to the wooden planks, but the stove was gone. The stovepipe, too, was gone, and the hole in the ceiling had been boarded over. It appeared as if no one had been there in a long time. A look of disappointment crossed her face.

"Well, this explains why the door wasn't locked," Dani said.

271

She sat on the lower bunk and leaned back on her hands. She watched her mother as she walked around the tiny cabin. After a few moments Emily came over and stood in front of her.

"This is where ... your father ... brought me after he found me in the woods."

Dani stared at her mother, shocked. This was the first time she had heard her mother admit that John David Marten was her father.

"We came back several times that year," Emily said, "in the winter, and then in the spring. Nobody but Gramma Davignon knew about it. Not even Grandpa. Not even *now*."

Dani nodded. She understood that her mother was telling her that this was a secret not to be shared with her friends.

"Is this where I was ... you know, conceived?" Dani asked, embarrassed.

Emily chuckled at the description, then nodded in agreement.

"Why couldn't you tell me?"

"I had to protect your father. My being pregnant would have been used by the district attorney as the motive for him killing Jack O'Neill."

"Have you ever heard from him?" Dani asked.

"No."

"Why wouldn't he want to see me?"

"Dani, he didn't even know I was pregnant."

"But I thought you said ..."

"I said the D.A. would say he killed Jack O'Neill because I was carrying his baby when Jack raped me. But nobody knew I was pregnant."

"So why did he kill him?"

"That I don't know," Emily said with a sigh. She paused for a moment, then added, "Well, actually, I suppose I do. He just did what any wild animal would do. Which is pretty much what he was."

"What was he really like?" Dani asked.

"I was just beginning to find out when all this happened. He was like two different people. In town, he was ... well, he didn't socialize much. He hated small talk. Actually, he hated just about any kind of talk." Emily laughed to herself.

"It was like teaching a bear to dance," she said. "It doesn't come naturally." She paused for a moment to think of him in this cabin. "But out here he was different. The way he walked, the way he jumped across a stream, the way he crouched down to examine tracks on the ground. It was likely watching a beautiful mountain lion, or a wolf."

Emily looked up at her daughter.

"To be honest," Emily said, "I still don't know if I loved him or not. We were so different."

They were both silent for a long moment. Dani did not want to speak, hoping that her silence would encourage her mother to go on.

"I don't think he could have lived out in the real world." Emily said. "And I don't suppose I could have spent my whole life in the woods. So where would that have left us?"

Emily walked to the door and stared out at the trees. Dani glanced around the cabin again, then checked her watch. It was past two o'clock. That didn't leave a lot of time for the long hike back.

"We'd better get going if we want to get home before dark," Dani said.

As she slid forward on the bunk her fingers ran across a series of grooves in the boards and she turned around to see what they were. She studied them for a moment, then read aloud, haltingly, for the light was exceedingly poor, two lines of verse.

We two, how long we were fooled
Long have we been absent, but now we return.

Upon hearing the words Emily spun around in the doorway. Her hands went to her cheeks.

"*Whitman,*" she whispered.

"What?" Dani said. "What does it mean?"

Emily rushed over to examine the words for herself.

273

"It's a poem by Walt Whitman," she said. "I haven't read it in years, but I gave John David a copy of *Leaves of Grass* once. He must have read it."

Emily ran her fingers over the carved letters. She quickly took out the map and traced the words onto the back with a pencil, then held them up to the doorway light. The letters had been carefully etched in the wood.

When would he have written this? Days afterward? Months? Years?

Emily searched the cabin for more clues, etchings on the logs, a note tucked in some corner, anything. But the cabin was bare. Finally Dani convinced her mother that they really had to get back. The left the cabin and walked back through the meadow and crossed the rocky stream.

The thought of those passing years filled Emily with a pang of great sadness. It began in her stomach and slowly crept up to her throat. She could no longer remember John David's voice or even what he looked like. Was it possible that she had passed him on the street and not recognized him? Once, back when she was in college, she saw a man that looked like him in the park near her grandfather's house on Hope Street. She had turned away, momentarily frightened by the apparition, and when she looked back he was gone. But that was more than ten years ago. All that was left were those words etched in the cabin bunk. And what if Emily hadn't returned to find them? Would he have been willing to let them go unheard?

Even as she walked, the tears began to flow from her eyes. She let them fall onto the ground beneath her feet. And when she could no longer see, she sat upon a boulder near a stream and allowed herself to cry. Dani stood nearby but remained silent. The water in the stream splashed over the rocks, racing on down the mountain to the Hudson River and the ocean beyond. A bluejay alighted upon a spruce bough and screamed once before flying away.

"You have a fool for a mother," Emily said, wiping the tears from her face with both hands.

Dani did not answer. She wanted to say something, but didn't want to grope for the right words.

274

Emily looked up at her daughter standing by the stream. The lean, muscular body seemed unbelievably perfect. The broad angular shoulders, the powerful calves and equine shins. She was as majestic as the trees that surrounded her.

"But *you* were meant to be," Emily concluded. "That much I know."

Chapter Thirty-One

In the weeks after Susan Davignon's death in 1956, Robert went through all of his wife's belongings and weeded out many things. He wasn't sure why he did it. It seemed disrespectful, but he told Julia that he had to concentrate on raising Emily. He gave Susan's clothes to the church and packed her jewelry into an old footlocker. He cleaned out the mahogany lowboy that contained her stationery and the fountain pen her father had given her as a graduation present and put them in a box with old letters. He had intended to give these things to Emily when she grew up, but the footlocker was placed in the attic of the house on Raquette Lake and long forgotten.

Thirty years later the roof on that house began to leak and Julia decided to clean up the attic before the men came to put on a new roof. Julia threw out racks of old clothes, a broken lamp, boxes of old textbooks and notes from college, and a huge stack of records. She found some of Emily's baby clothes and put them aside for her. Then she found the footlocker. She wasn't sure if she had ever noticed it before. It had been packed away before she and Robert were married and the movers handled it when they came to Henoga Valley. She had been too busy when they left New York City to look at all these things, but now she opened the locker and carefully studied its contents. She immediately recognized the fountain pen, and earrings she had given Susan for Christmas when they were freshmen at college. She found a small stack of the mass cards from Susan's funeral held together by a rubber band that crumbled when she touched it. Julia slowly ran her fingers over one of the mass cards, feeling the raised letters. She found Susan's address book stuffed with odd little bits of paper, which made Julia laugh because it reminded her of how Susan often wrote notes to herself. In college her desk had been covered with messages, classroom assignments, deadlines, notes for reports. Julia leafed through the address book and smiled at the old phone numbers. STUart399. HObart 511. She was just about to close the address book when she noticed the corner of an envelope sticking out from between two of the pages. Julia grabbed the tip and pulled it out. The envelope was yellow with age. She turned it over and gasped when she saw her own name penned on the front in Susan's neat handwriting. The envelope had already been opened. Julia reached inside and pulled out an undated letter.

Dear Julia,

We have been so close for so long that I think of you more as a sister than as a friend. And because we have been so close, what you and Robert have done hurts me that much more. I'm sorry that I have to write a letter instead of talking to you face to face. But I can't bring myself to do that. I know about the affair and the abortion. I don't care whose fault it was. Robert doesn't even know that I know, but I think it would be best if you just moved out of the building.

Susan

Julia was so shocked by the letter that she nearly fainted. The muscles in her neck constricted like a scarf pulled taut and a knot formed in her stomach. *Oh my God, she knew about us!* The air in the attic suddenly grew hot and Julia gasped for air. She stumbled down the stairs to the hallway and then down the hall to her bedroom, holding onto the wall as she went. She sat on the edge of her bed and read the letter or several times, rocking back and forth, crying. She could hear Susan's voice scolding her over a span of thirty years. She looked again at the envelope and a second wave of panic rushed over her. *Who opened it?* Had Robert kept it from her all these years? Or, had Emily found it back when she used to spend so much time playing up in the attic?

The realization that Susan knew of her affair with Robert struck Julia like a slap in the face. Susan had died almost a year after the affair. *Did she know right away?* Julia couldn't

278

remember anything Susan said or did in the last year of her life that indicated she knew about the affair. She tried to force herself to picture those events, but she felt like she was imagining them. How could she remember a sidelong glance now, so many years later? So many memories had vanished into the vast abyss of time. All that remained was the letter, which she reread a dozen more times.

Julia's life suddenly became a source of great shame. She felt as if she had stolen Susan's life. *I shouldn't be here,* she thought, wandering around the house. *This house doesn't belong to me. It belongs to Susan.* Julia felt like an intruder. She thought of the past three decades and was deluged by an endless stream of questions. *When was the letter written, and why had Susan decided not to send it? Or did she die before she had the chance to put it in the mail?*

Another woman might have considered the discovery of the lost letter as nothing more than a coincidence, but Julia did not believe in coincidences. Everything in life was somehow connected to everything else. The fact that it had rained, briefly, on the morning of her wedding to Robert was a sign from God, though not nearly as ominous as it would have been if it had rained the entire day. A cloudless sky on the morning of one of Emily's birthday parties was a sign of the child's purity. The tree in the yard struck by lightening the week after they moved to Henoga Valley had such frightening implications that she went to mass every morning for months. And so the storm that caused the roof to leak had been 'sent' to Henoga Valley on a mission, to speak for the dead and chastise her after thirty years.

Julia felt a dreadful urge to query Robert or Emily about the letter and therefore decided to avoid them to keep herself from blurting it out. She knew that the secret wanted to be free, that it wanted to jump from one person to the next. Whoever she asked would be the one who *hadn't* seen the letter, and then the secret would have spread to another person.

She had to escape. She told Robert that her mother was ill and then drove down to Glens Falls to visit her for a week. *You remember her, don't you mother? Susan Harkins? Emily's real mother. She was my college roommate.* But although Mrs.

Behrens knew of Susan, she could not remember having met her.

"Was she that tall girl with the red hair?" Mrs. Behrens asked.

"No, mother. That was Alice Morrow, from high school."

"Oh, yes. Alice. I remember *her*," she said, pleased, as if that small measure of success was somehow useful.

After a week in Glens Falls Julia decided to drive up to Plattsburgh and wander around the campus. She checked the faculty roster but could not find anyone who had taught there thirty-five years earlier. She walked through the corridors of MacDonough Hall, trying to imagine Susan and her together again in this dormitory. Although she tried to focus on these events, she found that it was like trying to recall a movie she had seen a long time ago.

It had been quite natural, Julia remembered, to fill in for Susan after she died. She did all the babysitting, even when she was coming off a shift. She washed the diapers, did all of the cooking and cleaning, and even started handling Robert's bills because he was indifferent to all domestic responsibilities. It was never a chore for Julia because she loved Emily as her own. And yet he did not seem to love *her*, and she was surprised when he asked her to marry him.

"But ... but you've never even told me that you love me," Julia said when he proposed.

"But I *do* love you. How could you doubt that ... after all we've been through?"

"I just don't know. How can I be sure ... how can we be sure ... that it wouldn't be a mistake?"

Robert explained how it was perfect for all of them. He was getting a raise and Julia could quit her job to take care of Emily. There was no question that he loved her, and couldn't wait to love her again, for of course they had been abstaining from sex, at Julia's insistence, out of respect for Susan. He understood that and fully agreed with her.

And for many years Julia had been able to put Susan's death behind her and raise Emily as her own daughter. Her inability to conceive was, for a time, a painful reminder of the past, as if her own womanhood had been stripped away. And, of course, Julia

280

had been able to accept her punishment, for it was certainly punishment, even if Robert thought it foolish to believe in such things. But she had gotten over that many years ago. Her marriage to Robert had been a good marriage. He had been kind and even thoughtful, sometimes, though he remained aloof. If it bothered him that they could not have any more children, he never showed it. Now the letter brought it all to the forefront again, reminding her that she did not belong in that house on the lake. She wasn't Robert's wife. She wasn't Emily's mother.

It was an unfortunate state of mind for Julia to be in during the long drive from Plattsburgh back to Henoga Valley. The winding mountain roads required undivided attention, even in the best of weather. A thunder shower had appeared out of the south and dropped several inches of rain in a matter of fifteen minutes. Although Julia had the wipers on high speed, she could barely see the road ahead. She felt the puddles of water tugging at her tires, and several times they nearly yanked her into the guardrails. She finally decided it was too dangerous to continue and pulled her car off onto the shoulder to wait out the storm. However, she inexplicably left the car lights on without her flashers, and to the driver of the tractor trailer that followed several minutes later her car appeared to be moving. It was, he later explained, natural to follow the taillights of the car in front of you, particularly in bad weather. By the time the truck driver realized he was following a parked car, it was too late. He yanked the steering wheel to the left in a desperate attempt to avoid the parked vehicle but caught the tail end of the car with his massive steel bumper. The force of the impact was so great that all of the windows simultaneously exploded. The car momentarily became airborne and spun around sideways in front of the truck, which, in spite of the brakes now being futilely applied, continued barreling forward. The collision and sudden braking forced the driver to lose control of the heavy rig, which careened back and forth on the mountain road like a giant snake. The truck caught the car in the middle of driver's side door and pushed it forward. The trailer whipped back and forth several times and it appeared that the truck might capsize. But instead, it plowed headlong into the guardrails at a bend in the road only

281

twenty yards from the initial impact. Julia's car was crushed so badly that the first rescue workers to reach the scene could not identify the make or model, and reported over their radios only that it was 'some kind of sedan.'

Chapter Thirty-Two

Diana Marten heard the grinding of bicycle tires on the gravel driveway and looked up from the kitchen sink. It was the middle of a weekday afternoon, an unusual time for the paperboy to come around collecting, but the paperboy's bike was the only one Diana had heard in that driveway since her own boys had left. She dried her hands and walked out to the porch. A tall girl with long dark hair was standing next to her ten-speed bike, her back to the porch, putting down the kickstand. Diana recognized her immediately as Danielle Davignon. She was wearing a Spandex bodysuit. Her broad muscular shoulders and powerful legs were unmistakable. Diana had seen the girl often since she and her mother returned to Henoga Valley. Diana had attended most of the girls' home basketball games and track meets, watching from a distance as the magnificent Danielle Davignon performed incredible athletic feats. Diana did not like basketball. It seemed a rather brutish sport for girls, but she loved to watch Dani compete in track. She ran the mile and two-miles races, the longest of the running events. Although several boys could keep up with her for the first half-mile, Danielle always appeared to gain strength as the races went on and she often won by half a lap or more. Even from a distance Diana could see how remarkably relaxed Danielle was on the track, her long ponytail bouncing from side to side. The unusual combination of powerful thighs and delicate footsteps reminded Diana of a deer bounding across an open field. On many occasions Diana had wanted to approach Danielle after a track meet and congratulate her, but she had never summoned the courage.

Dani turned from her bike and started to walk toward the house when she noticed Mrs. Marten on the porch. She stopped abruptly and the two of them stared at each other for several moments. Neither one seemed to know what to say. Finally, Danielle spoke.

"Mrs. Marten?" she said, although she knew who the woman was. "I'm Danielle Davignon."

Diana shook her head in recognition, although she appeared to be in shock. Danielle walked up onto the porch.

"I just wanted to introduce myself," Danielle said. She knew that her mother and Mrs. Marten had never met, at least not formally, but she had seen the woman at her grandmother's funeral a few weeks before and had recognized her. Dani still hadn't decided what she should say to the woman, but she had ridden by the house so many times that she finally decided to just stop and say hello. She was surprised to see tears running down the woman's cheeks. Dani walked up to her and they held each other in a long embrace. Diana rubbed Dani's back several times, not wanting to let go of her.

"Let me look at you, up close," Diana said, wiping the tears from her face. "My God, you're stunning."

Dani was embarrassed by such comments and did not respond. Diana took her inside the house and sat her down at the kitchen table. They talked for several minutes about Gramma Davignon and Emily, and school, but they were both anxious to talk about the past. About John David Marten. Diana went into the living room and returned with two photo albums, which they studied for the next two hours. Dani examined every picture in detail, wanting to know why each picture was taken and what had been said. She ran her fingers over the photos as if to touch her father.

"*Is* he your father?" Diana asked. She had wanted to know for years, and there had never been a delicate way to find out.

"Yes," Dani replied, then cautioned her grandmother about the need for secrecy. "My mother didn't tell me until this summer."

Dani flipped back through several pages to a picture of John David in his high school baseball uniform. It had been taken just before the sectional championship game. He was standing in front of the dugout with his right arm draped around Jack O'Neill's shoulder and his left leaning on a bat. Jack was holding his bat over his shoulder and both boys stood with their legs crossed at the ankles.

"Would you like to have that picture?" Diana Marten asked.

"Could I?" Dani said.

284

Diana carefully peeled back the plastic sheathing and removed the photograph.

"They were such good friends," Diana said. "And they were good boys, both of them. In spite of what everybody says."

"Have you seen him since he disappeared?"

Diana shook her head no.

"I hope you aren't waiting for him to show up," Diana said. "I'm afraid he'll disappoint you."

"But what about that girl over in Newcomb? Don't you think it was John David who rescued her?"

"It's a nice thought. But anyone could have done it, knowing that they would blame it on John David. Dutch, that's your grandfather, he told me about an incident a couple of years ago when a bear broke into camps up near Big Moose Lake. The bear was killed a couple of weeks later and everyone said it was John David, but Dutch heard it was killed by a couple of guys from Old Forge."

Dani looked at the photograph again.

"Are *any* of the stories true?" she asked.

"I don't know, dear," Diana said. "Some, maybe. I never knew what to believe because people up here are known for telling stories. He's 'J.D. Marten' now. He's just another one of their stories."

"But some of it has to be true."

"Well, I'm pretty sure the hunting part is. I know he shot his first deer when he was nine years old. We weren't any poorer than a lot of other people around here, but we couldn't always afford to buy meat at the store, either. But after John David starting hunting we never went without meat. I never asked how he got them because half the time it was out of hunting season. The funny thing is that he brought the meat home already butchered. Whenever I would ask for even the least bit of information, he'd say, 'Mom, you don't want to know.' Which sounded so ominous that I *didn't* want to know. Now I wish I knew."

"What about the Indian?" Dani said.

"How do you know about the Indian?" Diana asked, surprised.

"My mother told me about him. She said my father met him when he was a boy and he was the one who taught him everything."

Diana Marten nodded her head.

"He mentioned this Indian once, when he was maybe eleven years old. His father had a fit about it. He said it didn't want his son hanging around any 'savages.' Of course, he was just jealous. But John David never mentioned the Indian in this house again."

"But he didn't stop talking to him, did he?"

"Oh, of course not. John David never listened to his father."

"What was his name? Mom couldn't remember."

"Michael Sabelle. He lived by himself over near Big Moose. But I'm not sure he's still alive."

They were silent for a moment. Dani once again studied the picture of her father and Jack O'Neill in their baseball uniforms.

"Do you blame my mother for coming between them?" Dani asked.

"No. It wasn't your mother's fault."

"She says it was."

"Your poor mother," Diana said. "I imagine she's been through a lot, what with all the publicity. She doesn't need a load of guilt on top of it. You tell her to come over and see me sometime. I'd love to meet her."

Diana walked out with Danielle and waited while she buckled her helmet.

"I've been to all your basketball games," Diana said. "And the track meets. I always wanted to cheer for you, but ... you know."

"I'd like you to come," Dani said.

"Aren't you afraid of what people would say?"

Dani shook her head no.

"What could they say that I haven't already heard?" Dani replied. "I'm not ashamed that he's my father."

"But you're still going to keep quiet about that," Diana said.

"Yeah. Let them go on guessing."

The two of them laughed at their secret. There was an awkward silence in which Diana realized Danielle wanted to ask something else.

Finally, Dani said, "Are you ... and Mr. Marten?"

"Still married? No, not really. We haven't gotten a divorce yet, but he lives in town now, in an apartment. I finally got up the nerve to throw him out. Should have done it long ago."

Dani hopped on her bike and fixed her toe into the stirrup.

"Not a lot of good men out there, are there?" Dani said with a chuckle.

"Oh, Dani, now don't get the wrong impression. There are plenty of good men." She looked at Dani for a moment, then added, laughing, "I'm certain of it."

Chapter Thirty-Three

One week before the start of her senior year at Henoga Valley High School, Danielle rode her bike up to Big Moose. She had discovered that Michael Sabelle was still alive and living alone in his log cabin on the edge of the wilderness. She got directions to Sabelle's cabin, which was the only house on a four-mile road off the county road. She had wanted to call him first, but his phone number was no longer listed in the directory.

She walked up onto the porch and knocked several times at the door. Finally, a man, who appeared to be only in his forties or fifties, answered the door.

"Pardon me," Danielle stammered, "I'm looking for Michael Sabelle. But I must be at the wrong place."

"No, you're in the right place. C'mon in."

"*You're* not Michael Sabelle, are you?"

"Well, yes and no. I'm *a* Michael Sabelle, but not *the* Michael Sabelle. I'm his son, but folks call me Mickey. Can you imagine, an Indian by the name of Mickey? Hate the name, but I've never been able to shake it."

"You don't look like an Indian," Danielle said. She hadn't meant it to sound derogatory. She was merely confused. The man had a closely cropped beard and shoulder-length hair tied in a braid, which he wore under a Yankees baseball cap.

"That's because I'm not wearing my feathers and war paint," Mickey said, smiling.

"No, no. I didn't mean that. I meant ... I don't know what I meant. But I didn't mean anything bad. And I didn't mean to call you an Indian. I should have said 'Native American.'"

"No offense taken. I was just doing my righteous indignation act. I like to embarrass white people whenever I can get the chance."

"Well it worked," Dani said, holding her hand to her chest. "I feel terrible."

"Hey, don't worry about it," Mickey said, waving his hand. "So, you're here to see my father. Let me guess. You must be another one of these high school kids doing a report on New

York State Native ... what should we call them? Native New Yorkers?"

"No. I wanted to ask him about John David Marten."

"*Marten?!* You're doing a report on Marten? Didn't somebody already write a book about him?"

"I'm not doing a report on anybody. I'm just interested in how he learned so much about the woods."

"Well, Dad's the one to tell you about that, but he's sleeping right now. He takes a morning nap and an afternoon nap, then he goes to bed around eight o'clock. So that doesn't leave much time for interviews. 'Course, he *is* ninety-three."

"I'm sorry. I guess I came at the wrong time. I wanted to call, but the number isn't listed."

"It's not listed because my father doesn't have a phone anymore. Got rid of it as soon as he gave up guiding. That's why I have to come down from Canada every couple of weeks to check on him."

"Doesn't any of your family still live around here?"

"We never did. The rest of us stayed on the reservation in Canada. Dad was the only one who came down here. He didn't like living on a reservation, and my mother didn't want to leave her family."

"Oh, how sad."

"It's not as bad as it sounds. His father did the same thing. Dad came back to visit us all the time and he always sent money. He made a lot more down here than he would have back on the reservation."

"Well, maybe I should just try again another time," Dani said.

Mickey glanced over her shoulder at the bicycle.

"Where'd you say you lived?" he asked.

"Henoga Valley."

"That's fourteen miles from here."

"I don't mind. I ride at least that far every day."

"You don't say. Well then, why don't you come back tomorrow around noon. Dad never sleeps through lunch."

And so the next day Dani again rode her bike to the Sabelle's cabin, arriving shortly before noon. Mickey greeted her in the driveway and walked her around to the back porch overlooking the lake. Michael Sabelle was sitting in a rocking chair, but he stood up as Dani climbed the stairs.

"I'd introduce you," Mickey said, "but I forgot to get your name."

"I'm Danielle," she said, shaking the old Indian's hand. "I've heard so much about you."

Mickey said, "The two of you sit and talk while I go fix us some lunch."

Dani sat down next to Sabelle, who slowly settled back into his chair.

"So, you want to know about John David Marten," he said. "And what makes you think I know him?"

"He told my mother that you taught him everything about the woods."

"Well, that's not really true. I only got him started. I met him when he was about ten years old, setting traps out in the swamp behind Moose Mountain. He didn't know the first thing about trapping," Sabelle said, laughing. "He'd put them any old place, near a rock, near a tree. Wouldn't even cover them. So I taught him to think like the animal he was trying to catch."

Sabelle stopped rocking and leaned forward in the chair.

"Take a fox, for example. You might think they're like wolves or dogs, but they're not. A wolf or a dog will walk in a straight line across a field, but a fox zigzags back and forth, checking out every little hole and mound." Sabelle illustrated with his hand. "The wolf is looking for big game. But the fox lives on mice and moles. If he didn't check out all the little holes, he'd never find anything to eat. So if you make a little mound in the middle of a field and place a trap near it, you'll have yourself a fox."

Danielle listened for another fifteen minutes while Sabelle explained various methods of trapping mink, racoons, bear and fishers. She realized after a few minutes that Sabelle must have thought that she wanted to learn about trapping. She was too polite to correct him, so she continued to listen until Mickey broke up the conversation with lunch.

"It's such a nice day, I thought we'd eat out here," he said.

291

He was carrying sandwiches and tea on a wooden tray. He looked at Dani and said, "So, it's trapping you're interested in. I wouldn't have guessed. Trapping isn't popular these days, particularly with girls."

"Well, actually, I'm *not* interested in trapping, really." Then, thinking she might be insulting Sabelle, she said, "I mean, I am interested, but not for myself. I just wanted to know more about John David Marten. When was the last time you saw him?"

"When was the last time anyone saw him?" Sabelle replied.

"Why are you so interested in him?" Mickey asked.

"I can't say."

"What? You're a little young to work for the FBI, aren't you?"

"It's personal."

"Well you can tell *us*," Mickey said, chuckling. "We'll keep your little secret."

Dani looked at the two men and sighed.

"He's my father," she said.

The two men looked at each other, obviously surprised.

"How do you know that?" Mickey asked.

"My mother told me," Dani said, annoyed. "How else would I know?"

"Who's your mother?" Sabelle asked, obviously confused.

"Emily Davignon."

Mickey stood up and walked over to the porch railing. He looked out over the lake for a moment, then he turned back to Dani and said, "So you're the baby I read about in that book?"

"You've read it, too?"

"Of course. Who around here hasn't?"

"So you can understand why I'm interested in finding him."

Sabelle put down his cup of tea and shifted his weight in the rocking chair.

"Did John David know about you?" he asked.

"No," Dani said. "My mother didn't even know she was pregnant until after Jack O'Neill was killed."

Mickey leaned against the porch railing and studied Dani for a moment.

292

"Not many people know that my father and John David Marten knew each other."

Emily looked over at Sabelle, who nodded in agreement.

"If I said I knew where he was," Sabelle said, "I'd be ... what do they call it?"

"Harboring a fugitive," Mickey said.

"Yeah, that's it. Of course, it doesn't matter much at my age," Sabelle said, laughing. "They wouldn't put an old Indian in jail."

"So you *do* know what happened to him," Dani said.

Sabelle looked at Mickey, who raised his eyebrows and shrugged his shoulders.

"Sure, go ahead," Mickey said, apparently answering his father's unspoken question. "Why not."

"He arrived here early in the morning a few days after that boy was killed," Sabelle said. "I called my family in Canada and told them that John David would be coming to stay with them for awhile. Then I gave him a small canoe and some provisions and John David took the wilderness route to Canada. He traveled only at night, so nobody ever saw him."

"Is he still there?" Dani asked, turning to Mickey.

"No," Mickey said. "He stayed with us for a few years, then headed out west. He wanted to move out to the Yukon or the Northwest Territories. We used to hear from him every once in a while, but not in the last eight or ten years. Last I knew he was a guide and doing quite well."

Dani suddenly felt stupid for having spent all those nights in the woods talking to the empty forest. But she was excited to hear some news about him. A guide, she thought. In the Yukon. That sounded like him.

"Do you have an address where I could write to him?" she asked.

"Giving out the address of a fugitive is not a good idea, Danielle," Mickey said. "You can't just start writing to him. The FBI could monitor the post office, even now, after all these years."

"Maybe I could just go out and visit him. Nobody would know about it."

Mickey said, "You have to understand why we're so protective. We adopted him into the tribe and we've done a good job of hiding him. No one out west is ever going to suspect that he's a fugitive. He's safe. You wouldn't want to jeopardize that, would you?"

"No, of course not," Dani said, obviously disappointed. Then it dawned on her that there might be another reason for them not wanting her to contact John David. "Does he have a family out there?"

Mickey nodded.

"So you don't want me to contact him because his wife doesn't even know that he's John David Marten. Is that it?"

"Well, sort of," Mickey said.

She thought for a moment, then said, "What if I gave you a letter? Couldn't you get it to him somehow? Couldn't you mail it from Canada and tell him to rip it up after he's read it? He wouldn't even have to tell his wife."

Mickey looked at his father and they both nodded.

"I suppose," Mickey said. "I'll be back here the week after next. You can leave the letter with my father and I'll pick it up then."

Dani stood up and hugged Mickey impulsively. Then she leaned over and hugged Sabelle in his chair.

"This means so much to me," she said to both of them, excited. "Thank you."

There was an awkward moment while they seemed to study her. She thought, perhaps they disapprove of the whole idea and are just pretending to go along with it. Maybe they don't even plan to *send* the letter.

"People look at me and I know what they're thinking," Dani said. "'Who's the father, Jack or John David?' I always pretend like I don't care, and I suppose I *shouldn't* care. But I know they're judging me. That's why I wanted to be just like John David, so that they would *know* that I was his daughter."

The two men listened in silence.

"Mom never told me that John David was my father until after I found his cabin in the woods."

"You found his cabin?!" Sabelle asked.

294

"Well, I found a meadow that Mom painted with John David in it. Then she came back with me and took me to the cabin."

"Is she married now?" Mickey asked.

"No. Not even close. I used to think it was because she was a man-hater, but now I think it's because she still loves John David."

"What makes you think that?" Mickey asked.

"The look on her face when we found a poem that John David carved in one of the bunks. Something about being fooled, and being absent for so long and then returning. Mom almost started to cry when she read it. *That's* when I finally put it all together."

There was another silence and Dani decided it was time to leave. She thanked Sabelle and Mickey again. They smiled at her but said nothing.

It was less than a week later when Danielle returned to Michael Sabelle's cabin. She found the old man sitting on the back porch.

"You didn't bring a letter?" Sabelle said, noticing her empty hands.

"No, I didn't."

"I would have thought you'd have a lot to say."

"I thought I did," Danielle said, "but after I left here last week I found out that I just had a lot of questions. I didn't want to write a letter with a list of questions."

"No, I suppose not. That wouldn't be much of a letter."

"You don't think I should try to get in touch with him, do you?" Dani asked.

"Who am I to say?" Sabelle answered gently. "I'm an old Indian living alone at the edge of the woods. All of my friends and most of my family are dead. I can understand why you would want to see your father. I would like to go fishing with my father now, too."

"It's just that, after I left here I realized that I had the wrong image of him," Dani said. "All this time I was thinking that he lived *here*, in the mountains. And that he .... sort of ... watched over people. Over me." She paused upon hearing her own thoughts. "Oh, I know this all sounds so *stupid*."

"No, it doesn't."

"I should just keep that image of him and leave well enough alone. I wanted the mythical J.D. Marten to be my father. The legend, the one who rescues kidnapped girls. I probably wouldn't like the real John David Marten."

Sabelle leaned back in his chair and rocked gently. He looked at Dani for several minutes and she turned her eyes downward, embarrassed.

"You would have liked the real John David," Sabelle said. "Your father was a great woodsman. If he had lived a hundred years ago he'd have been the greatest of the Adirondack guides. Your father could walk through the forest without making a sound. And what he did better than any man I have ever known, was disappear in the woods. He used to play tricks on me when he was just a boy, sneak up on me when I was hunting and tap me on the shoulder. I'd never hear him coming."

Dani smiled to hear a real story about him. She had always imagined him somber, but Sabelle made him sound playful.

"And he was smart, like a wolf. You'd turn around and see him there, staring at you with those eyes. But you'd never hear him coming." Sabelle started to chuckle. "I had all I could do to not to laugh out loud when the sheriff said they were tracking him. He could have been following them and they wouldn't have known it."

"Did he really kill Jack O'Neill?"

"That I don't know," Sabelle said.

"Why wouldn't he tell you?"

"Let me tell you something about him. When he was little and came to visit me, he used to talk constantly. I taught him how to listen. When he got older we could spend a whole day fishing and hardly a word would pass between us. I would reach for a worm and he'd already be holding up the can. He learned to talk by thinking. So when he showed up that morning and asked for a canoe, I didn't ask him why. If he had wanted me to know more, he'd have told me."

"He probably didn't tell you anything so that you wouldn't be involved."

"Maybe."

Dani stood up and walked to the porch stairs. Her arms were folded in front of her chest. She looked out over the lake that her father had used in his escape and envisioned him paddling away, disappearing into the forest.

"He has always seemed so real to me," she said quietly.

Chapter Thirty-Four

It was several weeks after Julia Davignon's death before Emily could bring herself to go over to her parents' house on Raquette Lake and pack up her mother's personal belongings. Her father was at the hospital when she arrived, but Emily had a key and let herself in. She brought with her several large cardboard boxes, which she carried up to the bedroom. She went through the closets, examining every article of clothing and reminiscing about the last time she had seen her mother wear it. The chenille bathrobe brought back an image of her mother sipping coffee at the kitchen table. A mauve sweatsuit reminded her of one of Dani's cross- country meets. Emily put aside several sweaters, all of which were too big for her but might fit Dani. Everything else went into the boxes for the Salvation Army. She cleaned out all of her mother's shoes from the closet and emptied the bureau drawers. As each box was filled she carried it downstairs and put it in the back of her Bronco. Then she went up into the attic and looked for clothes that might have been stored up there.

Emily had not been up in the attic of the old house for many years. A flood of memories overcame her as she climbed the narrow staircase. The old familiar solitude returned like a childhood friend, the gentle stillness that had always ebbed and flowed with the weather. The rain tapping on the roof in September, the gentle rattling of maple leaves in the tree near the window. And on cold November afternoons, the wind whistling through the uncaulked attic window. And Sarah.

The attic, she now realized, had been a gift from her mother. Emily had always been reclusive, which was a great concern to her parents, so it must have been difficult for her mother to disregard conventional wisdom and allow Emily to hide away under these eaves.

When all of the items were packed into the Bronco, Emily went into the kitchen to write her father a note. She looked around the counter for a pencil and paper and noticed her mother's purse tucked in the corner by the toaster. Blood stains

299

were still evident on the dark blue leather. Emily reached over slowly and pulled the purse toward her. She unzipped it and dumped its contents onto the counter. Susan's yellowed letter, still in the envelope, landed on top of the pile. Emily's heart started to pound when she recognized the letter from the old footlocker. She remembered finding it when she was nine years old, and feeling like a spy opening it with a knife. She remembered the word *abortion* and how she had to look it up in the dictionary, which had only confused her because there were so many different meanings of the word. It had been Jennifer Baker who finally explained it to her, in her offhand and somewhat vulgar way, but it had been several weeks before Emily *believed* her.

Emily looked at the note again. She remembered wanting to tear up the letter, but it had seemed too important a document to destroy. So she had placed it back in the footlocker and never again opened the hideous black box. She pushed the footlocker into a corner and covered it with boxes of old books. And there it remained, the ugly secret that her three parents shared, for thirty years.

Except that they *hadn't* shared the secret, Emily now realized. *She* was the one who opened the letter. That meant that Julia had never before seen it. And neither had her father.

And so, instead of leaving a note of her own for her father, Emily left the contents of the purse spilled out upon the counter. With her mother's letter on top of the pile.

Part III

Chapter Thirty-Five

Danielle Davignon had always been a most unflappable young lady, not in the least prone to hysterics. Once a black bear wandered into their campsite and she calmly coaxed it away from the tent with a piece of brook trout. So when Dani's mother heard a deep guttural scream one morning in October, she naturally assumed that Dani must have been badly injured. Dani had gone downstairs to fix breakfast while her mother showered. Upon hearing the scream, Emily turned off the water and shouted to Dani, but all she heard were Dani's hysterics. Emily quickly covered herself with a towel and ran downstairs. Dani was standing over the newspaper at the kitchen table, trembling and ashen.

"What is it, Dani?!" Emily asked. She suddenly remembered when President Kennedy had been assassinated and a knot formed in her stomach. But even an attempt on the life of a president would not have shocked her as much as the headline that read, *J.D. Marten Surrenders.* Emily had to reach for the chair to steady herself. The words seemed to rise off the page like a ghost.

"Mom?" Dani said, crying. "What did I do?"

"Oh, God, Dani. I don't know." She did not even understand her daughter's remarks.

Emily picked up the paper and quickly read the article. Most of the story was about things that had happened eighteen years ago. There had been no new tips, no manhunt. Sheriff Cooney was quoted as saying that John David had walked in the front door of the sheriff's office at the county office building and said to a receptionist, 'I heard you were looking for me.'

"Dear, God, what have *I* done?" Emily said.

"*You?!* You didn't do anything. What do you mean 'you?'"

"It's not important," Emily said. She turned to Dani and said, "Look, I have to go down and see him."

"I'm coming too."

"Dani, you can't. Not now."

"*Mom!*"

"Dani, I need to talk to him first about some things. I'll bring you by later. But there's going to be a lot of newspaper people."

"Mom, I can handle it."

"I know you can, dear. But just go to school and I'll take you over later. I promise."

"I can't think about *school!*" Dani said. She sat next to her mother and took the paper. "I shouldn't have started this. I shouldn't have gone to see Sabelle."

"What?" Emily asked. "You went to see Sabelle?! When?!"

Dani told her mother about her two visits during the summer. She told her how John David had escaped through the mountains to the Abenaki reservation in Canada, and how he had been a guide somewhere out in western Canada for years.

"Why didn't you tell me about this?" Emily asked.

"I was waiting for the right time. I thought you might be mad at me for telling someone else that John David is my father."

Emily quizzed her daughter about everything Sabelle and Mickey had said.

"So," Emily said, when Dani had finished, "he heard about you and came back."

"But what about his family?" Dani said. "How could he do this to them?"

Emily placed a hand on her face and stared down at the paper.

"I gotta think," she said.

Dani asked, "If he wanted to see me, why wouldn't he just ... you know, stop by the house or something? Why did he have to turn himself in?"

But Emily could not answer these questions. It had been eighteen years since she had seen John David. She had no idea what he might be thinking. Emily told Dani that she could stay home from school. She gave Dani instructions to stay in the house and close the blinds, but she could see from her expression that she wasn't going to obey.

"Oh, all right," she said, too rushed to argue. "You can come with me."

The jail was in the Hamilton County Courthouse, which had been built in 1878. There weren't any visitation rooms, just four cells in the basement. John David was the only prisoner in the jail. The building inspector had long complained that the jail didn't meet New York State code, but the sheriff argued that they weren't going to build a million-dollar prison for a handful of prisoners, most of whom were drunks drying out after a night on River Street. Visitors were checked for contraband and then allowed to go one at a time to see their relative. The visitor sat in a wooden chair next to the prisoner's cell.

Dani sat in the waiting area while Emily went in to see John David. Emily was stopped by a guard as she entered the corridor.

"I have to check you, ma'am," he said, holding up a metal detector.

"Officer," Emily said politely. "Mr. Marten turned himself in. A man who turns himself in after eighteen years on the run wouldn't try to break out of jail the next day."

"Just following protocol, ma'am," he said, running the wand over her.

The guard opened the door and let Emily into the corridor. He followed her a few steps and then stopped and stood at attention, leaning against the wall with his hands behind his back.

"Last cell on the right," he said, nodding toward the end of the corridor.

Emily walked slowly down the tiled corridor past the empty cells. Her footsteps echoed on the cold brick walls. When she reached the last cell, she leaned against the bars. John David was sitting on the bunk, leaning against the wall.

"Hello, Emily," he said. He stood up slowly and walked over to her.

"Is it really you?" she whispered, as if asking herself rather than him. He seemed taller than she had remembered, and heavier. His hair was past his shoulders and he had grown a beard, which was turning gray. His hands were dark and leathery, like the bottom of a dog's paw. He looked like a bear standing on its hind legs, and Emily instinctively stepped back.

305

"I won't hurt you," he said.

"No, of course you wouldn't," Emily said, embarrassed. She stepped forward and reached up to touch his face, but the guard shouted for her to keep her distance. Emily sat in the wooden chair.

John David's nose and eyes were the same and there was something clearly familiar about him, but she might not have recognized him if they passed on the street. She stared at him for a moment, then asked, "Why?"

"I heard a rumor about me having a daughter. Thought maybe I'd check it out."

"Sabelle told you?"

"Yeah."

"Oh, John David, I never would have said anything to Danielle if I had known it was going to get back to you. You shouldn't have come back."

"Nice welcome," John David said, but he didn't sound hurt.

"I'm sorry. I didn't mean it that way. It's just that ... well, what about your family? What's this going to do to *them*?"

"Emily, I don't have a family."

"But Dani said ..." Emily immediately understood the lie. She stared at John David for a moment, trying to recall him as a teenager. She tried to remember how she had felt when they were alone in his cabin, but it was too long ago. All she felt *now* was fear, a terrible black ache deep in her bowels.

"I brought Dani with me," Emily said. "She wants to meet you. You mean so much to her, even though she's never even met you. She's been hiking out into the woods trying to find you." The tears started streaming down her face. "I told her you were her father because it was what she wanted to hear. But we could have a lawyer order a blood test ... and ... well, then ..."

"But she is my daughter," John David said. "Anyone could see that."

Emily smiled. Yes, of course, it would be obvious. Even to Dani. "I see that you read *Whitman*," she said.

"Many times. Usually I didn't know what he was talking about. But I didn't really care, cause every time I read it I could hear your voice, like you were still there, reading it out loud."

Emily fell silent again. She stared off in the distance for a moment, then turned to John David.

"When did you carve the poem in the bunk?" Emily asked.

"About fifteen years ago. Right after I came back from Canada."

Emily stood up and patted her blouse nervously. She looked around the jail as if she had lost something.

"I don't know what to say," she finally said, looking at the floor. "I don't even know what to think. I suppose I should go call a lawyer."

"I'd appreciate that."

Emily touched the back of John David's hand and then walked quickly down the corridor. She and Dani exchanged an apprehensive glance at the cell block door.

"Is everything okay?" Dani asked. "You didn't stay very long."

"Yes, yes, everything's fine. He'd like to see you now."

"Are you *sure?* You could have stayed longer."

Emily kissed her daughter on the cheek and then watched as Dani walked slowly down the row of cells, her hands partially covering her face. She could see Dani lean over and peek into the cell. But from behind the soundproof door that separated the waiting room from the cell block, Emily could not hear the surprise in her daughter's voice when she recognized her long-absent father.

"*Mickey?!*"

Chapter Thirty-Six

On the night that Jack O'Neill died, a young John David Marten quietly went about the task of loading his backpack. It was only two o'clock in the morning. Daylight was still three hours away and John David knew that the body of his best friend would not likely be discovered until then. Though it was still summer, John David busied himself with rolling up a winter coat and gloves and packing them into the backpack. He heard his mother at the top of the stairs and his pulse quickened. She would be alarmed if she saw him packing a winter coat in June.

"It's just me, Mom," he whispered loudly. "Go back to bed."

"What are you doing at *this* hour?"

"I gotta leave early in the morning, so I'm packing now."

"Just don't wake your father," Diana said. After a moment, she added, "Goodnight. I love you."

"I love you, too," John David answered.

It struck Diana as odd that John David would say *I love you*, since he was awkward with affection. But she smiled in the darkness and went back to bed. John David waited until he heard his mother return to her bedroom and then turned out the kitchen light. He sat in the dark for another fifteen minutes to make sure she was asleep, then he slipped quietly out the back door.

The night air was brisk in spite of the approaching summer. The moon, nearly full, was high above the trees. On the way out the door, John David had grabbed his little brother's squirt gun and filled it with his own urine in the backyard. He knew that the police would be using bloodhounds to track him and he wanted to make sure they followed him to the right place. He used the gun to spray the trail with his scent every few hundred yards. John David picked up a stash of steel leghold traps near the base of Raquette River Mountain. He climbed up the state hiking trail, knowing that it would be easy for the police to follow him. Near the summit he placed a trap in a narrow spot between two boulders and covered it with leaves. Then he sprayed the boulders with his urine. If the dog missed the trap

309

on his first pass, he'd surely step in it sniffing around the boulders. Just before leaving, his conscience got the better of him and he wrapped duct tape around the jaws of the trap. He knew the trap would hurt the dog enough to stop tracking him, even with the tape. There was no point in breaking the animal's paw, he decided.

John David crossed the summit of the mountain and headed down the northern slope. The state hiking trail veered to the west, but John David turned where a larger boulder protruded onto the trail and disappeared into the thick brush. To the casual observer he would have appeared to be bushwhacking, but he was actually following a trail that he had started three years ago. The path was narrow, no wider than his boot, and the branches completely hid it from view. But the branches had been trained by his previous trips. They slid over his backpack and allowed him to pass with little effort, but someone following him even six inches to one side of this trail would quickly become entangled in the mesh of pine and spruce branches. He followed the invisible trail across a sharp ravine that overlooked the Raquette River. He debated sitting there and watching the search party to assess their manhunt, but he finally decided that the trap was likely to stop them if they only had one dog. He'd set additional traps in case they brought more than one dog. Before starting out again, John David took off his hiking boots and put on a pair of calf-high moccasins that Sabelle had made for him. The moccasins were flat on the bottom and did not leave telltale prints like his hiking boots did.

John David looked to the eastern sky. The sun was already beginning to crest over the distant hills. He assumed that the police would not have a search party organized for several more hours. At that point, he would have to hide for the rest of the day in case they used helicopters or airplanes to search the forest. Although he considered it unlikely that they could spot him from the air under the dense canopy of spruce and yellow birch, he decided not to take any chances.

Just before nine o'clock, John David found a large spruce tree with thick branches that hung to the ground. He climbed underneath them and went to sleep. He awoke late in the afternoon to the sound of a helicopter, which he knew meant that a search had commenced. He had heard helicopters over the forest before, mostly training missions from the SAC base in Plattsburgh, but they were rare events. He took a transistor radio from his backpack and tuned it to station in Plattsburgh, which was the only one that came in Henoga Valley. The news reported that Jack O'Neill had been killed, but made no mention of John David. He turned the radio off to save the batteries.

Later in the day, after the sun had set, John David climbed out from beneath the spruce tree and started toward Sabelle's cabin. Big Moose was another fifteen miles to the north, and John David moved slowly through the woods. He carried a tiny candle lantern, which gave off a faint yellow glow. The lantern gave him enough light to see the trail but would be difficult to spot from an airplane.

John David reached Sabelle's cabin two days later. Sabelle answered the knock at the back door and let him into the kitchen.

"I heard about your friend on the radio," Sabelle said. "I was hoping you had nothing to do with it."

"No such luck."

"Where are you headed?" Sabelle asked.

"North, then out west, I suppose."

"Forget the west. You won't know anybody out there. Go to the Abenaki Reservation. My people will take care of you." Sabelle thought for a moment, then asked, "Does anybody in town know that you know me?"

"No. I didn't tell anybody, just like you asked." After a moment, he added, "Except Emily. But I don't think she ever told anyone."

"You never know about that," Sabelle scolded. "Nobody can keep a secret. You will have to leave tonight, as soon as it gets dark. I will call the tribal elders and let them know you are coming."

Sabelle and John David hurried about with their plans. Sabelle took out an old map that his father had given him, outlining an ancient Abenaki trail from the Adirondacks to Canada.

311

"It's overgrown in most places, but you should be able to follow it," he said.

Sabelle gave John David a small canoe that would be perfect for the first leg of the trip. He instructed him to hug the shoreline. There were no other cabins on the lake, so he didn't have to worry about being spotted.

"I should like to take this trip with you," Sabelle said. "The last time I followed it all the way home was with my father, when I was just a boy. We were running away, too."

"From what?" John David asked.

Sabelle sat in his chair, which meant that the story took more than a few minutes. But John David couldn't leave the cabin until after dark, so it didn't matter. He sat in the chair next to Sabelle.

"My father was an Abenaki, but my mother was white. They met when she was sixteen and he was twenty-three. Her father owned the Adirondack Lumber Company and my father worked for him during the logging season. He refused to let his daughter be seen with an Indian, but she used to sneak away and meet him down by the lake. My father wanted her to run away with him and get married. He said they could move up north to the reservation, but my mother could no more imagine life on an Indian Reservation than she could living on the moon. The idea of running away scared her. The unfortunate thing is that she got pregnant and her parents sent her to live with relatives in Virginia. She didn't return to Henoga Valley for almost three years. By *that* time the story was that she had married a man down south and he had died in a hunting accident. Course, none of it was true, but nobody around here knew it 'cept her parents. I heard that my father tried to see Sarah once after she came back. He went right up to the house and knocked on the front door like a fool. The next day her father sent some men over to his place to convince him not to see her anymore. Sons a bitches, they cut off his little finger, right above the first knuckle.

"Why didn't he go to the sheriff?"

"You gotta be kidding. An Indian going to the police about a problem with the white man? Hell, he might as well have been black as red. Anyway, those men, they told him every time he so

312

much as talked to Sarah they'd cut off another finger. I guess they must have convinced him, 'cause he kept his distance. But he heard over the years how my grandfather would whip me with his belt if I did the slightest thing wrong, which was just about all the time, seeing how I was a half-breed and couldn't do nothing right. My mother tried to stop her old man, but then he'd start beatin' on *her* and swearing at her for bringing a half-breed into the world. Then one day my father saw the old man slap me on the face, right down on Main Street. I don't even remember what for. But that night my father met the old man outside his house and beat the shit outta him. Nearly killed the sonofabitch. Then he went inside and told my mother that he was taking me away. He asked her to come with him. She was still too afraid, but she agreed to let him take me away. I remember her coming into my room and waking me up to get me dressed. She was crying, saying that I was going to go away with my father. I guess there wasn't time to give me the whole story. But I never saw her again."

"What happened to her?"

"She drowned herself the very next day. Got all dressed up in winter woolens, even put on a heavy coat and took the rowboat out to the middle of the lake. Some people saw her from the shore. They said she stood up in the middle of the boat and with her hands together, like she was praying. Then she just stepped over the side of the boat."

"Wait a minute. I've heard this story. But the way I heard it, the boy was *kidnapped* by the Indian, who wanted to get revenge on the grandfather for firing him."

"That's the way everybody around here heard the story. I never met anyone who knew the truth."

Sabelle paused and slowly rubbed the arm of his chair.

"I didn't come back here until I was in my twenties. I even worked with some guys I knew when I was a little boy, but I never told anybody that I was the kid who disappeared. It was like being a ghost."

Sabelle turned and looked at John David.

"You ain't never been much of a white man," Sabelle said. "You might as well become an Abenaki."

313

And when the darkness came, John David Marten carried a small canoe to the edge of the water. He stood there for a moment and looked back toward Sabelle's cabin. He could see Sabelle in the window, and they waved to each other. Then John David climbed into the tiny vessel and paddled off into the deep woods.

Chapter Thirty-Seven

Mark Welton was in his Springfield office with one of his law partners when his secretary's voice came over the intercom stating that a Ms. Davignon was on the line.

"*Who?!*" Mark said, not able to believe his ears.

"She said her name was Emily Davignon."

"Isn't she that artist you used to talk about?" the partner asked.

"Yes, she's the one."

Mark shooed his partner out of the office and grabbed the phone.

"Emily?"

"Yes."

"Good God, I can't believe it. You haven't answered one of my letters in the past ten years."

"I've been busy," Emily said, not bothering to pretend. "I called to ask a favor. I need you to defend John David Marten."

"Marten?! *J.D. Marten?* They finally caught him?"

"Not exactly. He turned himself in."

"I don't believe it," Mark said. "Why haven't I seen it in the papers?"

"It just happened last night. I'm at the jail right now."

"I can be there this afternoon," Mark said, looking at his watch. He mentally rescheduled his appointments. He had several important clients who were going to be angry, but the chance to see Emily again, not to mention defending the legendary J. D. Marten, was too good to pass up. He was about to say something to Emily about their 'misunderstanding.' He had thought about it for many years. He wanted to tell her that he had been so stupid when he was younger. But then he heard the click on the other end of the line. Emily had already hung up.

It was not out of a sense of nostalgia that Emily called Mark Welton to defend John David Marten. If there had been anyone else she could have counted on to defend John David, she wouldn't have called Mark. But in the decade since they had last

315

seen each other, Mark had become a prominent defense attorney. His first big break had come defending William Houghton, a Massachusetts state senator with a pit bull personality and gubernatorial aspirations, who had been charged with soliciting a prostitute in Boston's red light district. Senator Houghton had made a name for himself by ferreting out waste in the state budget. He was vilified for having proposed cuts in public education and increasing the cost of state college tuition. He was seen by others as a prophet who could lead the state back to fiscal responsibility. The newspapers had made his arrest the top story. The senator, who was going through an expensive divorce at the time, was not a wealthy man and could ill afford another expensive attorney. So he hired Mark Welton on the recommendation of a friend who had gone to law school with him.

Mark pursued every detail of the case with zeal. He discovered that the wife of the officer who made the arrest worked for the University of Massachusetts, which the senator had vociferously targeted for budget cuts. Then he found someone who lived in the red-light district who would testify that the senator had asked him for directions to a state-funded drug rehabilitation house only minutes before he was arrested.

"It is a tragic day in American jurisprudence," Mark said during his closing arguments before the court, "when a public servant is arrested for performing his elected duty. Senator Houghton was willing to enter the most dangerous part of Boston to examine first hand how drug rehabilitation is administered in the trenches. If it is a *crime* to question the effectiveness of an annual $14.3 million expenditure for drug rehabilitation, then you must find my client guilty. If it is a *crime* to solicit a woman of ill-repute for *directions*, then you must find my client guilty." Then, knowing that every one of the twelve jurors was nominally a Christian, Mark added, "But as Jesus taught us two thousand years ago, it is not immoral to be seen in the presence of those who are themselves immoral. A senator's reputation has been tarnished for all time by these charges, brought down upon him by those who wish to stop him. There is nothing we can do to rectify that injustice. But we, the residents of the state

316

of Massachusetts, owe Senator Houghton not only a debt of gratitude for his public service, but a sincere apology for having cast a pall over his career."

Senator Houghton was acquitted in six and one-half minutes. It still stands a Massachusetts state record.

There were numerous other cases that added to Welton's fame. He defended a school teacher who was accused of soliciting sex from a student. The girl claimed that the teacher had promised to improve her grade if she agreed to have sex with him, but Welton presented copies of the girl's work to the jury and claimed that she was trying to get revenge for his giving her a failing grade. He defended a prep school senior on a rape charge by personally reviewing the forensic laboratory's proficiency testing reports and finding two instances where the lab had made a mistake.

"The defense does not prove a client innocent," Welton told the freshman class at Harvard Law School, pacing back and forth like the professor he was subconsciously impersonating. "You can seldom prove innocence, any more than you can prove the existence of God. It's your job to prove the existence of a *reasonable doubt*." Mark stopped and looked up at the class, sitting in semicircular rows of the amphitheater. He was delighted to have been invited to speak at Harvard Law School. He had applied to the school himself, though they hadn't accepted him.

"And what *is* a reasonable doubt," he asked them rhetorically, "in a society where everyone has an opinion? Political opinions, foreign policy opinions, monetary policy opinions, opinions about the likelihood of the Red Sox winning a World Series. The philosopher Philip Bailey once said, 'Where doubt, there truth is... 'tis her shadow.' If we are to believe Mr. Bailey, any jury willing to spend the time to look for the truth should already be equipped with doubt. Our job, as attorneys for the defense, is not to create doubt, but to *preserve* that native doubt."

The fact that Senator Houghton was widely known to employ the services of prostitutes, or that the school teacher he defended was later convicted in a separate case of statutory rape, did little to dispel Mark Welton's theories on the nature of doubt. It did, however, solidify his reputation as a lawyer who could get you off the hook.

By the time Mark Welton arrived at the Henoga Valley Courthouse, the newspapers and television reporters had already been notified. Mark was unable to park his Jaguar in the tiny courthouse parking lot because it was packed with a half dozen television trucks, with wires and cables running all over the sidewalk. Mark drove on past and parked in the Grand Union parking lot. A little boy was pushing a shopping cart toward the van next to Mark's Jaguar.

"Scratch the paint and I'll sue your little butt, kid," Mark said, leaning over and smiling broadly. The boy's mother ran up and grabbed her son by the arm.

"Cute little guy you got there, ma'am," Mark said after her, but she didn't look back.

A reporter recognized Mark as he walked up the courthouse stairs.

"Mr. Welton, will you be defending J.D. Marten?" the reporter shouted.

"I've been retained," Mark said curtly. His words implied that he was too rushed to talk to reporters, yet he managed to pause for a moment and answer several questions before climbing the last of the stairs.

Emily was not there to meet him, which wasn't a surprise. He had tried to call her on his cellular phone when he was thirty miles from Henoga Valley, but he discovered that the Adirondacks were not in cellular phone range. 'Can you believe this shit?' he said to himself in the car.

Mark introduced himself to Sheriff Cooney with considerable accolades. How pleased he was to meet a legend, Mark said. He pumped the sheriff's hand vigorously and even grabbed it with his other hand, which caused the sheriff to look down at the mass of flesh wriggling between them, like two snakes trying to consume each other. Cooney was not accustomed to men using both hands to shake.

"What is the actual charge?" Mark asked, still shaking the sheriff's hand.

"What the hell do you mean?" Cooney said. "Where have you been for the past twenty years? Mars?" He roared with laughter at his own joke and looked around the room, signaling his deputies to join in.

"Worse, *Connecticut!*" Mark said. They all laughed even louder, and Mark slapped the sheriff playfully on the shoulder even while thinking to himself, *you dumb lard ass.*

"No, seriously," Mark said, still chuckling, "what's the actual charge?"

"Jaywalking," Cooney said, "and murder, when we get around to it."

"Get around to it? When are you going to get around to it?" Mark's voice was still playful.

"When we get around to it," the sheriff added. And the deputies laughed again.

Mark smiled at them as if this were a class reunion and they were his old buddies. But he was thinking *I'm giving up $500 an hour to talk to Gomer Pyle.*

"Did my client confess," Mark asked playfully, "without an attorney present?"

"Nothing formal yet," Cooney answered. He had the feeling that he was being set up. "He just turned himself in."

"Has he made any statements?"

"None."

Mark nodded his head and asked to use a phone. He called Emily and left a message on her answering machine for her to meet him at the courthouse. Then he followed a woman deputy along a narrow corridor to the jail cells. He noticed the splendid fit of the deputy's pants and made a comment on the attractive uniforms.

Mark had tried to picture J.D. Marten on the drive up from Connecticut. He still pictured him as a teenager, though of course he'd be almost forty years old by now. Emily hadn't said anything about him over the phone, so it was hard to gauge how much he might have changed from the pictures he had seen in Sawyer's book. But nothing could have prepared him for the vision of J.D. Marten he found sitting in the cell at the end of the corridor.

"Buckskins!" were the first words out of his mouth when he saw Emily forty-five minutes later. He was giddy with excitement. "He's wearing *buckskins!* God how I love this job."

"Yeah, I noticed that," Emily said.

"But, hey! Look at *you!*" Mark said. He held her by the shoulders. "You look great."

"You look good, too, Mark. Tell me about your meeting with John David."

"I'm meeting with the district attorney in about an hour. As far as I can see, they have no case. No eyewitnesses to the crime. An eighteen- year old murder weapon."

"They found the murder weapon?" Emily said. "I didn't know they found the murder weapon."

"Apparently they never announced it," Mark said. "They found it in a hollow tree near the murder scene, but it was years later."

"So what happens from here?"

"I don't think *they* know. They weren't expecting him to drop in like this, so no one has done much to prepare a case. He's a local legend and they have no case. A law student could defend him."

"What about the fact that he ran away?" Emily asked.

"It's not a crime to be absent from Henoga Valley for eighteen years. If it were, *I'd* be in jail, too."

Mark saw a man enter the courthouse with several assistants. His instinct's told him that the man was the local DA.

"I think my date has arrived," he said to Emily. "But can we get together later? Dinner maybe?"

Emily agreed and they hugged awkwardly. Emily watched as Mark walked down the hall and introduced himself to the group of three men and one woman. He had changed so much since she last saw him. He wasn't a kid in jeans anymore. His dark gray suit was hand tailored, his shoes looked Italian. He had a gold Seiko watch on his wrist. The DA had a frown on his face when Mark walked over to introduce himself, probably thinking 'what the hell is this media lawyer doing way up here, the son of a bitch.' But Mark must have said something funny and they were all laughing. The woman in the crowd had a lovesick look that disgusted Emily. She turned and left the courthouse by a side entrance.

"Well, Mr. Vesey," Mark said, "you've got quite a team here. I'm going to be outnumbered. Any chance you can let me have Ms. Amarini to help even up the sides?"

"No chance, Mr. Welton. I'm sure you can afford to bring in a dozen law clerks of your own. By the way, who's paying your retainer."

"I'm doing this case gratis," Mark said.

"I see," Mr. Vesey said. "Publicity *is* its own reward."

"Well spoken. Now, let's get to the issue of bail. Has it been set?"

"Yes and no. There isn't going to be any bail?"

"What do you mean?" Mark asked, pretending to be surprised. He had anticipated that they might do this.

"Mr. Marten has a record of running off. And seeing as how the Sheriff and the State Police have had some difficulty catching him in the past, I would say it was a prudent decision."

"He turned himself in!" Mark said. "Why would he turn himself in and then run away?"

"Maybe he likes toying with the police. Maybe he was bored. How should I know? But how do you think *I* would look trying to explain it to those reporters outside if I let him go on bail and then he disappears? What do I say, 'Oh, don't worry, he'll be back again in another twenty years?'"

Andrew Vesey was forty-two years old, no more than five-foot eight inches tall and small-boned. He had been in private practice for ten years before being elected Hamilton County District Attorney five years earlier. He had prosecuted two murder cases in his career, one that resulted from a drunken fist fight and another in which a couple of teenagers robbed an elderly man. But in both cases there had been witnesses who testified and the trials were virtually uncontested. The chance to prosecute J.D. Marten was an opportunity for the kind of publicity that careers are built on.

"He's not going to run away, I assure you. I'll post the bond myself," Mark said.

"Look, Mr. Welton. If it makes you feel any better, go talk

321

to the judge yourself. But before you do, you'd better go back and ask J.D. Marten. You might find out that he doesn't want to be bailed."

To Mark's surprise, Vesey was right.

Chapter Thirty-Eight

It took Danielle several seconds to comprehend why Mickey Sabelle was sitting in the jail cell. Her first thought was that Mickey was protecting his 'adopted' brother by assuming his identity. But even as these thoughts raced through her mind, she realized they made no sense. Then it dawned on her that there really wasn't any Mickey Sabelle.

"That's a name we should keep to ourselves," John David whispered in response to her question. "We don't want old Sabelle to get in trouble with the law."

"Why are you doing this?" Dani asked.

"I have a family now," John David said with a wry smile.

"I thought you had a family out west," Dani said. She instantly realized that, if there was no Mickey Sabelle, then anything he told her would be suspect. "I suppose that isn't true, either."

Dani could see from the look on her father's face that there was no family out west. But, for whatever reason, there he was, J.D. Marten, her father, sitting in a jail cell in ragged buckskins that looked like they had never been washed. The pants and shirts were crudely sewn with leather stitching. He looked just like she pictured him, except for the beard. Then she remembered that 'Mickey' had been wearing jeans and a T shirt when she met him at Sabelle's cabin.

"So, where'd you get the cute outfit?" she asked.

"Just something I threw together," John David answered. But he noticed her sarcasm.

"Newspapers would love to have a photograph, I'm sure."

"I doubt the sheriff will let them in."

Dani looked at the floor and then rubbed her hands together.

"So, did you really go up to Canada?" she asked. But her father cut her off by holding his index finger to his lips.

"Nobody knows where I've been these last eighteen years," he whispered. "It would be best if we keep it that way."

"What about that girl in Newcomb?" Dani asked.

"What girl?"

"Oh, never mind."

Dani slumped in the chair next to the jail cell. She could see the guard at the end of the corridor, leaning against the wall with his hands behind his back. She instinctively lowered her voice.

"You have another cabin somewhere out there, don't you?" Dani said.

"Why do you think that?"

"Cause you boarded up the hole in the roof of the cabin we found after you took out the woodstove. My guess is that you still use that cabin every once in a while, and that's why you fixed the roof. And you took the woodstove to your new cabin."

John David chuckled but did not answer her.

"You really don't say much, do you?"

"I'm a little out of practice," her father replied.

"Mom said that you *never* were much of a talker."

"I suppose not."

"How come you never tried to see us before now? You read Sawyer's book. It says right in there that either you or Jack O'Neill is my father. You had to know what was going on."

John David got up from the bunk and walked over to the bars. Dani looked up at him from the old wooden chair. He stood there for a moment in silence. He appeared to be thinking of a reply.

"Do you like to fish?" he said finally.

"What?!"

"Do you like to fish?" John David repeated.

"What does that have to do with anything?"

"I was just wondering. I know a pond up north, a big pond, very deep, almost a lake, where you can still catch lake trout. There are no roads. You have to hike for the better part of three days to get there. I think you might like to see it."

Danielle nodded her head. "Sure, why not," she mumbled.

She was beginning to put it all together. Her mother had warned her that J.D. Marten was someone that a newspaper reporter had invented. She thought of the reporters who had gathered in front of the courthouse. The man they were looking for didn't exist, but that didn't matter to them. They would be quick to latch onto the story that J.D. Marten had lived in the remote Adirondacks for nearly twenty years. The buckskins were definitely for their sake.

"You are so very clever," Dani said, looking down at the floor.

She stood up and turned to her father. His hair was out of the braid and it hung loose around his shoulders. With the beard and the buckskins, he appeared like a bear in a zoo. But he smiled at her, and his mouth was gentle and kind.

"Hey, I'd better go," Dani said. "Mom's waiting."

She did not wait for a reply. But when Danielle was a few steps down the corridor, John David called her back. She reappeared in front of his cell.

"What?"

"Can I give you a little ... fatherly advice?"

"I suppose," Dani said. She sounded impatient. First day back on the job, she thought, and already he wants to start giving me advice.

John David lowered his voice to barely a whisper.

"When you camp in the woods by yourself," he said, "don't talk so loud at night. Some of the wolves are beginning to laugh at you behind your back."

Dani stared at him with her mouth agape. And then he winked at her.

Chapter Thirty-Nine

Mark Welton climbed the stairs to Sheriff Cooney's office on the second floor. He had scheduled an appointment with the sheriff to review the physical evidence against John David.

"Okay, what are we looking at?" Mark said, sitting down in front of the sheriff's gray metal desk.

Sheriff Cooney opened the file on his desk. He handed Mark a series of photographs of Jack O'Neill, some of which had been taken in the park, others at the morgue. Mark studied the pictures for several minutes, turning them sideways and upside down.

"Pretty brutal," Mark said.

"Yep. Crime of passion written all over it."

"Must take a lot of passion to kill your best friend."

"Most murders take place right in the family," the sheriff said. "Particularly knives. No one uses knives anymore, except between family and friends. But I don't suppose I need to tell you that."

Mark nodded his head in agreement.

"No marks on the arms?" Mark asked.

"Nope. He didn't put up a fight."

Mark leafed through the sheriff's 1971 report. He seemed to pause on one page and read it several times.

"Tell me about the fight between Jack O'Neill and J.D. Marten. The one that took place earlier in the evening."

"John David heard about the rape from Emily around four o'clock in the afternoon. Around ten o'clock that night, he showed up at Jack's house. They had an argument, a lot of shouting. He left the house a few minutes later. Jack's mother was there but she didn't see what happened, and Jack wouldn't tell her. Then Jack left the house an hour later and was killed sometime around midnight."

"The fight at ten o'clock doesn't seem like much of a fight. Any punches thrown?"

"Not that I know of. But John David was a lot stronger. And he had a reputation for fighting. Jack might have figured that he couldn't take John David in a fistfight, so maybe he got the knife and went after him."

"In that case, the 'murder' would have been self-defense," Mark said. "So why would J.D. Marten run off, and why would he turn himself in now? It would have been a lot easier to plead self-defense eighteen years ago."

The sheriff had been leaning back in his chair with his hands behind his head. He dropped his hands to the desk and leaned forward.

"John David Marten wasn't the kind of kid who would think that far ahead," he said. "Jack might have, but not John David. Kids like John David Marten don't hire expensive lawyers from Connecticut. A kid like that figures if he gets in trouble, he's going to end up in jail. And he's usually right."

"Do you think this is a simple case of self-defense?"

The sheriff held up his hands in mock bewilderment.

"No, not really. I'm just offering possibilities 'cause I don't have any evidence. Just a knife and an argument, and the knife probably didn't even belong to John David."

Sheriff Cooney explained his theory of the cheap knife to Mark.

"For all it's worth, I think it was somebody else's knife," Cooney said. "Maybe Jack's, maybe someone else's."

"Somebody else?! Who?"

"Somebody John David was willing to protect."

"But if he was covering up for someone, why would he blow that cover now?"

"Because of the girl," Cooney said, "his *daughter*. She's the reason he came back."

"It doesn't make any sense. He could have seen her anytime he wanted to."

"Not out in the open. Not if he wanted to act like a real father."

"What about Emily," Mark said. The question was as much for his own interest as it was for the case. "Does he love her?"

"You'll hear a lot of theories around here on that one," Cooney said. "Personally, I doubt *she* was in love with him. They're not exactly cut from the same cloth."

328

"So what was this all about? Why was Emily seeing him?"

The sheriff leaned back in his chair and pulled out a small pocket knife and used it to clean his nails.

"You develop a lot of theories when you sit on a case like this one for so long," he said. "I think she used John David to make Jack O'Neill jealous and it worked better than she planned. But I'm going to tell you something, Mr. Welton. We don't have a case. It could be John David, it could be Emily, it could be someone else altogether. But there isn't going to be a trial with the evidence we have. So in a few weeks John David Marten will walk out of here a free man, and my theories will be no better'n everyone else's."

Mark Welton stood up and looked at the sheriff for a moment. It had been a long time since he was speechless.

"But maybe justice has been served," Sheriff Cooney added. "It happens sometimes. John David's own father pushed a man down an embankment in the middle of winter and the poor son of a bitch froze to death, but no one could prove he did it. Then about eight, ten years ago, Marten skidded off the lake road one night, drunker'n a skunk. No one saw his car cause of the snow drifts. He set out there in his car all night before someone found him the next morning. He lost three toes to frostbite. Was that justice? Lotta people think so. Maybe John David killed Jack and just finished serving an eighteen-year sentence. Hell, I don't know. Maybe we don't need all you lawyers and judges. Maybe in the end it all takes care of itself."

He extended his hand to the sheriff. Mark thought about responding, but decided not to. It was a nice little theory. It was comforting, even if it wasn't true.

"But stick around for a few days and enjoy the mountains," the sheriff added, standing up to shake Mark's hand. "They're lovely this time a year."

329

Chapter Forty

Several days after John David Marten was arrested, Mark Welton drove to Albany County Airport and waited in the concourse for a flight from Miami. He had received a phone call from Peggy O'Neill, asking him to meet her at the airport. Mark stood on the concourse with a small white placard with *Mrs. O'Neill* written on it. But Mark would have spotted her without the sign. She was tall, with streaks of gray in her blond hair, and her eyes darted about nervously.

"Thanks for driving down here to meet me," Mrs. O'Neill said. "I'd like to have come up to Henoga Valley, but it's been so long. I'm sure I wouldn't recognize the place ... everyone's probably moved away."

"I'm told it has changed a lot," Mark said.

They walked to a restaurant in the airport and sat at a table in the corner.

Peggy O'Neill started to speak. Her voice cracked and she turned to look out the window. Mark had no idea what to expect.

"I got a phone call from John David a couple of weeks ago," she finally managed to say. A tear formed in her eye, but she blinked and it disappeared. He called to tell me he was going to turn himself in. He wanted to let me know so that I wouldn't be shocked when I read about it."

"That was nice of him," Mark said. He was genuinely touched.

"There's something you need to know," Peggy said. "Something I didn't tell the police. I meant to, but everything happened so quickly, and they just went after John David. And, of course, they never found him."

Mark waited for a moment, knowing that the woman was simply working out how she was going to tell him.

"I *saw* the boys fight the night Jack was killed. John David came over to the house around ten o'clock. I was upstairs working on a quilt, but I heard Jack and John David's voices in the living room. I heard them shouting, so I ran downstairs. I

331

couldn't believe my eyes. They were screaming at each other at the top of their lungs. I'd never seen them like that before."

Peggy O'Neill looked at Mark Welton. She could tell by the blank expression that he didn't know what to make of it.

"They were like *brothers*."

"Brothers sometimes kill each other," Mark said.

"They never fought like that. They were so angry that they didn't even notice me."

"What was the fight about?" Mark asked.

Peggy O'Neill looked out the window again. Another tear formed in her eye, but this time she failed to catch it before it ran down her cheek.

"I didn't hear the first part," she said, wiping the tear away with the palm of her hand, "but when I got to the foot of the stairs I heard John David scream 'She just visited the cabin because she wanted to take pictures. I never had sex with her.' And then there was a pause and Jack called him a 'lying son of a bitch.' And then John David said something like, 'so that's what this is all about. You raped her to get even with me.' Then John David hit Jack, not a punch, but he slapped Jack across the face so hard that it sounded like a gun going off. Jack fell back onto the couch."

Peggy stopped talking and looked down at the table.

"What did Jack do?" Mark asked.

"Nothing. He just sat there on the couch, with John David standing in front of him. Then John David said something about ... I don't remember the exact words, something like ... 'how could you, Jack?' But his voice wasn't angry anymore. It was just ... *disappointed*. He turned and walked past me on his way out the door. I looked right into his eyes and what I saw was grief, not anger. That's how I know he didn't killed Jack."

"Can I get a statement from you?"

"No. I don't want to repeat this story. I'm telling *you* this because I don't want John David to go to jail. If there *is* a trial, I'll get on the stand and say that I saw the boys that night and I know John David wasn't in a murderous frame of mind. I want *you* to tell the district attorney that he can't get a conviction because I'm going to say John David is innocent."

"Did John David call to ask for your help?" Mark asked.

"No. He didn't even say that he was innocent." She paused for a moment and looked down at the table. She traced a circle on the table top, then looked up at Mark. "But that's because he knows that I know."

There was a brief silence between them. An elderly man entered the restaurant with a young child, probably his grandson. They held hands, and the boy guided the man to the table behind Mrs. O'Neill.

"How's Emily's daughter?" Peggy said. Her voice cracked and she swallowed hard.

"She's ..."

Mark's voice abruptly stopped when he realized the implication of Mrs. O'Neill story and why she had come to Albany. Danielle Davignon was *her* son's daughter, not John David's.

"Oh my God," he said quietly, raising his hand to his forehead.

Peggy O'Neill realized that she had made her point. She got up from the table and pulled her purse strap over her shoulder. She stood next to the table for a moment and looked out over the runway, tapping the table with her fingers.

"That little girl doesn't need to know the truth," she finally said. She choked on the words and swallowed again. She did not look at Mark, but kept her eyes fixed on the window. "And *I* don't need to know who killed my son. Everybody has suffered enough."

Mark Welton looked up at the woman. Her face was blank and lifeless. Her eyes had grown cold.

"I'll see what I can do," was all he could think of to say.

Chapter Forty-One

Emily heard the knock on her front door while she was standing in the kitchen. She glanced up at the clock above the sink. It was only nine o'clock in the morning. She was surprised because she hadn't been expecting Mark until eleven. She walked through the living room and glanced out the window. The car in the driveway was a Volvo. The only person in Henoga Valley who drove a Volvo was her father. She froze for a moment, then slowly walked to the front door.

It had been more than three years since her mother died. Emily had not spoken to her father since the day she left the contents of her mother's purse spilled on the kitchen counter. At first she had expected him to call, to offer an explanation, but weeks passed, and then months. And then Emily knew that there would be no explanation. It had always been beneath him to explain his actions.

"Aren't you going to invite me in?" he asked after she had held the door open for several seconds.

"Sure."

Emily stepped to the side to let him in. Robert Davignon walked into the parlor and looked around the room. He noticed that Emily was smiling.

"Something amusing?" he asked.

"Sort of. You come in here and look all around, but by the time you get in your car you won't remember a single detail."

"I didn't come here to get in an argument."

"Why *did* you come then?"

Robert did not answer right away. He walked over to the sofa and looked at the picture hanging above it. It was one of Emily's.

"You painted this?" he said.

Emily nodded her head.

"It's very good."

"Oh?"

"What? Did I say something wrong?" Dr. Davignon said. "Was that a faux pas?"

"Well, did you mean it was *good*, or that you *liked* it?" Emily replied.

"What's the difference?" her father answered, irritated.

"Art isn't really *good* or *bad*," Emily said. "You either like it or you don't. But liking it doesn't make it good, and disliking it doesn't make it bad."

Robert Davignon sat down on the sofa.

"There isn't such a thing as a casual remark with you, is there?" he said. "Don't you ever just let things slide?"

"I've let a lot of things slide," Emily said. "Too many things."

Robert nodded slowly. He hadn't wanted to start an argument, but after not talking to his daughter for three years, he wasn't surprised that the conversation was starting out this way.

"You're so much like your mother, it's scary," he said. "It's almost like she's still here."

"I wouldn't know," Emily said coldly. "I never met her."

They were both quiet for a moment. Emily knew that her father had come over to tell her something about her mother. Their banter was just delaying the real conversation. She watched her father pick at his nails nervously. Finally he turned and looked at Emily.

"I never knew about that letter," he said. "Your mother ... Julia ... didn't know about it either. She must have found it just before she died."

Robert paused, waiting for Emily to interject. But she remained silent.

"Julia wasn't aware that your mother knew of the affair. *I* was not aware."

"What difference does it make?" Emily asked.

"It makes a lot of difference. First of all, Julia and I didn't really have an *affair*. It was a one time thing and we both felt terrible about it. I know she wouldn't have married me after your mother died if she had known that Susan knew about the affair."

"What difference would it have made then?"

"I'm just saying that Julia was..." His voice trailed off. Finally he added, "She was a good woman. Both of your mothers were good women. You shouldn't think less of Julia because of that letter."

"But I *do* think less of her because of it. How could I not?"

"Hey, not everybody can be perfect like you," her father said. "She had her faults, I have mine. We all have them."

"You don't have to be proud of them."

"Nobody's proud of this thing. I'm certainly not. I'm just saying that, after everything Julia did for you, you shouldn't let this mistake ruin the relationship you had with her."

"I forgave her. You don't have to worry about our relationship."

"As opposed to *our* relationship."

Emily sat in a chair across from her father. She brushed her hair back from her face.

"Of course we don't actually have a relationship," she said. "You saw the letter three years ago. Why did it take you so long to come over here and talk to me about it? I've had to make excuses to Danielle why we never see you."

"I didn't know how to talk to you about it. I didn't know what to say."

"I guess that's why you never talked to me about sex."

"I left that up to your mother. I thought she could do a better job."

"You left everything up to Mom."

"I was pretty busy in those days," Robert said angrily.

"Don't give me any of that bull," Emily said, waving her hands. "It's not like you had a litter to take care of. There was only me, and I certainly didn't require a lot of attention."

"Hey, I made a point of being home for your birthdays, didn't I?" Robert said.

"Birthdays?! That's what being a parent means to you. *Birthdays?!"*

"Okay, okay," Robert said, conceding, "But there's a natural separation of duties when you're married. I was working. Your mother handled everything in the home. You don't know anything about marriage, so don't go criticizing mine."

"Oh, *that* was nasty. You think I'm still single cause I want to be?!" Emily shouted. *"I'd* like to have gotten married. *I'd*

337

like to have someone to come home to. But the men I meet are just big babies. They want somebody to be their mother. Cook for them. Do the cleaning. I already had a baby. I didn't need another one."

"Not all men are like that."

"No, you're right. Some drink, some beat their wives, some go off golfing every weekend. Some do all three. They're a real catch."

"God, you have such a twisted view of men," her father said. He was genuinely surprised to discover that his daughter's opinion of men was so low.

"All I know is what I see," Emily said. "And I never met a man I could ..." Her voice trailed off.

"What?"

Emily did not answer. She got up from her chair and walked into the kitchen. Her father followed her. Emily turned around and met him in the doorway between the rooms.

"I appreciate your deep concern for my spinsterhood," Emily hissed, "but if it's all the same to you, I'd rather we just dropped this."

"Have you talked to John David?" her father asked.

"What do you care about John David?" Emily said. "What is this, like, you found out something about me by reading Sawyer's book?"

"I never read that thing. It's just that, well, you two were some kind of thing once. I thought maybe there was something there."

Emily stared at her father for a moment. This discussion was so out of place, she thought. So unlike him. He had never shown an interest in her social life.

"I don't mean to butt in," he added, "but I heard that there wasn't enough evidence to convict him. I heard that a grand jury isn't even likely to indict him."

Emily continued to stare at her father in disbelief. Finally she said, "So, if they can't convict him, he must be innocent."

"That's what the law says," Robert argued. "You're innocent until proven guilty. Don't tell me you have a problem with the constitution."

"You're innocent until somebody finds a letter thirty years later. Somebody always knows. You can't escape it. I couldn't love a man who would commit murder, even if he was doing it to avenge my ... my... honor, or whatever he thought he was avenging. It doesn't matter if they can't convict him."

"Did you ever think that maybe he's just plain innocent?" Robert asked.

"I don't believe that. I saw John David that afternoon. *I* was the one who told him that Jack raped me. I know how angry he was."

"So you'll be the jury. You'll convict him without seeing any evidence."

Emily burst into tears and slumped against the kitchen wall. Her father moved toward her, but she pushed him away with the palm of her hand.

"I made him do it," she said. "I'm to blame." She covered her face with her hand.

"He shouldn't have come back," she said, her chest heaving with sobs.

Chapter Forty-Two

District Attorney Vesey got up from the chair in Sheriff Cooney's office and walked over to the window. He looked down at the horde of reporters on the steps of the county building. They gathered every afternoon around three o'clock, just in time to see Danielle Davignon come to visit her father. They were crowded around the dark-haired girl now, thrusting microphones at her face and shouting out questions. Each time a microphone came at her she backed away slightly, but her face showed defiance.

"So that's all there is?" Vesey said, turning his attention to the sheriff.

"Fraid so," the sheriff replied.

He was, of course, referring to the paucity of evidence with which to charge John David Marten. Marten had been in the county jail for more than two weeks and the reporters were bombarding Vesey with questions about when he would be formally charged.

"I could *reopen* the investigation," Cooney added.

"What are the chances of finding anything new at this point?"

"Somebody might remember something."

"Do you think anyone in this town would testify against J.D. Marten?" Vesey asked.

"Not likely," the sheriff said.

"Yeah, me neither. I spoke to John David's attorney last week. He says Jack O'Neill's *mother* will testify on John David's behalf. Can you believe that?"

"Does he have a statement?" Cooney asked.

"No."

"Could be bluffing. A guy like Welton doesn't earn the big bucks without learning how to bluff."

"Yeah, I thought about that," Vesey said. "But then he showed me a copy of Mrs. O'Neill's airline ticket to Albany. How could he get a copy of something like that if he hadn't met with her?"

Vesey turned back to the window and watched the crowd below. A smile came to his face. After a moment he walked back to the sheriff's desk and sat in a chair next to the sheriff's desk.

"Well, I can't use the DNA evidence," he said. "If it means anything, it exonerates him. Not that it means anything one way or the other."

The knife had been sent to the New York State Forensic lab in Albany for analysis. It had been analyzed for the presence of DNA that might identify the killer. DNA is extremely stable molecule. Samples extracted from mummies have been used to identify bacteria that were present thousands of years ago. The use of DNA evidence was already routine and crime labs had become sophisticated in gleaning information from drops of blood or strands of hair. The DNA from a single hair follicle could be 'amplified' to produce enough DNA to perform a detailed analysis.

In the case of the knife, scrapings from the blade hinge had provided enough DNA to match it with a sample extracted from blood stains on the shirt Jack O'Neill was wearing the night he was killed. But there were additional bands, representing a second DNA fingerprint. Vesey had tried to get a blood sample from J.D. Marten, but Mark Welton had obtained a temporary injunction on the process. The amplification process might detect small amounts of DNA, like those found in skin cells from the hand of the killer who wielded the knife. But it could also detect DNA from kids who had climbed up into the tree and gotten stuck in the hollow.

"Hell, they might be analyzing DNA from squirrel shit for all we know," Mark had argued to the judge.

Vesey was still debating fighting the temporary injunction, but he did not look forward to arguing the DNA evidence in front of a jury. He knew Welton's 'squirrel shit' defense would make the prosecution look foolish.

"Let me tell you," Vesey said, "this goddam DNA isn't all it's cracked up to be."

The comment brought a smile from the sheriff. Vesey noticed it. He also noticed Cooney's general lack of enthusiasm for the case.

"It's funny," Vesey said, "the way J.D. Marten just showed up after all these years. And by coincidence, we don't have a case. Do you think somehow he *knew* we didn't have a case?"

"Hey, you think I like it?" Cooney said, bristling at the implication that he might have talked to J.D. Marten. "This is the second time the kid has made a fool of me."

"Well think about it. The kid disappears for the better part of twenty years. As far as we can tell, no one has seen him in all that time. Not even his own mother. Then one day he walks into your office and gives himself up. Strangest thing *I've* ever seen."

"I didn't make any deals with him," Cooney said, "if that's what you're suggesting."

"I'm not suggesting anything. I just can't help but wonder if he didn't somehow know that we had zilch for a case."

"It sounds like you're accusing me," Cooney said. "How would he know if I didn't tell him?"

Vesey did not respond right away.

"Well, maybe it was a lucky guess," he finally said. "But I'll tell you something else that's odd about this case. Yesterday the mayor of this pisspot town came into my office. He started telling me that it would be a shame if J.D. Marten went to jail because he's the biggest tourist attraction we ever had. Like I was putting Mickey Mantle on trial. He said the murder was a long time ago and pretty much forgotten. Nobody really cared anymore."

Cooney shook his head in mock disbelief. But in fact he knew that a lot of people felt that way.

"Like it or not, Marten's a hero around here," Cooney said. "You learn to live with it after a while."

"Yeah, tell me about it."

Cooney leaned back in his chair and eyed the DA. "You went to school with Marten, didn't you?" Cooney asked. "You're about the same age."

"He was a few years younger than me. I was in college

343

when Jack O'Neill was killed. But I remember when I was a senior in high school and John David got into a fight with a kid in my class. Frank Tomecki. Jesus, Marten almost killed him. And he was only a freshman at the time."

"Yeah, I remember hearing about that incident," Cooney said.

"I hated that sonofabitch Tomecki," Vesey said, laughing in spite of himself. He stood up and put on his jacket, straightening the cuffs with a smart little tug. "Looks like there's no point in my convening a grand jury," he said. "The judge would just chew me out for taking up everybody's time."

Cooney nodded.

"What do we do with Marten?" Cooney asked. The district attorney knew that what Cooney really meant was 'how do we announce this to the reporters?'

"Well, he's your guest," Vesey said, smiling.

Chapter Forty-Three

Dani sat at the kitchen table and watched her mother cut up cucumbers for a salad.

"You should leave the skins on," Dani said.

"I don't like the skins."

"All the nutrients are in the skins," Dani protested.

"What about bananas? What about oranges? Where would it all end?"

"I would hope with cucumbers," Dani said.

"From now on I'll save all the skins and you can garnish your salad with them."

They were silent for a moment. The only sound in the kitchen was the clicking sound of Emily's knife on the cutting board.

"How come you don't go to see Dad?" Dani finally blurted out.

Emily put down the knife at looked at Dani.

"I *have* been to see him."

"Not very often," Dani scolded. *She* had been to the jail every day for the past two weeks.

Emily wiped her hands and came over to the table. She sat next to her daughter and touched her hand.

"Dani, I'm sure it's very exciting for you to have your father back, but I have to warn you that we're not going to be a family, the way you might have been thinking. Your father and I were very fond of each other once, but it was a long time ago, and so much has happened since then."

"Like *what?* It's not like you've been seeing anyone for ... oh, about a *decade*."

"It's not that simple."

"Why isn't it? Why is everything, like, so complicated with you?"

"Don't say 'like,' dear."

"Sorry, it, like, slipped."

Emily got up from the table and went back to preparing the salad.

345

"I *know* you love him," Dani said quietly.

"Oh? And how do you know that?"

"I'm not stupid," Dani said. "I saw the look on your face when we found that poem carved in the bunk."

"That doesn't mean anything."

"Yes it does."

"Dani, you really don't know what you're talking about," Emily said angrily.

"But I'm hitting a sore spot," Dani replied victoriously.

"Let's just drop it."

Dani walked over to the counter and started helping her mother prepare the dinner. Emily finished cutting tomatoes for the salad while Dani set the table. They worked in silence for several minutes.

"So, will you go see him?" Dani said, breaking the silence. "It would mean a lot to him."

"I'll go!" Emily said, exasperated. "But he didn't come back to see *me*. He came back to see you."

"Yeah, well, he ran away because of ..." Dani stopped before finishing the sentence.

The two women stood across from each other at the kitchen table. Emily stared at her daughter.

"Your dreams are very beautiful, Dani," Emily said. "I hope they stay with you for a long time. But as you get older you're bound to lose some of them. I just hope you're not too disappointed when it happens."

"I just hope I'm never that *old*," Dani said.

Chapter Forty-Four

As soon as the district attorney left the sheriff's office, Cooney stepped out into the outer office to summon a deputy. He was about to send for John David Marten and have him brought to his office before releasing him. But as soon as he popped his head out the door, his secretary ran over to him.

"There's a man here to see you," she said. "He's a doctor."

"Can it wait a minute?"

"He said it's about John David."

Cooney was surprised. He looked beyond the secretary to the man, who was sitting in a chair with his back to them. Cooney knew he wasn't one of the local doctors. He was dressed in a tan cotton suit and wore elegant, well-polished oxfords. He appeared to be in his late-thirties or early forties. Cooney walked over and faced the man.

"You wanted to see me?" he said, extending his hand.

The doctor stood up and shook Cooney's hand.

"Yes, sheriff." He looked around, then said, "Is there somewhere we can talk?"

Cooney led the man to his office and closed the door. He motioned to a chair and the man say down.

"So, you know something about Mr. Marten?" Cooney asked.

"I don't know where to begin," the man said. "I suppose I should introduce myself. My name is Michael Missek. I'm a cardiothoracic surgeon in Cooperstown, but I used to live here back in the sixties. My father was the minister of the Methodist Church. Perhaps you remember him?"

"Oh yeah, of course," Cooney said, nodding his head, but obviously lying.

Dr. Missek was silent for a moment. He looked down at his hands, rubbing the palm of his left hand with the thumb of his right.

"When I was a senior in high school," he said, "I got a job as an orderly at the hospital here in town. I did a little bit of

347

everything. I wheeled the patients around, I changed beds, I picked up the laundry from the OR."

"Sounds exciting," Cooney said dryly.

"Oh, it was. I mean, the *work* wasn't, it was scut work. But it got my foot in the door. I wanted to go to medical school, and I needed the experience on my résumé. It was a great job. I was lucky to get it."

"I see."

"I used to work every Friday night. I'd pull a night shift, from nine at night until six-thirty in the morning. The best part about that shift was that Dr. Davignon would let me come into the operating room and assist on any Friday night emergencies. Not *really* assist, all I did was help the nurse who was assisting him in the operating room, but sometimes it was so minor that I was the only one assisting him. He even let me suture cuts on the drunks who'd gotten beat up on River Street. Can you imagine, a high school kid tying sutures? Jesus, what a job that was."

"That's very nice," Cooney said, but he sounded impatient.

"Of course, after the surgery, it was my job to clean up. I had to separate the surgical tools and send them down to be sterilized, wash the room down, and take the surgical gowns from the locker room down to the laundry."

"They kept you busy."

"They did. And I did a very good job. That's why Dr. Davignon let me assist him. He knew how meticulous I was. He knew that I would pay attention to every detail, to everything that he said. You probably didn't know this, sheriff, but Dr. Davignon was a much better surgeon than Henoga Valley had a right to expect. I didn't realize that until I started my own surgical training. People around here couldn't appreciate what a good surgeon he was, they didn't have anyone to compare him to. He should have been a professor in a medical center. I think he enjoyed having me around to teach. I became his only student, and I knew it was an honor. He even gave me some of his textbooks to read, from his private library."

"He's a good man," Cooney said. "We should do a testimonial or something."

348

Dr. Missek detected the sarcasm.

"You'll have to excuse me," he said. "I'll get to the point." Once again he started to rub his palm with the thumb from his other hand. "I was working at the hospital the night Jack O'Neill died, like I did every Friday night. Around midnight, a male nurse who worked there, the only male nurse, by the way, met me in the hall and chewed me out for leaving soiled scrubs in the locker room. There was a basket at one end of the locker room, and the doctors would put their scrubs in it to be taken down to the laundry. I checked the basket every night when I came on and when I left in the morning. I told the nurse that I had checked the locker room at nine when I came in and the basket was empty. But he didn't like me. He thought I was a real suckup. He said, 'Well, if you ever want to be a surgeon, you'd better start being more observant.' So, of course, I was a little pissed. I went down to the locker room, and he was right. There were surgical scrubs in the laundry bin. But I can tell you they *weren't* there three hours earlier."

"So maybe there was a case that night, between nine and midnight." The discovery of bloody gowns in a hospital did not seem particularly important to the sheriff.

Missek shook his head.

"*No* one was admitted that night," he said. "Not before midnight, not after midnight."

"Any chance you could have missed the scrubs the first time?" the sheriff asked. He noticed again the doctor's shoes. Cooney believed you could tell a lot about a man by his shoes. Any guy who pays attention to his shoes has an eye for details. Missek's were not even scuffed. Didn't look like they had *ever* been scuffed.

"Not a chance," the doctor said. Cooney believed him.

"So what does it mean?" Cooney asked.

"The scrubs were an extra large. The only people in that hospital who wore extra large were Dr. Davignon and that male nurse I was telling you about. The other surgeon, Dr. Emerson, was a little guy, maybe five- foot-six. He wore mediums. I took the scrubs out of the basket and put them in a bin to take to the laundry. That's when I noticed they were covered in blood. Fresh blood."

"Is *that* surprising? This is a hospital."

"Not ordinarily," Missek said. "But these were only scrubs. There were no surgical gowns,"

"What's the difference?" asked the sheriff

"I know this is probably a little confusing, but let me explain. The scrubs you wear in place of street clothes. They look like pajamas. But in most operations, a surgeon will put a full surgical gown over the scrubs. If you get blood on the scrubs, it's because it soaked through the gown."

"But you didn't see any surgical gowns in the basket," Cooney said. He was beginning to understand the doctor's thinking."

"Exactly. After an operation, the gown would go in a basket outside the operating room and the scrubs would go in the basket in the locker room."

"Could somebody else have emptied the basket outside the operating room."

"Nobody did. I checked, thinking I might have missed something."

"Doesn't seem like much to go on," Cooney said, scratching the inside of his ear.

"No, that's true. And it *is* possible that he performed a procedure without a surgical gown. It happens all the time in the emergency room. But there weren't any emergencies that night. *None.*"

"You checked on that."

"Yes."

"So where do *you* think the blood came from, doctor?"

Dr. Missek looked up at the sheriff.

"I think it was Jack O'Neill's blood," he said. "The park where Jack was killed isn't more than a five minute walk from the hospital."

"Would you testify against Dr. Davignon?" Cooney asked.

Dr. Missek paused for a moment.

"I don't think it would make much of a case," he said. "To most people, blood on a doctor's surgical scrubs is not incriminating."

"So why are you telling me this *now*, after all these years?" Cooney asked.

"I know I should have come forward sooner. But even now, I'd have a hard time accusing Dr. Davignon of murder. And in the back of my mind I keep thinking there must be another explanation, one that makes perfect sense."

"Like it was some kind of accident that Jack was stabbed in the chest," Cooney said, sarcastically.

"I've thought about it hundreds of times over the years," Missek said. "But it didn't make a difference as long as John David was missing. His running away was more incriminating than the blood I found."

"But now that John David is back, your conscience is bothering you."

The doctor was sitting slightly hunched over with his elbows on his knees. He looked up at the sheriff with a blank expression.

"I wouldn't want to see him go to jail if he is innocent," Missek said.

"So why didn't you say something eighteen years ago? It might have changed a lot of things."

"I was scared. I didn't know what to do, or who to talk to. I didn't even tell my parents. You don't just accuse a prominent surgeon of murder because of blood on some scrubs. I never actually saw him wearing them, either. I mean, who was I to accuse Dr. Davignon of murder? Beside, he could have, you know, *treated* Jack, or something."

"You didn't want to jeopardize your job at the hospital, did you? If you were wrong."

"You can't accuse someone like Dr. Davignon of murder and then ask him for a recommendation when you find out later you made a mistake."

"What about the gowns. Did you try to retrieve them?"

Missek shook his head.

"It probably would have been too late anyway," Missek said.

351

"Yeah, probably." Cooney sensed he was lying. A little hospital probably didn't do the laundry in the middle of the night, but what was the point of arguing it now.

"Besides, the next morning I heard that John David had run away, and like everybody else I assumed he must have done it."

"But that didn't help you explain the surgical gowns, did it?" Cooney asked.

"No," Missek said quietly.

The two men studied each other briefly. They had never met before, both men were sure of it. The sheriff saw a doctor, once a young boy growing up in this town, now in the waning days of his youth. His hair was flecked with gray, his eyes looked a little tired. His shoulders were slightly stooped. Michael Missek saw a sheriff whose life was enviably simple. He could bring men before a judge without having to decide personally if they were innocent or guilty. He could excuse an unpleasant task by saying that he was just doing his job.

The sheriff turned his swivel chair and stood up. He walked around the side of his desk and extended his hand.

"Well, doctor," he said. "Thank you for coming in."

Missek stood up and shook his hand.

"What's going to happen to John David?" Missek asked.

The sheriff snorted in contempt. He considered giving the doctor a lecture on the timeliness of his conscience, but he decided that enough had been said. And so he simply ignored the question and led Dr. Missek to the door.

Chapter Forty-Five

The Adirondack wind turns cold even before the last of the mountain birch leaves have fallen away, and one morning in November the residents of Henoga Valley wake up and find six inches of snow on the ground. The children announce the arrival of winter with shouts of joy, but their parents' reaction is mostly an assessment of unfinished business. Regardless of how long they have lived in the Adirondacks, the abrupt arrival of winter catches them unprepared. Gas grills are wheeled through the snow and men reach into gutters to remove frigid, wet clumps of leaves. Storm windows are, more often than not, put in place the weekend after the first storm has struck.

High in the mountains the snow has already begun to accumulate. The ground is hard, the shallow mountain streams have frozen over. Spruce boughs are laden with snow and dip more acutely toward the earth. Beneath this nacreous veil field mice dart, but the surface shows no sign of their gentle lives.

The winter of 1857 was particularly long, even by Adirondack standards. The first snowfall came in late October and remained on the ground until the second week in April. There were no blizzards that year, but snow piled up. Three inches one day, seven more a couple of days later, and forty-two inches in January alone. The short spells of warm weather that usually break up the winter months never came.

The snow actually made travel in Henoga Valley much easier than it was during the rest of the year. The dirt roads were filled with choking dust during the summer months and impassable after the spring rains. But during the winter the snow was packed with a six-foot high wooden roller pulled by a team of four horses wearing rubber shoes over their hooves. The snow made a perfect base for the sleighs, which glided around the village at a remarkable pace.

William Spencer made pig iron all summer long in the blast furnaces on the other side of the river, then used the winter months to haul the iron to Lake Champlain. When the snow melted on the lake, the iron was shipped to Whitehall and then

Albany. This dependence on the weather meant that there was a six-month lag between the time Spencer made his iron and when he was finally able to sell it. Spencer covered this shortfall with loans from several commercial banks, but he always lived at the edge of his credit limit. Sometimes the men who worked for him went several months without getting paid. But they were trappers and hunters, a few farmers. Mining was a cash job, the only way to earn real cash, and so they were patient.

The winter of 1857 ended as abruptly as it had begun. In April the temperature rose to 63°F and remained there for almost a week. The frozen roads turned to slush and then to mud. The white ice on the rivers turned gunmetal gray and the children were warned to stay off it. Up in the high peaks the frozen snow, which had piled up as high as twelve feet in the ravines, began to soften. And then the sky darkened and rain began to fall. The Raquette River rose quickly and by late afternoon it crested over the dam that powered the furnace bellows. William Spencer, afraid that the swollen river would wash away the dam, ordered his men to open the floodgates. The rain continued for another two hours while then men stood on the overlook at the end of River Street, debating among themselves when it would stop. And when the rain *did* stop, they patted each other on the back. They had known all along that the dam would hold. Four and one-half feet thick. They were proud of that dam. No amount of flooding could wash it away, they bragged.

The snow in the mountains absorbed the rain like a sponge and held it back for many hours. But eventually the rain exceeded the capacity of the snow to hold it. Chunks of ice and wet snow slipped into the streams and immediately melted. The water tumbled down the mountain and over the ground, forming cataracts on nearly every precipice. It collected speed as it raced down over the rocky soil, uprooting trees and sweeping dead logs from their supine berths. It rushed toward the village of Henoga Valley, carrying the trees, the logs, the chunks of ice and stone, even animals. The Raquette River began to rise again, quickly.

By late afternoon the river had risen another two and a half feet. The men once again gathered at the overlook on the end of

354

River Street, but someone cautioned that the overlook itself was in danger of being washed away, so they climbed the hill to the south of town where they could see the river and the dam. They watched in silent awe, for the force of the rushing water was greater than anything they had ever seen. Each of them knew that the dam could not withstand such an incredible force, but no one dared utter those words. And when the dam *did* give way, it yielded gracefully. The huge stones opened like a pair of hands and the water rushed onward, tearing and ripping the earth and trees in its path.

When the storm was over and the water had subsided, the children of Henoga Valley went down to the dam and climbed upon the stones, now strewn about the river bed. They brought with them their fishing poles and cast their lines into the swirling pools of water. The sun emerged and beat hot upon their winter-white skin, and the cool mountain air was filled with their laughter.

Chapter Forty-Six

The deputy unlocked John David's cell and motioned for him to come out. He shackled John David's wrists and ankles and led him to Cooney's office on the second floor. The sheriff was sitting behind his desk. He asked the deputy to remove the cuffs, but the man instinctively hesitated.

"It's okay," Cooney assured him.

John David watched the deputy remove the cuffs. After he had left John David turned back to the sheriff. The two men smiled at each other.

"Sure you don't want a lawyer present?" Cooney asked.

"Do I need one?"

The sheriff dismissed the question with a wave of his hand. Of course not, he seemed to say.

"You want a cup of coffee?" Cooney asked. John David shook his head no.

"I'm going to release you this afternoon," Cooney said.

John David turned away from the sheriff and stared at the floor.

"No one came forward to testify against you," the sheriff said. "Not that I expected anyone to come forward, what with you being a hero and all."

"I'm not a hero," John David said quietly.

"Oh yes you are," Cooney said. "A genuine, grade A, first class hero. You killed the man who raped your girlfriend. That was the *honorable* thing to do. People up here understand that kind of thing. We ain't liberal sissies like those people down in New York City. We need more of your kind, to set an example for the children."

Cooney's voice was so genuine that it was difficult for John David to decide if he was being sarcastic.

"I'm not a hero," John David repeated.

"Maybe, maybe not," Cooney conceded. Then, using his thumb like a hitchhiker to point to the window by his desk, he said, "But everyone out *there* thinks you are."

John David looked to the window. It was an unusually

357

warm October afternoon and the unscreened window in Cooney's office was fully open. A gentle breeze blew a red and yellow sugar maple leaf came to rest on the sill, and a second gust pushed it inside. John David bent over and picked it up, twirling the stem in his fingers.

"Of course, you and I know you're not a hero," Cooney said. "Cause you didn't even kill Jack O'Neill."

John David looked surprised to hear those words.

"Oh, yeah," Cooney said, nodding his head. "*I* know you didn't do it. It took me a while to figure it out. Years, in fact. And, of course, by that time it was too late to gather evidence to convict the real killer." Cooney leaned forward with his forearms on the desk. "I know you're not going to say anything in this room that would help me convict Dr. Davignon. Not after all these years of protecting him. So I'll just do all the talking and you can sit there and listen."

Cooney sat back in his chair and leaned on one of the arm rests. John David stared at him.

"You're running away was very noble," Cooney said. "You probably saved the doctor's ass. You sure as hell fooled me. It was seven years before I found the murder weapon, and that's when I began to doubt that you did it." Cooney studied John David's face for some expression, but he found none to interpret.

"I know you didn't do it for the doctor," Cooney said. "You did it for Emily. You wanted to protect her. So it must be really hard on you knowing that she will never know that you didn't kill Jack. She just thinks you're one of those guys who kills someone for messing with his girl. And with her being the artistic kind, she isn't going to renew a romance with a murderer like you. Is she?"

John David did not answer.

"And you can't tell her what really happened, either," Cooney added. "There wouldn't be much point in protecting her from the truth all these years and *then* telling her. Hell, if you were going to do that, you should have told her the truth in the beginning."

Cooney waited for a response, but he was not surprised by John David's silence.

"It's funny, how we get at the truth sometimes," Cooney said. "Kinda makes you wonder what we really know about anyone."

To the sheriff's surprise, John David nodded his head in agreement.

Cooney slapped his knees with both hands and rose from his chair.

"Well, I've got to go talk to some reporters," he said. "Now, I could tell them I think you're innocent. That, of course, would only start them asking a lot of questions, and that's not what you want at this point. And, to be honest with you, I really don't want them to know just how badly I botched this investigation eighteen years ago. So I'm going to go out there on the front steps and tell the reporters that we don't have enough evidence to indict you and just leave it at that. Then you're going to walk out of here, and for the rest of your life you get to play the part of the hero- murderer."

John David looked up at the sheriff, who was now standing directly in front of him.

"So, when do we get started?" John David asked.

"Whenever you're ready," Cooney replied.

John David stood up and the two men headed for the door. Cooney reached for the doorknob, then paused for a moment.

"You know," he said, holding one finger up, "there's one other little thing you could help me with, if you have a moment. You're not in a hurry, are you?"

John David smiled.

"There's one other case that I would like to close before I retire," he said. "I was hoping you could shed a little light on it."

The sheriff led John David to a small table in the corner of the office. An object lay wrapped in a bath towel on the table.

"We had a kidnapping here a couple of years ago," Cooney said. "Over near Newcomb. Maybe you heard about it."

John David returned a blank stare.

"Turned out okay, though" Cooney said. "We found the kid a couple of days later. But she had the most incredible story to tell. Said somebody, who she never actually *saw*, killed the man with these arrows." Cooney flipped open the towel to reveal the

359

two arrows that had been retrieved from the body of the kidnapper. They had been delivered to his office from the Essex County sheriff that morning.

"One of these went right past the girl's face and pinned the sonofabitchin kidnapper to a tree."

"Nice shot," John David said.

"*Very* nice shot," Cooney said. "And whoever shot these arrows knew exactly where the little girl and her kidnapper were headed. He had to have known, 'cause he climbed a tree ahead of time to clear away branches to give himself a clean shot."

John David nodded. He appeared to be impressed.

"Lot of good hunters out there," Cooney said, "but not many who could predict where a man was going far enough in advance to get there before them, climb a tree, and cut some branches to get a clear line of sight. *Very* few men could do something like that. Unless, of course, he tracked the man on his way in. Then he would have a pretty good idea which way he was going out. Don't you agree?"

"Sounds reasonable," John David agreed. He would have liked to compliment the sheriff on his detective work, but he realized how perceptive Cooney was. Every word spoken was a clue. John David continued to study the arrows in silence.

Cooney said, "A professor down at some college in Schenectady tells me these are genuine Mohawk Indian arrows. *I* wouldn't know, but I thought you might take a look at them and tell me what you think."

John David reached down and picked up one of the arrows. He held it in his hands and ran his fingers down the shaft. He picked at the leather cords with his thumbnail that held the arrowhead and feathers in place.

"I'm sure you don't have any idea who fired these arrows," Cooney said. "I'm not asking you about that. I'm just wondering if that professor knows what he's talking about."

John David looked at the sheriff and then studied the arrow in his hands.

"Whadya think?" Cooney asked. "Genuine Mohawk Indian arrows, or is that professor full of shit?"

John David chuckled softly. Cooney was genuinely surprised at his reaction.

"Are you telling me they're not Indian arrows?" Cooney asked.

"They're Indian all right," John David replied. "But they're not Mohawk."

Now it was the sheriff who had a blank stare on his face. He was obviously confused.

"They're *Abenaki*," John David said, and then handed the arrow back to the sheriff.

Chapter Forty-Seven

An evening several weeks before the start of summer, but so warm and full of rich vernal humors. It was three weeks before the class of 1971 was to graduate from Henoga Valley High School, and Jack O'Neill had learned that afternoon that he was valedictorian of his class. He had beaten Emily Davignon by one one-thousandth of a point. Jack was present in the main office when the guidance counselor performed the final calculations. She recalculated the numbers three times because they were so close, and Jack's mood rose with each tally. He fought back the urge to whoop aloud. Emily had not been present. She would, quite likely, have declined even if she had been invited, which she was not.

The women who worked in the principal's office were ecstatic. They loved Jack and they knew how much he wanted to be valedictorian. They all agreed he was a much more appropriate valedictorian than the sullen and often difficult Emily Davignon. Who knew what kind of valedictory speech *she* might have given? Some protest speech, no doubt, one that would have put a damper on the spirit of commencement. How thrilled these women were that Jack O'Neill would deliver the speech. *He* would never forget to mention all of the teachers and staff and what they had done for the class of 1971. They could almost predict what he would say.

Jack knew that it was his responsibility to break the news to Emily. She would, of course, hear about it the next morning from the principal, just before he announced it in school, but Jack thought that it would be better if he told her. Jack picked up Emily that evening and took her to the Barkeater, where they sat for almost an hour. The conversation was surprisingly lively. Witnesses would later comment that they seemed to be having a good time. So good a time that Jack could not bring himself to mention their class ranking. But afterward, in the car, they stopped by the old train station near the edge of town and Jack finally told her.

"Congratulations," Emily said, subdued, but genuinely happy. "You deserve it. You've worked very hard."

"We *both* have," Jack said. "We both deserve it."

"Oh, no," Emily said, shaking her head. "There can be only one. I'm sure that's the rule."

"Well, of course, it *is* the rule, but it's a stupid rule. I really wish it was you."

Emily looked at Jack in disbelief.

"You don't have to lie to me," she said.

"Still, if I was going to lose to anyone, I would have liked it to have been you."

"Winning, losing, losing, winning," Emily mocked.

"I know, there I go again. I didn't mean 'losing' in the traditional sense."

"I don't feel like I lost anything in the nontraditional sense. I got exactly the kind of education I wanted. I might have gotten better grades if I'd kissed a few more asses."

"Are you saying that *I* kissed ass?"

"No! I wasn't talking about you. I was just saying that I could have gotten better grades if I really wanted to."

"So you let me win, is that it? Are you saying you let me win?" No one had 'let' Jack win anything since he was six years old. He'd have quit a game if he thought an older boy was letting him win.

"Jack, I wasn't competing," Emily said, her voice rising. "I never cared about winning or losing, particularly when it involved *schoolwork*."

"You're right, you're right" Jack said, apologetically. He leaned across the front seat of the car and kissed Emily fully on the lips. They lingered for a moment, their lips pressed together. Jack reached over and placed his hand on Emily's hip. Their relationship had become increasing physical in recent weeks, and Jack had been hoping that maybe he'd get lucky by graduation. But Emily stiffened and removed his hand.

"Jesus, you *are* mad about it," Jack said. "You say that you aren't, but you *are*. You wanted to win just as badly as I did. You just won't admit it, that's all."

"I'm not mad about it, Jack. I don't care. I really don't care."

"Yeah, well, then why are you pushing me away?"

"What does one thing have to do with the other?" she asked. "Maybe I'm just not in the mood."

"You're *never* in the mood," Jack said. His voice was thick with sarcasm. "You'll be a virgin till you're thirty."

"What makes you think I'm a virgin *now*?" Emily asked.

And at that moment, for some inexplicable reason, the one thing that came to Jack's mind was John David Marten. Perhaps it was because Jack had heard the rumors, the *taunting* rumors, that Emily was seeing John David behind his back. He had dared not ask either of them about it. Emily would have seen such a question as a lack of self-confidence, a sign of weakness. And Jack was unwilling to show Emily *any* sign of weakness. But there had also been rumors that Emily spent weekends with John David in his cabin, and, of course, the two of them did have lunch together almost every day. Jack had, more than once, fumed in solitude over the possibility, that Emily might reject *him* for the intellectually inferior John David Marten. John David, the big ape, who had never been out on a date in his fucking life. How could she find that big gorilla *attractive*? Wasn't she doing this, screwing around with his best friend, just to piss him off?

"What? Did you let John David pop your little cherry?" Jack said.

"That's disgusting," Emily shouted. "You're a pig."

And she slapped him in the face with such force that his nose immediately began to bleed. The shock of the blow angered Jack and he lunged at Emily. In an instant they were wrestling in the car. Emily must have screamed, though neither of them would later remember any sound at all. Jack found his hand over Emily's mouth. She kicked and tore at his face with her fingers. She grabbed a handful of hair and yanked it hard, but he seemed not to notice. His face was contorted in foaming rage and his eyes had narrowed to feral slits. She bit him at the base of the thumb. Jack released his grip instinctively, but his hand quickly pounced again on her mouth. Had she screamed again? His hand gripped her mouth so tightly that Emily thought he might break her jaw. Emily was surprised by Jack's strength. She was, of course, quite small and should not have been surprised that an athlete like Jack was so powerful. But she had never felt physically intimidated by anyone before and could not have imagined such violence. She was powerless to even turn her head, which was now pressed against the seat. She felt that if he were to suddenly twist her head he might snap her neck. She continued to kick and flail until, it seemed, she lost consciousness.

And then Jack found himself on top of her, ripping her underpants from beneath her denim skirt. He would later remember that it did not feel like his own body, and that the body upon which he forced himself was not someone he had known for many years. It did not seem at all violent to him. It did not seem at all cruel.

And when it was over Emily dragged herself to an upright position by pulling on the back of the car seat. Jack had drawn away from her, his pants still awkwardly bundled around his knees. He might have said something. Emily couldn't be sure. She could see his chest heaving, but the only sound that fell upon her ears was the wind outside the car. An eerie wail, like a child crying in the distance.

But the night was perfectly still, there was no wind. It was her voice, her cry.

Emily twisted and reached for the door handle. She flung it open and fell out onto the gravel parking lot, her panties wrapped around one ankle. Jack, still trying to pull his pants up in the crowded confines of the car, shouted after her. Emily scrambled across the gravel parking lot on her knees, the stones tearing away pieces of flesh. She stumbled to her feet and ran behind the old train station.

Jack started the car and drove around to the back side of the station to look for her. He left the headlights on and got out of the car.

"Emily, c'mon," he shouted. "Get back in the car." His voice sounded angry, impatient.

But there was no answer.

Where would she run to, he wondered? Just beyond the station was the woods. Would she have run out there, in the dark? Would she keep on running? What if she did? What if she disappeared into the woods and something happened to her out there? Everyone would blame *him*. He ran to the edge of the woods and called her name several times. But the woods were dark and perfectly still.

"Emily!" he called, but his voice was muffled. "Emily, c'mon. I won't hurt you."

An owl flew from a nearby branch and startled him.

"Emily, c'mon, you can't stay out here. I gotta take you home."

Then he heard her, off to his left, coming out of the woods. He ran over a few steps and nearly ran into a black bear lumbering toward him. The bears often came to the abandoned station at night, to pick over the garbage left by the kids who drank beer and ate potato chips on the old platform.

"Holy shit!" Jack said, staggering away from the bear. He tripped and fell over backward, but his legs kept pumping as if to push him back to his car on his ass. Jack turned and jumped to his feet and ran back to the car. The bear eyed him nonchalantly and then wandered over to the platform to look for scraps. It did not bother to look up when Jack drove away.

It was several minutes before Emily crawled out from behind the Syringa that grew alongside the old station. The bear blocked her path. They stood less than ten feet apart, but the bear was accustomed to humans and did not appear alarmed. It stared at her for a moment, then returned its attention to the bag of stale pork rind held beneath its claws. Emily instinctively knew that the bear did not wish to harm her and she was therefore not afraid. And the only thing Emily would ever remember about that evening was the way in which the bear's oily black fur reflected the moonlight.

Chapter Forty-Eight

Jack O'Neill was uncharacteristically quiet in school over the next three days. He accepted congratulations on his valediction with a cryptic grin, and it was obvious that something was troubling him. One could not help but notice that Emily Davignon was simultaneously absent from school for the remainder of that week, and it was therefore not surprising that the rumors had begun to circulate that they had broken up. It was inconceivable that the two events, both exceedingly rare, were unrelated. When John David himself asked Jack if he was 'okay' (for it would have been impossible for him to ask a personal question, even of his best friend), Jack brushed him away. The principal of the school was so concerned that he personally called the Davignon house, and was told that Emily had come down with a 'bug.'

The exchange between Jack and John David on the night of the murder could hardly be described as an argument, for exceedingly few words actually passed between them. John David had been to Emily's house that afternoon. He had been concerned by her absence from school and her 'inability to come to the phone,' and he sensed that something was wrong. He doubted that Emily would be sufficiently disturbed about a breakup with Jack to miss three days of school. She hadn't been absent since the second grade. Emily's mother had reluctantly allowed him in to see her. John David and Emily walked down to the pond where she told him about the rape. Later that evening he stormed into the O'Neill house and confronted Jack. Mrs. O'Neill had been upstairs and had heard the shouting, but by the time she reached the bottom of the stairs, the argument was nearly over.

"Jack, what's going *on*?" she asked her son after John David left.

"Nothing," he snapped.

"What do you mean, 'nothing?' *Something* is going on." She lowered her voice to barely a whisper. "What did you do?"

"I didn't do anything?"

"Then what was John David talking about?"

"Mom, I don't know! Now will you leave me alone?!"

Peggy O'Neill went back upstairs and paced around her sewing room. She could hear her younger children playing with friends in the backyard, their laughter pealing in the distance. The house was empty except for her and Jack. She had never seen John David and her son fight and the sight of it sickened her. The sound of John David slapping Jack had been so loud, like the time the old wooden swing set in the yard snapped with three of her children on it. An angry red welt covered one side of Jack's face. Peggy walked through the upstairs bedrooms, rubbing her arms. It wasn't the fight that bothered her, it was the word 'rape.' She hadn't heard the entire conversation, but she distinctly heard that word. She could not remember it ever having been uttered in her house, in any context. It sounded harsh, like the tearing of cloth, and it was not something she could associate with her boy.

Jack left the house moments later and did not return until all of the younger O'Neill children were in bed. Jack's father was usually late getting back from Albany on Friday nights, so Peggy O'Neill was up alone when Jack returned. It was late, after eleven o'clock, and she decided to go downstairs and check on him. The house had a front and rear staircase, the latter exiting through a door into the kitchen. Peggy crept down the stairs and heard Jack dial the kitchen phone. She stopped on the stairs and, through the closed door, she could hear him talking on the phone.

"I need to see you," he pleaded. "I know you're mad at me ... and probably don't want to talk, but if you do ... if you change your mind ... I'll be in the park."

There was a brief period of silence. Peggy assumed that Emily was speaking, but when Jack said, 'are you there?' she realized that Jack was doing all the talking.

"Emily, I'm sorry," she heard him say. "I ... I don't know why I did ... what I did. I can't explain it. It's just that you were making me ... and ... and I ..." His voiced trailed off. "But if you want to ... if I could ... if I could *undo* ... but of course, I can't. Not now. But still, maybe if we talked, maybe we could straighten this thing out ... and you ..."

There was another silence, some more incoherent rambling, and then Jack hung up the phone. Peggy heard him go out the back door a moment later. She knew now that what John David had said earlier must be true, that her son had committed an unspeakable act. She didn't know what to do, or even what to think. There had been difficult times before raising her boys, but now they seemed trifling. Nothing remotely like this had ever happened before. She wanted to run after Jack and bring him back to the house, but she was afraid. His crime spoke of such violence, such *shame*, that she was powerless to intervene. *How could this be possible* she thought? *How could my son, the valedictorian of his class, the most popular boy in the high school, how could he do something like this?*

Across town, in the house on Raquette Lake, the phone was gently returned to the cradle. Other than a quiet 'hello,' the woman had said nothing. When Jack intoned *Emily?* and the voice affirmed with a *um*, Jack rambled on as if he *was* talking to Emily. He never suspected that it was, in fact, Emily's mother on the other end of the line. Julia never mentioned this phone call to her daughter, not even years later when the two women were finally able to once again talk about the summer of 1971. But Julia did call her husband at the hospital and told him about the troubling things she had just heard. She did not in any way suggest to Robert that he should go over to the park and meet the O'Neill boy, and Robert never admitted to her that he had. And yet, what motive could she have had for telling her husband about that phone call? Had she not been aware of how angry Robert had been since Tuesday night? Was it possible that she had not noticed he was yet in a murderous state of mind, as perhaps any father would have been, three days after his daughter was raped?

And that was how it came to be that Dr. Davignon was in the park with Jack O'Neill on a warm moonlit night in June. He told a staff nurse that he was going out to get a sandwich, which he often did because the food in the hospital vending machine was awful. Dr. Davignon did, in fact, walk to the Neba roast beef

371

sandwich shop not far from the hospital. On his way back he circled around through the park and saw up ahead the figure of a young man sitting on the park bench. The moon was nearly full, and when it appeared from behind the clouds it revealed his face clearly. Dr. Davignon approached the bench slowly. His soft-soled shoes made no sound. He was, in fact, only a few feet away from the bench when Jack noticed him.

"Dr. Davignon?!" Jack said, startled. He stood up, a reflexive habit of a well-mannered youth. The doctor did not answer. Jack stammered a few greetings, as if they had met by chance on a summer night. But Jack soon realized that it had not been serendipitous. He sat back down on the park bench. Then his face fell into his hands and he began to cry.

"You probably want to kill me, don't you?" Jack said. The question sounded so innocent, as if issued from a teenager who had left his father's golf clubs in the rain.

"It crossed my mind," Dr. Davignon said. Actually, he felt more like punching the boy, but he could not bring himself to move.

"You should," Jack whispered. "Somebody should." His voice was so full with remorse that, for a brief moment, the doctor felt pity for him.

He did not, however, *express* pity. Instead, he heard himself say, "Well, it won't be me. I took an oath."

Robert Davignon would later have great difficulty trying to understand why he said that, and even what he had meant. Like all physicians, he had taken the Hippocratic oath to 'do no harm' when he graduated from medical school. But the words, spoken in a moonlit park, sounded as if the task of ending Jack's life was beneath him.

And then he saw the knife in Jack's hand. He saw the knife at the same instant that he heard Jack say *Tell Emily that I am truly sorry.* Jack's hand struck his chest in a desperate act of contrition. The knife was preternaturally accurate. Its blade slipped between two ribs and severed Jack's aorta at the point where it joined the heart.

Dr. Davignon saw Jack slump over on the bench, but several seconds passed before he fully understood what had happened.

372

In all his years as a surgeon he had never heard of anyone committing suicide by stabbing themselves in the chest. But it *had* happened, right in front of his eyes. The brass plate on the knife protruded grotesquely from Jack's chest.

"Oh, God," he said. He pulled the knife out of Jack's chest, as if removing it would reverse the suicide. It was an untrained act, an inexplicable reflex. A surgeon would be expected to have known *not* to remove the knife, which might staunch the flow of blood. Dr. Davignon recognized his error immediately and tried to stop the bleeding by placing both hands over the wound. He was immediately covered with blood.

Dr. Davignon began to panic. He was quite certain, by the rapidity of the collapse, that Jack was already dead. But it was not, at this moment, the boy's death that frightened him. It was the fact that he was present with the boy who had raped his daughter, and that he had placed his hand on the knife. His fingerprints were on the murder weapon. How would anyone not think that *he* had killed the boy?

He backed away from the body, terrified.

"Oh, God," he said. "What's happening here?"

He looked down on the knife that had fallen to the grass after he pulled it from Jack's chest. He couldn't leave it there, not with his fingerprints all over it. He had to pick it up again, he had to get *rid* of it.

And then suddenly John David Marten rushed forward from the shadows. He had received a frantic call from Peggy O'Neill, who begged him to follow her son to the park. She had been worried that something terrible would happen, and she didn't want her son alone again with Emily. John David had arrived at the park moments after Jack and hid in a stand of cedars fifty yards away. When he saw Jack stab himself, he ran over to him. He pulled the lifeless body of his friend to his chest and cradled it

"I didn't do it," Dr. Davignon said. "I didn't kill him."

"I know," John David said.

"We have to get him to the hospital," the doctor said.

But John David shook his head and said, quietly, what they both knew. "It's too late."

373

John David let the body of Jack O'Neill slip back down onto the park bench. He stood up and turned to the doctor. The men looked at each other for a moment, assessing the dilemma. Neither one of them would, under the circumstances, be a credible witness to a suicide.

John David looked at the knife laying in the grass.

"Don't touch it," Dr. Davignon warned. "It doesn't have your fingerprints."

"It might as well have," John David said, picking it up off the grass. Dr. Davignon had no idea what he meant. He was unaware of Emily's visits to John David's cabin.

John David gripped the knife tightly in his fist.

"What are you *doing?*" the doctor asked, incredulous.

"You'd better get back to the hospital," John David said.

"What about you? What about the police? What will we tell *them?* They're not going to believe that this was a suicide."

"You won't have to say anything," John David said. "They won't be looking for *you.*"

"How do you know?" the doctor asked.

John David never answered him, and his eyes, narrowed and down- turned, did not invite further questioning.

Chapter Forty-Nine

The sudden appearance of Sheriff Cooney on the steps of the county building sparked a rush of reporters. They had been waiting on the steps for several hours, ever since someone in the DA's office had hinted that there might be too little evidence to indict Marten. The sheriff appeared at the front door and confirmed the rumor. He explained that the files would remain open, and if, at some later date, new evidence were to appear, the case would be reopened. Several of the reporters shouted out questions, but the sheriff had nothing else to offer. No, Marten would not be charged, he said. Yes, Marten was a free man. No, the case wasn't *closed.* It would never be closed until someone was convicted. The reporters knew the answers to these questions. They were wasting everyone's time by asking them.

"Look, there's nothing more to say," Cooney said, waving as if to swat them away. He turned and reentered the building. The same crowd of reporters rushed John David Marten when he appeared, clad in buckskins, ten minutes later.

"J.D., how does it feel to be a free man after all these years on the run?" one reporter asked.

John David looked at the man as if he did not comprehend the question. He had always been a free man. No one had chased him in years. He didn't answer the question.

"Can you speculate on who would have had reason to kill your best friend?" someone shouted.

John David did not respond.

"Are you protecting Emily Davignon?" said another voice.

Still, no response.

"Where have you been all these years? Have you lived in the mountains by yourself?"

Nothing.

"Was it *you* who rescued the girl over in Newcomb?"

John David looked at each of the reporters as the questions were shouted at him. He was a polite man and might have formulated an answer to at least some of the questions if he'd been given enough time. But the questions came at him so fast that all he could do was look at the reporters and acknowledge that he *heard* them. He appeared, perhaps, mildly retarded.

"Are you in love with Emily Davignon?"

John David would not dream of answering so personal a question.

"Have you been in contact with her over the years?"

John David managed to shake his head no. The answer clearly surprised the reporters.

"Is Danielle really your daughter?" one of them asked.

There was a pause in the questions, as if the crowd realized that J.D. Marten needed time to answer. But at that moment a Bronco came roaring down the street and screeched to a halt in front of the courthouse. Sheriff Cooney had called Danielle just before he had talked to the reporters. She had run out the door and hopped into her mother's Bronco. Her mother was upstairs in the bathroom taking a shower, and although Danielle thought of leaving a message, she quickly decided that there wasn't enough time. She knew her father would be besieged by reporters.

There were no parking places left in front of the county building when Dani pulled up in the Bronco. Television crews had even parked on the lawn. So Danielle stopped the car in the middle of the street. She threw it into park and laid on the horn, then hopped out of the idling car and stood on the runner to look over the roof.

"*Dad!*" she yelled, waving wildly. She laid on the horn again. "*Over here!*"

The reporters turned to Danielle. A cameraman turned his camera on her and adjusted the focus. Several reporters started toward the car, thinking that she would join her father on the steps of the courthouse. John David used the moment to excuse himself. He stepped back from the crowd of reporters and walked around the edge of the group. They suddenly noticed that he was on the move and began to follow him. But he was surprisingly quick for a big man. He was in the Bronco in seconds and the two of them drove off down the street.

"Where are you taking me?" John David asked.

376

"I don't know," Dani said. "But I couldn't leave you out there, with them."

"They don't mean any harm."

"They don't mean any good, either," Dani said. She looked in her rearview mirror and saw a group of reporters running to their cars. Dani maneuvered the Bronco down a side street and followed it to where it turned onto the road leading out of the village. She checked the rear view mirror again. No one was following her yet.

"I can't take you to our house," Dani said, thinking out loud. "They'll know to look for you there."

"It doesn't matter," John David said. "I'm not actually running away from them."

"Yeah, I know," Dani said. She pulled out onto the county road and sped out of the village. "But there's also my mother."

"I understand."

"How can you understand?" Dani said. "I don't understand, and I've been living with her for the past eighteen years."

John David did not respond.

"I know that she loves you," Dani added. "I'm sure of it. That's why she hasn't been serious about anyone else all these years. *You* were special. You were a legend. Nobody else could compete with you."

"*I* can't compete with me," John David said. "Not in real life."

"No, I don't mean all that hunting stuff, or escaping the police. I mean ..." Dani's voice trailed off. She didn't know what she meant. She didn't know her own father well. "I don't care that you killed a man," Dani said. "I know you wouldn't have done it if you didn't have to. That's what's important. But Mom, I dunno. She's different."

John David stared out the windshield in silence. Dani realized she wasn't going to get a response.

"What *is* it with you and Mom?" Dani said, exasperated. "You guys really don't communicate very well. What did you two do when you were together, just work on making me?"

"Don't be disrespectful of your mother," John David said.

Danielle apologized. She had one hand on the steering

wheel and with the other she rolled down her window. The sudden burst of air blew her thick hair around her head. John David opened his window to balance the currents and Dani's hair settled back into place.

"I love the fresh air," Dani said, turning to him. "This thing has air conditioning, but I never use it. I even open the windows when it's raining. Mom gets so pissed when I do that."

John David smiled at her.

"We're a lot alike, you and me," Dani said. "That's what you're thinking, isn't it?"

"Actually, I was thinking that I would have liked to have watched you grow up," he said.

Danielle slowed down and pulled the Bronco off the side of the road. She let it coast to a stop in the grass by the Raquette River and then turned off the engine. She now had both hands on the wheel, which she gripped so tightly that her knuckles turned white. She rocked back and forth slightly, and then suddenly her face contorted as if she were overcome with pain. A hand went to her face and covered her eyes. She slumped against the steering wheel, sobbing.

Although Danielle had grown up without a father, she had always been able to hide any remorse. Classmates had, over the years, asked about her real father. Innocent questions, of course, but nevertheless painful, and ever more painful as she got older. It had always seemed hypothetical, like asking a blind woman if she regrets not being able to see. Even the girls whose parents were divorced knew where their fathers were. Knew *who* they were. But Danielle Davignon felt as though she had been dropped onto the earth from a spaceship.

For years Dani had not known if J. D. Marten was her father, but she was utterly convinced that he had to be. She was the daughter of J. D. Marten, and though some kids might talk about her behind her back, might say spiteful things about her in the girls room, not knowing that she was behind one of the stalls, they would nevertheless hold her in awe. It might not have mattered if she and her mother had stayed in Rhode Island, where few of her friends had ever heard of the Adirondacks, and only a few would have remembered J.D. Marten. But it mattered in Henoga Valley. The name *J.D. Marten* meant that the vast wilderness, the mountains, the streams, the rocky ledges, they were her father. She pushed herself to excel in sports so that everyone would know that Danielle Davignon was not just a girl, she was a wild animal. And the daughter of a wild animal. When she walked onto a basketball court she could feel the other girls staring at her, nervous and afraid. When she stood at the starting line before a race, the boys against whom she competed gave her a little more room. For wasn't the lioness the most dangerous member of the pride?

And then quite suddenly J.D. Marten was no longer a myth. He was there for everyone to see. For two weeks the people in town spoke of little else. Dressed in buckskins, with hair down to his shoulders. Living in the Adirondacks for nearly twenty years without ever having been seen. Of course, rumors had begun almost as soon as John David turned himself in that he *had* been seen over the years, by hunters and backpackers, fishermen, even a Boy Scout troop camping along the Raquette River. A man in his early thirties called one of the television stations and said that he'd been rescued by J. D. Marten when he was in college. He said that he had been hiking alone in the Adirondacks and had gotten way off the trail. Marten found him late in the afternoon, tired and wandering in a great circle, and led him back to the trail. *Did you know at the time that it was J. D. Marten?* he was asked. *No*, the man said, *he wouldn't tell me his name. And he wasn't wearing buckskins, either. But I recognize him now from his picture.* John David's own mother insisted that she had *not* seen her son for all those years, but just about everyone agreed that she had to be lying.

Danielle Davignon realized that she *was* the reason he had come back. He had never come to see her before because he hadn't known he had a daughter. But once he heard the truth, he was even willing to face a prison sentence just to be with her. Her classmates, even her closest friends, were so in awe that they found it difficult to talk to her about him. *Their* fathers were mere mortals who went to work and mowed the grass on weekends, and complained about how sloppy their kids were.

379

But Dani's father lived in the mountains and dressed in animal skins.

In spite of her mother's warnings, Danielle allowed herself to believe that her father would come to live with them, that he and her mother would marry. It was fate, Dani believed, and, like many teenagers, she was at the peak of her ability to believe in fate. Her mother's doomed love, her father's noble, if ill-advised, act of justice, her own pathetic creation. It was all part of a plan.

Danielle even came to believe that she had been imbued with the power to forgive. Her expression of love to her father on Sabelle's porch, even though she had not known at the time that he was her father, absolved him of his crime. The police would not be able to convict him, she reasoned, because *she* had forgiven him.

And yet, she was unable to convince her mother to do the same. She could not have been more indifferent. She acted as if John David Marten's presence in the county jail were no more newsworthy than the occasional appearance of a moose in Henoga Valley. It was obvious that she was avoiding Dani's father, that she was incapable of loving a man who could commit murder. It was this futility that caused Danielle to slump against the steering wheel of her car in tears.

John David Marten reached over and pulled her to his chest. He stroked her hair gently, brushing it away from her face, and rocked her ever so slowly, back and forth. After a minute Danielle stopped crying and sat upright. She wiped the tears from her face and stared at her father, who stared back in silence. Slowly, a smile came to his face, but no words issued forth from his lips.

The quiet of the autumn afternoon was split by the sudden grinding of tires on the gravel. Danielle turned around and saw three cars and a news van pull off the road right next to the river. Several men and women were already jumping out of their cars and rushing over to the Bronco. A man wrestled with a bulky video camera, hoisting it onto his shoulder like a beer keg. Several more cars pulled up behind the first group and it appeared as though a traffic jam was forming. Dani looked at her father in shock, but he was already getting out of the Bronco. He closed the car door and blew her a kiss.

"I'll call you when they're all gone," he whispered.

"They'll *never* leave," Dani said.

"Yeah they will. They'll get tired pretty quick. Trust me."

Several reporters had already surrounded the car and were shouting questions, shouting so loud that they had to raise their voices over each other in hopes of being heard. John David turned around and faced them. He nearly laughed at their movements, for they were lunging at him like puppies.

"Hey, anybody want to see my cabin?" Dani heard him say.

The reporters all said yes.

"Well, let's wait for the others," John David said.

Moments later they were all assembled, eleven reporters with microphones in hand and cameramen with camcorders and battery packs. They slid down the short embankment to the river's edge and listened while John David explained how to cross the river. The river was pretty shallow this time of year, he explained, but they should step on the rocks closest to the surface of the water. He even suggested that they remove their shoes and socks and carry them to the other side, which several of them did.

John David led them across the water, though he was clearly better able to hop from rock to rock without getting his feet wet. Perhaps the soles of his moccasins gripped the stones better than their hard soled shoes, or maybe he was simply more agile for having lived so long in the woods. The reporters were quite wet by the time they reached the other shore, and even those who had rolled up their pants found that they had gotten wetter than expected. One woman, who was wearing shoes that were clearly not designed for hiking, lost her footing midstream and sat in more than a foot of water. John David suggested that she not continue, but she was determined not to be left behind.

Danielle watched as they crossed the Raquette River and assembled on the far shore. John David waved to her just before they crossed the grassy floodplain and disappeared into the thick forest. It seemed odd to her that he would, on the spur of the moment, be willing to lead them up the steep slope of Moose

Mountain, through the narrow ravine overgrown with spruce and witch hazel and into the swamp beyond. She was familiar with that area. A difficult hike, she thought. He would have his hands full with *that* group, in *that* forest. But she reasoned that he had made the offer to get them away from her, to rescue her. Dani smiled as the group disappeared from view into her father's beloved forest.

And later that night, when the eleven o'clock news reported that the New York State Police were still searching for a group of reporters lost in the Adirondack Mountains, Danielle Davignon laughed so hard, and so long, that she threw up on the living room floor.

Epilogue

John David Marten attended every one of his daughter's sporting events during her senior year at Henoga Valley High School. At the basketball games he sat at the end of the highest row, quietly, his hands folded in his lap. He wore denim jeans and flannel shirts and looked much like the other men from Henoga Valley. Visitors from other schools would inquire as to which one was J. D. Marten, and they seemed disappointed when he was pointed out. *Are you sure that's him?* He looked uncomfortable in the gymnasium and always left moments before the final buzzer sounded. During cross country and track meets he sat near the grove of birch trees where the mysterious *Ondama Field* plaque had appeared many years earlier.

Regardless of how close and exciting the events were John David did not cheer or yell, or draw attention to himself in any way. He accepted the greetings of the other parents, but it was obvious that he was uncomfortable. He avoided old classmates. *He's spent so much time in the woods by himself that he doesn't know what to do around people,* was the rumor. *But he seems harmless.*

It was also rumored that John David turned down a huge sum of money, hundreds of thousands, perhaps millions of dollars, to tell his story. The exact amount was unknown since John David denied the story.

And Emily, who had been an infrequent spectator at her daughter's events over the years, also became a regular attendant during Danielle's last year in high school. She sat on the opposite side of the gymnasium and did not wave to John David. But she studied him from a distance, out of the corner of her eye, always wondering if he was staring at her. He seemed not to look, but it was, as one might expect, impossible to tell what John David Marten was looking at. With time Emily anticipated running into him in the parking lot. She expected him to appear out of the darkness as she was getting into her car. More than once she actually hesitated while putting the key in the door. But he never showed up.

Danielle finally accepted her guidance counselor's advice and stopped trying to bring her parents back together. She was therefore completely stunned to see them sitting together in the birch grove just before the start of her final track meet. Dani was warming up for her race and she glanced up to her father's customary spot. She had seen him there moments before, alone, and she had waved to him. Each time she jogged around the infield she looked up at the birch grove and waved. And then, on her fourth pass, she saw her mother sitting next to him. Dani stopped and stared at them in disbelief. When they waved to her in unison, Dani threw up her arms in victory and danced around the infield.

On the last lap of the 3200 meter race that she was certain to have won, for Danielle Davignon was undefeated in competition on the boys team, Dani was accidentally tripped by a boy from another school. Dani typically jumped out at the start of a race and set a pace that wore the competition down, but lately the other track coaches had been sending a team of three boys against her to box her in on the inside lane and slow down the pace. One boy ran in front of her, one immediately behind her, and the third ran alongside her. Dani had to be careful when breaking out of the box. If she touched another runner she could be disqualified. The boxing tactic had worked quite successfully against her in several races that spring, although in the end Danielle always maneuvered away from the group. But this time the boys managed to keep the box intact for seven laps. The plan was to keep her boxed in until the last one hundred yards, at which point the race would become a sprint. Somebody might be able to beat her in a sprint.

At the start of the final lap, the boy running behind Dani came too close to her. His leg caught Dani's and tripped her. She fell so hard onto the track that her legs came up over her back. Her knees and arms were badly scraped, and by the time she got back to her feet the group of boys was more than one hundred yards away. She could have dropped out of the race and no one would have criticized her. But Dani knew that *he* was out there, up on the hill by the grove of trees, watching her. She jumped to her feet and took off down the track, blood streaming

384

down her shins. She raced to catch the group of boys, pounding the track, *sprinting* the final four hundred yards. Dani's stride grew in length and her long hair streamed from her head. Her muscles were no longer bound by human sinew and she became a magnificent thoroughbred, tall and sleek and powerful. The crowd must have witnessed this transformation, for they cheered wildly.

And then he appeared at the edge of the track. Dani saw him as she came around the final turn. She had nearly overtaken the boys. They were less than twenty yards ahead of her now, but it was obvious that she was *not* going to win. She had lost too much time in the fall. At first Dani did not recognize her father, standing as he was in a crowd of people at the edge of the track. *Their* faces were contorted in anger against the boy who had tripped her. *He should be disqualified,* they screamed, their mouths foaming with spittle. *They should all be disqualified.* Spectators were hurling epithets at the boys. A fight even broke out between parents from the competing schools, and a mass of people rushed onto the track in a futile attempt to block the boys from crossing the finish line.

Dani stared at her father as she rounded the final turn. She was disappointed that she was going to lose, disappointed that she had let herself get boxed in where she could be tripped, even accidentally. But the smile on her father's face was graced with pride, so markedly in contrast to the anger that surrounded him. Dani smiled back at him. She was still smiling when she crossed the finish line moments later. And when the boy who had tripped her came over to apologize, which he did profusely, and comically, with his head bowed in remorse, she tussled his hair as if he were but a naughty child asking forgiveness.

And when the crowd noticed that Danielle Davignon was not angry, they fell silent, ashamed of their wrath. And then they applauded her charity.

About the Author

Brian Freed grew up on the edge of the Adirondack Mountains in upstate New York and has been a student of Adirondack folklore for over twenty years. He currently lives in Colorado with his wife, Gisele and their four children. Dr. Freed is a professor of medicine and immunology and Director of the Clinical Immunology and Histocompatibility Laboratory at the University of Colorado Health Sciences Center in Denver. *BMFreed@aol.com*

9 781587 210662